ALL
THE
GLORY

How Jason Bradley Went
From Hero to Zero
in Ten Seconds Flat

Books by Elle Casey

CONTEMPORARY URBAN FANTASY

War of the Fae (10-book series)
Ten Things You Should Know About Dragons
(short story, The Dragon Chronicles)
My Vampire Summer
Aces High

DYSTOPIAN

Apocalypsis (4-book series)

SCIENCE FICTION

Drifters' Alliance (ongoing series)
Winner Takes All (short story prequel to Drifters' Alliance,
Dark Beyond the Stars Anthology)
The Ivory Tower (short story standalone, Beyond the Stars: A
Planet Too Far Anthology)

ROMANCE

By Degrees
Rebel Wheels (3-book series)
Just One Night (romantic serial)
Just One Week
Love in New York (3-book series)
Shine Not Burn (2-book series)
Bourbon Street Boys (4-book series)
Desperate Measures
Mismatched

ROMANTIC SUSPENSE

*All the Glory: How Jason Bradley Went from
Hero to Zero in Ten Seconds Flat*
Don't Make Me Beautiful
Wrecked (2-book series)

PARANORMAL

Duality (2-book series)
Monkey Business (short story)
Dreampath (short story standalone, The
Telepath Chronicles)
Pocket Full of Sunshine (short story & screenplay)

ALL THE GLORY

How Jason Bradley Went
From Hero to Zero
in Ten Seconds Flat

ELLE CASEY

DEDICATION

For those betrayed.
May you find peace, love, and the strength to forgive.

PROLOGUE

THIS IS THE STORY ABOUT how Jason Bradley went from hero to zero in ten seconds flat. It's his story, not mine, but he insists I'm better at the telling part, so here I am. Hopefully I won't suck at it because his story, his version of it, is important. Like, really important.

You're probably wondering who I am, how I got to be the special, chosen one telling this sordid tale. Well, let's just say I'm the only one who really knows the whole thing from start to finish. Lucky me, right? Yeah, well, we'll get to the details of me later, but first, let me tell you a little bit about who Jason *used* to be in all his glory, or so the whole world thought. Then you'll be able to truly appreciate who he came to be in the end of things...

"SET! ... BLUE, TWENTY-THREE! ... BLUE twenty-three! ... Hut! Hut!"

The ball got snapped and the quarterback grabbed it, running backwards a few steps so he could survey the field. The defense was all over Jason, or at least they were trying to be all over Jason, but as usual he was slicker than a greased farm animal that oinks.

He managed to find a hole and get through it, breaking free of the pack and wide open, running so fast his legs were a blur. That's how he got his nickname. The Blur. Totally original, right?

Ugh. If I had been in charge of nicknames on the day he earned that one, I would have called him Mister Bighead. But no one ever asked me what I thought about Jason, least of all Jason himself. We were not friends. And yes, that's an understatement.

I'm not a big fan of football, but like eighty percent of the kids at our high school, I go to the games. The home games, anyway. Our school is very competitive and we make it to State almost every year. The atmosphere in the stadium is always really energized, the snack stand makes pretty decent nachos, and I got extra credit in phys ed class for going, so yeah ... that explains my presence there pretty succinctly.

Jason made it to the state championships as a sophomore playing first string wide receiver on the varsity team. It was his senior year that really came into focus for people, though.

See, he was being courted by some colleges already, even though he still had all of senior year ahead of him, and they were coming out to see the games. Even for non-football people like me, it was pretty exciting news. We'd sit in the stands and try to figure out who the scouts were and where they might be from.

Rumor had it that he was a shoo-in for one of the top five, Auburn, Florida, Michigan ... I found out later directly from him that one of those wasn't actually on the list of interested parties, but it's really not relevant to the story ... mostly because he didn't end up going to any of those places and because after he did what he did, no one cared about his YAC. Yes, that's a real word for those of you who don't give a flying crap about football like me — it's yards after catch, which used to be a really big deal in Jason's life. After *The Incident*, no one even wanted to admit they'd talked to him.

But I'm getting ahead of myself. Back to the game...

Jason was running, his legs a blur, his gloved hands going up as the ball sailed over the field and all the heads of his competitors. It always amazed me how he seemed impossibly far away and then at the last second the ball would drop and his hands would just be there. I didn't have to like the guy to admire his mad skills. I liked to call him mister grabbyhands in my head sometimes. I never said it out loud because my friend Bobby would for sure have thought I was talking about something else, which I wasn't.

Jason was really close to the end zone. The game was almost over and the score was tied. A giant bulldozer of a guy on the opposing team was headed his way, arms going out, ready to take a flying leap.

My hands clenched in my lap and I let out a mighty scream. I had no idea where it came from. I didn't even like Jason at that point in our lives, maybe even outright disliked him. If he got nailed before he scored it was really no big deal to me. Part of me wished it would happen. His big old head could have used a little shrinkage at that point.

But of course that didn't happen. Jason was the golden boy and he did what all golden boys do; he leapt into the air, snatched the ball, and then took off like some superhero sans cape into the end zone.

Guys dove behind him trying to take him out, but they all missed. They always came up empty, miscalculating and under-estimating the speed at which his feet could eat up the ground.

That game was the last one that Jason would ever play. I saw him after. His face was flushed with exertion and self-importance. Everyone was patting him on the back, and a couple people hit him on the butt too.

For the record, I never understood that special social permis-sion our football-fanatic society has … allowing men to touch each other in such an intimate way just because they're on a football field. You'd never see a guy doing that at the mall or at school in the hallways. Or maybe you would and then you'd see him getting his ass beat down. You sure do see it in football, though. Fully grown men strut around wearing those tighty-whitey stretchy pants, spanking each other and saying *Good job*. It makes zero rational sense.

Stupid football. Stupid football players.

I saw Jason at a party after that game. Normally, I avoid big parties at strangers' houses, but my friend Bobby convinced me to go. I drove my beater Toyota over there and paid my five bucks and pretended to have a beer but drank cream soda instead.

It was at that party that I talked to Jason face-to-face for the first time in forever. Even though I'd known of him for years, both of us living in the same neighborhood and attending the same schools, I'd never really spoken to him after third grade. It wasn't that I actively avoided him, but guys like Jason don't talk to peo-ple like me unless they have to. I was invisible. Usually. But not this night.

I WAS COMING OUT OF the bathroom and he was standing in the hallway for some reason. I've never been in a bathroom that had a door that opened outwards, but that night I was. And I was so busy making sure I didn't have toilet paper stuck to the bottom of my shoe, I wasn't paying any attention to who might be on the other side of the door.

It swung open and made contact with something hard. My eyes bugged out and my heart stopped for just a second. *What the ... That can't be good.*

"Holy shit, watch it, would ya? Jesus."

I stuck my head around the door and saw Jason standing there, holding his forehead. We were the only ones around, which was really weird because the house was full of people, not only from our school but others.

"Oh, crap. I'm sorry. Did I hit you in the head?" I look at the door, wondering how it was that I could have managed that. Seems like I should have hit his foot first.

"Yes, you hit me in the head." He was rubbing his eyebrow above his right eye, and it struck me that I could have ended his football career with one ill-timed bathroom door opening. A wide receiver missing vision in one eye probably isn't as effective as a guy with two functioning eyeballs. It kind of put the whole thing into perspective for me. I felt really bad. Football was his life, after all.

"I'm sorry, Jason. Really. I should have opened it more slowly but I was worried about the toilet paper."

Yeah. I said that.

I wanted to bang my own head against the door, but that would have been even more embarrassing and I was already doing pretty well in that area.

He slowly dropped his hand away and let it fall to his side. "The toilet paper?"

My grin came out kind of crooked. My mom hates it when I do that. She says it makes me look like I'm mental, but it's automatic; I can't help it. When I'm feeling awkward, I look awkward. I can always be counted on to have the corresponding facial expression for each and every embarrassing event.

I quickly decided a short explanation was in order. Everyone worries about toilet paper on shoes, right? *He won't think I'm weird. Maybe.*

"I always check before I leave the bathroom to make sure I don't have any paper stuck to my shoe."

He stared at me for a couple seconds and then grinned. "I always check my zipper."

My awkward smile morphed into something more normal-looking. The fact that he didn't hate me for almost knocking his eye out made me go all warm.

I opened my mouth to tell him I thought that was probably a good idea, but we were interrupted by his girlfriend.

Brittney Blake. Do I really need to describe her for you? I'll just cut to the chase and say that she's exactly the kind of girl you'd expect to see going out with the hottest football star our school had seen in twenty years. And she was wicked jealous of any girl who thought she was good enough to talk to her boyfriend.

"Jason, what are you doing?" She had a red Solo cup in her hand and if her heavily-lidded eyes were any indication, she wasn't fake-drinking the beer like I was.

I dropped my gaze to the floor. I hated myself in that moment, that I felt the need to apologize for stepping outside of my social strata and being bold enough to engage in conversation with The Jason ... Her Jason. But life is what it is and I often find it impossible to control my reactions to social pressure.

"Ease up, Britt, we were just having a conversation about toilet paper."

She snorted. "Toilet paper. Wow. That's sexy." Then she laughed.

My face was burning up. The only way I could stop myself from saying what probably should have been said and/or bitch-slapping her was to focus on something else. I stared down the hallway and thankfully caught sight of Bobby.

Coming more fully out of the bathroom, I shut the door behind me and moved to walk around the happy couple who were now making out. "Okay, well, see ya."

Jason lifted his head and looked at me. "Check your zipper."

I froze, my gaze going down to my pants. The relief that washed through me at finding everything all copacetic down there was unbelievable. I had no idea why the idea of Jason Bradley catching me with my barn door open would have been such a tragedy. He's just a guy.

Breaking out in the cold sweat of relief, I gave him my mentally unbalanced smile once again. "Ha, ha. Thanks. I think I'm good."

He went back to his saliva swapping, and I fast-walked to the end of the hallway, grabbing Bobby by the arm and steering him into another room, grateful to be putting some distance between myself and The Blur.

I WAS READY TO GO right then, but Bobby was busy making his move on this guy he'd had his eye on all the summer, and he wasn't going to leave until either he had permission to text or had copped a feel.

It was always a crap shoot for Bobby, looking for love. When you're a guy looking for a girl, you can be reasonably sure you're being rejected because you're just not good looking enough. With Bobby, he was a guy looking for a guy, and he had to worry about not only not being good looking enough but getting his ass beat. His gaydar was pretty good, but it wasn't perfect and he has a few scars to show for it.

An hour or a few later, I kind of lost track with all the wandering around I was doing, he finally gave up. "Come on, let's go," he said, linking an arm through mine.

I was relieved to be ditching that party. Nobody I cared about was around but him. I have a very small circle of friends; he was pretty much it most of the time. Can two people make a circle? It felt like it then, but later I realized friendship circles are pretty lopsided when there are only two points of reference.

Bobby and I have been friends since kindergarten, and his preferred method of walking when he's with me is with arms linked and hips connected. I think I'm part friend, part security blanket, part Siamese twin.

"Thank the tiny baby Jesus," I said, digging through my bag for my keys. They're usually not hard to find; I have a ridiculous number of keychains connected to them. "This place was getting scary." Not two minutes ago I saw a girl barf into a houseplant. I seriously go bonkers if I see that stuff land on the floor, and by the looks of the people stumbling around, it was only a matter of time before I'd be forced to bear witness to that nightmare.

I remembered where my keys were at precisely the same moment that some loud voices came to my ears from the front door area.

"What are you doing?" Bobby asked, twisting his head around to see what all the commotion was about. "I thought you were ready to go."

"I am. I just remembered that my keys are in that bowl at the door."

"Come on," he said, pulling me through the living room and over to the shouting match in the foyer.

When we arrived, we saw Brittney throwing a tantrum, demanding her keys from the big guy at the door. I recognized him as one of the students who wears a football jersey in school on game days, but I didn't know his name or what position he played. I would have guessed his job was to tackle people. He was about the size of one and a half Jasons or four Bobbys. Bobby's very twiggy.

The big guy's voice was higher than I would have guessed it would be. "You've been drinking, so you don't get your keys. That's the deal. Now get out of my face, Brittney, or I'm going to punch your boyfriend."

I was wishing I had some popcorn, because this was getting interesting, but my ability to spectate got cancelled when Jason looked over at me and pointed.

"She lives near me. She can drive us home."

Brittney followed the direction of his finger and then made one of those faces like she smelled something really stinky.

"I'm not riding with ... no." She shook her head. "No way. I need my car tomorrow. I have cheer practice early in the morning."

The big door guy sat down and smiled. "Not my problem." He looked over her shoulder. "Next!"

No one was standing in line, but it was pretty effective as a dismissal. Jason grabbed Brittney over the back of her shoulders and steered her in my direction.

Bobby's arm squeezed mine until I was close to losing circulation.

"You mind giving us a ride?" Jason asked when they stopped in front of us.

Brittney stared at the ceiling, pretty much fuming. Then she took out her phone and texted someone.

"Sure, no problem." I didn't even know that Jason was aware of the fact that we lived in the same 'hood. He'd never even given me a second look driving by.

I'm forced to do a lot of yardwork, so I saw his car all the time. I always knew when Jason was home or going out somewhere. It wasn't that I stalked him, but his loud Camaro was kind of hard to miss when it rumbled by.

"And Britt too?" He looked down at his girlfriend to get her approval of his plan.

A girl walked up behind Brittney and interrupted her answer. "Ready to go?" she asked.

We all stood there, staring at her. The interloper.

"Yes, I'm ready." Brittney smiled at her boyfriend, completely ignoring Bobby and me. "You coming?" she asked.

Jason frowned. "I already got us a ride."

Brittney's smile disappeared as quickly as it arrived. Maybe even quicker. "I'm not riding with them. I'm riding with Tiff. You are too."

Tiff is Brittney's best friend. They're like clones of each other, making me wonder if Jason ever got them mixed up. People talked about them like they were one unit. Tiff and Britt. Britt-n-Tiff. They sounded like an annoying clothing label.

I got the distinct impression that Jason didn't like having Brittney make his decisions for him. His expression was pretty clear, but his words sealed the deal.

"No thanks. I'm riding with them." He gestured towards us with his chin.

Bobby squeezed me again. I was pretty sure he was close to squealing.

See, Bobby loves drama and he adores football players. This was a dream come true for him; Jason Bradley in my car with him in the backseat. That's what he was imagining. I knew it then and he confirmed it for me later. Too bad he lets his brain get away from him sometimes.

I could see the steam starting to gather and spill out of Brittney's ears, so I detached myself from Bobby's death grip and showed the beefcake at the door my cup of cream soda, which he sniffed and tasted to verify its non-alcohol status. After his nod of approval, I reached into the bowl, snagging my keys.

"Well, I'm outta here," I said with feigned cool. "Whoever is going with me better come now." I walked away like I didn't have a care in the world, like my stomach wasn't in knots about Jason riding in my crappy car and Brittney coming after me with the fury of a thousand angry cheerleader girlfriends.

The grass was wet with dew, making me realize that it was a lot later than I had imagined. A quick check of my phone told me it was two in the morning. It made me wonder if somebody slipped something into my cream soda at the party causing me to go into some kind of drug-induced time warp. *How did I last so long at this lame partay?*

"Sorry about that," Jason said, catching up to Bobby and me as I reached the side of my car. "She can be a real pain the ass when she's had too much to drink."

"Aren't you worried about her getting home?" I asked, realizing that he'd totally just abandoned her. What kind of boyfriend does that?

He slipped down my scale of awesomeness in that moment. Not that he was all that high up to begin with, but I reserved a special place in Doucheville for guys who ditched girls when they were vulnerable.

"Tiffany took her. I saw her get in the car. She'll be fine."

Slightly mollified, I unlocked my door and got in, leaning over to unlock Bobby's. At least, I *thought* I was letting Bobby in next to me, but Jason grabbed the handle and helped himself to the front seat.

Bobby's face fell, but he stepped over and got into the back seat.

I put the key in the ignition and then paused. Bobby's expression in the mirror was killing me.

Sighing, I stopped my ignition sequence and leaned back against my seat, turning my head to the right. "Jason, do you mind getting in the back?"

The entire car went silent. Muffled sounds of party people yelling and laughing came through the windows.

"Why?" Jason asked.

Tons of things raced through my head a split second after he asked that question. Should I lie and say that there's something wrong with the seat? With the seatbelt? Should I make up some lame story about how I drive better with people in the back? Should I joke and say I want to be his chauffeur for the night?

My eyes bugged out at that thought. Talk about labeling oneself a leper. *No.* I just had to tell the truth.

"Because that's Bobby's seat."

Bobby's jaw dropped open as he stared at my reflection in the mirror. I knew exactly what was going through his mind. He couldn't believe I just told the school's favorite son that he wasn't wanted.

"He your boyfriend?" Jason asked, kind of laughing. "I thought he was gay."

I sighed heavily. Jason was now the favorite son of Doucheville as far as I was concerned. "Just get in the back, please. Or find another ride."

He opened the door, got out, and stood at the curb for a few seconds staring into the window.

"I cannot believe you just did that," Bobby said in a loud whisper, leaning between the front seats. "You are completely crayzola crayon."

"Just get up here, gaylord, or I'm going to go through all this humiliation for no reason." Gaylord is the nickname Bobby gave himself five years ago. If there's anybody crayzola crayon crazy in this car, it's him, not me.

"Let's tell him I'm your boyfriend," Bobby said before opening his door. "Really blow his mind."

"No. Just get in, would you? I'm tired and I want to go home." I stared straight ahead, wondering if I would be forevermore branded head pariah with Jason's entire squad of friends and hangers-on. That would make life interesting. Just the kind of interesting I like to avoid, in fact.

Bobby got in the front seat and shut the door. We exchanged a look when the back door opened and Jason got in, but then I faced the windshield again. Sometimes Bobby makes me laugh at inappropriate times, and I didn't want Jason to think we were mocking him. Disliking someone and mocking him are totally different things, and I didn't want any misunderstandings between us. As if it mattered. I can be really silly sometimes.

Halfway through the ride home, I got up the nerve to look in my rearview mirror at the back seat. I was used to seeing girls back there or Bobby, so it was weird how Jason seemed to take up half the entire space. Being a wide receiver, he's shorter and lighter than a lot of the guys on the team, but he's by no means small. Weight training class was mandatory for all the football players, and Jason has the kind of body that takes to that stuff naturally. His shoulders are broad and the muscles in his arms are obvious even when he's not flexing.

Seeing him back there being all fit, reminded me how I was always telling myself I should get to the gym and work on my own muscles. I always came up with other things to do instead, though. I'm not lazy so much as easily bored.

We pulled onto Bobby's street and I slowed down as I reached his driveway. Bobby turned around and grinned at Jason as I drew to a stop.

"So, you going to be in big trouble with Brittney or what?" he asked.

Jason huffed out some air, like he was annoyed. "Probably."

"She's so drunk, she'll probably forget it even happened," Bobby said, trying to reassure him.

"You don't know Brittney very well, do you?"

"Tell her that she got mad at you and didn't want you to come along. We'll totally back you up, won't we?" Bobby looked at me and wiggled his eyebrows.

"Tiffany will set her straight," Jason said, sounding like it was a foregone conclusion he was resigned to suffer. "Don't worry about it. I'm not."

Bobby turned back around and quickly texted something before opening his door. "Come on up front," he said to Jason.

My phone beeped and I pulled it out of my bag enough to read the message. *Don't do anything I wouldn't do.*

I rolled my eyes. As if.

"I thought that was your seat," Jason said, making me wish I could go bury my head in Bobby's front yard. How embarrassing. Did I really say that?

"I hereby bequeath it to you. Use it wisely." Bobby started to walk away but then he stopped and turned to face us. "Oh, but don't touch the radio. The radio channel selection privilege does not come with the front seat privilege. I learned that lesson the hard way."

He shook his hand like it was stinging, making me wish I had a go-go-gadget boxing glove I could shoot out at him. *Pop!* Right in the kisser. But I didn't have one of those handy dandy gadgets, so I just shot him the shit-eye instead. *Way to make me look like a desperate loser, Gaylord.*

Bobby giggled all the way to his front door. I swear I could still hear him haw-hawing, even with the thing closed up tight behind him.

Jason got out of the back and sat in the front next to me, slamming the door shut way harder than necessary.

"Wow. This thing is like a tin can," he said.

"The tin can that brought your sorry ass home," I mumbled. Before I'd been nervous about having Jason in my car. Now I just was annoyed he was there and wanted him out.

I took off from the curb and barely got out onto the road when Jason reached his fingers up towards my stereo buttons.

I slapped his hand away and glared at him for a couple seconds. "No touching!" Then I went back to watching the road. *Only ten more blocks to go.*

He jerked his hand back and laughed. "No touching? What does that even mean?"

"It means what it means."

"That makes no sense." He sounded like he was still laughing inside that stupid big head of his. I couldn't tell if he was mocking me or just feeling a little dizzy over the beer he drank. Whatever it was, it was making me mad.

I tried to explain so his tiny brain would understand. "It makes perfect sense. Do not touch my stereo and I won't slap your hand. Simple math."

"Put it on yourself, then," he said.

"No. I like the silence."

"You're sure talking a lot for someone who likes silence."

"You're the one talking, not me." The ridiculousness of the situation did attract my attention. I just couldn't stop once we got started.

"How do you know where I live?" he asked.

I was grateful for the change of subject. "Because we're neighbors? Because we've lived down the street from each other for over ten years?" Pretty much disgusted with him at this point, I couldn't wait to get to his house and get rid of him. I pressed on the accelerator to make the time stuck with him go by faster.

A full minute passed before he responded. "I knew that, you know. That we're neighbors. I just didn't know if you knew."

"Oh, yeah?" My liar-liar-pants-on-fire alarm started going off in my brain. "Where do I live, then, if you know me so well?" I was probably being a bitch, but I couldn't help it. I imagined he was lying to me like he probably lied to everyone. I was busy cooking up this whole persona for him during this short car ride, and none of it was very pretty.

"Riiiight there," he said, pointing to my house. "The house with all the flowers. You're out there every single weekend planting those things. They look nice."

And just like that, he made me feel very small and very stupid and very mean-girl.

"Yep, that's me," I say, trying to play it off. "The gardener girl."

"The constant gardener. Loved that movie," he said, kind of wistfully.

I was speechless. Nothing I'd imagined about him before was consistent with who he was right then. Was he being a different person for me as some kind of one-act play, or was I seeing the real guy? There was no way for me to know for sure then, but I know the truth now.

But we're not to *now* yet. I still have things to tell you about *then*.

TWO WEEKS WENT BY BEFORE I talked to Jason again. During those two weeks I fantasized that I'd be out constant gardening and he'd pull up in his Camaro and we'd shoot the breeze like old friends. But that never happened. We weren't old friends and he had a life that didn't include me.

Bobby came over, though, of course. I gardened while he did his cuticles and worried about sun exposure. We hung out and analyzed the living daylights out of that night with Jason.

Our final conclusion was that it was one of those moments in your life where the Universe reminds you in a fairly obvious way that things won't always be the same and people aren't always what you expect them to be. At the time we came to this brilliant conclusion, we had no idea how poignantly awful and true that insight would turn out to be for all of us.

It was game day again. Friday. The weather was perfect. The heated talk around school was that this was Jason's big game. *The Game.* The one where the college scouts would all be attending and filming and making decisions over.

Not being a football player, I really had no idea what this would feel like for him, but I imagined it was a pretty big deal. He was probably nervous. A piece of me wanted to drive over to his house after school and tell him good luck. But he wouldn't have been there, anyway. I found out later that he was at the stadium, in the locker rooms reserved for the home team.

I went to the game with Bobby, getting there early so we could have a good seat in the nosebleed area, the top row of the stands on the fifty yard line. We liked being able to see the entire game without anything blocking our view, and the players looking like tiny ants running around the field. We'd hold up our first fingers and thumbs and pretend to squish them as they ran around after that stupid ball. Silly little ants. *Squish!*

The crowd was buzzing, even more so than usual. Bobby was twisted around so he could look out into the parking lot behind us. He banged me on the arm a bunch of times to tell me what he was looking at as I stared down at the groups of people huddled on the sidelines. The game should have started a while ago, but the players weren't even out on the field yet.

"Check it out," Bobby said. "Trouble."

I turned around to see cop cars pouring into the parking lot.

"Whoa. What the hell is that all about?" I turned around more fully and stood up. "It better not be a bomb."

Bobby and I held onto the back railing and watched as the squad cars parked with their lights flashing and several police officers got out. The wind ruffled my hair, and I had the strangest sensation that something evil had just blown into town. I tried to brush off the feeling, but it wouldn't leave.

"I have no idea." Bobby looked at me for a second before he took his phone out and started tapping away at the keyboard.

"Who are you texting?"

"Caroline. Maybe she knows something."

Caroline was the one cheerleader who communicated with those of us on the lower echelon of the school's hierarchy. Her little brother is gay so she has a special place in her heart for guys like Bobby.

A couple seconds later there was a response.

Bobby looked up at me, worry in his eyes.

"What?" I asked, suddenly concerned myself. I hadn't seen this expression on Bobby's face often, so I knew it must be a big deal, whatever it was.

"It's Jason."

Jason and I weren't friends. I didn't even really like him. But in that moment, my heart kind of seized up and I felt sick to my stomach. If nothing else, he was a neighbor. A neighbor who called me the Constant Gardener.

"What about Jason?" I asked, my voice kind of messed up.

Bobby was looking out into the parking lot. "Look," he said, pointing down below us.

And that's when I saw Jason being led out of the building in handcuffs and put into a police car.

THE GAME NEVER STARTED. AN announcement was made over the loudspeaker that it had been cancelled due to an emergency. That was it; that was all they gave us, after calling in an entire battalion of cops.

The stands were full of grouchy adults who apparently lived for this baloney, but all the people my age were more interested in speculating about the reason for the cancellation. The most plausible they came up with was some sort of football player prank gone awry, but that didn't really explain the level of police response we saw, or Jason being hauled off in handcuffs. I mean, that would have to've been a pretty serious prank, for it to end up like that. I thought maybe it was some sort of fight, but that really didn't make sense either because Jason had never been the fighting type before and there would have been more than one person in cuffs, right? And all kinds of injuries?

I had to find out what had happened. Bobby's texts had come up empty. Apparently, the cheerleaders were all on lock-down or something. They never came out on the field either that night.

Good thing the powers-that-be cancelled the game, because I wasn't sure how those players would have found the will to go on without all those pom-poms fluffing around and miniskirts flying up.

"Bobby, do you mind hitching a ride with someone else? I don't feel very good right now."

"Yeah, sure, you go ahead. Text me later." He hugged me and kissed me on the forehead. "I'm here for you if you need me." Somehow he knew that it was the Jason thing bothering me, but he also knew well enough not to say anything about it. There was a time to tease and a time to chill and he was good about recognizing the difference.

I left the stadium and drove home without the radio on, hoping that when I turned the corner, I'd see something up the street at Jason's house shedding some light on the tragedy that had befallen him.

His house was dark. I drove past a couple times, but with all the lights off, it looked like neither Jason nor his dad were home. Jason's mom died when he was a kid, so it was just the two of them. I felt really bad for him then. If I'd been the one arrested, I'd definitely want my mom there on the other side of the bars.

I went back home and up to my room after kissing my parents good night. Then I went online with my laptop and surfed the local news channels, hoping to find out what had happened at the stadium.

That's when I saw the newsflash.

At first it was only on one site, but within an hour, it was picked up by every station.

LOCAL FOOTBALL STAR ARRESTED FOR ALLEGED MURDER OF HIS COACH.

I kept reading the headlines over and over, different iterations of the same theme, getting sicker and sicker as the seconds ticked by. There was a roaring in my ears, and I could actually hear my pulse slamming away in my veins.

My door opened and my mother stuck her head in. "Babe. Did you see the news about Jason Bradley?"

I nodded, afraid that if I said anything out loud I might sound crazy. It was like I was falling apart, bits of me flying out into the air and dissipating like smoke from a blown-out candle. He was just in my car two weeks ago. He loved *The Constant Gardener*. He was funny, and he checked his zipper before he left the bathroom, which to me was a lot like checking for toilet paper on a shoe.

And he murdered someone? His coach, of all people? How was that even remotely possible?

"Can you believe it?" my mom said, opening the door more fully and crossing her arms over her chest. "It all sounds so improbable."

"I know," I said, my voice coming out scratchy.

"You okay?" she asked, frowning at me.

I nodded more vigorously so she wouldn't question me. I wasn't in the mood for a mom-interrogation. "Yeah. I'm fine. I hardly knew him." My gaze slid over to the screen and another headline. "I guess I didn't know him at all."

"We never really know people, do we?" She sighed. "I guess that means the neighborhood is going to be a zoo with the press, for a while at least. Just try to stay clear of it, okay?"

For some reason this struck me as very disloyal and insensitive, but I nodded anyway. "Okay. I will."

"G'night, sweetie," she said. "Need anything before I hit the hay?"

"Nope. Sleep tight," I said.

"Don't let the bed bugs bite," she said back.

That was our thing. I was pretty sure that if she ever didn't say it to me, that I'd have nightmares, or bedbugs would actually start biting me. For some reason tonight it took on special meaning. I wondered if there were bedbugs and anyone to wish them away where Jason would be sleeping tonight.

She shut the door behind her and my room went silent. There was a video I could play on the news website if I wanted to. The thumbnail showed a woman news reporter with a microphone in her hand. The piece was about the football player who killed his coach. They were saying *allegedly*, but their stories kept reading as if he'd already been found guilty. The headline over the video jumped out at me.

Coach Alan Fielding of Banner High School found slain in his stadium office. Alleged killer is Jason Bradley, recently taken into custody after he was found standing over the lifeless body of the beloved coach and mentor to thousands of our city's young men.

I never knew the coach, since he pretty much stayed with football exclusively, but I'd heard he was a nice guy. Tough but fair. He was a big proponent of charity work, so all the guys on the team had to do this Big Brother thing where they mentored kids from bad neighborhoods and taught them about sports and stuff.

Even never having met him, I was mad at Jason for killing him. The news articles were turning my neighbor into someone I didn't know. My mom was probably right. Maybe I never knew him at all.

It made me supremely depressed. I texted Bobby and told him that I was going to need copious amounts of chocolate tomorrow to get over this, and then I felt even worse when I realized that Jason wouldn't be eating any chocolate tonight and for sure felt a hell of a lot worse than I did. This wasn't about me; it was about him. I was so glad to be me that night, which was a first. Normally I was wishing I was someone else, some*where* else.

I thought about Jason and who he was, or who I thought he was. He'd never struck me as the violent type, not even on the field. He always helped people up off the ground and never joined in the shoving matches that sometimes erupted on the field.

Maybe he was provoked. But what could that coach have done to make Jason want to murder him? Did he tell Jason he was going to ride the bench, maybe? Did Jason see his NFL career going in the toilet because of something the coach was going to do, and that was what made him lose it?

Just the very idea made me dislike Jason even more, to imagine him doing something like that, having that attitude. And then I felt bad for jumping to those conclusions without even hearing his side of the story.

Nothing was making sense, so I stopped trying to make it sensical. Instead I put on my p.j.s and shut off my light, climbing into bed and hoping for a very quick transition into unconsciousness.

I fell asleep to tortured dreams about bad people I couldn't see attacking me and calling me a loser.

I WOKE UP DETERMINED ... DETERMINED to find out the truth, or some version of it, anyway. I texted Bobby and he showed up a half hour later, dressed for trouble-making. I can always count on Bobby.

"Where are we going? Will we be storming any ramparts? Because if so, I need to stop by my house and get my rappelling gear."

I couldn't help but smile at the vision of him sliding down a rope. He'd totally scream like a girl the entire way and then complain about his manicure.

"Do you even have any rappelling gear?"

"No, but my dad does, and I'd be overjoyed to steal it."

Bobby's dad was less than thrilled with Bobby's life choices. That's my nice way of saying that Bobby's dad is a dick who really shouldn't be allowed in the house, but since he paid the mortgage, there wasn't really much Bobby could do about it.

"No storming of ramparts today. Maybe tomorrow, though."

Depending on what we find out.

I didn't know why, but at this point I was imagining myself as some kind of superhero. After downing sixteen ounces of orange juice and eating a way-too-sugary breakfast bar, I'd decided that there was no way Jason Bradley, the guy who'd lived down the street from me for the past bunch of years, had killed his coach. Not on the eve of his biggest game. Not without a really good reason.

I needed to find out what that reason was. It was possible I was suffering a minor breakdown in that moment, but I didn't give it a second thought.

Yeah ... for sure I might have been a little crazy that day. I was picturing myself breaking him out of jail and running away while someone solved the mystery and absolved him of his crimes. I had twenty bucks to my name and a quarter tank of gas, but that didn't stop the fantasy from taking hold.

Regardless of the source of my madness, I knew down to the deepest part of my heart that if I'd been falsely accused of a crime, I'd want people to get to the bottom of it and spread the truth instead of the rumors, and school was going to be lousy with lies and conjecture on Monday. If I had to be his PR person at Banner High, then so be it. I was filled with a fire that I didn't quite understand, but I let it burn bright anyway.

We got to the police station where the news people said he was being held. There was a crowd of people outside, most of them with microphones or cameras. There were a few people from school, including Brittney. I didn't see a single footballer, though. That seemed really weird at the time.

Bobby and I sidled up as close to Brittney as we could, trying to eavesdrop on her conversation with Tiffany and some other girls.

She was alternately crying, blowing her nose, and whining about the story as she heard it.

"They said he actually did it. He actually *killed* the coach. I just can't get over it. I was dating a murderer! He could have murdered *me!* Do you know how many times I was alone with him? Oh my god, I feel like I'm going to vomit. I can practically feel his hands closing around my throat right now." She made a gagging sound, and all her friends cleared a path to the grass.

"I really feel like slapping her right now," Bobby said quietly in my ear.

"You and me both." I shook my head in disappointment as she bent over and gagged.

Nothing came out. She was totally faking, thank God.

"All she cares about is herself," I said. Jason had terrible taste in girlfriends, that much was clear.

The crowd parted, pulling my attention away from Brittney. I recognized Jason's dad as he came down the stairs from inside the building. When he saw Brittney, he changed his angle of approach and moved in her direction.

One of her friends tapped her on the shoulder and she looked up. When her expression transitioned to one of fear and revulsion, I really, really wanted to punch her lights out. I almost didn't want to hear what she was going to say next, but Bobby had other ideas for us.

Bobby shoved me so hard I tripped and had to take several steps to right myself. I ended up standing right behind Mr. Bradley.

"He'd really like to see you, Brittney. Can you come inside for a minute?"

Her face went pale. Then she stammered. "Ummm ... hi, Mr. Bradley. Ummm ... no, I can't. I was just leaving." She grabbed Tiffany's shirt and nearly tore it off her in her hurry to leave. "I have to go. I have ... cheer practice."

I let out a big rush of air.

Sooo pissed. That's what I was. Pissed times a hundred. A thousand million. Her boyfriend, the one she hung all over in school and lifted her skirt for every weekend if the rumors were true, was rotting in a cell inside that building and she didn't have time to go see him? What. A. Lowlife. Bitch.

Mr. Bradley watched her go and then slowly turned around.

Bobby pinched me really hard on the back and whisper-yelled in my ear. "Ask him!"

I reached back and slapped him away, already making the plan in my mind.

As Mr. Bradley started walking by, I touched his arm. Before the reporters could descend, I leaned in and said quickly, "I'd love to go see him, Mr. Bradley ... if that's okay with you."

He looked down at me in confusion. Then his brow smoothed out and he gave me a humorless smile. "You're the constant gardener."

His comment made me blush. My face went red hot as I realized he and his son had been talking about me in their house. I wondered if it was recently or something that had happened years ago.

"I guess."

He tilted his head and then his smile seemed more genuine. "Sure. He could use a friend right now." He took me by the elbow and we plowed through the group of people asking really rude questions about his son.

"Did he always have it in for the coach?!"

"Did he tell you he was angry with the coach before the game?!"

"Did he kill him because he got benched?!"

I felt terrible, especially with that last question. I was guilty of thinking the same thing. Shame washed over me as I realized I was just as much an asshole as they were.

Innocent until proven guilty is a joke. Until this happened, I never realized that we're all assholes when we're in the clear, when it's not us being accused. There's this weird and twisted type of satisfaction a person can get inside, when hearing bad news while not *being* the bad news. Like, hey, I'm not a murderer, I'm not sitting in a jail cell right now. Aren't I awesome? Check out how bold and rude I can be, sitting here in my safe little not-accused bubble.

"Where are his other friends?" I asked as we mounted the stairs into the police station.

"Great question." Jason's dad sounded massively stressed.

His reaction made me feel better, like finally someone was expressing the appropriate response for the situation. Me, I was more a kaleidoscope of emotions ... angry, bitter, confused, scared, freaked out, and then sad, all in the space of thirty seconds. Thinking about how Jason must be feeling made my conflicted emotions even worse. Now was not the time to be self-centered. I knew that, and yet I found myself going there again and again.

Guilt assailed me when I realized that I had imagined for a moment that I should be pitied, even when — unlike Jason — I could walk down the sidewalk to my car and drive home whenever I felt like it.

I can be such an a-hole sometimes. Disappointment in my lack of humanity made me want to turn around and run away. I didn't want Jason to see me being this awful person when he already had enough on his plate. But I kept going, anyway. I continued to walk up those stairs and into that building because I knew if I didn't, I'd never be able to live with myself after.

Being inside a police station on a field trip is nothing like being in one when a person you know is being held in a cell there. My heart was beating gangnam-style in my chest and I could literally feel the perspiration coming out of my pores. I was probably sporting a really attractive sweat mustache too, but I was too afraid to lift my hand and wipe it off. The way my fingers were trembling, I could accidentally pick my nose and really make a fabulous impression on Jason's dad.

My steps were robotic, maybe even militaristic in their precision. I didn't want to piss anyone off and get kicked out before I saw Jason. I had no idea what I was going to say to him, but I needed to see him. Maybe to let him know he had at least one person on the outside rooting for him. Maybe to confirm this nightmare was real and I wasn't Alice lost down in a rabbit hole somewhere.

We were led down some corridors with walls of concrete block and into a room with a metal table and chairs. The paint on the walls was a very light green that reminded me of a hospital. There were two cameras, high up in the far corners of the room, and a big glass window on the other side. It was a surreal moment where I thought I was on the set of *Bones* or some TV show like that, ready to be involved in some sort of interrogation.

Mr. Bradley and I sat down in two of the chairs on the same side of the table. The police officer who guided us in left the room and shut the door behind him.

An awkward silence ensued.

I glanced over at Jason's dad and saw his jaw muscles twitching like mad. He rubbed his hands together, bunching one up as a fist and massaging it with the other. The muscle fibers in his arms jumped and moved around.

He's a big man like his son. I almost felt afraid to be alone with him, but then reminded myself that we were in a police station with cameras and a two-way mirror and everything. There were probably five guys on the other side of it watching our every move, recording our every word. Besides ... he wasn't the guy accused of murder.

"Thanks for coming," he finally said, looking at me. His eyes were very bloodshot and there were dark smudges underneath.

"Sure." I didn't know what else to say. Normally, I'm fine around adults, but on this particular day I was tongue-tied, afraid I'd say the wrong thing. I mean, what's the right thing to say to a guy whose son has just been arrested for murder? There is no right thing, so I said nothing.

The door opened, saving me from brain vomiting on Mr. Bradley, and the first sound I heard was chains. It made my blood run cold.

Jason walked into the entrance and just stood there, looking first at me and then his father. His hair was a mess. I don't know why I found that so shocking ... maybe because Jason always looked so fresh and clean and today he looked just plain terrible. Like he'd been in jail all night, which is exactly where he had been. The reality of it made my throat close up and I nearly choked with it.

"What's she doing here? Where's Brittney?"

If there had been a hole in the floor, even a pretty small one, I would have crawled into it. Even though I'm claustrophobic, I would have dived in, head first. I'd never felt so in-the-wrong-place-at-the-wrong-time as I did in that moment. An imposter. A wannabe of the highest degree.

But I immediately told myself that this feeling was ridiculous because I wasn't there to be his girlfriend. I was just there to let him know he had someone at school on his side, or at least willing to listen to his version of events.

"Come in and sit down," Mr. Bradley said, standing up and motioning to his son.

The police officer behind Jason took him by the elbow and led him in. It was slow-going because Jason had both handcuffs and leg irons on. He was still in his street clothes, but his hair was all over the place. His right eye was swollen and going purple. There was what looked like dried blood near his chin.

I was instantly sick to my stomach, queasy. I wanted to stand and run out of the room, but at the last second reminded myself why I was there and didn't. I stayed because I wanted answers, and I wanted to make sure that no one lied about Jason at school. He might have been a big-headed douche a lot of the time, but everyone deserves to have the truth told about them. And he had a black eye. I told myself that had to mean something.

Jason said down, scowling. He slouched in his chair, and I thought at the time that I'd never seen him look so small, so collapsed in on himself. Even when we were in third grade, he always seemed larger than life to me. Today, he looked positively tiny. Defeated. Like nothing would ever be right in his life again. I wanted to cry for him, Argentina.

"Son, don't lose your manners, even though you've lost your place temporarily."

His father's strict tone made me feel just the tiniest bit better, like maybe someone would stay strong in Jason's life and be someone he could lean on. Because for sure Jason looked like he needed it. It was almost surreal how different he seemed. Did murder do this to a human being? Change him fundamentally from the person he could never be again?

My guess was, yes. It definitely did. Maybe even just being accused of the crime could do that, because I still wasn't convinced that Jason had done anything. It had to be a case of mistaken identity or whatever. No way could the kid who lived down the street from me be a murderer. That happened to other people living on *other* streets.

Jason turned in his seat and swung his hands up to rest on the table. "Yes, sir." He kept his gaze down, aimed at his lap between his arms.

"Your *friend*," he meant me, "came by here to support you. Brittney ... couldn't be here."

It was on the tip of my tongue to say that she took off and left him in the dust because she was worried about her reputation, but I didn't. I did hope that he'd find out in the future, though. She didn't deserve him, and he didn't deserve to be burdened with her. He already had enough of a shit storm going on in his life.

"What's your name, hon?" Mr. Bradley asked me.

"Katy. Katherine Mary Magdalina Guckenberger, actually. But I prefer Katy."

He smiled. "That's a mouthful."

I sigh. "Tell me about it. I can't wait to get married."

It totally slipped out without warning. My brain was not properly connected to my mouth, apparently. My face flamed red once more.

Thank the little tiny baby Jesus Mr. Bradley had bigger things to concern him than my brain bloop. He moved on like I hadn't just said something totally lame, like I hadn't just hinted that I had some weird and twisted motive to be in this room with his son.

Gah. Where is that hole in the floor, anyway?

"How have they treated you?" Mr. Bradley asked.

"Fine."

No mention of the black eye. I wondered if that meant Mr. Bradley already knew how it had happened.

"Did you eat?"

"Yes."

"Do you have access to bathrooms?"

Jason finally looked up. "Jesus Christ, Dad, do you really care if I used the toilet or not? Is that your biggest issue right now?"

Anguished. That's what he was. It made my heart hurt just to see that expression on his beautiful, beat up face. He was never so emotional before that I could remember. Even when they won State last year, he just smiled when pretty much the rest of the team was crying like a bunch of babies.

It had nothing to do with me, but I wanted him to have his easy life back. I wanted him to be walking around town with his great, big, blown-up head, knowing he was the shit for every girl who passed by. No kid should have to deal with what he had on his plate right then.

"I'm just trying to have a conversation. Relax, Son. Relax." He took Jason's hands and covered them with his own. It was touching and sad. I'd have bet a million bucks right then that these two men never held hands like this before today. Before the coach was dead. They'd smack each other on the butts and say *Good game!* but they wouldn't hold hands. It was blowing my mind how crazy the world was in that moment, and how it seemed like I was the only one who could see it.

Jason sat that way for a few seconds, but then leaned back in his chair, pulling his hands off the table and resting them in his lap. He looked over at me.

"I know why he's here. Why are you here?"

I tried to smile, but my face wouldn't cooperate. I gave up and tried to answer in a way that wouldn't make me sound like a psycho.

"I just ... wanted to show you some support. See if I can do anything for you."

His smile was bitter. "I think Brittney had the better idea."

"What's that?" I asked, wishing immediately after that I hadn't.

"Get lost. Stay gone. Don't let my shit mess up your life too."

"Jason ..."

"Dad, shut the hell up, okay?" Jason's attention shifted lightning quick to his father. "I did it, okay? I fucking killed the guy. It's over for me and you too if you get all caught up in it." He looked at me and scowled. "You should go."

"Listen, Son ...," Mr. Bradley's volume went up and sternness came in, "... I'm your father. I'm not going anywhere, and this young lady deserves your thanks and your respect, at the very least. She risked a lot coming in here and that's not *nothing*."

I watched shamelessly as Jason's face underwent a transformation. I could literally see the emotions battling inside him. The storm cloud that had surrounded him went darker, then his face went red, and finally when it seemed like he was going to blow, he lost all his mojo. His shoulders sagged and his head dropped, chin to chest.

"I'm sorry," he whispered, lifting his head after a few seconds to look at me. There were tears in his red-rimmed eyes. "I shouldn't have said that. Thanks for coming."

I nodded, the only thing I could do and hold back my own tears at the same time. My heart felt like it was collapsing in on itself with the pain. I wanted this to be all over for him, to be just a bad dream, but no matter how many times I pinched my wrist, it just wouldn't work. We were all three really here. In the jailhouse. Listening to the sounds of Jason's chains clinking together.

The door opened again before anything else could be said, and a police officer in plain clothes told us we had to leave. Jason was pulled to his feet by his upper arm, and he shuffled out of the room in front of us, the chains on his body making clanking sounds all the way down the hall until he disappeared behind a heavy metal door.

It seemed so final when it banged closed. It crossed my mind that I might never see him again after that moment. I hated myself for not saying more when I'd had the chance. For not telling him that I believed in him.

And then I laughed at myself. What does that even mean, to believe in someone? It was just garbage from movies that I'd swallowed my whole life and never questioned. Just like my freedom. Just like my ability to walk out of this place and never come back.

I never appreciated that stuff before now, and I wasn't even sure I could fully grasp how big it was. After all, I wasn't the person being led away in chains. The only thing clinking on me was my ridiculous key-chain collection. It felt really silly and immature for the first time since I started building it eight months ago.

I walked out with Jason's dad and didn't stop until I was at my car. Bobby was sitting on the hood waiting for me.

A few reporters followed us, but thankfully not so closely that Mr. Bradley couldn't say a few things in private.

"I really appreciate you coming, and even though he was kind of pigheaded about it, I know Jason does too. So, thank you. Thanks a lot." He got a little choked up at the end, so I kind of just went with my gut and threw my arms around him awkwardly. My bag banged against our sides with the momentum of my movements.

"I'm happy to. I can come back if you want. I'd like to."

"That would be great," he said over my shoulder. His grip around my back was like iron. I felt for second that I was his anchor before he let me go.

"Want my number?" I asked, wondering if I was overstepping my bounds.

He pulled his cell out of his pocket and handed it to me. "That'd be great."

I quickly entered the digits and then called myself, letting it ring a few times before I hit the red button. Now I could get in touch with him too if necessary. "Call me if you need anything," I said, handing it back.

"Will do. He has his arraignment Monday."

"What time?" I wasn't sure what an arraignment was, but I'd for sure be looking it up online when I got home.

"In the morning. Not sure what time."

I put my hand on his arm when his eyes suddenly got all watery.

"Don't worry, Mr. Bradley. Everything is going to work out." I prayed I wasn't lying when I said that.

"Let's hope so," he said, and then he walked away.

OBBY AND I TALKED ABOUT The Incident, as we came to call it between us, all weekend. The news channels were loaded with conjecture, but so far no one knew the hows or the whys.

I knew Jason had done it; he'd said as much in that room with me and his father. But I wanted to know why. I felt like I *needed* to know, like I'd never be able to rest until I did. There had to be a reason. Not just a reason, but a good reason why he'd snapped.

Bobby and I reminisced about some of our years with Jason. We both had the same image in our minds; he was a privileged kid with everything going for him, charm enough for three guys, and a body and face that made every girl and gay want to be on his arm.

But he wasn't always a douchebag. He'd stuck up for Bobby once, when we were all pretty young. Bobby reminded me and the memory came back like a movie in my head.

Jason pushed a kid down on the playground for calling Bobby a fag-bag. Back then we weren't very creative with our name-calling, but that didn't make it hurt any less, and Jason knew that. He was to some degree the champion of the underdogs in our younger years, always coming to our rescue when kids got too rough — and that happened more often than I care to remember. I think Bobby and I must have had the words *Easy Victim* stamped on our backs or something. It was only when the whole world started showering Jason with accolades that he kind of stopped having time for the superhero act.

Bobby and I decided after discussing it for the entire day Sunday and into the morning Monday on the way to school that Jason was still a champion, deep down inside. That meant he had a story to tell, and I for one wanted to hear what it was.

Turns out, so did everyone else at school. Every single conversation I heard in the halls and in the classrooms was about him. Suddenly upcoming dances, exams, and the latest break-ups were no longer front-page news. Most of the words spoken about Jason were dark. I heard *murderer*, and *cold-blooded*, and *sociopath* more than one time, often from people I was pretty sure he'd had on his BFF list three days ago.

Brittney was really playing it up. I felt like punching her in the boob every time I looked at her. She was crying pretty much the entire day, but whenever someone tried to placate her, it was to tell her she would be fine, that her life wasn't over.

What about Jason? was all I could think. *What about his life being over?* No one seemed to care about that part of the equation.

The football players were being more circumspect. When they talked it was at a whisper. Try as I might, I wasn't able to pick up any of their thoughts, but none of them looked happy. I couldn't tell who they were mad at until I saw one of them in a back hallway with his arms around Brittney.

I ducked behind a wall of lockers and shamelessly eavesdropped.

"Babe, you're going to be fine. It's not you dead in the ground, it's the coach, okay?"

"But it could have been me! It could have been! I was dating a murderer. I slept with him! Oh, God, I feel so dirty!"

"Shhhh, shhhh, don't worry. The law's got him now. He'll be punished for what he did to the coach. For what he did to you. You're going to be all right..."

Some other people were coming from another hall and being loud about it, so Brittney and Trace, her comforter, broke apart and walked away.

It took everything I had not to run after her and bonk her over her stupid air-head with my books.

"Here you are, you little sneak!"

I jumped a mile and turned around lashing out at my attacker like a madwoman with some crazy-ass girl slaps.

"Ow, ow, ow!" Bobby yelled, holding up his hands and curving himself into an s-shape of self-defense. "Put away your smack-o-matic! You know I bruise easy!"

I dropped my arms and huffed out an anxiety-filled breath. My pulse was going nuts. "Do *not* sneak up on me, Bobby Garrity. You *know* that always freaks me out."

"Sorry, geez." He dropped his arm-shield and hiked his backpack up higher on his shoulder. It's a Hannah Montana design complete with tiny stuffed animal keychains hanging from all the zippers. I nearly gag every time I see it, which is exactly why he keeps carrying it around every day. He didn't care that he looked like a Hannah-obsessed, third-grade girl. As far as he was concerned, he was a conversation piece.

I was about to lecture him further when my phone buzzed in my pocket. Normally I didn't risk having it confiscated and kept it off during school hours, but I was hoping Mr. Bradley would call me and update me about Jason so I left it on vibrate. There was really no reason why he would call me, but I didn't let that stop me from dreaming.

"Who's that?" Bobby asked.

I read the text. *Arraignment not so good. You can visit after school if you want. This is Chuck, by the way. Jason's father.*

I smiled a little at that. As if I wouldn't know who he was. Humility in a situation like this was kind of crazy, but nice all the same.

"Who, who, who? Come on, don't make me beg." Bobby was twisting around trying to read my screen.

"It's Jason's dad. He says I can visit Jason after school."

Bobby stopped dancing around and just stood there.

"What?" I finally said, hating the expression on his face.

"Are you sure you want to do that?"

It pissed me off that he would even ask. "Of course I do. Why would you even say that?"

"Hey, don't shoot me, okay? I'm just wondering if you've played this all out in your head or if you're just kind of mesmerized by the muscles."

"What does that even mean?" We had two minutes before our next class, so I walked away, expecting him to follow and harass me some more.

He didn't disappoint. "It meeeeans, that if you keep going over there and hanging out with him, you risk the wrath of Britt-n-Tiff and possibly other people. Do you know what your motivations are? Are they good ones?"

I sighed loud in annoyance.

Bobby sighed too, mocking me. "Let's just say that it won't enhance your reputation here in the hallowed halls, so it better be worth it."

"Screw my reputation." I was fuming at this point, not so much at him but at the truth of what he was saying. I was so disappointed in my fellow man at that point.

"Okaaaay, then. Screw the reputation. Got it. Check. Noted." He followed me all the way to American History. "Call me later?"

"Maybe," I responded, opening the door.

"Toodles." He was gone before I could say anything else.

I turned to watch him swish and sway down the hallway, his stupid tiny stuffed animals hanging from his backpack swishing and swaying right along with him. He was impossible to stay mad at, not that I was really mad at him to begin with.

I shook my head at his antics. If anyone should be concerned about his reputation, it was him, not me. He delighted in taunting people over his life choices, his wardrobe, his backpack flair. He dared them to say anything about it. He was loud, he was proud, and he never took any poop from anyone.

He could hardly blame me if I'd turned out to be exactly like him. A best friend tends to have that kind of influence on a person.

I took my seat in the classroom and had to work really hard to not turn around and stare at the empty spot in the back row where Jason should have been. Instead, I watched the clock and the minute hand slowly making its way around its face. Ninety more minutes and I'd be able to leave to go see Jason. I wondered if he'd be any happier to see me today than he had been on Friday.

I MET MR. BRADLEY IN the parking lot of the jail on the out-skirts of town. Jason had been moved after his arraignment to the county facility instead of the small, local police station.

It was seriously depressing for me to drive up to that drab, menacing-looking place. I could only imagine what it must have been like for Jason to arrive in cuffs, knowing he was going to be staying there for the foreseeable future. Apparently he pled not guilty *on the advice of counsel.* At the time I heard this from Mr. Bradley, I wondered if he had some sort of guidance counselor at the jail, but I learned later it was a lawyer that was the counsel person.

"I'm glad you came," Mr. Bradley said, holding out his hand to shake mine after I got out of my car. We were parked next to each other in a mostly empty part of the lot.

I stared down at his proffered hand, thinking how weird it was that we were shaking hands. I took it anyway and did what he expected of me, shifting my backpack to the other arm to make it easier.

"I'm happy to be here. Thanks for calling me." I didn't tell my parents where I was going. They were better off thinking I was hanging out with Bobby after school than getting involved with a murder suspect. My mother would give birth to a farm animal if she knew where I was right now. My father would probably just frown, but sometimes that frown is just as powerful as a full-on freak-out from my mom.

We walked to the building together from the parking lot, following the sidewalks that were all at right angles to each other. It was silly, but it bugged me that there were no curves, no flowers, no hope of any kind there.

"You're not the only one I called, you know," Mr. Bradley said. "But it's funny how all his other friends seem to have very busy schedules all of a sudden."

My heart started aching for both Jason and his dad then. It was a dull pounding, timed with the rhythm of my pulse. "Yeah. That stuff happens, I guess." What else was I going to say? That everyone at school had already written Jason off as a cold-blooded killer, too dangerous to even admit to knowing?

Mr. Bradley's voice went bitter. "They all have college football careers to watch out for. You know how it is."

"Yeah," I said, at the same time hating them for that narrow-mindedness. Maybe it was easy for me, not being a big important football star, but still... With friends like that, why bother?

"Apparently they were all big fans of the coach."

"Understandable," I said, not sure it was. But I couldn't just say nothing, and I definitely couldn't say, *What a bunch of douchebag numbnuts*, because I was taught not to cuss around adults, even though I did a hell of a lot of it with my friends and in my head.

"We were fans too, Jason and I. I just can't understand ..." He stopped there, leaving the rest to my imagination.

"Did he say anything to you? Jason, I mean?" We came even with the front doors as I finished my question. I wanted to know his answer and then I didn't at the same time. It was so confusing.

"Nothing. Just that he did it and he didn't want to talk about it." He paused as he grabbed the rectangular door handle. "I cannot understand how he could have come to this place in his life. I never imagined ..." He stopped there, shaking his head.

Even though it was really warm out, a chill settled into my bones. How much could I possibly know Jason Bradley when his own father didn't even know him? Was this a smart thing to do? Visit him in jail? I knew my mother was going to shit a toaster when she found out, and she *would* find out, that was for sure. Nothing gets past her, like, *ever*.

"Maybe we'll find out how it all happened or why," I said, not sure that we ever would.

"Let's hope so," he responded, opening the door so I could go in before him.

WE HAD TO WAIT A long time before Jason joined us in the room that had all the same features as the one in the local jail but bigger. I texted Bobby pretty much the entire time, relieving Mr. Bradley of the chore of conversation. He was really stressed out. He kept staring at the door, waiting for it to open.

When it finally did, I put the phone in my bag and stared at Jason as he shuffled in. He wasn't wearing his own street clothes anymore. Now he was in a bright red jumpsuit with slippers on his feet. His eyes were bloodshot and his black eye looked even worse.

Mr. Bradley started clearing his throat over and over. I caught his Adam's apple bobbing up and down as he tried to control his emotions. It scared me because I wasn't used to seeing adults look so lost.

Jason sat down in his metal chair across from us and rested his hands in his lap. At first he kept his eyes down, but then he glanced up at me. "Thanks for coming again."

"You're welcome," I said. So polite. So lame.

He cast his eyes down.

"Is your lawyer coming?" Mr. Bradley asked.

"No. He's got other cases."

I looked from father to son and back to father again. "Is he using one of those free lawyers?" I'd seen them on TV a thousand times, those court-appointed defense attorneys you get if you can't afford a real one of your own. It was weird to realize that I knew somewhat how this system worked.

"For now." Mr. Bradley explained. "I have to see if I can get a second mortgage on the house. If I can, then we'll get him a better one."

"Don't bother," Jason said, looking up again. "I told you there's no point."

"Son, don't say that." Mr. Bradley leaned in closer, putting his arms on the table in front of him. "We can get you out of this. Self-defense or whatever it was, I know you're not guilty."

Jason looked up, his eyes red-rimmed. "Of course I'm guilty, Dad. Don't kid yourself. I fucking killed him, okay? I punched him over and over and he slammed his head into the desk. He never woke up. I did it. I'm a murderer." He turned his head slightly to look at me, his anger simmering just below the surface. "You got that? A murderer. So you can stop showing up and feeling sorry for me."

I blinked a few times, letting my brain absorb not only the facts but the rejection. I kind of went cold, but only because the emotions were just too much to process on the spot like that.

"Did you hear me?" he asked, sounding angrier.

"Son..."

Jason whipped his head over to stare his father down with a malevolent glare. "Just ... shut up, okay, Dad? Sorry to say that, but shut the hell up. I don't want to hear it." Jason stood and looked over his shoulder at the door.

"Sit down," I said, not really knowing what I was going to say until I said it. "I drove all the way over here from school to see you, and you can at least have the decency to talk for two minutes."

Ha! There I was, sitting in jail ordering a murderer around! I was temporarily insane, apparently. But it made me appreciate on the tiniest level that sometimes we can be a different person in a split second when the pressure is on. Maybe that was what happened with Jason and the coach. It made me braver, fueled the fire that was burning in my chest.

Jason looked down at me with an expression on his face like I was nuts, which to be fair, I probably was to say that.

"Decency?"

"Yes," I said, sticking my chin out, "decency. Just because you're a murderer doesn't mean you don't have to be polite to people anymore." Or maybe it did, but this was the only argument I could come up with.

Jason's face went all wonky for a few seconds, like he was going to cry or scream or something ... and then his features smoothed out and he kind of smiled. "You're seriously strange, you know that?"

I could sense Mr. Bradley looking at me, so I turned my head to face him. "Sorry. That was rude."

His eyebrows went up and he shook his head. "No, you were right on the money." He looked up at his son. "Can you sit down please? We're here to talk. No pressure. We can discuss school, or how you're feeling, or football, whatever you want."

Jason dropped into the seat and scowled. "Not football. Do not talk to me about football ever again."

That told me more about what Jason was going through than anything else he'd said. *No more football.* The thing that had been the centerpiece of his life, of his teenage reality ... gone. Poof. Like it never existed.

The door opened and a man stuck his head in. "Hello! Mr. Bradley?"

Jason's dad lifted his head and his expression lightened up. He seemed happy to see whoever this was. "Oh, hey. You want to come in?"

"Actually, I'd like to speak with you outside if you have a minute." He nodded at Jason. "Hello, Jason. How're you holding up?"

Jason shrugged but didn't say anything.

"You okay in here alone?" Mr. Bradley asked me, standing in front of his chair.

"Sure. No problem." Only after I agreed did I realize I was telling him I was fine alone in a room with a self-proclaimed murderer. It probably should have freaked me out, but it didn't. This was Jason sitting here before me, not some deranged psychopath. I did kind of wonder why none of the adults around me were concerned, though, especially since he admitted to the crime. But no way was I going to mention rules or whatever. Jason needed to know I wasn't afraid, even if I might have been just the littlest bit.

"There's a guard just outside the door who's watching," the guy in the doorway said to me as if he'd read my mind. "Don't worry, you'll be fine."

I hated him in that moment since he gave voice to my temporary thoughts. And Jason heard it too, which made it ten times worse.

"Of course I'll be fine." I scolded him with my squinted-up eyes. "Don't be ridiculous."

They guy's eyebrows went up, but then Mr. Bradley was standing in front of him and his attention was pulled away.

A moment later Jason and I were alone in the room, him in handcuffs and me in a panic. I had no idea what to say to him. There were no words that could express my pity or my sadness over what had happened, and I didn't even know what *had* happened.

"I'd never hurt you, you know," Jason said finally after a very long minute of silence. He sounded awkward. Embarrassed. Ashamed.

I tried to laugh it off. "I know that. Please. As if." I rolled my eyes, but my grip on my bag went tighter all on its own. Not that there was anything inside that would have helped me if he did decide to attack me. They'd searched it at the main door and pulled out my nail file and my mascara. I had no idea that mascara was such a dangerous weapon until today.

Jason stared at the table for a while before he asked his next question. "Is everyone at school talking about it?"

I nodded. "Yeah. Everyone. It's like the biggest news since Obama."

"Great." He turned his head and stared at the side wall. "Brittney say anything to you?"

"Brittney? No. I heard her talking to some guy, but whatever." I wished as soon as the words were out that I'd kept my big mouth shut. Jason didn't need to hear what a b-word his girlfriend was right now.

"She dumped me you know. Did it through my dad. Sent him a frigging text message."

I pressed my lips together trying to keep my opinion to myself, but it didn't work. "What a bitch."

He laughed. "Yeah, well ... can't blame her, can you?"

"Hell yes, I can blame her. Where's the loyalty?" I did some sort of half-grunt, half-snort that Bobby would have roasted me for. So not lady-like.

He stared at me for a long time after that. So long that I started squirming in my chair. But I didn't look away. I couldn't. He needed to see that I meant what I said.

"Loyalty," he finally said.

"Yes. Loyalty."

"It's a funny thing, isn't it?" He cocked his head to the side a little.

I frowned, not sure I understood. "I don't know. Is it?"

He nodded. "It is. Trust me. It is."

My heart started racing. I knew he was talking about the coach somehow, telling me something about what happened without actually saying it. "You're a loyal person too, you know. I don't know you that well, but I know that."

"Apparently not," he said, sounding bitter.

I took my bag off my shoulder and from across my chest and dropped it on the floor next to me so I could pull my chair in closer. "You are. And you're a good person, Jason, so whatever you did, I know you did it for a good reason." I desperately wanted him to believe that.

He looked at me like I was an asshole, a scowl of disgust on his face. "How can you say that? I *murdered* someone. With my *bare hands.*" He held them up for me to see. The handcuffs banged against the metal table making a loud clatter.

I shrugged, refusing to look at them, like it wasn't the biggest deal in the entire world that he murdered someone, which it was.

"Like I said. It can't have been in cold blood. He said something or he did something that was wrong." I prayed it wasn't him putting Jason on the bench during the big game, because as much as I liked Jason and as much as I appreciated him defending my best friend all those years ago, that was not a good reason to kill a man.

Jason's eyes took on a faraway look and then went red. Tears welled up and then just fell down his face. He didn't make a move to wipe them away.

"I trusted him," he finally said, his voice hoarse.

"Everyone does," I said in almost a whisper. "Did, I mean." I cringed at my use of the past tense. What a jerk I can be sometimes.

Jason turned what looked like fury on me. "We were wrong. We were all wrong."

The door opened and Jason's father came in followed by that other guy, stopping our conversation or whatever it was that was happening in its tracks.

Relief washed through me. Things had gotten suddenly intense, and I hadn't been prepared. I wanted to know what he was talking about and then I didn't, too.

"Jace, your attorney wants to talk to you alone." He looked over at me. "Katy, do you mind waiting outside?"

I leaned down and grabbed my bag, feeling guilty over the fact that I was happy to be interrupted. Jason had sounded like he was about to lose it, and I didn't want that for him. I didn't fear for my safety, but I knew he was walking the fine line between sanity and not, and I didn't want to be the one to inspire him over the edge.

"Yeah, sure, no problem," I said.

As I was walking by Jason, I stopped and put my hand on his arm. I didn't want to disappear without saying anything. I knew what he'd shared was a lot, and I'd keep those words to myself as long as I lived. I could do that for him. I could be loyal as hell when the need arose.

"I'm not going anywhere, Jason," I said, squeezing his forearm, sensing the strong muscles under the stiff material of his jumpsuit. "I'll see you again real soon."

"Don't bother," he muttered.

For some reason, I had this flash in my mind that he was Bobby and not himself. That's the only explanation for my next move.

I lifted my hand and bapped him on the back of the head with it. "Stop feeling sorry for yourself, butthead. And you can stop being ungrateful while you're at it, too."

I walked out of the totally quiet room leaving three stunned-into-silence men behind me.

I LEFT THE COUNTY JAIL before Mr. Bradley came out. I was too embarrassed about losing my cool and assaulting his son to hang around and wait for him to appear. I chanted prayers all the way home that Mr. Bradley wouldn't come by and tell my parents what I'd done.

Thankfully, the rest of the evening passed without incident. Mr. Bradley never showed up, and Bobby agreed to wait until tomorrow to grill me about my visit.

When I went to bed, I lay there staring at the ceiling, hugging my old teddy bear to my chest like I used to when I was tiny. I'd rescued him before bedtime from a bookshelf where he'd been banished a few years ago when I'd decided I was too old and so-phisticated to sleep with baby toys.

Not normally a very religious person, I was moved to break my normal routine of falling asleep to visions of sheep jumping over a line of monster trucks and prayed for my friend instead.

Dear God. Can I call you God? I was a little worried about be-ing too casual since we really weren't on speaking terms, but I figured he wouldn't mind in the end and kept on going. *Anyway, I have this friend. You know him. He's Jason. He broke probably your biggest rule or commandment or whatever you call it on Friday night. I've heard you're a forgiving kind of deity, so I'm hoping that applies to him. I don't think he meant to do it, or if he did, there's a good reason for it. I know the rule is that there is no good reason to end someone, but I don't really believe that rule. I mean, not that I'm in a position to judge, but I feel like I have heard of lots of monsters who don't deserve to be here with people who, you know, don't hurt other people or whatever. So if you could find it in your ... heart or ... whatever organ you use, if you even have organs, could you forgive him? Help him out? Let everyone see who he really is? Including me? That would be really cool. Okay ... that's all I have for tonight ... high five ... peace out. Oh, and thanks.*

I fell into a restless, dream-filled sleep where Jason's face kept coming back up, floating before me with the red jumpsuit below it, him saying, *I trusted him. I trusted the coach. I trusted him.*

I went ahead and classified it as a nightmare when the next scene in my brain was Jason being buried alive, with me standing there holding one of the shovels of dirt.

TUESDAY WAS A RAINY, CRAPPY day. The perfect weather for my terrible mood. Not only was I tired from a partially sleepless and partially nightmare-filled night, but my car decided it didn't want to start when I tried to leave for school.

I called Bobby, irritated beyond reason. I couldn't keep the snappishness out of my voice. "Can you borrow your mom's car and come over here and get me?"

"Well, good morning, Miss Merry Sunshine. And how are you this lovely day?" His voice was way too chipper, grating on my nerves like nails on a chalkboard.

"My life is poop on a stick, thanks for asking. Are you coming or not?"

"Let me see. Hold on." I waited while he screeched down the stairs at his mother. He came back on the line a few seconds later. "She says yes, but we have to put some gas in it."

"I have five bucks."

"*Done!* said the king with a stroke. I'll be there in ten."

"Make it five. I can't be late."

"Bossy pants? Hello? Okay, fine. I'll be there, but don't expect me to be beautiful. You're cutting into my regimen."

By regimen he meant the fifteen minutes he spends putting lotion and crap on his face every morning. He constantly worried about wrinkles. He says his mother's face is like the map of the highways and byways running through the northeast United States and he has to do whatever he can to avoid that same fate.

While I waited for Bobby to show up, I texted Mr. Bradley. It felt a little strange doing it, but I forged ahead anyway. He didn't seem to mind me visiting his son. Hopefully the slap-on-the-head situation hadn't changed his opinion of me too drastically.

When can I visit Jason again?

Just as Bobby was pulling up to the front of my house, the answer came back.

Next week. Monday again. 4:30. Meet you there?

I texted back an affirmative as I went out to the car, getting in beside Bobby and hitting *Send*. I was disappointed it wasn't today or even tomorrow, but decided I should be grateful he was letting me see Jason at all.

"Who you texting, yo?" Bobby asked, using his best ghetto accent.

"Jason's dad. Setting up our next visit."

Bobby didn't say anything for a while, which was a sure sign he had something to say. Otherwise, he would have been prattling on about nothing.

"Go ahead and just say it," I sighed out. "Stop playing like you're not about to get all up in my bidness."

"I'm just worried is all." He patted me on the leg. "You're getting very involved, and right now the only ones who know that are Jason and his dad and me. But pretty soon people at school will know and then you'll get labeled." He looked over at me with concern in his eyes, the genuine kind, not the goofing around kind. It reminded me way too much of an expression I've seen on my mother's face.

My temper started to rise over the fact that he felt the need to chastise me, as if I were just a stupid little kid who needed adult guidance.

"Labeled?" I did my best to keep my anger hidden. "Labeled as what?"

He shrugged. "I don't know. Groupie or something?" He glanced over at me to gauge my reaction.

I ignored his look, staring out the front window and trying not to get angry over the utter stupidity of high school people — a completely pointless exercise if there ever was one. It's a fact; high schoolers be stupid.

"So?" I finally said. "Who cares?"

Yeah. That was my brilliant repartée. Now you know why I'm not involved in Debate Club activities.

"*You* will, eventually. Being invisible is not the same as being a pariah, you know."

I didn't respond because he was completely right, and obviously this was something that I'd already thought about. It kind of deflated my angry balloon a little. Being mad at Bobby made no sense, and being mad at the world made even less sense. I wasn't going to change anyone else's view of things, but I could control my own.

The fact that I was pretty much totally involved wouldn't change, no matter what Bobby said, no matter how logical his arguments might be. It *couldn't* change. I was fully committed to being Jason's friend at this point, and there was no going back in my mind. No way could I not show up at Jason's new home-away-from-home, especially now that I'd slapped him around. I had to see this thing through, for better or for worse.

I only gave a passing thought at that time to the fact that I was officially saying goodbye to my high-school life as I knew it. Looking back, I've wondered if I would have made a different decision, had I known what I was in for.

THE REST OF THE CAR ride to school passed with zero conversation and lots of loud music, mostly of the Katy Perry variety because Bobby is such a huge fan and my brain was too busy thinking about Jason's fucked-up life to bitch about the lack of variety.

We parked in the farthest lot from the school, the place reserved for people who don't have regular paid parking stickers. I was sweating and all the crankier for it, dripping wet by the time I reached the main sidewalk leading up to the closest building. I hate starting the day off with my shirt plastered to my body. Nothing good ever came of that in my experience.

It was terrible timing that we ended up walking just behind a group of football players talking in their normal, loud, nobody-matters-but-us kind of way.

"I'll fucking kick his face in if I ever see it again," said one of them, his swagger advertising to the world that he was just the man for the job.

"When's the memorial for Coach?" another one asked. "This Wednesday, right?"

That's when I knew they were talking about *The Incident*. The murder. *Jason*. My pulse quickened as did my pace.

"Yeah, it's Wednesday," said the future potential face-kicker.

"Did you guys hear that Jason might show up?" said a third guy. "That's what Brittney said. She's totally freaking out, poor girl."

My jaw dropped open at that utter lie, and I was instantly fuming. Brittney seriously needed a boob punch in the worst way.

Bobby grabbed my arm when he noticed me speeding up even more. "Easy, sister. Just let it go," he said in a quiet voice.

I yanked my arm away from him and ignored his advice completely. That was probably a stupid move, but I'd pretty much abandoned being circumspect at that point. I slap murderers around and then I stick up for them when they're being maligned. *Boom*. That's how I roll. Chaos? Yes, give me more of that, please.

"Hey, assholes!" I shouted, coming up behind the group of five football players. It was a little harder to breathe, the closer I got. I never talked to these types of guys if I could help it. Now I was calling a whole group of them out.

They kept going, in complete denial that I could be speaking to any of them.

Typical.

I could have stopped there and walked on with my head down, pretending like nothing had ever happened, and no one would have been the wiser except maybe Bobby, — who, for the record, looked like he was about to have an apoplectic fit — but instead I raised my voice and gave it another try.

"Hey, assholes on the football team! Yeah, I'm talking to you!"

Several people walking nearby slowed down and moved to get in a better position for spectating. I'd thrown down the gauntlet, and I could tell it was finally sinking into the group's collective football brain that I meant it for them, as they slowed and looked at each other in confusion.

The biggest one, the guy who issued the threat to kick Jason's face in, turned around first.

"Say what?" he asked, and then he laughed. "Check this," he said, hitting his buddy on the arm and then pointing at me.

They all stopped and turned around, facing Bobby and me.

I kept going until I was just feet away, shifting so that I was in front of Bobby. This wasn't his fight; no need for him to get pummeled.

I had to look up to meet their eyes since none of them were less than a foot taller than me. The big one was probably six and a half feet, so a full foot plus a few bonus inches bigger. Talk about David and Goliath. All I could think when I stared up at his giant, square-shaped head was that he *had* to be sprinkling steroid powder on his Lucky Charms in the morning. His neck was as thick as my waist.

"Jesus, how many years can they hold you back before you can't compete anymore?" I muttered, my head cranked way back so I could still see his face.

"What'd you say?" one of the other guys asked. He sounded confused.

I decided to stick to my first line of attack. "I said, *Hey assholes*, but that's not all I have to say." I gripped the strap of my backpack really hard with both hands.

Expressions darkened. A couple of the footballers dropped their backpacks to the ground. It crossed my mind that I was about thirty seconds away from being killed, and boy, wouldn't they be hypocrites if they did that to me? That tiny measure of satisfaction did nothing to cure the almost-heart attack I was suffering as they all stared me down.

I did find some courage in the fact that they didn't want to be in jail next to their former teammate any more than I wanted to be buried in the same cemetery as their former coach. I wasn't seriously worried about a throw-down, at least not with all these witnesses standing around. No, here I had the freedom to tell them all about themselves without fear of a premature death anytime soon. I'd worry about later, later. It was time they got a little dose of reality, served up fresh and hot, courtesy of little old me.

"What's your fucking problem?" one of them asked, rocking side to side like a drunk rooster and flopping his hands around a little near his crotch. "You on the rag or something? Lost your mind with temporary insanity?"

Ugh. Where are all the metal chairs when you need one? I used to laugh at professional wrestling, but today would have been a good day for some chair-to-head bashing.

I smiled in a bitter, I-couldn't-be-more-disappointed-in-the-male-gender way, shaking my head. "Typical. A girl tells you that you're an asshole and it's all on her. It couldn't possibly be that you're an *actual*, bona fide asshole, could it?"

"Get to the point," the biggest one said. He was a lot less roost-er-ish, but his steady calm made him more scary.

My heart was pounding so hard it was like it wanted to get out of my chest and run away on its own, abandon my stupid mouth to its fate. It was making my shirt quiver with every beat.

My voice came out high and reedy as my ears flamed hot red. "The point is that you guys are a bunch of disloyal, hypocritical assholes who aren't fit to wipe Jason Bradley's ass, let alone be on his team." I hitched my backpack up higher on my shoulder because it was sliding down with the weight of my books. Taking a deep breath did nothing to calm my nerves.

They stared at me for a few seconds and then, frustratingly, started laughing.

"Check her out," the smallest one said. "Shorty got her box all up on his kickstand, coming in here scolding us." He shook his head at me like I was the one to be pitied. "Guy's a murderer, yo. Killed a good man. He better not ever show his face to any of us ever again or he's gonna find hisself buried too." He looked at all his friends, nodding and getting encouragement before turning back to face me. "Balee dat."

That was his grand finish, and they all kept nodding like a bunch of stupid bobble heads right along with him.

"Hisself? *Hisself?* Seriously? Do you not even hear yourself? Is grammar optional now?" I was disgusted with them being turncoats and on top of that, barely educated. Football players at our school always got a free pass, in part because of that stupid coach who did something to Jason that was bad enough he got smacked down for it.

I didn't mean to be minimizing the seriousness of what had happened to the dude in my head, but this whole situation just felt horrifically, terribly wrong. I knew for a fact that these guys used to call Jason their brother, for shit's sake.

"Come on, man, you're wasting your time," one of them said to the small guy. "She ain't worth it and neither is he."

But the small guy was not so easily dissuaded. He walked up to me and stopped when he was way too close. Putting his finger into my face, he leaned down so we were just inches apart. "You watch your mouth, bitch, or you'll end up sorry, I can promise you that."

I smacked his finger out of the way, my voice no longer all goofy. Something inside me took over and helped me sound all badass. I think I was channeling Zena the warrior princess.

"Get your dirty finger out of my face, asshole. God knows where that thing's been. I don't want to catch anything nasty."

He turned partway around. "You saw her hit me, right? You all saw that. That's assault and battery."

"Yeah, we saw it," said one of his friends. "Let's go talk to Principal Lindberg."

I started laughing, forced to bend over to the side a little to save my stomach muscles and not bump into the guy's massive chest. I think it was the adrenaline that was pumping through my heart and veins that made the wrong emotion start emoting. When I should have been quaking in my Converse and crying, I was giggling like a loon.

"Yeah, go ahead, dick cheese. Tattle on me." I stood up with a big old smile and waved all of them off with one big sweeping gesture of my arm. "Big bad fucking athletes? *Pffff*, right. Bunch of children is what you are. Good luck making it to State without Jason." I shook my head, so ashamed of them. "Assholes."

Bobby grabbed my backpack at that point and pulled me away from the group. "Iiiii think we're done here," he said under his breath. "Come on, sweetie pie. Off to class now." He pushed me around the group of kids who'd gathered to watch the show, but I stared the players down the entire way past them.

"Fucking *cowards*," I spat out, flipping them off at the same time.

The little guy leapt towards me like he was going to tackle me, but his friends held him back.

My responding laugh was fueled purely by the energy boost that surviving that mess gave me, because I was back to sweating bullets and shaking all over.

When we reached the school and stepped inside, Bobby grabbed me by the backpack, spun me around, and slapped me right across the face.

I stood there pressing my hand to my stinging cheek in stunned silence, all the fight in me fleeing for parts unknown. I could hear my heart beating in my ears. It was very possible I was smelling something not very nice from my armpit area too. Suffice to say, I was not in a good place.

"Don't you *ever* do that again, do you hear me?!" Bobby's voice had gone up to levels that I was pretty sure could damage a dog's sensitive ears. He was crying too, obviously nearing the edge of a full-on panic attack. "You almost got yourself killed!" He grabbed me by the arm and dragged me down the hallway as the double-doors behind us opened and students started coming in.

"I had to say *something*," I whined, my feet slapping on the linoleum as I unsuccessfully tried to slow him down.

"No, you didn't. At least not *that*." We turned several corners until we were in a back hallway not often frequented by anyone but smokers trying to hide from teachers.

"It was fine," I said, trying to reassure him and myself at the same time. "I'm fine, see?" I held up my hands and let him assess my totally unscathed body parts. I was only trembling a little by then. He probably didn't even notice.

Bobby folded his arms across his scrawny chest. "Listen ... I get it that you have some sort of bond with Jason or that you feel some sort of responsibility, okay? I get that." His arms came apart and his hands started flying all around his head next. "What I *don't* get is the death wish. Do you think that you'll somehow start a fight, get arrested, and be able to share a cell with him or something?"

"No. Don't be ridiculous." The very idea made my face burn red. Would people really think that about me? That I could be that stupid and naive? How humiliating.

"Okay then. *Think*. Think about what you're doing before you do it." He started tapping his toe then, hands on hips.

"You heard what they were saying, Bobby. I couldn't just let it go."

"Of course you can. It's just *talk*." He grabbed me by the upper arms and shook me a couple times. "You make me so *crazy* sometimes! Assholes like that talk all the time. Talk means *nothing*. But letting yourself get kicked out of school or worse *is* something. Something bad. *Very* bad." He finally quit shaking me, which was a good thing because I was starting to get a headache. "Do you think your parents will let you visit Jason if you're suspended? Or expelled?"

I dropped my gaze to the floor, fully chagrined and feeling about as smart as a kindergartner. "They don't know I'm visiting, so maybe it wouldn't matter."

"If you get yourself kicked out of school, I'll tell them. I totally will."

I lifted my head in a hurry at that. "What? Are you serious?"

"Yes, I'm serious. I will tattle and tattle and *tattle*. 'Til my tongue falls out, I will tattle like a tattling mofo b-word."

"Why would you do that?" The loyalty argument was rising to my lips as he answered.

"Because I love you. And when you see someone you care about making bad decisions, when they need you, you intervene, even when it means you can get hurt in the process and they might even hate you for it."

I could not stay mad at him after that little speech. It was like the sun burst out from behind some dark clouds and shined warm rays right onto my cold face, thawing me out. He made total sense in a world I was starting to think would never make sense again.

Instead of arguing like I'd planned to, I turned him sideways, laced my arm through his, and guided him back to the main part of school. "I agree with you completely." It felt so good to say that. To know that one other person and I were on the same wavelength. "And now when anyone asks me why I'm standing by Jason during this debacle I'll have the perfect answer."

He eyed me suspiciously. "So you'll stop trying to take on the football team single-handedly?"

"Yes. I think." I shook my head, ridding it of my vigilante visions. "No, I know I will. I'll stop, I promise."

"And you'll stop looking for trouble when none of that crap matters?"

"Yes. And thank you for putting things into perspective for me."

He smiled big and the bounce came back into his step. "Wow. That was way easier than I thought it would be. And you're very welcome, by the way. I'll send you my bill later. Lucky for you I'm running a special on perspective re-calibration this week, otherwise I'm pretty sure you wouldn't be able to afford me."

"I look forward to getting it." I was trying not to laugh at the way Bobby was swishing again. At the very least, I could always count on him for entertainment, but today, he'd shown me he was worth his weight in gold. Friends like Bobby are really hard to come by, and as much as I didn't really like what he was saying, I knew he was right.

If I was going to be helpful to Jason, it wouldn't be by fighting wars that had no good outcome. It would be by just *being there*. Being a friend like Bobby always was to me. Maybe the best I'd be able to do would be that, and I'd just have to pray that it would be good enough. What everybody else thought didn't matter. If they were the type to turn their backs on a friend when he needed them most, they weren't worth my time anyway.

I floated to my first class of the day, hanging on the arm of my BFF. The euphoria didn't last that long, though. Unfortunately, my newfound perspective did *not* come with an automatic erasure of what I'd started out in the parking lot. I had one good period of classes before the foo doo really hit the fan.

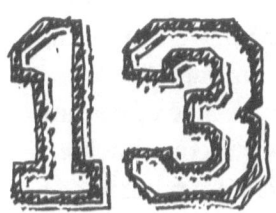

I WAS WALKING DOWN THE hall to my Algebra II class when something hit me really hard in the middle of my back, sending me flying.

It was not pretty. One minute I was upright, the next I was bent in half backwards, my head whiplashing in reverse and my pelvis charging forward.

My knees hit the linoleum first and the rest of me went down like a really bad version of a break-dancing worm. My backpack was the last to succumb to gravity, landing on my neck, the full force of thirty pounds of books denting my spine.

There were several gasps of surprised horror and then some evil laughs. Once I could breathe again, I rolled over to find Brittney standing behind me.

"God, you're clumsy, aren't you?" Standing on one side of her was her evil twin Tiffany and on the other was one of the football players I saw her with earlier.

I was overwhelmed by a mixture of both extreme humiliation and a fury I'd never known in my seventeen years of life. For just a moment, I pictured myself leaping up and choking the life out of Brittney, and it was very satisfying for the nanosecond my brain forgot that murder is wrong.

It took me a while to get on my feet. Everything ached. Bobby's wise words echoed in my brain and cooled my fury just enough to take the edge off.

"You did that," I said once I was steady.

Yes, master of the obvious, that's me.

"I don't know what you're talking about. A little friendly advice, though? Watch your back."

"Literally," I said, my sense of humor overriding my ability to come up with tough, witty comebacks.

"What?" She scrunched up her face and pulled her chin back into her neck.

"I mean, you just punched me in the back, so ... yeah ..." I waited for her to catch up, but it just seemed to frustrate her more that I had nothing else to say.

You might think I was taking the high road here, following Bobby's sage advice to turn the other cheek or whatever, but in reality I was just so stunned from being physically attacked by a deranged Barbie-ho that I couldn't think of anything else to say.

"Whatever. Don't think I don't know what you're doing," she said, practically spitting out the words. "So pitiful."

"Ooookay ..." I wasn't sure what she was getting at, but had a strong feeling I wasn't going to like it. I started chanting in my head silently to keep from bitch-slapping her with all these witnesses around. *Be like Bobby. Be like Bobby. Be like Bobby...*

"You can't get a real guy to like you so you bottom fish at prison, trying to hook up with murderers."

Tiffany looked a little uncomfortable at that, but the footballer laughed. "Yo, that's cold," he said, making ridiculous snorting sounds as the humor overtook him.

I had so many things to say, so many little factoids to drop on Brittney's head at that moment, I didn't know where to start. I opened my mouth to let her have it, starting first with her complete lack of loyalty, when a heavy hand landed on my shoulder and everyone's expressions went slack.

"Are we having a problem here?" asked a female voice behind me. An adult one.

"No, ma'am," said the footballer, taking a few steps back and then turning around. "Gotta go, late to class."

"Good idea," said the teacher, one I hadn't had for classes before but knew to be in a freshman civics classroom across the hall from where we were standing. "You too, Tiffany ... Brittney ... get to class."

Brittney glared at me for a second before turning on her hundred-watt smile for the teacher. "Sure, no problem." She and her evil twin disappeared into the crowd of students moving past us, leaving a cloud of perfumed lotion in their wake.

I turned around to face my fate.

The teacher was staring at me like she expected an explanation, one of her eyebrows arched up high into her forehead.

"What? I didn't do anything," I said. "She punched me and I fell."

"She punched you?" The teacher raised her gaze, trying to see over the sea of students between us and Brittney.

"Never mind," I said, regretting saying anything. "Just let it go. I have to get to class."

I tried to move away, but she grabbed me by the arm. "Not so fast. Come into my classroom. I want to talk to you."

I looked at my watch, trying to be really obvious. "Okay but ..."

"I know you have class. If you're going to be late, I'll write you a note."

I had no idea what a freshman civics teacher would want with me other than to scold me, but if it got me out of part of my math class, that was fine with me. Scold away. Just don't make me do any word problems.

The classroom was empty. All of the teachers had some periods where they were supposed to work on grading papers and stuff. I guess it was just my luck that I got my ass kicked right outside her door during her free period.

Aaaand the shit just keeps getting better and better.

Bobby would say this was karma kicking my butt right now and I should just sit here and take it, so that's what I did.

"Take a seat," she said, gesturing to an empty desk in the front row.

I DROPPED MY BACKPACK TO the floor and slid into the seat as the teacher perched one butt-cheek on her desk directly in front of me. I noted how her butt fat pushed out and strained the polyester material of her pants and felt sorry for her. She probably got mocked hard behind her back for her choice in clothing. Her blouse was of the same material and had a big bow at the neck. There were way too many flowers on that shirt, reminding me of my now-dead grandmother's sofa material.

"You're Katy Guckenberger," she said.

I blinked a few times, trying to bite back the smartass comments that quickly leapt to mind.

"Yeah," I said, proud that I'd been able to control myself.

"Do you know who I am?"

I shrugged, letting my gaze roam the room a bit. I took in a poster of the U.S. Constitution, some pictures of some presidents, and a model of a large boat in the corner of the room.

"You're a civics teacher."

"Yes, I am. I also teach American History. My name is Melody Davis. You can call me Melody if you want."

That made me squirm in my seat. Calling a teacher by her first name was a serious no-no in my world. Besides, it wasn't like she was young like some of the new teachers. Calling them by their first names didn't seem as big an offense, seeing as how they were just a few years older than we are. But this lady? She had to be, like forty or something. No way in hell was I calling her anything but Ms. Davis.

"Uh, thanks," I said, trying to ease us past this awkward conversation and into me leaving.

"Do you know why I called you in here?"

"Because I tripped and fell outside your door?" I lifted my eyebrows up into my forehead in an effort to look as innocent as possible, playing 'let's pretend you didn't catch me about to enter into a Barbie smackdown'.

"No, not exactly. Although I am concerned that you've hurt yourself." She looked down at my knees. "Are you okay?"

"I'm fine. Really. It's nothing." I moved to stand, but she held up a hand to stop me.

"I also wanted to talk to you about this Jason Bradley business."

My heart stopped beating for a second and then started again, racing to catch up to its regular rhythm. Was I wearing a sign or something?

"I don't know what you're talking about." I figured my best bet was to play dumb. I could do that pretty convincingly. All anyone had to do was ask my Algebra teacher to confirm this fact.

"I saw you on TV going into the jail with Jason's father. It aired on this morning's news again."

I could feel the blood leaving my face. My parents were definitely going to see that. I had to at least text my mom before she found out from another source. My hand itched to pull my cell out of my pocket.

My mind started to stray. Ms. Davis might have been saying something, but all I could do was sit there and think about what I was going to say to my parents ... how I could tell my mom

I was hanging out with a murderer without having her freak right the hell out.

Hey Mom, listen, I know you wanted me to be more social and everything, find something to work on as an after-school thing, so I decided to, you know, hang out at the jail with our old neighbor.

It was never going to work. There wasn't a single thing I could say to my parents to make this okay with them.

"Are you listening?" Ms. Davis said, tilting her head to the side as she stared at me.

"Oh. Sorry. I kind of went off on my own track there for a second."

She frowned but continued. "I was saying that if you have any questions about the process, about what Jason is going to go through legally speaking, you could talk to me about it."

I couldn't think of what to say to that, so I just sat there and waited to hear more.

"I graduated from law school a few years back, but preferred teaching to practicing, so here I am." She shrugged and then gestured around her room. "Trying to tap into all these young minds and get them interested in their country's government and history."

"Wow. Talk about ...," I almost said *boring*, "... interesting."

She laughed. "I know, I know. You're thinking it's lame, but it's really not."

I readjusted myself in my chair, embarrassed that she, like so many other adults, had the ability to hear my unspoken thoughts.

"Most kids never have the luck — or the bad luck, I should say — to see the process up close and personal. And based on what I'm hearing and seeing in the hallways, none of your friends are going to get involved. But if *you're* planning to do that, I can help."

"If I'm planning to do what?" I was so confused at this point. Up was down, down was up. Teachers gave a shit and my neighbor murdered a football coach.

"Get involved." She leaned towards me, bending almost in half. "Standing by Jason during his trial."

"His trial?" Until then I hadn't really thought about a trial.

A real courtroom where people would be watching and Jason would be on the stand, like the countless television shows I'd seen where the guilty went to prison or the electric chair and the innocent were set free.

Jason admitted to doing it. He wasn't going to be set free.

I suddenly felt sick. Standing, I reached down to grab my bag. "Thanks, Ms. Davis, that's really nice, but I don't think I need any help." I threw the bag over my shoulder and side-stepped away until there was enough distance between us for me to turn around and not be totally rude.

"He entered a plea of not guilty," she said at my retreating back.

I tried to ignore her and get to the door, but she kept talking.

"But he confessed. What do you think is going to happen with that?"

I paused at her words, my foot refusing to cross the threshold. I had no idea how things really worked in a genuine courtroom, but common sense told me this was not a good combination.

"There are legalities, things that he's going to have to deal with. I was just thinking that you might want some support. It's hard to be the only one standing against a sea of hate."

"Okay, thanks," I said, just before pretty much running out of the classroom. My survival instincts or something inside me that wanted to be in another life at that moment told me to get the hell away and stay away. There was way too much cold, hard truth flying around that classroom.

I ran all the way to Algebra, falling into my chair as the bell rang signaling the beginning of class.

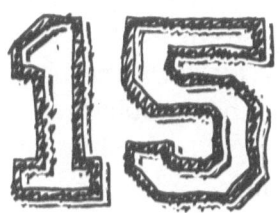

THURSDAY, AFTER A COUPLE OF mind-numbingly awful days at school listening to people talking not only about Jason but about *me* being a murderer-lover, I got a text from Jason's dad. It was the first bright moment in an otherwise very dark week.

Jason's coming home tonight. Feel free to drop by. Only if you want to.

He must have made bail. That was the talk of the town, whether he'd be allowed to wait at home for his trial to begin or whether he'd have to stay in prison. I'd said a prayer every night and every morning that he'd be allowed to come home, and it kind of freaked me out that my prayers had been answered. Or maybe it was Jason's prayers or his father's that had done the trick. I doubted anyone else was sending that particular plea to The Big Man upstairs. At this point the coach was being proclaimed a saint by every single news organization.

That last line of the text, *only if you want to*, haunted me for the hour it took me to build up the guts to text back. I didn't know what my problem was, but after listening to the hundredth person slander my name and the thousandth person give me the shit-eye, I didn't have the same enthusiasm for the cause as I'd had earlier in the week. That meant I was the world's biggest jerk, I knew that, which made the whole situation that much worse. Once again, I was back to worrying about myself and not the person who really mattered. I was at an all-time low, humanity-wise.

I finally texted Mr. Bradley back after realizing what an a-hole I was being by leaving him hanging. It didn't hurt seeing Brittney making out with Trace right in the middle of the hallway as if Jason had never existed for her, either. It pissed me off enough to forget about my own minor problems. The coward in me hoped Mr. Bradley was thinking it took me so long to respond because I was in class or something.

I'll be there after dinner, I said before tucking my phone away into my bag. It scared me to think someone would find my cell and retrieve my messages off it. It was bad enough people were speculating about my involvement. I preferred to keep them in the dark about the extent of it. As much as I felt the need to support Jason, I didn't want to be painted by the same brush as he was right now. I know it sounds like an excuse, but I wanted to be able to focus on Jason and not on defending my choice to support him.

I opened my locker to pull out the books I'd need for homework and a white piece of folded-up paper floated to the ground. Frowning, I picked it up. Bobby was the only one who ever left me notes, and usually they were on his favorite purple paper.

You no what they say. An eye for an eye bitch.

My ears were burning as soon as I started reading the words. The assholes were getting seriously bold, and they didn't even have the decency to check their spelling. *Ugh.*

I looked to my left and right, but no one was paying me any special attention. The handwriting seemed purposely weird, as if the person were trying to hide his or her identity.

Slamming the door shut, I shoved the paper into my backpack's side pocket. Making a big deal out of this was exactly what this person wanted, so that wasn't going to be a part of my plan. I refused to be manipulated like that.

Bobby told me to ignore all the haters, and until I knew exactly who was hating me to the level that they'd put a note in my locker, I was going to do exactly that. I was going to act like this didn't scare the shit out of me and make me want to be home-schooled. Besides, if my parents found out about this crap and how I basically brought it on myself, they'd kill me; I wouldn't have to worry about anyone here doing it.

My parents still hadn't found out about my involvement in this whole thing. Every time my father went to turn on the news, I jumped up with another ridiculous story about something that didn't happen at school — a complete fabrication — or ideas about my future ... a future that I honestly couldn't really see that clearly right now. I acted like it was nothing but smooth sailing and positive days ahead. I was ready for adulthood, or so I pretended.

I yammered on and on about colleges and scholarships and majors until my parents were starry-eyed about my total change of heart. Before, whenever they tried to broach the subject, I feigned intestinal problems and disappeared into the bathroom. Now I was all about sororities and school mascots and SAT scores. By the time Thursday rolled around I was ready to shoot myself and put me out of all our misery.

The longer I kept them away from the reality of my life, the worse the pressure between us got. I wanted to tell them, but I worried they'd order me to stay away from Jason, and that wouldn't have been fair to him. And in the grand scheme of things, I felt his life needed more fairness in it than mine did. I decided to do my best to keep them ignorant and I'd deal with the doo when it hit the fan later.

I didn't tell Bobby about Jason getting out on bond, figuring he'd lecture me about the whole thing, about my plan to visit him at home. He was on Jason's side, but more like a silent observer type. He'd been hearing vague threats being issued against me in school and had decided that with a target already on his back, he had no hope of escaping alive if he was too open with his support.

I was disappointed with his choice, but I got where it was coming from. It seemed like most people were interested only in self-preservation, and since it was a natural human reaction, I could hardly fault them for it. Besides, some of the truth had gotten around school along with the rumors; Jason had admitted to the murder. He *was* a murderer.

It was all over the news. There was no arguing this fact and anyone who tried to would have been laughed or beaten out of school. I know I kept my mouth shut about everything. It wasn't that I was ashamed; it was just that there wasn't anything to say. Jason's life was over. Now all that was left was to know if he was going to die for what he did or spend the rest of his life in prison.

The prosecutor was calling for a death sentence. The very idea of it had me waking up in the middle of the night drenched in cold sweats. I could only imagine what it was doing to Jason.

After dinner that night I got on my computer for a few minutes, checking to see if the news had picked up the latest on Jason's situation. Sure enough, the reporters were talking about how he'd been granted bail and it had been paid for by his father. People speculated about how he'd come up with the money, but no one knew for sure.

Talk turned to Jason's mother, wondering where she was and whether she'd met an untimely end like the coach had. I wanted to punch my laptop screen reading that. Some of those news stations really pushed it too far trying to get an audience. I officially boycotted two of them that day, refusing to take part in their disgusting publicity schemes.

Innocent until proven guilty ... what a joke. I slammed my laptop closed before I could read anything else. I needed to get to Jason's before it got too late.

My nerves were getting the better of me, even though I was trying to act like a quick visit to my neighbor's house was no big deal. My intestines churned and burned. *Breathe in, breathe out. Relax, idiot. It's just a visit with a friend. Forget the part about him being a murderer.*

"I'm just going outside to ... uh ... go for a run." I bent down to tie one of the laces on the running shoes I never used. I felt like I was going to vomit, I was so nervous. I didn't know what was bothering me most ... the fact that I was lying to my parents, that I was about to approach a crowd of reporters, or that I was planning to hang out with an admitted murderer who called me The Constant Gardener. It was completely insane and my stomach knew it better than my brain, apparently.

My father looked at me over the back of the couch. "You? Running? That's a first."

I rolled my eyes at him, playing the annoyed teen to the hilt. "I noticed some cottage cheese on my thighs this morning." Actually I have plenty of cottage cheese on my thighs *and* my butt, but my parents love me too much to ever say that. They liked to call me 'soft and sweet' but kids calling me fatty-fatty-two-by-four-can't-fit-through-the-bathroom-door since I was in sixth grade kind of put things into perspective.

"Stay away from the Bradley place," my mother shouted from the kitchen.

"Why?" I asked, annoyed enough that I forgot to play it cool.

She stuck her head around the corner. "Do I really need to say it? It's a circus over there with all those media vans." She gestured out our front window. "Look! One of them is practically parked on our lawn." She put her kitchen towel down and made as if to go have a word with the a-hole reporters.

I held up a hand. "I'll go tell them to move. I'm going running, and for the record, I'm not letting those dickheads decide where I go and don't go." It was the closest I could come to telling them what I was up to. I wasn't ready to risk being told I couldn't be around Jason or his dad anymore. Admitting that I might go in that direction felt like less of a lie.

"Good girl," my father said, clicking the TV on with the remote. "Give it to 'em good." He was no longer paying attention to anything we said or did.

I took his encouragement as a sign that on the day that I confessed, my dad would be on my side supporting me. I left the house with a slightly lighter step as a result.

And that tiny bit of euphoria lasted all of three seconds ... the time it took me to get to the end of my driveway and into the range of the reporters who didn't have any respect for people's front lawns.

"ARE YOU FRIENDS WITH JASON Bradley?" the woman standing next to the van parked by my mailbox asked. She gestured to a guy lounging around the hood area of the vehicle and he picked up a big camera, hefting it onto his shoulder.

"You need to get off my lawn," I said, walking in the opposite direction from Jason's house.

"The street is a public place. Are you friends with him? Do you go to Banner High?"

I looked at her van again and immediately got pissed off with her casual dismissal of my grass. Maybe I was being petty, but I couldn't help it.

"Listen, lady, I don't know who you are, but your van's wheels are on my *lawn* not the street. If you don't move them off, I'm going to get a steak knife and cut a hole in them, got it?"

She put a microphone to her lips and turned to her cameraman, a look of feigned shock on her face. "Did you hear that? I've just been threatened with a knife. Right down the street from Jason Bradley's house. Do you think there's something in the water here?"

The camera man pulled his face out from behind the lens. "Seriously, Karen? You're going with that?"

Her face morphed into one I've seen in horror films a couple times. "Shut the hell up, Will. Just do your job and run the camera."

I stood on the lawn, pulling my phone out of my running bra. Yes, even though I never run, I do have a running bra. Call it wishful shopping.

"I'm calling the cops to report you as a trespasser right now." I pressed random buttons, not at all interested in calling the cops over to my house. I'd never get to Jason's place if I had to deal with that bullcrap.

The woman rolled her eyes. "Fine." She turned to her cameraman. "Will, move the van."

"Yes, ma'am," he said, the distinct flavor of disrespect lacing his words. I liked him a lot more after that, even though he was a blood-sucking parasite newsperson guy.

She glared for a few seconds in his direction and then dropped her microphone to her side, stepping gingerly through the grass as her high heels sank into the soft ground. When she was just a few feet away from me, her voice softened into something that I think was supposed to make me feel like we were suddenly BFFs.

"You could be on the news, you know. Just a couple sound bites and we'd be good."

From here I could see that she had gobs of make-up on, making her skin appear to be made of mannequin plastic. She looked way better from far away. Not only was her voice fake, her face was too. *Ugh.*

"I don't want to be on your version of the news," I said, moving off to start my fake-run. I couldn't wait to put some distance between us. It was as if just being in her presence made me somehow agreeing with her tactics and attitude.

"What's that supposed to mean?" she yelled at my back.

"The kind where people are guilty until proven innocent!" I yelled over my shoulder, running to the corner and crossing the street. My thighs jiggled, and I prayed that the cameraman was too busy moving the van off my grass to be filming it. I'm really not good at grand exits.

"You have a lot to learn about life!" she yelled, apparently not yet ready to give it up. "And the news!"

"Blow me!" I yelled loud enough for the whole neighborhood to hear.

Adrenaline was coursing through my veins. I could have sprinted all the way to Jason's house on the high I was living, but instead I slowed down to a fast walk. No need to get crazy about this running thing.

A plan was slowly forming in my mind as I turned the next corner, taking the street behind Jason's backyard neighbor. I knew for a fact that Mr. Baumgarten, the old dude who lived there, was out of town. My next-door neighbor was watching his dog for him until the following week. All I had to do was get into his backyard and I'd be home free. He had to have some kind of patio furniture I could use to get over the fence, right?

Unfortunately, I wasn't the only one with this great idea.

I GOT THROUGH MR. BAUMGARTEN'S side yard and up to the gate dividing it off from the backyard, no problem. But as soon as I pushed the slatted wood door open, I knew there was going to be an issue. Three guys were there at the back fence, using high-powered lenses on big-ass cameras to get pictures of the inside of Jason's house.

Dicks.

I hung out in the shadows and chewed my lip. I needed to get over that fence, but I wasn't ready to have anyone know that's what I was doing.

Inspiration struck when I remembered that my other neighbor, Mrs. Cook, used a key hidden in Mr. B's garden to put his mail inside. If I could just get into Mr. Baumgarten's place, I could scare them off by making them think it was my house. Trespassing was a popular threat tonight.

I went around to the front of the house and started searching through the mulch at the edge of the garden. I was expecting a fake rock, but the only thing there was a dog turd, and no way was I touching anything near that.

Sighing in frustration, I looked out into the street. Cars drove by and a couple people stared at me. Pretty soon *I* was going to be busted as the trespasser if I didn't find a way inside that house soon. I glanced down at the garden again and watched as a snail started crawling over the dog turd.

A snail crawling over a dog turd?

I grabbed a nearby twig and poked the nasty pile. The entire thing moved as one disgusting unit.

"Why you sneaky little perverted bastard," I said, whispering to the absent Mr. Baumgarten with a huge grin on my face. Picking up the turd with way more confidence than a person should be allowed to have where dog excrement is concerned, I confirmed my suspicions; it was faux poo. Brown, turd-like plastic with a front door key in the hollowed-out interior, accessed through the bottom.

Less than a minute later I was inside and opening up the back door, acting like I owned the joint.

"Hey! What are you guys doing in my yard? Get the hell out of here!"

Two of them ran. One of them took his time. I made a big show of getting my phone out and taking a picture of him.

"I just got your picture. I'm sending it to the cops. You're trespassing, asshole."

"Yeah, yeah, whatever," the guy said.

I snorted. *Some people.* Zero professionalism.

It was a lot of work keeping the smile off my face. Never mind the fact that I was breaking and entering. I told myself I was an official neighbor, not like those cheesedicks who came from out of town to camera-stalk one of our own.

As soon as the last guy was gone, I ran out the door and over to the back fence, grabbing a patio chair and dragging it along with me. Falling over the other side into Jason's yard only resulted in one largish scratch on my arm, so I considered my mission a success.

I looked up at his house and kind of stopped for a few seconds. *Now what?* I asked myself.

I KNOCKED ON THE BRADLEY'S porch door like it was no big deal that I was in their closed-off back yard. My plastered-on giant smile was supposed to stun them into not realizing how psycho that was.

"What are you doing out in the back yard?" Jason said as soon as he opened the door. Apparently the power-level of my smile was zilch-o in this house.

I pushed inside, worried the photographers would be back before I could get under cover of his roof and four walls.

"Just avoiding all the press."

"But how did you get back there?"

Jason's father came into the hallway and smiled. "Hello, Katy. Nice to see you." He looked back at the door behind me and his smile slipped.

Time for a distraction.

"Yeah! I'm so glad you invited me. So what are you guys up to? Did you have dinner yet? What'd you have? We had pizza. It's always pizza on Thursday nights at chez Guckenberger."

Word diarrhea. That was my big plan. Flood them with the sound of my voice spewing nonsense and they'll forget all about the part where I broke into their neighbor's house and climbed their fence.

"How'd you get into the back yard?" Jason asked again.

I sighed, rolling my eyes in his direction. "Can't you see I'm trying to distract you from asking for details? Jesus, get a clue."

Mr. Bradley laughed and then acted like he was just choking. "I'm going to be in the living room if you need me." He turned and left us standing there in the hallway.

A wave of silent awkwardness filled the small space.

"So are you going to tell me or not?" Jason finally said. It was a challenge for him at this point, to figure out my secret. I could tell by his tone.

"If it's that important to you..." This was my attempt to make him feel stupid so he'd stop asking.

"It is." He wasn't falling for that either, persistent little twad that he was.

"Fine. I'll tell you. Do you have any juice? I'm parched."

He moved past me into the hallway, back in the direction he'd come.

Having him that close made butterflies take up residence in my belly. I wasn't sure whether they were the nervous kind or the excited kind. I couldn't remember ever being close enough to Jason that I could feel the heat of his body like that. I admit, it wasn't entirely unpleasant.

"I have juice if you have a confession."

I think he was trying to be funny, but the humor just kind of died with the word *confession*. Things we'd say without thinking in another life suddenly meant so much more in this one.

It made me want to stop fighting with him and just make him happy. "Yeah, sure. I'll ... uh ... tell you how I got back there. After the juice."

I stood in the corner of the kitchen as Jason went through the motions of filling my drink order. He'd probably done that a thousand times in this place, but today he was doing it as a confessed murderer. I couldn't stop thinking about how much his life had changed since last week. It didn't seem fair that mine was going on as normal, right along with everyone else's that we knew. Well ... except for Coach and his family, of course.

I blocked my mind from thinking about them. If I got too sympathetic, I'd never have it in me to support Jason. I refused to think about what that said about me as a person, that I'd choose a side even when on the surface it seemed like the wrong one.

I took the glass of juice from him and tried to be casual about drinking it. I'd take a sip and look around. Take another and look around some more. This would be the longest juice-drinking event in the history of the world if I had anything to say about it.

He stared at me the entire time. The longer I took to finish, the higher his right eyebrow got. It was pretty much in his hair by the time I got to the end of the glass.

The last sip of the juice took me almost an entire minute to finish. I watched the clock, every second ticking away getting me closer and closer to my complete humiliation.

He'd think I was desperate to be in here with him. He'd laugh at me. He'd feel sorry for me for being such a dork. It was going to be terrible, I was absolutely sure of it. I saw no good coming from the telling of the truth. My mind raced to come up with a decent lie.

"Just tell me," he said, as if he could sense my distress. "How bad can it be? You jumped the fence, right?"

I put the juice glass down on the counter. "Yep. Jumped the fence." I wiped my mouth with a swipe from the back of my first finger, trying to look graceful about having a juice mustache.

He folded his arms and leaned on the counter. "I'm pretty sure there's more to the story."

I couldn't come up with a lie that sounded like anything he would believe, so I just went with what I had.

"All right, fine." I had to stare at the floor to get it out. "I took Mr. Baumgarten's turd key, went inside his house, then came out the back door, used his patio chair, and climbed on it to get over."

"You could have just walked through his side gate. He never even closes the damn thing."

I shook my head, sorry to have to be the one to tell him this. "I tried. There were reporters at your back fence."

Jason frowned. "So ... I don't get it. Why'd you go inside his place?"

I sighed heavily. "Because, I had to act like I lived in there to scare them away."

He nodded, taking my glass from the counter. "Slick," he said, before walking around the kitchen island to put my dirty glass in the dishwasher.

Suddenly it didn't seem so awful. "Thanks."

"I'm still not clear on where the turds come in, though."

Aaaaand just as suddenly it did seem so awful. My face heated up to the point that it felt like it might actually be getting a sunburn, like a permanent one that wasn't going to go away after the embarrassment wore off.

My voice sounded funny when it finally started working again. "He hides his key in a plastic dog turd in the garden."

Jason laughed. He laughed first just a little and then a lot.

I laughed a little too when it became too awkward not to. "What's so funny?"

He turned around and fixed his eyes on me, leaning back on the counter. "I'm just picturing you having the balls to pick up a bunch of dog shit to try and find a key."

My chin went up, horrified that he'd actually picture me doing this. "I'll have you know that I didn't touch *anything* until I saw a snail climbing over it."

"A snail ... climbing ... what?" His laughter died off, but his smile didn't.

"Must we, really?" I looked around his kitchen. "Nice kitchen you have here."

He pushed himself off the counter and walked to another exit from the room. "Come on. I'll give you a tour."

Thrilled to be moving on from my B&E and the picking up of turds, I followed him into the dining room. Jason might be a lot of things, but he was still a gentleman. Bobby would have given me the third degree until he'd gotten every detail out of my brain.

"This is one of the rooms we never use." He gestured to the table and chairs that all had a slight layer of dust on them. The waning light coming through the back windows emphasized all the faults in the room, including a big scratch on the wood and fingerprint smears on a photo on the wall.

I moved closer to that picture, noticing three people in it. "Is that your mom?" I asked as soon as I recognized him as the kid. He was wearing a sweater I knew he'd never be caught dead in these days.

"Yeah. She had cancer when I was little. Died when I was eight."

"I'm sorry to hear that." I faced him, knowing that I didn't understand how that felt but wanting him to see that I meant it when I said I was sorry. She'd died shortly after Jason moved in, but at the time I'd been so young, and death had been such a foreign concept. Had I noticed his pain? Did I see him grieving? I couldn't remember.

"Thanks." He left me standing there and went into the next room. The sound of the TV got louder as I moved closer to it.

"This is the family room. That's my father. I think you've already met."

I waved awkwardly as we passed through the room. Mr. Bradley waved too but said nothing, watching us go by for a second before going back to his program.

"This is the front hallway, powder room, and stairs." He stopped at the bottom with his hand on the railing.

I waited there with him in the front hall, wondering what the hell he was doing just standing there and looking at me.

"Well?" I threw up my arms and shrugged my shoulders. "Do you have an upstairs or what?"

"I wasn't sure you'd want to go up there," he said, a very serious expression on his face.

"Why not? You got dead bodies up there or something?"

I hated myself a split second later for saying the first thing that came to my mind, but then I didn't feel so bad when he laughed.

"You're crazy, you know that?" Instead of waiting for a response, he preceded me up the stairs, taking them two at a time.

His leg muscles bulged with the effort. I could see the movement of them under his jeans and it gave me a secret thrill. I immediately chastised myself internally for even looking. I was not here to cop a feel or anything else stupid like that. He really does have a nice butt, though. That was the first time I'd taken notice of that fact.

"There'd better not be any bodies up there, that's all I'm sayin'," I mumbled under my breath, taking the stairs like a normal person. I liked listening to him laugh, and I felt like a million bucks when he did it again.

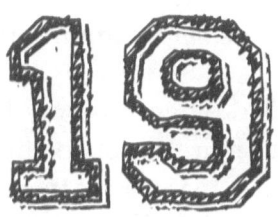

"THAT'S MY DAD'S ROOM," HE said, pointing down the hall to the right. "That's the bathroom and laundry room," he said, pointing to the door in front of us. "And that's my bedroom." He walked down the hall to the left a little and stopped in an open doorway.

My feet made whispering sounds as I made my way down the carpeted hall. I stopped opposite Jason and leaned into his room with just my head. I wondered how many other girls from school had gotten this far into Jason's life. Probably a few.

"Definitely a guy's room," I said, my nose scrunching up as I took in all the dust and trophies. It was the best I could come up with as far as a response. Not very witty, but functional. That's me.

"Does it smell?" he asked.

I looked up to find him serious. "Smell?"

His expression changed, and I could have sworn I saw embarrassment before his cool mask went on again. "I just thought ... you said it was a guy's ... never mind."

I walked inside it, not sure he wanted me there, but going anyway. Lifting my nose, I gave the air a good whiff. "It does smell, now that you mention it."

"Shut up," he said, coming in behind me. His dissipating embarrassment was still present in his voice. It gave me courage.

"It smells like ... cologne ...," I turned slowly, keeping my nose in the air, "... an Airwick apple-scented candle and ... shoes." I finished sniffing and smiled at him. "Smelly ones."

"You're ridiculous," he said, jumping up and landing on his back on the bed.

I walked over to his desk and ran my hand over some of his things. There was a blue spiral notebook that looked hardly used, a keyboard to a computer that wasn't there anymore — the cords where hanging out of a hole in his desk — and a pen. The rest of the surface was empty and dusty. I slowly drew my name in it. K-A-T-Y. I put a heart after my name without thinking and then quickly rubbed it away before he could see it.

Hearts? Are you serious?

"What happened to the 'puter?" I asked, running my hand over the notebook and away from the evidence of my serious lack of maturity. I really wanted to look inside the book but felt like it would be pushing the boundaries of privacy to turn the cover over.

"Confiscated. Evidence, I guess."

The truth of why I was there — nerd girl from down the street running her fingers over his stuff like she belonged there, drawing hearts in the dust — came right to the forefront.

I turned to look at him and lowered myself into his desk chair. I hugged the back of it and rested my chin on the top rung of the seat's ladder back. "What else did they take?" When I realized that with every word my head was bouncing up like some kind of freaky puppet, I moved my arms to rest there instead.

He laced his hands behind his head and kind of shrugged, his arms flopping up like chicken wings, as he acted like it was an easy question. "Shit that doesn't matter. None of it matters."

He shifted his gaze to the ceiling.

"Are you glad to be back home?" I asked, my voice annoyingly soft.

"Yes and no." He sighed loudly.

I tried not to take it as a sign that I was irritating the hell out of him with my questions.

"Why no? I'd think you'd be much happier to be here than in ... you know." I couldn't say the word. It was so harsh. So awful. So real for him and not for me.

"You can say it," he said, looking at me now. "Prison. I was in prison. I *belong* in prison."

"I wish you'd quit saying that." I was kind of mad at him at that point, being so harsh and so blatantly in-my-face about the whole thing. Couldn't he pretend for a few minutes even for himself that it wasn't as bad as it really was? It made me glare when I really didn't mean to.

"Why?" he asked. "It's the truth."

"Yeah, let's talk about the truth." My tone was taunting. "Like why you're telling everyone that you're guilty."

Boom! Yes, I did that. I dropped that truth-bomb right there in the middle of his bedroom, right in his face. No more beating around the bush. It was time to get ugly, apparently. I had no idea what I was thinking except that I probably wasn't ... thinking, that is.

He sat up and turned sideways on the bed, staring into the palms of his hands. "I'm telling the truth." He looked over at me, and all I could see was anguish there. "If you're living in some kind of fantasy world where I admit secretly to you that I didn't do it, you need to wake the hell up. Go home and go on with your life without me in it."

I swallowed with difficulty. Not because I was scared, exactly, but because he was being so intense. And we were talking about murder, after all.

"I'm not," I said, my voice barely above a whisper.

"Then why do you keep talking about it? Do you think I'm not torturing myself enough that you need to add to it?"

"I'm not trying to torture you, Jason." A mixture of embarrassment, anger, and sadness was just about overwhelming me.

I was completely out of my league here. Tears threatened. Why did I think I could manage this? I must have been high on permanent marker.

"Then why?" he asked, sounding almost as tortured as I felt.

"Because!" I shouted, before I could get control of my volume.

We both looked at the door, but nothing happened. I was hoping Mr. Bradley's television was too loud for him to hear me freaking out.

"Because," I said more normally. "I know you."

He stared at me for a long time after that. His jaw muscles got really tense and then they relaxed. Then they tensed up again. His eyes became very bloodshot and filled with tears that didn't fall.

"I have spent the better part of ten years ignoring you," he said finally, his voice very hoarse.

My heart kind of broke there. For both of us. There was no use denying the truth.

"On purpose?" I asked, waiting for him to confirm my worst fears ... that I'm so lame and so dorky, a person would purposely go out of his way to *not* interact with me. A murderer, no less.

He shook his head. "No. Not on purpose."

I shrugged, relief washing over me. I hate it when my insecurities get the better of me like they did in that moment. I knew I shouldn't care what other people thought of me, but I couldn't help being human, being a person who wanted to be liked.

"But I did that," Jason continued. "I ignored you. We've lived right down the street from each other since we were kids."

"So?" I shrugged again, trying to make him feel better for being kind of a stuck-up jerk. "Lots of people live in the 'hood and don't hang out with me. I'm cool with that."

"Not right here on our street. I could have given you a lift to school."

"I already had a lift to school." *Usually.* I left that part out. My car wasn't the most reliable and Bobby's mom didn't always give him hers.

"Stop trying to make me feel better," he said, sounding pissed.

I took a deep breath in and let it out slowly. I couldn't have a normal conversation with him because I was constantly thinking that I had to watch what I said. I'd already stuck my foot in my mouth enough for one night. For one lifetime, really. But I felt like he needed to know where I was coming from. That's why I kept talking when I probably should have just shut up and nodded.

"I'm not trying to make you feel better. Maybe you should feel like a dick because you didn't talk to me or give me a ride or whatever ... but that's how it's done, right? I mean, everyone does that. You're not any more of a jerk than anyone else in your situation is."

"In my situation?"

I stared at him blinking several times in rapid succession, waiting for him to stop playing idiot with me. But he just kept staring back, like he expected me to fill him in on the details.

"You know what I'm talking about. Don't make me say it." Now I was embarrassed, like it was my fault, like I was the one doing the judging all along.

"No, I really don't." He looked kind of confused and really charming.

How does a girl tell a guy all about himself without sounding like a bitch? I wasn't sure then and I'm still not sure now. But I gave it a shot anyway because I was the queen of saying shit I shouldn't.

"Jason, you have it all."

"Excuse me?"

"You know what I mean. You have it all. Just like all your friends. You guys are in all your glory."

"My friends? Glory? What?"

I was getting more mad at him, each time he parroted something back at me.

"Yes. Your friends. Your girlfriend. Her friends. You guys have it all. All the glory."

"What is this *all* of which you speak?" A tiny smile quirked up the edge of his mouth.

I wasn't going to be placated by his charm, though. He was mocking me and it pissed me off. "You have popularity, looks, athletic talent, a great family ..."

"Hold up, hold up ..." He held his hand out in between us. "Back up ... I have what? Say that stuff again ... I think I missed something."

He was totally luring me in and I was the one dumb enough to dig the hole to fall into.

"Popularity?" I said, my neck starting to get hot.

"No, not that one..."

"Athletic talent?" My voice started squeaking.

"Nooope. Not that one either."

"A good family?" My face was so red at this point I was sweating.

He shook his head, a barely concealed and very satisfied smile taunting me. "No, there was something else you said..."

"Nope, that's all I said. You must be mistaken."

"You said *looks*."

I frowned, like he was nuts. "No, I didn't."

"Yes, you did. You said I have looks."

I shook my head, channeling pity into my eyes as best I could. "See, that's your conceit coming out again. You thought I said that, but I didn't. I said *books*. You have books." I gestured to his shelves that actually only had trophies on them.

"Ah," he said, nodding, "I see. So I *don't* have looks."

"No."

"I'm just butt-ugly, is that it?"

Finally the heat in my face started to calm down. He wasn't mocking me anymore. It was more like he was mocking himself, which I was much more comfortable with.

"No, you're not *butt*-ugly. I mean ... I wouldn't use the word *butt* necessarily."

Both of us sat there trying not to be the one to laugh first. For a few seconds I thought we were just going to be best buds now, smiling and laughing and joking around.

But then his face fell, and the happiness I thought I'd seen was replaced with anger.

"Why are you here?" he asked.

I wrestled with myself for a second or two trying to find the right answer. Maybe it was ten seconds. I struggled mainly because I wasn't even really sure of the answer myself, but also because I could tell he was in a very vulnerable place. I didn't want to be the one to injure him more than he was already injured.

"I just thought you could use a friend."

"And you're my friend." He was staring at me, like he was testing me. Maybe like he wasn't sure he believed it himself.

"Yes. I'm your friend."

"Even though I've been a dick to you for most of our lives."

I sighed. It seemed like I was doing a lot of that, but it couldn't be helped. This was a very frustrating situation.

"Jason, I think we've already determined that you've been acting like most guys in your situation would and that I'm okay with that. Stop beating yourself up about it, okay? It's getting annoying if you want the truth."

He laughed kind of bitterly as he stared at his hands in his lap. "I do want the truth."

I leaned over in my chair, trying to get his attention.

He finally rewarded me by twisting his head to the side a little. We stared at each other.

"I'll make you a deal," I said, my heartbeat quickening for some reason.

"Okay."

"From now on and forever, we swear to always tell each other the truth."

His eyes searched mine. He looked desperate, like he had something more to lose in this bargain than I did. I couldn't figure out why he'd feel that way when the deal was mutual and he'd already sworn up and down he'd told me the truth about the coach. At least not then.

"What if we can't tell each other the truth?" he asked. "What if you don't want to tell me something because it's better for me not to know it?"

"That's fine. Then I won't say it at all. But I won't blow sunshine up your ass, either."

"So this is the no-sunshine-up-the-ass deal?"

"Yes. That's exactly what it is." I held out my hand for him to shake. "Are you in?" My fingers weren't trembling, thank all that is holy, even though my insides were a mess.

He turned more fully around so he was facing me, his hand coming out to envelop mine.

I remember very clearly how warm his skin was, his hand so large it swallowed mine whole. I could see bruises and scabs from a fight on his knuckles, and I realized I was striking a bargain with the hand that had killed our high school football coach. I held on anyway, even though it felt like my heart was going to explode with all the craziness.

"I swear I will not blow sunshine up your ass," Jason said.

"And I swear I will not blow sunshine up your ass either," I said, feeling like one of the most momentous things I've ever done was happening in that moment.

"I didn't want to mention it before, but you have some salad in your teeth." Jason kept holding onto my hand, staring me in the eye, not even blinking as he delivered that line.

I pulled my hand away and leaned back. "You are such a dick."

He started laughing so hard, he rolled backwards and then fell off the end of his bed at my feet.

I stood and left the room in a fake-huff, looking for the bathroom he had gestured to earlier. Embarrassment doesn't even begin to cover what I was feeling as I pictured myself smiling over and over with a green tooth.

"I'm just kidding!" he yelled.

I found the bathroom and locked myself in. Leaning with my back against the door, I realized that Jason and I really were on the road to being friends.

At first I was smiling so hard my face was hurting, but then I realized that my new friend was being put on trial for murder and facing the death penalty. My smile disappeared and I felt like crying instead.

WHEN I FINALLY GOT UP the nerve to go back to Jason's room, his dad was there standing outside the doorway. I was really glad that green stuff in the teeth thing was total b.s., otherwise I would have had a hard time smiling at him ever again.

"I think it's time we call it a night," he said. He gestured towards the stairs. "Can I walk you home?"

Jason's expression turned into something resembling a storm cloud. "She came in over the back fence to avoid the press. Maybe she should go back out the same way."

I shook my head, looking at Jason's dad. "No, don't be silly. I'll go out the front door."

Truth.

Jason and I had dedicated ourselves to the truth. That meant I had to stop hiding who I was and what I was doing from everyone, not just him.

I walked towards the stairs before I could second-guess myself.

As I went down to the front door, I thought of all the ways I could break the news to my parents about what I was doing. In my mind, the best-case scenario was engaging them in this casual conversation where I explained everything, after asking them to sit with me in the living room. We'd be mature adults, just discussing me hanging out with a murderer like we were talking about the weather.

"I'm going to be spending some time with Jason," I'd say.

"Do you mean the boy who killed your high school football coach?" my mother would ask, smiling with her hands folded in her lap.

"Yes, that's the one."

"Be careful, sweetie. And make sure you do your homework too," my father would say, before shifting his attention back to the television.

Yeaaahhhh, right. And then monkeys flew out of butts everywhere.

It took only two seconds after walking out of Jason's front door for me to realize I was living in a seriously naive fantasy world. Monkeys do not fly out of butts, and my parents were not going to be one bit happy about what I'd been up to.

Microphones were shoved in my face, and the front porch was lit up like a theater stage with all the lights.

"Are you Jason's sister? Are you Jason's girlfriend? Are you a friend of the family? What did Jason say to you? Did he confess to you? Did you talk about the murder?"

The ridiculously harsh and way-too-personal questions went on and on. I blocked out the rest of them to maintain my sanity. It was way too tempting to shout something back at them, even though I knew people like this would feel no shame at anything I said.

"Excuse us! Please move!" Mr. Bradley yelled, holding up one arm to shield my face while putting the other around my back and urging me on.

I held my arms up in front of me, trying to see past the bright lights. I couldn't see any faces, I could only hear voices. They were getting more demanding with every passing second. Panic welled up in my chest and made me feel like I was going to suffocate from it. People pushed against me and crowded me. The air was getting too thin.

"Sorry about this," Mr. Bradley said under his breath, just before a microphone hit me in the face.

"Ow!" I yelled, tasting blood on my lip. I was in shock that someone had been so desperate they'd do something like that, even if it was an accident.

"Oh, for crying out loud!" Mr. Bradley yelled, stopping us in our tracks. He turned me around to look at my face. "You're bleeding," he said, his face contorting into one of extreme anger. He looked out into the crowd of reporters. Tons of pictures were taken, flashes going off and shutters whining. *Chick-eh, chick-eh, chick-eh...*

"Don't you people have any respect for anyone?"

"Who is she, Bradley? Family member?"

Chick-eh, chick-eh, chick-eh... More pictures. Those people were vultures.

He shook his head in disgust and looked back at me. "Are you sure you want to go this way?"

I nodded. "Just point me in the right direction and I'll start running." I looked down at my feet. "Got my speed-racers on."

He glanced down and then back up again, looking like he was going to say something about my shoes, but instead he grabbed me into a big bear hug. His words came right into my ear as he leaned down and squeezed. "Thank you so much, Katy. You're an angel."

He let me go and then shoved a couple people out of the way to clear a path for me.

I took off running for my house and didn't stop until I was inside with the door locked behind me. My breath was coming in gasps, and I knew my face was white from fear and exhaustion. That was the most exercise I'd gotten in years. Cottage cheese be gone!

My father heard the door slam and turned around. As soon as he took in my appearance, his expression went from mildly curious to concerned.

He jumped up from the couch and came to me, yelling, "Marjorie!"

The doorbell rang.

My dad put his hand on my arm and leaned over towards the front door handle.

"Don't answer it!" I yelled, right in his face.

He froze in place, blinking rapidly as he slowly stood up straight.

I tried to calm my tone down so he wouldn't go ballistic on me. "Just ... leave it." I put my hand on the door to keep him from opening it. "It's some reporters."

He let his hand fall away from the handle and pulled his shoulders back. "Are you telling me that some reporter did this to you?" He pointed at my lip.

My mother came around from behind him and stared at me. "You're bleeding." She looked from me to my father, a questioning expression frozen on her face.

I held up my hands like two stop signs, trying to stave off the inevitable ... the massive ass-chewing that was about to turn my butt-cheeks into two bloody stumps.

Okay, bad visual, but you get what I'm saying.

"I can explain everything. Let's just go sit down and talk about it."

The doorbell rang again. And again and again.

I was trying to get my parents to calm down and be reasonable, but every time that damn doorbell rang, it intensified their suspicion and worry. It filled me with a rage that I cannot explain. Even after all these months of looking back on it, I don't understand why I didn't just let that bell ring.

I swung around and grabbed the door, hauling it open.

The lights and the microphones were there, along with all the obnoxious questions. I picked out the one that I heard most clearly, the one that bothered me more than the others.

"Are you Jason's girlfriend?"

It bothered me because I wasn't his girlfriend, and I didn't want people thinking that was why I was going over there visiting him. Not because I was embarrassed, though. The truth was, I still considered Jason as being out of my league, even though he was a criminal now. I hated to think about what that said about my confidence level or self-respect or whatever; it was what it was and no amount of common sense was going to change things for me. At least not then.

"No!" I yelled out at the sea of reporters, my voice causing everyone to go instantly quiet. All I could hear now were the sounds of camera shutters going off.

Chick-eh, chick-eh, chick-eh...Chick-eh, chick-eh, chick-eh...

The flashes made it impossible to see who was invading my privacy. "I'm Jason's *friend!* He used to have a lot of them, but they've all disappeared. Funny, isn't it, how when times get tough, you find out who your real friends are?" I realized I was getting all preachy and that was just lame. I'd probably already said too much. "Now you have your answer, so you can leave me and my family *alone!*" I slammed the door in their faces. Or at least, I tried to slam the door in their faces, but there was a foot in the way.

I banged the door several times, but this stupid reporter's shoe was stopping me.

My father shoved me to the side and pulled the door open again.

There was a guy standing there, the same cheesedick who'd been slow to leave Mr. Baumgarten's backyard. He held his camera up and took a picture of my father's enraged face.

Chick-eh.

My mom and I watched in shock as my father cocked his right arm back and punched the guy right in the gut.

My dad. The resource specialist at the local community college. That's a librarian in case you didn't know. He totally kicked that guy's ass with one punch.

When the cheesedick leaned over gasping for air, his camera went down and out, extending into our foyer.

I snatched it out of his hands and yelled, "Shut the door!" at my dad.

He did exactly as I ordered, and *that* is how we ended up locked inside our house with a paparazzi's camera, and me standing there with a whole lot of explaining to do.

THAT WHOLE VISION I HAD of my parents and me sitting down and discussing the situation like rational adults? Yeah. That was some kind of weird-ass fantasy.

The yelling started before I even passed the threshold into the living room.

"What the hell is going on?!" my father screamed, following behind me.

"Not so loud, honey, there's still reporters out there." My mom rushed over to make sure the blinds were tightly closed. She removed the tie-backs for the drapes and closed them too, something that made both my father and me stop freaking out for a second.

My mom never did that. Curtains were for show, she said, not to actually be used. Those tiebacks had probably only ever been touched twice in all the years they'd been there, once when they were put up and today.

"Can we just sit down and discuss this rationally?" I asked, trying to sound super mature. I put the camera down on the small table near the entrance to the family room.

"How about you just start explaining yourself. Did I hear that reporter ask you what you were doing at *Jason's* house?" My father's face was beet red.

"I thought you were out running," my mom said, sounding kind of lost.

My father snorted. "Yeah, right. Because she's a runner."

"Hey!" my mother and I yelled at the same time.

My father shook his head and then mussed up his hair. "Sorry. Sorry, that was uncalled for ..." He turned around and around, like he was trying to get his bearings.

"I think we all should sit down," said my mother the peace-maker. "Let's discuss this and figure out what we're going to do with all these wolves at the door."

I walked around the couch and took the armchair facing the coffee table, to the left of the sofa. My parents came over and sat side by side, both of them staring at me.

"So ...," I started, wondering how much I should say and how much I could get away with withholding. I decided *not much*, when the look on my father's face told me I'd better not mess around.

"I ... uh ... was over at Jason's house, and when I tried to leave, I kind of got surrounded by those press guys and someone bumped me on the mouth with a microphone. No bigiddy."

"No bigiddy? No *bigiddy?*" My father's volume increased with every word. "That's called battery, Katy, and it's not even my biggest concern if you can believe that!"

"Easy, Mike," my mom said, placing a hand on his arm, "easy." She looked up at me, speaking in a carefully-measured tone. "I think what your father is trying to say is that we don't understand why you're over at Jason's house in the first place."

My father glared at my mom. "I wasn't having trouble saying it, I just didn't get the chance yet."

My mom glared back at him, all her easy-going mom-ness suddenly absent. "Do you want to take this upstairs?"

That's code in my parents' world for fight-club. Their bedroom is where all the work of raising a family happened, the good, the bad, and the ugly. I'll let you decide which part of their fight and make-up process is which.

My father sighed heavily and turned to me. "Start talking, missy."

I was doomed. When my name got changed to Missy, all bets were off. Both of my parents were staring at me with serious expressions and they were holding hands. No one in the history of the world has ever gotten past that wall of oneness before and no one ever would, so I didn't even bother to bullshit them.

"Jason is my friend. He's been accused of a terrible crime, and he needs support. That's why I was there. It's also why I visited him in jail."

My mom's jaw dropped open, but no words came out.

"If I've read the articles correctly, he wasn't just accused ... he *admitted* to killing his coach." My father was challenging me, waiting to see if I'd fall into the lie-trap. No way was I even going to try.

"Yes. He's admitted it publicly and to me."

Both my parents opened their mouths to jump all over me, but I held my hand up and kept talking to cut them off.

"But! He's entered a plea of not-guilty, which means innocent until *proven* guilty, *and* I think there's something else going on there. I don't trust his confession." *There.* I'd said it. I'd given a voice to the unrest in my heart. It was both thrilling and scary-as-snakes at the same time.

My mom glanced at my dad, whose face looked like a lobster, and then turned to me. "Something else?" she asked. "What do you mean?"

"It doesn't matter what she means," my father burst out, "because she's not going to spend time hanging around with a murderer! And that's *final!*" He stood up and stormed out of the room, pausing only when he was at the doorway. His finger came up and jabbed the air in my general direction. "You are forbidden from visiting that boy ever, do you understand?"

I stood up, full of righteous indignation. "No, I do *not* understand!" I seriously wanted to punch something right then. Maybe my father. It struck me then how passions can overtake some-one's good sense and make them want to do something they'd never dream of doing on a normal day.

My mom jumped to her feet and held her arms out wide at her sides, one hand in my face, and one pointed towards my dad's. "That's enough! There will *no* more shouting at one another in this house!"

We were at an impasse. All of us were pissed, all of our faces on fire, and I'm sure all of us feeling completely justified in our positions.

"Now! Get your buns back here and sit down ... both of you. Or I'm on strike and you'll be doing your own cooking and laun-dry for the foreseeable future while I take a cruise to Alaska."

My dad and I exchanged a look.

"You hate snow," I said.

"Alaska?" My father walked slowly into the room. "I tried to get you to take an Alaskan cruise with me five years ago and you said you had no interest in icebergs and salmon fishing."

"That's not the point!" my mother yelled, apparently giving herself a pass from the no-shouting rule she'd just implemented. "Sit down!"

Dad and I rushed to do what we were told. My mother didn't lose her shit very often, but when she did and threats about no more dinner started flying around, we listened. My dad and I once went through a two-week punishment together, and for the first three days it was fine; but after that we both realized that Mom is the glue that holds everything together and neither of us was willing to live falling apart like that again.

My mom lowered herself primly to the couch. "Now, we are going to talk about this in calm voices and without grand state-ments of what will or won't be happening in the future, and we will not go to sleep until it's resolved."

"Alaskan cruise," my dad mumbled, shaking his head.

My mom looked at me. "Katy ... tell us about Jason. Is he okay?"

I folded my hands in my lap, trying to look as adult as pos-sible. "He's not good. I mean, he's healthy, but he's ... worried. I think."

"I'll bet he is," my father said, snorting under his breath.

"Mike. I'm not kidding."

My father wilted a little under my mom's glare.

Anxiety welled up inside me, and I had this desperate thought that I had only one chance to convince them about something I didn't even really understand myself. The words poured out of my mouth in a rush.

"When we were little, he was like ... superman. He was cool. He never let anyone pick on Bobby or me. And then we got older, we weren't really friends, but he was still nicer than everyone else, and he knows I garden a lot and him and his dad call me The Constant Gardner, and then something terrible happened and he made a big mistake. I don't know what *exactly* happened, but I know it's something. People don't just kill people for no reason, right?" I looked back and forth from my dad to my mom. "Right?"

"The news is saying he killed the coach because he was going to bench him for the big game," my father said.

"Do you honestly believe that?" I asked, disgusted both with the news vultures and my father for just unquestioningly believing that crap. I conveniently forgot the fact that I'd been thinking the very same thing a few days ago, a-hole that I was.

"I don't know." My father was offended at the insinuation that he's an idiot coming loud and clear through my tone. "I don't know this boy. And I don't think you know him either."

"You've never mentioned him," my mom said, I think trying to be fair. "He wasn't one of your friends before he was a murder suspect."

I waved her off. "Listen, we live in different social stratospheres, okay? That's normal. It's totally *normal*." I pounded my fist on my thigh. "It was the same for you when you were in school." I switched to a pleading tone. "Mom, you said so yourself ... when you went to your twenty-year class reunion, everyone was totally different. The real world showed you that popularity meant nothing." I shifted my gaze to my dad. "Jason is living in that real world right now. I'm living in it. This thing that happened to the coach ... it changes everything." I realized as I said it that it was so true. Jason and I would never be the same after this, either individually or together.

"I don't agree that it has to change *your* life," my father said.

My chin went up automatically. "I'm sorry, but it's not your decision what happens with my life."

My mom's eyeballs kind of popped out of her head a little, but my dad was the first one to respond.

"Excuse me?"

Ooops. Went a little too far there.

I struggled to fix what I had just messed up. "What I meant was that I am grown-up enough to make my own decisions about this kind of thing, and I've made my decision. I'm going to stand by Jason through thick and thin, and I don't care what the news says or what the kids at school say. He needs a friend and I am that friend. It's a done deal." I was totally ready for a cape and some tights at that point.

"Need I remind you that you are only seventeen years old?"

I could see the anger simmering beneath my father's calm exterior, but I didn't let it sway me from my mission.

"I'll be eighteen in six months, but it makes no difference. I have to do what I have to do, and I just hope you can support me in this. You've been telling me for years that I need to get out of the house and do something worthwhile, so now I'm doing it."

"I didn't mean hang out with *murderers!*" my father shouted, jumping to his feet again. "I meant like glee club or something!"

"Glee club? Are you serious?" I stood up too, ready to get the hell out of this ridiculous place. *Glee Club. As if.*

"All right, that's enough!" my mom shouted, also standing. She gave my father the evil eye and then turned it on me. "No more arguing. No more threats. Here's what's going to happen..."

My breath got stuck in my lungs and wouldn't come out. I could hear a ringing in my ears as the pressure mounted. My father was breathing like a bull ready to plow us both over.

"Katy, you will be permitted to visit Jason, if, and I mean only *if*, you discuss each meeting with us first and gain our agreement."

The breath left my lungs like air departing a soggy balloon. "Great. I guess I know what that means." It meant tying sheets together and rappelling out of my window in the middle of the night.

"No, you don't," she said, wiping the smile off my dad's face. "We agree to be fair, to listen to what you have to say, and to try and understand what you're doing and why you're doing it. Because you are a mature almost-adult, as you've mentioned, and we recognize that you need practice having adult independence before the day you actually leave this shelter we've provided for you and strike out on your own."

My father rolled his eyes.

My mom turned to face him, effectively blocking me out. I was an observer in a moment that would normally be left for their bedroom.

"God forbid if Katy were ever accused of a terrible crime, we would want her friends to support her. If they all disappeared and left her here with us, it would be as bad as prison. We have always believed in a person's right to be proven guilty before being treated as a criminal, right?"

My father nodded, but he still had that stubborn look in his eye. "But he's admitted he did it."

"You can't...!" I started, but my mom cut me off with a hand and a glare. She's really good at that.

She went back to counseling my dad, this time with a sweeter tone. Her eyes went soft and she stepped in closer, taking him by the hands. "As you well know, people often give confessions and later recant them. Innocent people admit guilt all the time. We cannot just assume he's guilty on that basis, especially considering he's pled *not guilty*."

My father's shoulders sagged and his face fell. "I really hate that you went to law school sometimes. You get all ... lawyery and it's seriously interfering in my ability to ever win an argument about anything."

She threw her arms around him and hugged him hard. His hands slipped around her lower back as he pulled her in close.

My mom spoke into his chest. "I don't want her going over there any more than you do, but imagine what it's like to be Chuck right now. He must be devastated. I'm upset with myself that I haven't gone over there and given him our support yet."

My mom pulled away from my dad and looked over her shoulder at me. "We'll go over as a family tomorrow morning."

I tried to calm the zip of electric happiness that shot through my body. It could be a trap. My parents are seriously awesome at setting them and I usually fell right into them too. "But I have school."

"You can miss a couple periods in the morning."

I wanted to leap for joy, but I was afraid to enjoy the victory too much. My dad was on a hair trigger, and it wouldn't take much for him to veto my mom's decision. They have some crazy rule that each one of them gets a no-questions-asked veto that cannot be argued against. I've only seen it used once in all the years I've been alive, but it was ironclad. No way did I want to invoke one of those.

"I'm going to do some homework and then go to bed."

My father looked down at my mom. "Who is that kid and what has she done with our daughter?"

"Ha, ha," I said, walking by them.

I was almost out of range when my dad grabbed my arm and pulled me back. Soon I was enveloped in a Katy sandwich, my parents the bread and me the meat.

"We love you, Katydid," my father mumbled into my hair. "We're not ogres. We just want to protect you from the terrible things out there in the world."

"You can't protect me forever," I said, my voice catching in my throat. How I wished their love could be enough to turn back time and stop Jason from making such a terrible mistake with his life.

"Yes, I can. I'm your father."

I know he meant it as a joke, but I had to show him I was an adult now. I looked up and stared him and my mom in the face. "Tell that to Mr. Bradley tomorrow. I'll bet he thought he could protect Jason too."

My mom's eyes teared up and she and my dad squeezed me so hard, I thought I was going to pee a little. When they finally let me go, I separated myself and grabbed the camera on the side table, intent on deleting any photos on the memory card before giving it back to its owner.

I went upstairs to my room with a lighter step but a heavier heart. Things just kept getting more complicated, and I didn't see my future being any better.

FORGET HOMEWORK. I WAS MORE interested in playing camera hacker than learning about matrices and determinants. *Pre-calc. Bleck.*

After texting Bobby, telling him I'd fill him in on all the drama at lunch tomorrow, I pulled the memory card from the camera and put it into the slot on the side of my computer. Images started loading into my photo program, and I hummed to myself as I waited.

Carwash ... mmm-mmm mmm-mmm mmm-mmm mmm-mmm... talkin' 'bout the car wash, yeah...

Inspiration struck as the old-school tunes kept rolling through my brain, so I opened up my music library and quickly put together a playlist that I thought Jason might like. Deciding that Facebook might be the best way to contact him, I did a search of his name.

His page was the first one that came up under my search, even though I was sure there were hundreds of Jason Bradleys around the country, maybe even the world. That meant I was probably one of a thousand people who'd gone looking for him online recently. It made my heart hurt to imagine why all those people suddenly cared about him. Surely it wasn't to 'friend' him. What a joke.

His page was loaded with new messages and images, all of which were sickening. It was clear Jason hadn't been online in awhile, otherwise for sure he would have deleted all of it. Hell, if it were me, I would have closed the account down entirely.

His wall was covered in people saying horrible things to him and about him. There was a meme that said, DEATH PENALTY in big letters, superimposed over Jason's yearbook photo from last year.

The whole thing made me nauseated, and I prayed silently that Jason would never see it. The police had taken his computer. Maybe he wouldn't be allowed to have one for a while. Maybe I could talk to his dad about getting onto Jason's account and deleting his Facebook page before he saw it.

I abandoned the idea of sending a friend request and instead decided to get a new email address for him. That way I could put stuff in there without anyone knowing about it, and his dad could get stuff off it for him. It was bold and crazy and definitely impulsive, but I didn't let those little nagging doubts stop me. Using Google, I signed up for a new account with my name as the owner.

I smiled in satisfaction after writing the user and password info down on a post-it note, feeling so super-spy it wasn't even funny. I sent a message to the new address with a link to the playlist on my cloud account. Hopefully his dad wouldn't think it was weird that I'd done all this. I'm not sure why I was more worried about Jason's father's reaction than Jason's himself, but I was. Everything was upside down and inside out, not making the least bit of sense.

Would his dad think I was a stalker? A wannabe girlfriend?

My stomach kind of flipped around at that thought. I didn't want that, I was sure of it. My interest in Jason was purely friend-oriented. I could ignore the knowledge that murder hadn't changed the fact that he was the hottest guy in school.

The pictures had finished loading, so I clicked over to my photo program and started sifting through the images. Anything was better than second-guessing my motivations where Jason was concerned. Jason and his fine butt.

Argh. I hated that I'd noticed that and couldn't forget it.

All of the most recent pictures were of my front door, my lawn, my dad's car, Jason's house, Jason's windows, Jason's fence and then several of me and Jason's dad coming out of the house with a crowd in the background. The camera guy even caught a shot of the microphone smashing into my face. I looked like a serious freak with my mouth hanging open and my eyes crossed. I deleted that one first.

The rest of the photos were taken during the daytime, of football players I recognized from my school. The pictures were either individual shots of players walking or several of them standing around in small groups. There were some younger boys hanging out near them, kind of on the outskirts of the groups, like they were fans of the players. I couldn't figure out where the shots were taken until I saw a sign in the background of one of the photos. I pressed the zoom key until I could read it.

"Big Brothers of South Banner," I said out loud into the room.

After a few seconds it rang a bell in my brain. Big Brothers of Banner was one of the coach's pet charities. It had been mentioned in the news about a million times since the murder last week. Yep, Jason had killed a saint.

I quickly shut my photo program down, and when the window popped up asking me whether I wanted to save or delete the photos from the camera's memory card, I selected *Delete*.

That'll teach that assmunch to invade our privacy.

After pulling it from the computer, I also laid both sides of it on a giant magnet I had in my room from a failed science project, circa sixth grade. I had no idea if a magnet could do anything helpful, but I saw on a CSI episode once that they were able to get photos off an erased memory card, and I didn't want that picture of me or Jason's father seeing the light of day. Magnets erase all kinds of digital stuff, I knew this for a fact. Putting one on top of our TV when I was twelve had totally messed up my dad's screen and made him cranky for a week.

I would have just kept the memory card or broken it into bits, but I didn't want to be accused of stealing on top of all the other shit I was sure to be accused of. After seeing what was on Jason's Facebook wall, I could only imagine the fresh horror that awaited me in school tomorrow. I was so glad it was going to be a Friday and I'd be missing first period.

After I put the card on my desk, I dressed in my pajamas, which consisted of a long t-shirt and sweat-shorts with the words *Hot Stuff* on the buttcheeks. The card was back in the camera ready to be delivered to its owner when he came knocking, which I was fairly certain he'd do tomorrow morning. If I were a vulture, that's what I'd do.

Sleep did not come easily to me that night. I tossed and turned for what seemed like hours. When I did finally succumb to endless visions of sheep jumping a white picket fence sometime after two in the morning, I had a horrible dream about the coach.

He was the coach, of that I was sure, but he had this giant, grotesquely-shaped head and claws for hands. Then, just as I was about to turn away, his face changed and it was Jason there looking like he was about to eat me alive.

I woke up screaming and never did get back to sleep that night.

AFTER SPENDING WAY TOO MUCH time staring at the sad state of my closet and finally picking out an outfit to wear, I went downstairs. My mother and father were already at the breakfast table, dressed and prepared to head over to Jason's house. My mother seemed peppy, and my father a mystery, hiding behind the morning paper.

"Did you call Jason's dad first?" I asked, pouring myself a bowl of muesli cereal. I hated the stuff, but it made my mom happy when I ate it, so I was going to make the effort. It was the least I could do after she spared me from being roasted over a pit of punishments last night.

"No. Should we have?" My mom paused in the middle of pouring me a glass of orange juice.

I shrugged, talking around a mouthful of cereal. "No. Maybe. I dunno."

My dad bent the newspaper so he could see me over it. "Having second thoughts? Because we could just walk away, let this thing just die off."

I rolled my eyes, trying to control my temper and keep my gaze directed towards my bowl of floating bits. Unfortunately my mouth wasn't on board with that plan. I crunched my oats a few more times before the sarcastic comment flew out.

"Yeah, sure. Literally, since they're going for lethal injection." I looked up at my father and narrowed my eyes.

"Don't start," my mother said, setting my orange juice down in front of me. "We're going over there, and we'll make our decision about next steps after we do that, okay? And I don't want you two at each other's throats about this either, or neither one of you are going to be happy with the result."

I chewed slowly, feeling guilty that I'd tried to make my dad feel bad. He was just being a parent. "Sorry," I mumbled.

My father put his paper back up and didn't say a word.

My mom and I shared a look. Her silent words told me she'd make sure he acted reasonably. My silent words were telling her *good luck with that.*

My dad had obviously decided this whole thing was a bad idea and he was only going along with our visit this morning to appease my mother. It was going to take some kind of miracle to get him to change his mind.

I wasn't too proud to use my mother's power to my advantage, but I wasn't so dumb that I thought it could last through anything. I made a vow right then to do everything I could to make my father happy, even if it meant swallowing a whole buffet's-worth of words I'd rather say aloud. Until Jason's situation was determined, I would be the model child.

Ugh. Even thinking it in my head made me want to gag.

"Are you feeling okay?" my mom asked, stepping over to rub my back. "You look at little green around the gills."

"I'm fine," I said, swirling my grains and nuts around in the pool of tepid milk. "Just worried about Jason is all."

My father's paper jerked like he'd just snorted.

I ignored him. "I'm going to get my stuff. Are you guys ready to go?" I stood and brought my bowl to the sink, dumping the uneaten cereal down the disposal before putting the dish in the washer.

"Five minutes," my mom said, heading off to her room. "I just need to brush my teeth."

I was almost out of the room before my father's voice stopped me.

"The question is, are you ready?"

I paused, my hand on the doorway to the kitchen. "What's that supposed to mean?"

My father folded up his paper and put it down next to his plate on the table, turning partway in his chair to face me when he was done.

"I'm worried that you have this schoolgirl fantasy view of what's going on here. That you see this cute boy who needs a friend and think you're going to ride in there and save the world and maybe get a new boyfriend while you're at it."

I couldn't keep the look of extreme disgust off my face. *Screw being the perfect daughter.*

"Are you serious?" I shook my head. "Jesus, Dad, I'm not ten, okay? Give me a break." I stormed down the hallway as I sent my last shot. "Thanks for ruining my morning, by the way!" My face was burning, possibly from the last part of his comment. I wasn't in this to get a new boyfriend. I didn't even *want* a boyfriend, and if I did, it definitely wouldn't be the guy everyone hated.

My father mumbled something in response, but I didn't hear it. Instead, I went to the bathroom attached to my bedroom and brushed my teeth, taking extra time to floss and use mouthwash too. I kept telling myself I wasn't using the mouthwash because I was hoping Jason would get close enough to smell my breath. I did it because gingivitis is a serious problem that I didn't want to have.

"GINGIVITIS," I SAID, BEFORE I could think straight.
Jason half-smiled, half-frowned at me. "Gingivitis?"

"Yeah." I nodded several times, enough that I probably looked like a crazed bobble head doll. We were standing face to face in front of the sink in his kitchen, pausing in the process of loading the dishwasher while our parents talked in the living room.

I hadn't meant to get this close to him, but he'd insisted on helping me clean up — something I was only doing to kiss up to all the freaked-out parents in the house — and then he was just there. Right in my face. Close enough to smell my breath, maybe. Hopefully not. I'd just had a bagel with lox and cream cheese on it.

"I use mouthwash because I'm afraid of getting gingivitis. Have you seen those commercials?" I fake-shuddered, trying to play off the fact that I was completely dorking-out.

"And you're telling me this because ..." Jason just stood there with a bagel plate in his hand, waiting for me to explain the spontaneous Rainman issue I appeared to be suffering. *I'm an excellent driver ... ack!*

If there was a magical power that could make the earth open up and swallow me whole, I'd want that one. And I'd have used it right then if I had it, too. The more I tried to salvage the situation, the worse it got.

"You were staring at my mouth," I explained, "so I thought maybe you smelled my mouthwash and I was explaining the reason why I use it."

"I was staring at the cream cheese on the edge of your lip, actually."

My hand flew to my face, wiping like crazy. "Are you serious? Oh my god, how embarrassing."

Jason started laughing his ass off, barely holding on to the plate in his hand.

I yanked it away and pushed him away from me, not sure now whether he was messing with me or I actually did have an eating disorder that caused everything that passed through my mouth to end up on my face.

"Shut up, you idiot. And go over there and get me those glasses off the table."

"Bossy, bossy," he said, doing what I told him to do without question.

He put the glasses in the top rack of the dishwasher while I rinsed my hands in the sink. My face was burning from embarrassment, so I kept my gaze off him and on anything else. There was a lopsided ceramic frog holding a steel-wool scrubbing pad on the edge of the sink that held my attention for a while.

"Sorry, I was just messing with you."

"I noticed." *Scrub, scrub, scrub. Just keep scrubbing.* My ears were burning.

"I can't seem to help myself. You're so gullible."

I scrubbed the soap on my hands around and around. "That's me. The gullible idiot."

He put his hand on my arm. "You're going to scrub your skin off if you don't stop."

My hands stilled and my wrists lowered to rest on the edge of the sink. "Sorry ... I'm just ... nervous, I guess."

He let me go and shut the dishwasher door. As he dried his hands off on a towel, he leaned his hip on the counter, facing me.

"What are you nervous about? You're not the one on trial for murder."

I think he meant it as a joke, but all it did was make me feel worse. I let the water run over my hands, watching the bubbles disappear from my skin. It was too awkward to look at him, so I pretended that the physics of the surface tension of my skin was fascinating to me.

I sighed. It was time for a little truthiness. "I'm worried my parents will tell me I can't come over here anymore."

"They gave you some shit, huh?" He sounded defeated.

"Mostly my father. But my mother's worried too."

"Do you blame them?"

My head jerked up at his tone. "They're not worried about you, about what you would do. They're worried about the rest of the world."

"I find that hard to believe." He threw the towel down and crossed his arms over his chest. "I murdered a grown man, Katy. With my bare hands." He pulled one hand out and looked at the back of it. "*This* bare hand."

The cuts and bruises were still there. This insane idea that they'd never go away, that they'd always be there to remind the world of what he'd done, popped into my head.

I reached out without thinking and placed my hand over his. I wasn't able to cover most of it because it was about twice the size of mine, but I did hide the injuries that were so blatantly supporting his claim of being a murderer.

His skin was cool, mine warmer from having been soaked in all that hot water. I pretended to be totally unaffected by his presence and by what he had done. Talk about a conflict. One made me hot and the other made me ice cold.

"Jason, I want you to stop saying that." I looked up into his eyes, refusing to be cowed by his good looks or the frown that he made after he heard my words.

"Stop saying what? The truth?"

I squeezed his hand a little. "No. I mean, yes. I mean ... *ergh!*" Everything was a jumble in my space-cadet brain. I couldn't remember what I was going to say or if I ever even knew in the first place.

"Ergh?" He smiled a little. "You want me to stop saying *ergh* or start saying *ergh*?"

My second hand joined my first and I leaned in closer, giving him my death glare. "I want you to stop focusing all of your attention on the past. *Ergh.* I want you to talk about something other than being a murderer. *Ergh.* I want you to admit that you're not the kind of person that just kills a guy for no reason. *Ergh* and double *ergh!*"

My heart was going wild in my chest. It went even nuttier when Jason stared back at me.

"You're hurting my hand."

"Oh. I'm sorry." I loosened my considerable grip.

"And you need to stop hoping for a miracle," he said, before adding, "*Ergh.*"

My mouth opened to respond, but the sound of our parents' voices coming back in our direction stopped me. I let my hands drop away and stepped towards the kitchen table, putting some distance between us.

"I'll discuss this with you later," I whispered, before turning to face the parents. I felt like my mom, issuing promises laced with warnings.

Jason smiled, apparently not feeling threatened at all. He had a lot to learn about me, that was for sure. I wasn't playing.

"You ready to go to school?" my father asked. He glanced at Jason and nodded once.

Jason returned the gesture.

I had no idea what that meant, man-code being a complete mystery to me. I checked the expressions on my mom's and Chuck's faces, but they were totally neutral. *Frigging parents. Always playing mind-games.*

"Yep. Ready to go." I walked over and picked up my backpack that I'd left on the floor. "See ya," I said to Jason casually as

I headed towards the front door, following our parents. No one but me knew that my heart was racing and my head pounding. I was working up one hell of a headache to bathe my brain in, just in time for second period.

"Yeah. Thanks for coming by," Jason said.

I turned around and caught the look on his face. My heart broke right in half at the sadness I saw there. He was staring at my backpack, and I would have been willing to bet the entire balance of my college savings account that he was wishing he could be heading off to Banner High too.

I thought of all the times I'd wished that I didn't have to go, and then a shiver passed through me as I realized I could have had that wish granted like Jason had.

Be careful what you wish for took on a whole new meaning for me that day.

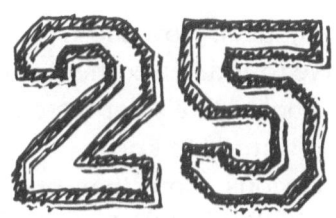

BOBBY MET ME AT THE entrance to the school, five minutes before the bell was about to ring. His outfit had me shaking my head. Apparently he had decided to go all out for the occasion of my re-introduction to the entire school as Jason's number-one supporter. Wearing not only black pants, a black shirt and a black satin vest, he was also sporting a small black hat with a black netted veil attached. The only things with any color on his entire body were a red rose in the hat and bright red lipstick to match. I kid you not, he looked like he was going to a funeral in a Tim Burton film. Three guesses whose funeral he had in mind.

"So, what is the dealio, sister? I've been in the dark for way too long. Rumor has it that you have some secrets." He stuck his arm in the crook of my elbow and dragged me along. "And you have four minutes, so start spilling your guts or we won't be friends anymore."

"As if you could lose me that easily," I said, trying to stall the inevitable.

"Don't play. I have chemistry next period and you know that class always makes me break out in hives."

I was trying to ignore all the obvious stares and whispers that followed us through the hallways, but it was tough. No one was making any effort to be cool.

"I visited Jason a couple times. No big deal."

Bobby looked at me, probably glaring, but I didn't check to see.

"Uh, wrong. *Very* big deal. How did it go?"

"Good, I guess." We rounded a corner to get to the long row of lockers that held my books. "He's depressed a little. Still confessing, if that's what you wanted to know."

"Of course I was curious about that, but I'm more interested in how he's dealing with the fact that you're the only one coming to see him."

As we got closer to my locker and the ring of students standing around it, I thought less about answering Bobby's question and more about what fresh horror awaited me.

"Oh, boy," Bobby said under his breath. "I was hoping to avoid this mess."

I pulled away from him, making his arm fall from mine. "Fine. Go if you have to."

He thrust his arm back through my elbow and pulled me along. "That's not what I meant, and you know it. Come on. Let's go kick some mean-girl butt."

The front of my locker had something smeared on it. Something red.

Bobby sighed really loudly and rolled his eyes as we approached. People moved to make room for me, some of them giving me the shit-eye, others looking ... scared. Maybe they thought because I was hanging out with a murderer it had somehow rubbed off and caused me to be dangerous too. Ironically, that made me want to punch someone.

"Oh, please, is that supposed to be blood?" Bobby asked really loudly. He held his hand up to it, palm towards the locker. "More like my latest nail color. I like it." He gestured towards the lock and looked at me. "Open it up. I want to see what the tiny-brained idiots have put in there today."

Several students looked at each other. I couldn't tell if their expressions said guilt or look-what-the-crazy-gay-boy-is-up-to-today. Bobby was always good for some entertainment. His silliness was taking some of the darkness out of the atmosphere, so I wasn't about to stop him.

I turned the lock with trepidation. People were whispering, but all I could hear with any clarity was the *click, click, click* as the dial passed through the numbers.

32 *click click click* ... 48 *click click click* 12 ...

Several slips of paper fell out of my locker and onto the ground. One of them had red smears on it, similar in color to the crap on the outside of my door.

Bobby kicked them into a pile and then leaned down, picking them all up in a stack.

"Okay, folks, F.Y.I. ... here's what we think about anonymous, cowardly notes, delivered by small-minded assholes who should have better things to do with their time than to try and bully someone into turning her back on a friend." He whipped a lighter out of his front pocket and set fire to the corner of the pile.

He waved the flaming mass over his head. "Here's our message to the cowards who can't say whatever it is they think they need to say to Katy's face ... *go to hell!*"

It was a glorious two seconds as all the faces in front of us angled up to watch the flame of honor and awesomeness burning bright in Bobby's hand.

Unfortunately, the moment was quickly lost when he waved his flaming standard a little too close to one of the school's fire-suppression sprinklers.

There was a *clack*, a *fizz*, and then water started spraying everywhere, first just over our heads and then out of all the sprinklers in the entire hall.

A fire-bell started clanging loud enough to give me an instant headache, and people began screaming in fright. Everyone who had books with them threw them up over their heads and ran.

Bobby got bumped and slammed around and ended up dropping the papers to the ground, and the fire got put out by the stampede of feet running by.

All I could do was stare at the pandemonium. As bodies flew by bumping into me, sending me left and right, I started laughing, thinking how ridiculous my life had become. In the mornings, I hang out with a murderer, then I move on to spending time with an arsonist who sets the school on fire. *I'm so not getting into college.*

"It's not even funny how royally screwed I am right now," Bobby said, sounding way more depressed about it than I was about my own future. He was standing there with water running down his hair and into his face. His formerly spiked hair was now wet-dog scraggly, hanging down to his chin, and his hat was leaning precariously off to the side.

I pushed some of the moppy mess behind his ear so I could see his eyes. "You are my hero, Bobby Garrity."

He pulled me into an intense hug, his wet hat whacking me on the ear.

"I wanted to be as brave as you are. I'm sorry I didn't go with you to Jason's."

I patted him on the back. "You win. You're the bravest kid in the entire school." I didn't tell him I was glad he hadn't gone with me to Jason's, because if he wanted to go in the future, he should go. Jason needed all the friends he could get. Besides, I liked the time I spent alone with my neighbor a little too much, probably. Bobby would be a nice buffer to keep my girly-emotions in check.

I smiled as I watched teachers coming out and running down the hallways with their purses and briefcases in hand. "You are so going to get suspended for this," I said, shaking my head at his bravado.

"Excellent. More time for shopping." Bobby's chin went up in defiance.

We were still laughing when the school police officer walked up, took Bobby by the elbow, and led him away.

"SO, AM I ALLOWED TO go to Jason's or what?" I asked my mom after school, glad my father wasn't around to share his opinion on the subject.

My mother paused in mid plant-watering to answer me. "Your father and I spoke last night and we decided that we would let you visit Jason on a limited basis."

"What's that mean?" I took an apple out of a bowl on the counter and bit into it, pretending like I enjoyed fruit and wasn't freaking out inside over what she was saying.

"You may go after school for a couple hours to do homework together, and on the weekend we can negotiate for additional time, but you are not to go over there when you should be in school and you cannot go over at all unless you ask one of us first and get permission."

"So you're going to keep me on lockdown, is that it? Treat me like I'm ten again?"

"No, we're going to protect your interests while also giving you the latitude to support a friend, as you've asked to be able to do. You might not like the rules, but you don't get to make them until you're eighteen. I think we're being more than fair."

I kept chewing the apple to keep from saying what I thought about these so-called fair rules, rules that were very much like the ones set for me when I was in fifth grade. Fact is, they weren't fair, but I had six months before I was able to do anything about it, and I knew if I pushed it, my father would get all up in my face and make them even more restrictive.

"Fine. I'm going over there now, if that's okay with you." I tried to keep the snark out of that last sentence, but I wasn't entirely successful, or so her burdened expression told me.

"Yes. Take your books. Chuck told us that Jason has a couple of tutors keeping him on track with all his classes at school."

"All of them?" I could just picture some old hippy coming to his house helping him with his ceramics class. That would be interesting.

"Not the electives but the ones that count towards his graduation requirements, yes."

I left without another word, worried she'd change her mind if I said anything else.

Instead of going to Mr. Baumgarten's house, I walked right down the street like I owned it and up to Jason's front door. There were only three reporters there, and I blazed past them so fast using my super-walk they didn't even get a chance to say anything before I was ringing the bell. Looking over my shoulder as I waited for an answer, I noticed that they all stayed on the street. It was nice not having my face attacked by microphones.

Mr. Bradley answered the door. "Katy!" he said, on his face a huge smile. "Come in, come in." He stepped back and closed the door behind me, acting like there weren't reporters using cameras with long lenses to snap photos of us at high speeds.

"Hey, Mr. Bradley."

"Call me Chuck." He looked up the stairs. "Jason! Katy's here!" He shifted his focus back to me. "I'll leave you kids alone. I'm doing some bookkeeping in the other room if you need me."

I nodded and waited in the front hall alone, taking in the ceramic tile floors and scuffed cream-colored paint on the walls. This house was missing a woman's touch. There were no pictures in the hallway, no crap on the table tops ... my mom would have had a heart attack over walls like that with all those scuff marks. I'd lost count of how many times she'd had our front hall re-painted.

For a few awkward seconds, I wondered whether Jason was going to choose to ignore me today and stay in his room, but then there were some pounding sounds and Jason's feet appeared as he came down the steps.

He wasn't wearing any shoes, and his jeans dragged the floor under his heels. His hair was wet as if he'd just taken a shower.

It seemed strangely intimate to see him this way. A silly part of me wondered if he'd taken the shower specifically for my visit. I just as quickly squelched that ridiculousness and banned it from my brain.

"Hey, what's up?" he asked, stopping at the bottom stair. The smell of his soap wafted up into my nostrils and I tried to inhale deeper without being obvious about it.

"My mom says I have two hours to help you with your homework," I blurted out.

He rolled his eyes and came down the last stair to the floor-level. "Fun, fun. Come on, let's go in the kitchen."

I was glad he hadn't suggested we go to his room, but at the same time I wondered if we'd always just hang out in the kitchen like two neighbors and not two friends.

"So what's new at Banner?" he asked. "Everyone talking about the cold-blooded killer?"

"Yep. You're still the biggest news the school has had since they discovered Mr. Williams was a closet transvestite." If Jason could joke about his situation, so could I. *So there.*

I reached down into my backpack that I'd dropped next to my chair and pulled out a book as I sat down.

"They giving you shit?" he asked me in a more serious voice. "My dad says you were on the news in front of our house, and that whole getting-punched-in-the-face-with-a-microphone shot was on every news channel all night."

I dropped the book on the table with a bang. "Nothing I can't handle." I turned to a random page and looked up at him. "You ready to do some work?" My tongue licked at the spot on my lip that was still a little swollen from said microphone incident.

He shook his head. "No." He was staring at me but then put all his attention on his cuticles.

"I heard you got tutors."

"Yeah. It's a joke." He snorted in disgust. "You should see the homework."

"Is it better or worse?"

"Way better. A single page. Four problems for math, nothing for anything else."

"What?" I slapped my book shut. "That's bullshit, man. You're getting a free ride?" A sound distinctively like one a pig makes escaped my nostrils. Not attractive at all. I was thinking of the mountain of physics homework alone that I had waiting for me in my bag and I'd have to do later after I got home.

He shrugged and leaned back in his chair. "I guess killers don't need to worry about having an education."

I couldn't decide how to react to that, but it didn't matter. Jason wasn't done.

He tipped his head back to stare at the ceiling. "Everyone used to be on my case all the time about grades, giving me extra help, making sure I could qualify not just to play but to get into a good school."

"But you had scholarships all lined up, right?"

His chair leaned back farther, making me think he was about to flip over.

"They're better if you have good grades to back them up. It's not easy to find an athlete who can play and do the classwork too."

"Because they're all dumbasses," I said, agreeing with him, or so I thought.

"No, not really." His chair rocked back and forth, back and forth on two legs. "It's because most people choose to do the least amount of work possible, regardless of how smart they are. And if you're good on the field or the court, you only need to do the minimum, and everything just falls into place."

"You mean people get bogus good grades so they can make the school proud."

Jason tipped his head and chair down to look at me. "Let me put it to you this way ... strong sports programs bring in the best teachers and the most bucks."

"For college maybe."

"Not just college. Don't fool yourself. You saw the car that Coach drove around, right?"

"Who didn't. Mercedes SUV, right?"

"Yeah. You don't think he paid for that out of his pocket, did you?"

I shrugged. "I guess I did. Maybe his family has money."

"Bullshit. He was given a new car to *borrow* every year." Jason put the word *borrow* in finger-quotes. "Same as the assistant coach. But you don't see that happening to the woman's softball coach, do you?"

"I have no idea what she drives."

"She drives a nineteen eighty Toyota Corolla, covered in dents."

"What about the track coach?" I asked, kind of joking. I imagined making a chart of all the coaches and their cars to prove some kind of point to the world.

"Track doesn't get shit either. It's football, basketball, sometimes baseball ... the sports that pay big money on the outside professionally."

"What about soccer?"

"Not there yet."

I chewed on my bottom lip as I considered what he was saying. "So you guys, the future possible professional athlete golden boys ... you help the coach get a slick ride ... and you get what?" I glanced over to the door that I knew led to his garage. "You get cars too?"

"Hell no. No one would risk being that obvious. They can't give us gifts, but they can take us out to dinner, buy us 'equipment'...," he used the finger quotes again, "... warm-ups, shoes for playing in, under armor, that kind of stuff. You should see my closet. It's loaded with shit I probably shouldn't have."

"So what's the point?" I asked, folding my arms over my book on top of the table.

"What do you mean what's the point?"

"Why are we even talking about this?"

He shrugged. "I don't know. You wanted to dive into the homework and I was telling you there's no point. I'm going to pass anyway. Or not." He looked out the window into his backyard. "It doesn't really matter at this point, anyway, does it?"

"Are we talking about the prison thing again?" His self-defeatist attitude was getting really annoying.

"Yeah. Sorry to be so boring about it." He glared back at me.

"Okay, so let's assume you're found guilty."

"I will be." His nostrils flared.

"Whatever. So what does that mean? You have to be in prison for what ... twenty years?"

"Minimum twenty-five."

"So? You'll only be a little old when you get out."

"Forty-three."

"See? You could get married and start having kids then. But you'll need a job and you won't get one as a football player. And since you'll need to *work* in the future, you have to make sure your grades don't suck."

"You really are living in a fantasy world," he said, sounding kind of bitter.

"Maybe." I stared him down.

"Not maybe. *Definitely*. It's hopeless."

"I made you an email account," I blurted out, no longer able to take the stare-down contest and horrible words floating out there in the air between us.

Prison. Future. Hopeless.

"What?"

Leaning down, I grabbed my iPad from inside my backpack and put it out on the table. "I actually made you a playlist of songs, but I wasn't sure how to get it to you off my cloud account." I kept talking to fill the weird silence. "We aren't friends on Facebook, and I didn't have your email address, so I just opened you up a new account and put a link to the playlist in a message."

I turned the iPad on and slide it over so he could see the screen.

He stared at the glass as different windows popped up at my command. I leaned in close enough that I could smell him again; not on purpose, but I didn't lean back either.

"I haven't been online since everything happened. My dad wouldn't let me, and the cops took my phone and computer."

I paused to look at him. "Am I breaking some kind of rule here, letting you see this?"

"No. He just told me he preferred I didn't look, and he's been so upset I didn't want to make it worse by giving him a hard time about it." Jason turned his head to face me, our noses just inches apart. "Is it bad? What they're saying about me?"

I shrugged and leaned back a little, trying to play my rapid pulse-rate and his horrible question off like they were no big deal.

"Yeah, I guess. I don't pay much attention to that stuff. People are assholes." I pressed the link to get to the Google mail sign-in page. Things were getting too intense. I felt like the room was shrinking, having him that close.

"Your user name is here," I pointed to the screen, "and your password is constantgardener99." My face pinked up a bit at that small admission that I appreciated him noticing me. I prayed silently that he wouldn't put two and two together and come up with four, i.e, desperate neighbor girl hungry for attention.

He signed in and clicked on the link in the message I sent without saying a word. It brought him to the playlist that automatically started playing. It shuffled the order so that the first one to come on wasn't the first one I'd put there.

A slow smile spread across Jason's face.

"You like?" I asked, smiling too, maybe a little embarrassed. Making a playlist suddenly seemed so ... intimate.

He started bobbing his head. "What is it? Have I heard this before?"

"It's *Return of the Mack* by Mack Morrison. From the nineties. Lots of gems from that decade."

"It's kind of hard not to dance to," he said. "Brittney always said I was a terrible dancer."

"Bitch." The word popped out before I could stop it.

He laughed and a huge grin lit up his face, erasing all the those sad creases that had settled in before. "You said it." He stood up and started moving around the kitchen. "Check this out. Can you believe she didn't like it?"

I hooked my arm over the back of the chair as I watched his stiff body movements qwerk and jerk him over the floor.

"Oh my. Maybe instead of saying 'bitch' I should have said 'starkly honest'."

He pointed at me. "Get on your feet. No fair judging unless you're ready to share your moves too." He clapped his hands and raised his arms above his head and did some kind of weird attempt at a hip swivel.

I got up and rolled my eyes as I let the rhythm take me. "*This* is how you dance." I moved my legs, feet, and hips in carefully-crafted, awesome synchronicity for a few seconds before waving a finger in his direction. "I don't know what that is you're doing over there."

"This is cutting a rug, busting a move, getting on my gliiiide," he said, dancing over in my direction.

"You look like you're having a seizure." I giggled as his head dropped back and his eyes rolled up into his head.

"Come on," he said, grabbing my hand and spinning me in a circle. "Dancing With the Stars, here we come."

I was laughing and sweating within seconds, spinning this way and that, trying not to fall or get stepped on. Jason's feet were everywhere, way too big for his own good.

"Ow!" I yelped, getting my big toe smashed for about the fifth time.

"Watch those giant toes of yours, lady. You're throwing off my groove." He attempted to do a spin and tripped, barely rescuing himself from a face plant by doing some sort of improvised push-up against the counter.

The song faded out and the next one in the shuffle order came on. I swallowed hard as the words started up.

We both stood there swaying and listening to the words, Hootie and the Blowfish talking about how old Hootie only wants to be with this girl who comes from a different world than he does.

Ack! What was I thinking when I made this thing!

"I love Hootie," Jason said, making a lame attempt at dancing to the rhythm. He either didn't notice the lyrics or was being a prince pretending like he didn't.

"Yeah. Me too." I was going to say something else to try and shift the subject away from the song, but the doorbell rang and did it for me, *thank all that is holy.*

"You get it," Jason said.

"Me?" I pointed at my chest.

"Yeah. If I get it they take a million pictures." He walked over the front window and pushed the blinds down to peek in between them. "It's Bobby."

I rushed to the door and pulled it open, or tried to anyway. There were two locks Jason had to lean over my shoulder to undo before it would work. My whole body went warm with the scent that filled my nose.

"Hello, kids," Bobby said, a huge grin on his face. "Can Jason play?"

I GRABBED BOBBY BY THE front of his shirt and dragged him into the foyer before shutting the door behind him. "What are you doing here?"

"Hey, man," Jason said holding up a hand for some sort of high five.

Bobby failed miserably, slapping his hand around with a loose wrist, never making a solid connection.

"Just came to hang out, see what's what. Get the answers to our upcoming chemistry exam." He winked at me. He was completely unashamed of his attempts at cheating his way through that class.

Jason laughed when Bobby's ears perked up at the next song.

"Rico Suave? Seriously? Are we going old-school today?" He started doing some kind of flamenco move on his way into the middle of the living room.

"Please stop," I said, "before you hurt yourself." I leaned on the wood frame that surrounded the entrance to the room.

"You guys hungry?" Jason asked, moving down the hallway towards the kitchen.

"No, I'm on a diet," Bobby said. "But I'll watch you guys eat." He danced his way down the hall behind Jason, and I took up the rear.

Bobby sat down at the table and I joined him. We both watched Jason go to the fridge and start pulling things out, putting them on the counter.

"Are you expecting guests?" Bobby asked as the items piled up.

"Nope. Just you guys."

Six ham and cheese sandwiches and a giant bowl of potato chips joined us at the table before Jason sat down with three big glasses and two liters of soda.

"Uhhh, what part of diet did you not understand?" Bobby said, cracking off half of a chip and nibbling on it.

"These are for me," Jason said, taking five of the sandwiches and putting them on a paper towel in front of him. He pushed the one remaining sandwich on a plate towards me.

I ate a chip and looked first at Bobby and then at Jason and back to Bobby again. Everything was too weird, all of us sitting at the table, acting like it was totally normal to eat after-school snacks together. If Jason hadn't murdered the coach, none of us would be here. It was so, so wrong of me to have a glimmer of happiness over the tragedy, but I did. It was awful.

Bobby put his overly-understanding face on. "So. You killed the coach, eh?"

I kicked him under the table.

"Ow!" He glared at me.

Jason's jaw clenched, and I wasn't sure he was going to answer at all, but then he did and it was actually worse than the question, something I wouldn't have guessed could be possible.

"Yep. I killed the coach. And I'm really sorry that he died, but there's nothing I can do about it now." He took a huge bite of his sandwich, pretty much leaving just the crust behind.

"Everyone wants to know why you did it." Bobby leaned his face down really close to the table. His eyes darted to the window and the back door. "They're speculating."

"Let 'em," Jason said, starting on his second sandwich. He kept staring at his plate, like he was planning his next move with his lunch. Something way more important than discussing his crime against humanity, or so it seemed.

I wanted to pretend like this was a normal conversation and eat my sandwich too, but I'd lost my appetite. Nothing about this could have been called normal. Not the conversation, not me and Bobby being here, not the way I was feeling, and not Jason acting like it was all okay.

"Just stop!" I said, way too loudly.

Both of them looked at me.

"Sorry. That was loud. I just … want to not dwell on the awful part of this."

"That's all there is," Bobby said. "Unless I'm missing something." He looked from Jason to me.

"Nope. It's all pretty much awful soul-destroying shit." Jason shoved about ten chips into his mouth at once.

"It's not completely hopeless, come on." I was practically pleading at this point. "Jason, you're alive, and you did something terrible, but I know it was a mistake. I *know* it was."

Jason put down his third sandwich and stared at me. "You just don't get it, do you?"

"She's kind of the hopeless romantic type," Bobby said, like he was commiserating with Jason.

I smacked both of them on their arms.

"Shut up, I am not. I'm just logical. Logic says you did *not* wake up the day of that game and decide you were going to kill the coach, goddammit!"

"*Oooph*. That's a commandment broken right there," Bobby said.

"You're right," Jason said, saving Bobby from getting slapped again. "I didn't wake up and think that."

"See?" I looked at Bobby and Jason, back and forth, a smile lighting up my face. Hope was practically exploding from my chest. "It wasn't pre-meditated, it wasn't planned, it wasn't part of who Jason is!"

"But he did it," Bobby said in a small, sad voice. "So I guess it is now."

I lost my happy right there. Boom. Gone. My heart became a black hole sucking in all the misery around me and filling me with it.

"Listen," said Jason, "I don't want you guys getting into a fight over this, okay? It's a done deal, whether we want it to be or not. I killed the ass... the coach and nothing is going to change that. Not all the wishing or second-guessing or hopeless romantic whatever in the world." He shoved another handful of chips into his mouth and stood up. "I'm going to go upstairs and work-out."

"That's my cue to leave," I said, standing and gathering up my stuff into my bag.

"But I just got here," Bobby whined, looking up at us.

"Yeah, and you got everyone all depressed, so come on." I nudged his shoulder. "Now you have to leave."

Bobby stood and hung his head. "I'm sorry for being a party pooper. I promise I won't rain on your love-parade ever again."

If Jason hadn't been standing right there, I would have clocked Bobby good, but since Jason *was* there watching, I just laughed it off. "Ha, ha. Very funny. Come on. We have tons of physics homework to get done and I don't understand any of it."

Bobby argued about whether he was going to help me as we made our way to the front door. I was glad for the distraction, so I let him roll with it.

"See you soon, maybe?" Jason asked me, his hand poised on the door handle.

"Tomorrow for sure," I said, sending him an apology with my eyes. I wasn't even sure what I was apologizing for; I just wanted his day to not suck as much as it did right then.

"Cool. See ya." He undid the locks and pulled the door open, remaining behind it as we went across the threshold.

When we stepped out onto the front porch and the door closed behind us, Bobby leaned towards me, whispering in my ear. "Now I see why you keep coming over here."

A spark lit up my heart. "You can see it too? That he's hiding something?"

"No. He's seriously hot, and now he's single and available too."

I pinched Bobby really hard on the back as he tried to escape me by running down the front porch stairs.

SATURDAY STARTED OUT AWESOME, SUN shining every-where, birds chirping, and a weather forecast that said we wouldn't be seeing any clouds or rain for days. I danced around my room, thinking of all the fun things I could do. That lasted all of ten seconds as it came to me that Jason had woken up to the same weather but probably wasn't dancing around his room or happy about all the things he could do. Because he couldn't do any of them.

My parents explained that technically he could leave his house and do things, but the press had other plans for Jason, should he ever show his face outside his door. And kids at school were still talking about how he'd get seriously injured or worse if he ever showed up where they were. That pretty much left out any place worth going in our town. No mall, no movies, no hanging out downtown, no zoo, no library, no bookstore, no *nothing*.

An idea began to form in my mind, but I had to be sure Jason didn't have other plans first. I texted his dad.

What is Jason doing today?

A few minutes later I got a response. *This is Jason. Working out. That's it.*

Feel like company?

My nerves got the better of me when it took him a long time to answer. I was ready to type *or not* when his answer came back.

Sure. If u dont have smthng better to do.

I thought about what I'd be doing today if Jason were his regular, non-murdering self and ignoring me like he'd always done before. I'd probably call Bobby and we'd drive around, maybe see a movie, or possibly go to the mall. My twiggy buddy wasn't much for outdoorsy things, and I was too unmotivated to come up with anything more interesting, usually.

My fingers were shaking a tiny bit as I typed out my response.

C u at lunch.

As I pounded down the stairs, my plan came together. If Jason couldn't go out, I'd do what I could to simulate being out. At least until his fame died down a little. Having a plan of sorts gave me hope, and hope felt like pure drugs at that point.

"What are you so energetic about this early on a Saturday morning?" my mom asked from her spot at the table.

"We usually don't see you before noon on the weekends," my father added.

"I have to do a lot of homework." I poured myself some cereal and joined them.

"Check her for a fever, Marjorie."

"Ha, ha, very funny." I didn't even look at him, worried he'd see in my eyes that I was lying about the whole homework thing. "I'm feeling fine."

"This doesn't have anything to do with a certain boy who lives down the street does it?" my mother asked.

"God, Mom ..." I stood up with my bowl and ate at the sink, using every bit of acting power I had in me to keep the truth from my face.

"Sorry. I was just asking."

"Are you planning on going over there?" my father asked.

The thing I'd been trying to avoid was happening; all eyes were on me, my parents no longer paying any attention to their sudoku puzzles or crosswords.

"I was thinking about it." *Munch, munch, munch, I sure do love this healthy cereal!* "We have this monster physics final and Jason's pretty good at that stuff." That part wasn't a lie. He *was* pretty good at it. I'd seen his tests when the teacher passed them back from the front of the classroom. Normally the exam papers that went all the way to the back row had low grades on them, but I'd never seen Jason get less than a B, at least in that subject.

"I don't want you over there all day," my father said, his voice getting stern.

"I'm not planning to, okay? Geez, I know you don't want me over there at all. You don't need to keep bringing it up." I was on edge. Normally I wouldn't be this reckless with talking back to my parents when I knew I had plans to go out later, but everything about Jason seemed to immediately get me out of control. I definitely needed to work on that.

"It's not that we don't want you over there, sweetie." My mom sighed. "We just worry about the long-term effects of this friendship."

"Forget long-term, how about short term?" my father said. "Say what you want, but our society does not look kindly on people who support criminals."

I had to literally bite my tongue to keep from yelling at him.

"All we're saying is ... be careful. That reporter or photographer or whatever he was who came over here to get his camera was not a nice person. He'd be more than happy to take pictures of you in compromising positions."

My face heated up flaming red instantly. "Mom! Jesus Christ, I'm not going to get myself into any compromising positions!" An image of Jason's naked torso flashed in my mind and made me feel like a total perv.

"Hey, easy there!" my father said.

"No, no, I didn't mean it like that," my mother said, sounding embarrassed. "Not compromising like sexual..."

"Mom! Could we please just drop it?" I practically threw my dish in the sink and fast-walked out of there as quickly as I could. Climbing the stairs to my room, I did everything I could to keep the images from re-forming in my mind, but my brain had other ideas.

Jason with his shirt off.

Jason in his boxers.

Gah!

Me in a bathing suit and Jason in his bathing suit and us holding hands.

Double gah!

I grabbed my phone off my desk and texted Bobby.

U in for lunch at J's?

I brushed my teeth and read his response after I spit.

No can do. Gotta go get reproed.

My eyes naturally rolled up into my head at that. Re-proed meant he was going to a local church that practiced what they called *re-programming*. Their goal was to heal gays of their homosexual proclivities.

It was this sick game played by Bobby and his father. Bobby would go and act like it was finally making a difference, telling everyone what they wanted to hear, and then he'd go to the mall and buy something really sparkly and try to hook up with a guy.

It made me totally upset, but this was a pattern that they'd established a long time ago, and nothing I said would ever change it. Bobby had been going through re-programming for almost five years at that point. It was sick and sad and completely wrong, but Bobby's father was not yet ready to accept the fact that Bobby was who he was and no priest or anyone else was going to change that. Bobby was way more charitable than I was about it. He kept saying that one day, his father would come around. I wasn't so sure.

Good luck with that, I texted.

U going to J's all day?

My defenses went up.

No!

I sent the message before I could tone it down, which was really stupid because no one can read the emotions in a text like Bobby can.

Feeling a little anxious? lolsies

I rolled my eyes. He was totally fishing, so I didn't bother to answer. Instead, I went online to check the latest news on Jason's case.

The first headline caught my eye and immediately made me feel sick to my stomach.

MURDERER'S GIRLFRIEND DEFENDS HER MAN.

My first thought was that somehow Brittney had experienced a major change of heart, but the photo under the caption immediately cleared up that little misunderstanding.

Some assbucket had snapped an action shot of me in the middle of forming a word that looked like it might have been *orange* or *ogre*. I couldn't have looked less attractive had I tried.

I prayed Jason wouldn't see it. Not only would he realize how truly heinous I can look in the wrong light, but he'd probably think I was telling people I was his new girlfriend. Even the thought of it made me get all flustered.

I didn't even bother to read the article, knowing it would piss me off way too much for such a sunny day. Instead, I texted Bobby one last time and then left for the store so I could gather up my supplies for my little plan.

I RANG THE DOORBELL, MY arms loaded down with my backpack from this year and the one I kept from the year before. I
ignored the sounds of camera shutters behind me. The press had
thinned, but that didn't mean there was any privacy for anyone
approaching the Bradley house. I could only imagine what the
headlines tomorrow would say.

GIRLFRIEND ARRIVES WITH LUGGAGE PLANNING GET-
AWAY WITH MURDERER BOYFRIEND.

I was over it, though. Screw those assholes. Always assuming
the press's goal was to get to the truth, I never used to think much
about reporters. Now I knew better. Now I knew their game plan
was sensationalism, pure and simple; and the more awful or out-
landish it was, the better.

No one had bothered to ask me the status of my relationship
with Jason before they published that garbage yesterday; they'd
just assumed it. Girlfriends of murderers probably sell way more
papers than friends of murderers or neighbors of murderers.
Whatever happened to fact-checking, I wanted to know.

My train of thought was derailed by the door opening. No one was there, but the hall was now plainly in view.

"You behind the door?" I asked.

"Yep," Jason said, "come on in."

I stepped inside and the door swung shut behind me. Jason was standing there in shorts and no shirt, and he was sweating. A lot.

My heart did a double back flip. I swallowed with difficulty. He looked like some guy in an ad for a sports drink. Guys in those ads are never anything less than stunning.

"You're naked," I said before I could stop myself.

He laughed. "You wish. Come on." He gestured for me to follow him and then ran up the stairs without even waiting for my response.

I left my backpacks at the bottom of the stairs and followed the sounds of Jason ahead of me. He'd disappeared into a room in the middle of the hallway.

When I got there, I leaned in the door a little. The room was full of exercise equipment, and he was lying down on a bench with a bar of weights over him. It kind of smelled, like old sweat and metal.

"Your dad home?"

"Nope. He'll be gone all day. Come spot me."

I walked into the room, not exactly sure what he wanted. I stopped at his feet.

He lifted his head, his hands gripping the bar above him. "What are you doing?"

I shrugged. "Spotting you."

"Kiiiind of difficult to do when you're nowhere near the bar."

I pointed at the weights. "You want me over there?"

"You've never spotted before, I take it."

I walked around and stood behind his head. "Do I look like I hang out at the gym?" I paused and then added, "Don't answer that."

He wiggled around, getting comfortable on the bench, and then tightened his grip on the bar. I could tell his attention was no longer on me. He was staring off into space while the sweat on his body was pooling in the curves of his ab muscles and dripping down his sides.

Sweat. Ew. Even on Jason it was gross. Kind of.

All of sudden the bar surged upwards and came off the things holding it on either side of Jason's shoulders. His face was getting redder and redder as he lowered the weights to his chest and then pushed them up again.

I figured he was done with just that one lift, seeing as how much effort he was putting into it, but instead he went for another one. Down the bar went and then up again. His lips were stretched into thin strips and pulled away from his gritted teeth. I never thought before that Jason could be unattractive, but I had been wrong. His expression made me laugh.

"What are you ...," he huffed and puffed as he pushed the bar up. "...laughing at?" He lowered the bar once more.

"You. Your face is seriously ugly right now. I never thought I'd see the day."

Jason was in the middle of pushing the bar up, but then it just stopped. Halfway between his chest and the bar's resting spots, it floated in the air.

Jason's face got redder and redder and redder. Then he started sputtering and spitting a little. His face went kind of purple.

"Spot me ... dammit," he grunted out.

My heart flipped. "Oh, shit. Me? You want me to help you?"

"Grrrrrr!" The muscles in his face, neck, arms, and chest were bulging out all over the place.

"I can't lift that thing!" I yelled. I grabbed the bar anyway and yanked on it.

"Up, not back!" Jason roared.

Using both hands, I lifted with all my might. Together, we slowly got the bar high enough that it could rest on the rack. It seated itself into the supports with a loud *clang*.

I was breathless from four seconds of effort even though he'd pretty much done all the work.

Jason's hands fell away and his arms flopped down to the floor, making them look like they were broken at the shoulders.

"Are you okay?" I asked, staring at him with worry creasing my brow.

His words came out with a lot of breath added to them. "You completely suck as a spotter, in case you didn't already know."

My heart was racing from the earlier panic, but I sounded cool as can be. "Thank you. And you're welcome for saving your life, by the way."

"If you're going to spot for me, you're going to have to build up some of those muscles in your arms." Jason looked up at me and then stared pointedly at my biceps.

I looked down at my right arm along with him. "I've got muscle."

Jason sat up. "The muscle of a spaghetti noodle maybe." He wiped his face off with a small white towel that had been lying on the floor next to the bench.

"I'll have you know that I've won every arm-wrestling competition I've ever entered."

He looked up at me, wiping his arms off. "Oh yeah? How many have you entered? One? When you were five?"

I snorted and looked around the room. "Whatever." It was when I was about seven, but I wasn't going to tell him that.

The room went silent for a few really long seconds before Jason spoke again. "You could work out with me." He paused. "If you want. I'm not saying you need to or anything."

I looked at him quickly, to see if he was mocking me. "You messing with me now? After I saved your bacon?"

He smiled and it made my heart squeeze a little in my chest.

"No. I'm saying that you could hang out here in my personal gym if you want. But only if you want. I know how sensitive girls are about working out and their weight and stuff."

I looked down at myself, wondering what he saw. I knew what I saw when I looked in the mirror — a girl who'd eaten way too many cookies and not enough carrot sticks for the past seventeen years.

"I wouldn't have the first idea how to work out. Plus, I hate sweating."

He laughed. "Sweating is kind of part of it. But you could just do high reps and low weights. It wouldn't be too bad. You'd just get a sheen."

"I don't know what high reps are but low weights sound like my kind of exercise."

He shrugged. "Come tomorrow with shorts on and I can show you some things."

A hint of a thrill ran through me. I hated exercise in all forms, but to be able to use Jason's gym and hang out with him while possibly losing a few pounds ... it could be fun.

"Ready for lunch?" I asked, trying to distract myself from visions of my sweaty workouts with a half-nude Jason. They were getting better and better with every passing second, curse my vivid imagination.

"Lunch?" He stood. "Sure. I guess. You like ham?"

"I have it all figured out. Come downstairs when you're ready." I started to leave the room.

"Ready? Am I supposed to get dressed up?"

"Just de-sweatify yourself and you'll be fine. And put a shirt on." I didn't add the last part that was on the top of my tongue: *So I can eat in peace and not be drooling over your muscles*. That would have made lunch awkward.

While Jason cleaned up, I opened up the contents of my backpacks and laid them out on his living room floor. I was glad his dad was gone for the day. I had no problem feeling kind of goofy around Jason so long as we were alone; it was the idea of having witnesses watch me being a dork that made me want to run back to my house and never return.

"What's this?" Jason asked, walking into the room as he toweled off his wet hair. The smell of his soap wafted into the room and made me smile. It was so uniquely Jason, and I was kind of touched that he'd bothered to take a shower. That had to mean something, at least that we were actual friends, right? That's what I told myself, anyway.

"A picnic." I couldn't look at him, afraid he'd make a face that said I was a complete loser. "It's so nice outside, I thought a picnic would be fun, but I knew that you probably wouldn't want to actually *go* outside and be mauled by those dogs out there, so I brought the sunshine in."

Verbal diarrhea. It always happened when I was worried I'd gone too far.

Jason walked over without saying anything, slowly lowering himself to the ground and criss-crossing his legs in front of him. He tossed his towel over the arm of a nearby chair.

"What's this?" he asked in a softer voice, picking up a framed picture that was lying next to the contents of the picnic blanket I had spread on the carpet.

"That's the sun."

I finally looked up at him. He was staring at the framed photo.

"Is this from today?"

"Yeah. I shot it with my camera and put it in a frame I already had." At the time I'd come up with the idea and went out into my backyard to grab the picture, I felt really inspired; now I just felt like a complete paste-eater. Who takes a picture of the sun and puts it in a frame?

"We can throw it out after," I said, my face heating up.

"Nah, I like it." He put the frame down on the ground next to the blanket, setting the back support up so picture stayed upright.

I started pulling the lids off the various containers I'd brought, trying not to let my heart read too much into his charitable response.

"Soooo, we have potato salad and egg salad ... I wasn't sure which one you'd like. Or you could eat them both, whatever. And I got some fried chicken. It's still pretty warm. And there's some pickles and chips. I know you like chips because I saw you inhaling them yesterday..."

Jason's hand on my arm stopped me from passing out from lack of oxygen.

"Thanks," he said.

I looked up, our eyes meeting.

"I mean it," he said. "You really thought of everything."

"You haven't seen what I brought for dessert yet." The words came out all soft. I hadn't meant for them to, but his eyes were kind of watery, and my heart was breaking over the idea that he might cry over my totally gay picnic.

His eyebrow went up. "Are you suggesting what I think you're suggesting?"

I shrugged his hand off me and slapped him on the leg. "Shut up. It's Rice Crispie treats, idiot." My face was so hot, it probably looked like Jason's had when he was lifting those weights. I couldn't look at him. I held up the open plastic tub for him to see. Then I pulled it away. "But you aren't getting any."

"Whaaaat? Come on, don't be cruel. Rice Crispie treats are my favorite dessert of all time."

I looked at him through narrowed eyes. "Seriously?"

He made a cross on his heart. "Swear to God."

"They're my favorite too."

He smiled. "I thought all girls' favorite desserts had chocolate in them."

I rolled my eyes, shaking my head at his ignorance. "I'm not all girls."

"Ain't that the truth," he said, pulling a drumstick out of the mass of tinfoil I'd wrapped the meat in.

"What's that supposed to mean?" I took a drumstick too and bit right into it.

After he put the entire end of the drumstick in his mouth and pulled all the meat, gristle and everything else off in one bite, he gestured at me with the bare bone. "Right there," he said with his mouth full. "Chicks don't usually just grab a leg of chicken and bite right into it."

I pulled the meat away from my face and looked at it. "What was I supposed to do with it? Use it as a wand?" I started waving it all over the place.

He laughed. "No. That's what Harry Potter dorks would do."

I immediately stopped. "Hey, I liked that series."

He shook his head, still laughing. "No, I'm just saying ... you're cool. Not like other girls."

I sighed, letting the drumstick drop to the paper plate in front of my crossed legs. Talk about the kiss of death. I'd now been deemed *cool*. Cool girls never get to see the hot guy naked. It was one of those universal truths. I shouldn't have been so bummed about it, but I clearly wasn't capable of controlling my emotions or reactions to things Jason said.

"You're lucky you're so damn good-looking," I mumbled.

"Why do you say that?" He finally stopped laughing.

"Because without those looks, you'd never get a girlfriend." He really wasn't smooth at all. A smooth guy would have shined me on and gotten more Rice Crispie treats out of me before revealing I'm a cool-girl.

His mouth dropped open, revealing the rest of his chewed up food.

"You are like ... not smooth at all." I took a spoonful of potato salad and plopped a small serving on my plate. At home, I would have eaten three times that much, but around Jason I was going to pretend I didn't eat like a horse.

"I'm smooth."

He sounded offended. I couldn't tell if the emotion was fake or not.

"No, you're not. You've insulted me like eight times already today and I haven't even been here a half-hour yet."

"I did?" He looked genuinely confused. "When? How?"

I waved my fork in the air. "Never mind. I'm over it already. Are you going to eat any of these salads? You'd better. I slaved over a cold grocery cart for, like, ten minutes."

He leaned over really far to grab the salads and put half the container of each on his plate. "Happy?" he asked.

"Very." I smiled, chewing up my chicken and potato salad mix.

We ate in companionable silence for a few minutes and I mostly forgot about the cool-girl comment. When Jason's plate was clean, he wiped his mouth off with the paper towel I gave him and then started leaning towards me.

I leaned away, keeping him from getting too close.

"What are you doing?" I asked, suspicion lacing my voice.

His grin looked devilish. "Just trying to get a Rice Crispie treat. You worried I'm making a move on ya?"

I frowned, pretending to be way cooler than I was. "Yeah, right. As if." I sat up straight again. "I told you. No Rice Crispie treats for you."

He play-frowned. "Pleeeease?"

"No." I lifted my chin.

He pointed to his face. "Look at this."

I looked at him, ignoring the way that face made me want to give him anything he asked for. "So?"

His expression dropped back to normal. "That didn't work on you?"

"Was it supposed to?"

He shook his head. "You're a strong woman. I've never known anyone who can resist the puppy dog eyes. It's patented, you know."

I lifted up the container that had the dessert in it. "It's going to take a lot more than patented puppy-dog eyes to get me to give you one of these babies." I took one out of the box and bit into it, rolling my eyes with the pleasure. "Mmmm, marshmallows and butter, get in my belly."

The next thing I knew I was on my back and the box of Rice Crispie treats were flying out of my hand. Blobs of sticky cereal fell all over the carpet behind me and in my hair.

"Tackle!" Jason yelled, half his body spread out over my torso.

"What the ...! Get off me, you giant ogre ... idiot ... *buttcheese!*" Obviously I panicked; I'm never eloquent when in a blind panic. I struggled to get out from underneath him, but it was about as easy as escaping an elephant who's decided to take a nap on you.

"Say uncle." Jason's face was inches from mine. I could smell the chicken on his breath.

"You have parsley in your teeth," I said, trying not to laugh.

He grinned really hard and leaned in closer. "Get it for me."

I twisted my head left and then right, trying to get away from him. "No! Get off!" Too close. His mouth was too close. I could have kissed him if I'd just lifted my head a half-inch.

He went still and then all I could feel was his breath on me. I opened my eyes and he was staring down at me. The mood went electric in half a second and then I *really* panicked. Fear took over.

"Get off, I'm serious."

"What if I don't want to?"

My body bucked up, trying to dislodge him. "Get off!" My voice had gone suddenly into a higher register.

Jason rolled off to the left, freeing me. "Okay, okay, no need to panic."

I sat up and tried to pretend I wasn't shaking all over. To keep my hands busy, I balled up all the tinfoil and put lids on plastic containers.

"I wasn't going to hurt you, you know."

My hands stilled. The pain and regret in his voice was impossible to miss.

When I looked up at him, I hated myself. He was devastated.

I reached out and touched his arm. "I know that. I know you'd never hurt me. That's not what ... that's not what freaked me out." My ears started burning as soon as the words were out.

"What was it? Are you claustrophobic?"

I gave him one of my awkward crooked grins. "Something like that." More like I'm afraid of being confined in small spaces with Jason's lips, but I'd never tell him that.

"Have you had this problem for a while?"

I shrugged. "No, not really." Like about a couple days, I'd say.

It was in that moment I finally admitted to myself that my feelings toward Jason weren't entire platonic. It didn't mean I was going to act on those not-so-friend-like feelings or anything, but there was no denying they were there.

Ugh. My parents would kill me if they ever found out. Bobby would kill me. *I* would kill me. And those reporters ... man ... they would roast me alive.

"Can you get help for it? Like therapy or whatever?"

"No, there's no help for me. Maybe time will fix it." Or not. Maybe time will make it worse.

This situation was hopeless, but I still felt like hanging on. I guess it was no mystery now why I felt that way. I liked Jason. He was my friend and would only ever be my friend, but it was useless denying the cold, hard facts; he lit a spark inside me that refused to be put out with common sense.

I was just going to have to smother that thing or at least ignore it. This wasn't like a regular I-like-a-guy situation where I could pretend it could work, even though we came from different worlds. I had a crush on a murderer who was probably going to be in jail for the better part of his life. Two strikes. Murderer ... unavailable. Man, I sure could pick 'em.

"Thanks for the picnic," he said. It sounded like an apology.

"You're welcome." I smiled big, to show him there were no hard feelings. "I have to take off." I started stuffing things into my backpack as fast as I could.

"Want to work-out tomorrow?" he asked, helping me put things into my bags.

"Sure," I said without thinking. "What time?"

"Before lunch? We could do another picnic if you want. Or not."

I stood and put one of the backpacks over my shoulder, handing him a Rice Crispie treat.

He took it from me as he held the other backpack out in front of him. "Thanks. I wish I could walk you home with this stuff. I'd carry it for you."

I took it from him. "Someday, you will." I prayed that it wouldn't be when he was forty-five years old.

"SO, WHAT WAS IT LIKE?" Bobby asked. He'd called me on the phone when I refused to text him all the details of my day with Jason.

"It was ... good."

"Hello, pregnant pause. Tell me what was so *not* good about it."

I sighed heavily. "It's seriously annoying when you read into my comments like that."

"Am I wrong? Something happened that made you mad or whatever, don't try to deny it."

I debated internally whether to say anything to him about it, but then decided I might as well, mostly because I hated being left alone with my own thoughts and no good input to help dissect them with.

"Fine. It was fine. But it was also not fine."

"Okay, that makes complete sense."

"He was just ... he's so not aware of how much his looks play into the equation."

"What equation?"

"I don't know ..." I was getting annoyed with myself, not quite knowing where my brain was going with all of this stuff. "...It's like he's gotten everything in life just because he's so good looking."

"So? That's the way the world works."

"Yeah, but he's completely oblivious to it and I find that extremely annoying."

"So? Let him live in his dream-world. How does that affect you?"

"It doesn't." I was pouting now. It shouldn't affect me. The fact that I wanted it to be my business was just sad.

"Ohhhh ... I seeeee." Bobby was using his omniscient tone with me.

"You see nothing. Go away."

"No, I get it. You like him, but you also don't like him because he's so shallow."

"I didn't say that."

"Then what are you saying?"

"I have no idea!" I yelled.

"Okaaaay, so ... shall I assume it's that time of the month now or ...?"

"No, you should assume that I'm just frustrated and confused and worried and that I'm therefore acting like any person would in that situation, thank-you-very-much."

There was a three-second pause and then Bobby started on another tack.

"You like him."

"Maybe." I knew I had to be honest to get to the bottom of my issues, whatever they were, so even though I was feeling seriously uncomfortable over my admission, I went ahead with it anyway.

"And does he like you?"

"Sure, as a dorky neighbor friend."

"Are you sure about that?"

"Don't sound so hopeful. It doesn't matter that he murdered the coach; we're still from different social worlds."

"Have we not watched *Pretty In Pink*, like, eighty-five times together? Social crossover can work."

"No, it can't work. We love that movie so much because it's *completely* unreal. You know the original version had Andie with Ducky, right? They re-shot the ending after the test-audience got pissed."

"I know. Pissed at reality. How lame is that?"

"Anyway, it doesn't matter how I feel or how he feels. He's about to go on trial for murder, and he'll lose if he keeps telling everyone he did it, and then he'll be in jail forever or until I'm seriously old and wrinkled. And that's a best-case scenario." I didn't even bother bringing up the death penalty. Or the fact that he really did murder a human being and I should be totally repulsed by that and not attracted to him.

"I'm not even going to mention that little annoying fact that he actually murdered a full-grown man." Bobby's ability to read my mind was seriously annoying on my best days. Today I wanted to give him the biggest wedgie of all time.

"Bobby ..." I was mad and sad at the same time and having a hard time putting it all into words. "...I know that, okay? I know he could be dangerous given the right ... or the wrong ... circumstance. But I also really truly believe deep down inside me that he's only capable of doing something like that under very certain situations. Like, drastic ones."

"Okay, so what were the drastic situations that made him kill Coach Fielding, then?"

I chewed my lip as I considered his question. "I wish I knew. I'd give my left nut to know."

"Which means absolutely nothing since you have no nuts."

"Okay fine. I'd give *your* left nut to know."

"I don't remember giving you the power to gift my nuts."

"Whatever. I know there was a reason and it wasn't because he got benched."

"Did he tell you that?"

"No. He hasn't told me anything."

Again, a long pause came over the line, but I didn't know what else to say. It felt like Bobby and I were pulling apart a little, but to try and bring him back close to me by talking about something stupid like school drama would have been dumb. We both would have seen right through it; none of that mattered to me anymore.

"Are you going to go over there again?" Bobby's voice was soft, like he'd read my mind again.

"Yes. We're going to start working out together."

"Oh." Bobby's voice perked up. "Well, that's exciting."

"Is it? Why?"

"No reason. Just ... you've always talked about getting fit and stuff and now you can."

"You want to come?"

"Are you kidding? Me? Sweat? No thank you. But I'd be happy to come watch Jason sweat, though. I'd bring popcorn for that."

"No pervy-watching. If you come, you have to lift weights just like us."

"Ahhhh, no thanks. Maybe in another century. Talk to you tomorrow?"

"Of course." And I meant it. Bobby was my anchor to reality.

"Tomorrow, take a selfie of you guys together and send it to me. Make sure to get his abs in the shot."

"Bye, Bobby."

"Bye, Katy. Sweet dreams."

SHOWED UP WITH JUST two sandwiches this time, wearing my yoga pants that had never been on me for anything but sleeping in. I left my running shoes at home, worried that I'd look too excited about working out when I was still pretty reticent about the whole sweating thing. There are many reasons why Bobby and I are best friends, our hatred of perspiration being one of them.

The door opened within seconds of me knocking on it, and Jason was standing there in full view of the cameras.

I stepped inside and pushed him back, shutting the door behind me. "What are you doing? Are you crazy?"

"What?" Jason looked down at me, confusion reigning.

My hands flew to my hips, and I knew I was probably doing a pretty good imitation of my mother, but I didn't let that stop me. "You want them to take more pictures?"

He shrugged. "What difference does it make?"

I sighed, letting my bag slide down my shoulders and dropping it on the floor by the stairs. "It just gives them more ammo to make up stories about you."

"What could they possibly say about me standing in my own doorway?"

I gestured to his workout shirt. "I don't know ... that you're getting bigger in preparation for your life in prison ... that you're hanging out having a good old time not feeling sorry about what you did..."

Jason took a step back away from me, and that shut me up instantly.

"Sorry," he said, his voice cold, "I didn't realize you were so angry about everything."

I shook my head and closed my eyes for a second. "That's not it." I looked up at him and tried to appear contrite. "You're allowed to have a life, okay? Innocent until proven guilty. But that's not how they see it, especially since you confessed."

Jason glared at me for a couple seconds, but then his shoulders slumped and his voice came out sounding tired. "I know. Come on." He turned and mounted the stairs, only this time he took them one at a time and very slowly. It was completely un-Jason-like.

I'd totally ruined the mood and we hadn't even started sweating yet. "I'm sorry. I'm a dick." I followed him up the stairs.

"No, you're not a dick." He went down the hall towards his workout room. "You're just being honest. I appreciate it. Everyone else around here is blowing so much sunshine up my ass I'm surprised I'm not glowing."

"You should get everyone to commit to the no-sunshine-up-the-ass pledge."

"I wish I could, but my father is barely hanging on. He needs to pretend everything's going to be okay, so I just let him talk. I let the lawyers talk. Everyone's talking a bunch of shit all the time and I just nod my head."

I couldn't think of anything to say to that. I could only imagine what my parents would go through if I were arrested for murder. It would destroy our entire family.

As I passed by Jason's room, the top of his dresser caught my eye. There on the top of it was the picture of the sun I'd taken the day before. I hadn't even realized that he'd kept it, but the fact that he'd put it in such a prominent place in his bedroom made me feel twice as bad for him as I already did. I vowed then to pump iron like nobody's business. I was going to sweat like a pig on steroids and not complain one bit.

That vow lasted all of five minutes.

"Jesus Christ, what'd you put on there, a thousand pounds?" I was straining against the bar hovering above my face.

"There are no weights on there. Zero. It's just the bar, Hercules. Forty-five pounds. Too much for ya?" He smirked. Or maybe he just smiled. I was feeling pretty negative on life right about then, so it was hard for me to judge.

"Errrgh..." I strained with all my might and barely got the bar off the supports.

"Errrgh. That's it. Let it out." Jason put his hand under the bar and helped me out, taking some of the pressure off. "Lower it down gently. Feel the burn in your arms and chest."

"Feel the burn," I grunted out. "Fuck the burn." My arms were shaking like crazy as I slowly lowered the bar to my chest. I didn't do it slowly because he told me to, but because I didn't want to crush my boobs and break all my ribs. That bar was freaking heavy.

Jason kept one of his hands in between mine the entire time I did that one repetition of what I later learned was called a bench press. Thank God he did, too, or I would have been stuck with that thing pinning me down until they found my dead body stinking up the place days later.

"You're not going for two?" he asked as I clanged the bar back into place and sat up.

"I kind of like my ribs the way they are, actually. Each of them in one piece." I was out of breath, believe it or not. I didn't even know it was possible to get out of breath lifting a weight one time, but I'm here to tell you it's true. A person *can* be that magnificently out of shape.

He laughed.

I slouched over, cringing as beads of sweat trickled down my back under my shirt. I was going to look like the very worst version of myself in about five minutes once all of the liquid from my body was on the exterior and plastering my shirt to my not-cut, stay pufft marshmallow body.

"Let's see where you are with your legs."

"How about we have a popsicle and skip the rest of my body instead?" I stood up and faced him as he moved over to a machine with a seat and some black weight-bars in a contraption behind it.

He busied himself with moving a thick metal pin out of the bottom of the rack and putting it on the ground. "Sorry. No pain, no gain."

"How about no pain, no *pain*, eh? That sounds like a great philosophy to me." I put on my extra-huge smile to try and convince him that I was making complete sense, which I was.

"More like no gain, no gain." He waved me over. "Come on. Have a seat. This one will be easy. I have a feeling you have strong legs."

I looked down at what I new to be bright white, somewhat sausagey, cottage-cheesey-looking legs hiding beneath my yoga pants and frowned. "And what, pray tell, is leading you to that conclusion?"

"Just get over here and sit down, would ya? Jesus, this is like working out with an eighty-year-old lady."

"Hey! I take exception to that." I walked over and sat down, hating the fact that he was probably right. I felt like an old lady. More like ninety years old, though. An eighty year old could have kicked my ass with one wrinkled hand tied behind her Quasimodo-hunched back.

Why did I hate this exercise thing so much? I wasn't really sure. My muscles probably appreciated it, if all the articles I'd read on Yahoo were true. I suppose the issue was that I was a firm believer in losing weight by reading about weight loss, and not actually doing any physical activity to get there. Plus, there was that whole sweating thing. *Ew.*

"Okay, so hook your feet under that cushioned bar down there and lift the bar up using your thigh muscles. Hang onto these handles if you need to so you don't pop off the seat."

He took my left hand and guided it down past my thigh to a spot below the seat where there was indeed a handle. My heart did a little shuck and jive at his touch, which pissed me off at myself. It fueled my inner beast and had that bar flying up.

"Whoa, easy now. I don't want you pulling something."

I dropped my legs and the bar and weights attached to it banged down loudly.

"Lower them *sloooowly*. You get more than half the workout on the lowering not the lifting."

"Why?"

"Gravity, maybe. I don't know. Try this."

He'd added weights that made it hard for my legs to lift the bar at all. "Too much," I grunted out.

"No, it's just right. Do as many as you can." He rested his hand on my shoulder as he leaned in. "Come on, you can do it."

Maybe it was him touching me or the fact that he seemed so excited about me just being there and trying, but whatever the cause, I felt suddenly inspired. I finished eight lifts before my legs refused to budge again.

"That was awesome, Katy! You did it!" He held up his hand for a high-five and I was barely able to participate. Not because I didn't want to, but because all that gripping-of-the-handles under my fat butt had been a workout in and of itself. My arm muscles were trembling right along with my legs.

"Time for a popsicle?" I asked, hope flavoring my tone.

"Nope. Time for bicep curls. Popsicles are for losers. Curls are for winners. Be a winner, Katy, not a loser."

I looked up at him ready to give him shit for being such a goofy pep-talker, but the expression on his face stopped me.

"Did I do something wrong?" I asked.

He turned away, his voice suddenly rough. "No. Nothing at all. Just ... let's go have a popsicle."

He started to leave the room.

I tried to leap up after him but my legs were not cooperating. I got two steps before they reminded me that they'd recently turned into rubber bands. "Wait!"

He was almost to the hallway.

"Wait, Jason! My legs won't work." I hobbled over to him as he paused.

Whatever was going on in his head, I wanted it to stop. He'd gone from totally excited about my leg lifts to depressed in, like, two seconds. Whatever was happening wasn't good.

"I need to do those curls. Like you said, my arms are like noodles." He didn't turn around so I went for my last ditch effort. "Look!"

Giving him a double bicep pose, I waited for him to turn around, which he finally did.

A ghost of a smile appeared on his face. "That's seriously pitiful, you know that right?"

"Yes!" I pointed at him in my excitement.

Tragedy averted!

"See? Show me how to curl. I'm ready to do like fifty reps. Right now." I did some miming of the exercise like I expected he'd tell me to do it. I was looking pretty good, if I do say so myself. It was an excellent distraction.

He came back into the room and slowly walked over to a rack of weights on tiny bars. "See if you can lift this."

I joined him and took the seemingly tiny thing from him. It fell to my thigh as it pulled my arm down.

"Too much?" he asked. He was just a foot away, and I could swear from his tone and expression that he was asking me about something other than the weight in my hand.

Too much? Was all of this too much for me?

"Nope. I can handle it," I said, also not talking about the weights.

"I don't think so." He took it away from me and gave me something much lighter.

I started pumping it up and down. "I can, you know. Handle whatever you give me. I have spirit like that. You can ask Bobby."

Jason gave me a courtesy laugh. "I don't need to ask him. I can see it for myself."

"Check this out," I said, exaggerating the strength it took to lift the weights. "Errrghh! *Booyah.* Feel that burn, baby."

He put his hand on it to stop me. "You're doing it wrong. Go nice and easy, don't totally flex your arm at the top and go slower on the way down."

"Like this?" I looked up at him for approval.

He was staring at my arm. "Yeah, like that."

I pumped a few more reps, trying to figure out how to bring up that awkward moment that had just happened a couple minutes earlier. I'm a bulldog like that sometimes, with serious lockjaw, not able to let certain things go; and anything that was going to get me closer to Jason's true story was definitely something I was hanging onto.

"Sooo ...," I said, trying to sound all casual, "...winners and losers. Be a winner not a loser."

He froze in the middle of picking up another, bigger weight. "What'd you say?"

I shrugged as best I could with my arm about to fall off. "I said ... be a winner ... why does that piss you off so much?"

"It doesn't piss me off. It's just an expression." He picked up a huge set of weights and started doing curls with me. It was kind of ridiculous how much bigger his barbell was than mine, but that wasn't what really caught my eye. It was the sight of his bicep bulging out and sliding up and down his arm, practically growing before my eyes that had me instantly distracted. I had to look at the wall to stop the drool from appearing and embarrassing me.

"I've never heard it before. Is it from Coach Fielding?"

Jason sighed heavily before answering me. "Yeah. He was full of that stuff."

"Stuff?"

"Shit. He was full of shit." Jason's lifts got more frantic, faster.

"Hey," I paused on my eighth rep and pointed at Jason's arm, "you need to lower it *sloooowly*. You're going too fast."

Jason's face was getting redder, and the sweat was starting to bead up on his forehead. He didn't respond and he didn't slow down.

I put my weights back on the rack and placed my hand on his arm. "Stop for a second."

Jason practically threw his barbell on the ground, making my ears ring with the loud clang of it.

"Fuck!" He stood there staring at the wall and gritting his teeth, making his jaw pump out over and over. When it finally stopped, his Adam's apple began going up and down, like he was trying not to cry.

"It's okay to be upset, you know." I didn't know what else to say. It probably wasn't the best thing either, since he didn't reply. My verbal diarrhea problem got away from me again, and I couldn't stop.

"What happened was bad, and he's gone, and a lot of people are very sad or mad about it. But you are a good person and you have a life to live and now you just have to find a way to move on from it. To face what's coming and keep your head up. You made a mistake. A *mistake*. It was a huge, awful one, but it wasn't on purpose. It was a *mistake*."

Maybe I thought if I said it enough times, it would finally mean something, but we both new differently. Some mistakes were too big to ever go away, to ever be forgiven.

His head whipped sideways so he could glare at me. "I'm not a good person. I'm a fraud. A fucking *fake*. You shouldn't even be here." He started to back away, but I stopped him in his tracks by grabbing his hand. I didn't even have time to think about what I was doing and then it was done.

We both stared at our joined hands as I spoke. "Listen, Jason, I'm here and I'm not going anywhere. Unless you don't want me around and then all you have to do is say it and I'll be gone. But don't shove me away because you think that's what's good for me or out of some misplaced sense of honor or whatever. I'm your friend and I'm sticking by you, no matter what."

The silence was deafening. I never knew what that meant until it happened to us, standing there in his workout room like that. His not talking was like a weight pressing down on us. I felt like I was waiting for a jury verdict in the most important trial of my life, and I wasn't even the one who'd killed someone.

"This is going to ruin both our lives," he finally said, his voice a shadow of its normal self.

I squeezed his hand. "This is going to *change* our lives, but it's not going to ruin them. I won't let it, and neither will you."

He and I looked up at the same time, our eyes meeting.

"Why are you my friend?" he asked, his eyes shining with unshed tears. "I don't deserve to have friends, so why you? Why now?"

I sighed heavily and tried to come up with an eloquent answer. When one didn't appear in my brain I just said what I was thinking. "Because it's easy to be friends with people who don't need them, and I was never very good at doing things the easy way. Besides, it's not right that everyone turned their backs on you without knowing the whole story. You're a good person, Jason."

"What if there is no story?" Jason asked, sounding very vulnerable. "What if you've already heard all of it? What then?"

"Are you asking me if I'll stop being your friend?"

He nodded.

I shrugged, acting like he wasn't asking me something stupendously, horrifically, amazingly huge. "Like I said ... I'm not going anywhere. Friends for life." In my head I heard the closing of a jail door and the turning of a very large lock, like I'd just sealed both our fates inside a very scary prison. It was seriously creepy and deep all at the same time.

He swallowed several times in quick succession. I could hear the noise of his throat working and see it too, so close to me. The warmth in the room increased substantially.

"I don't think I deserve to have you here. In my life, I mean."

I let his hand go and crossed my arms over my chest. "Well, I do, so deal with it."

His face morphed from one expression to another in rapid succession. First he seemed sad, then confused, than surprised and finally, maybe, happy.

"You're stubborn," he finally said. "I didn't know that about you before."

"There's a lot you didn't know about me before. Like for example how much I hate sweating."

"I know that now."

I smiled. "Yes. Now you know." Why that made me feel awesome, I don't know.

He readjusted his feet to face me more fully. "And I also know you're forgiving, funny, dedicated, creative, sneaky, and pretty." He reached up and pushed an errant piece of hair out of my face over towards my ear.

My ears, by the way, started burning like they were on fire. Never before had any guy other than Bobby come right out and said I was pretty, and never in a million years would I have expected it to come out of Jason's mouth.

"I'm not pretty. Shut up." I suddenly couldn't take my eyes off the carpet. It was very important and interesting carpet that needed all of my attention.

Jason took a step towards me and put both of his hands on my upper arms. "Yes, you are. You're really pretty. I don't know why I didn't notice that about you before."

I looked up at him and crossed my eyes. "Seriously, Jason? Did you just say that?" I shook my head. "So not smooth."

He smiled his most charming smile. "Sorry. What I *meant* to say was that I always thought you were cute there in your garden with those big gardening gloves on and that floppy hat, but I never realized just how cute you were until I saw you pumping iron here in my room."

The space between us became positively electric. I'm not big on physics or chemistry, but something was for sure happening to electrons and protons and neurons or whatever. I was about to have a heart attack with how close he was and that look he was getting in his eye.

"What are you doing?" I asked in a near-whisper.

"I'm thinking about kissing you," he said, equally quietly. It was like we were afraid we'd be caught or that speaking in normal tones would wake us up to the reality that this was just not supposed to be happening.

"I'm not sure that's a good idea," I said, my brain on auto-pilot.

"Me neither," he said, just before lowering his head down to mine and pressing his lips against my mouth.

MY LIPS STARTED TO TREMBLE the very second they sensed his mouth there. His touch was feather-light, but that didn't matter. It was like the weight of the entire world accompanied that kiss.

I backed away.

"Too much?" he asked, looking chagrined.

I nodded, refusing to allow my fingers to come up and touch my lips. I wanted to do that so badly, to make the tingling go away, or maybe to hold in the feeling and enjoy it for another second.

"I just think ... it's not a good idea right now," I said.

Lie! It felt like a lie, but I had to say it. Things were just too complicated for me. I needed time to figure things out. I didn't want to believe I was here just for that kiss. I wanted to be a good friend, a real friend, not a stupid girl sucked in by his pretty face or his dark situation.

He took a step back. "I get it. Really, I do." He bent over and picked up a small towel that was on the floor.

I felt terrible. He was acting like I'd rejected him for being a murderer and that wasn't really what had happened, even if it probably should have.

"Jason, I don't want you to get the wrong idea."

"Hey, it's cool." He tried to laugh but it sounded strained. "Trust me, I wouldn't want to get involved with me either if I were in your shoes. It's fine."

He started to leave the room, so I took a few big steps on shaky legs and grabbed him by the arm. "That's not it."

He stopped and turned towards me. "Okay, so what is it?" He was understandably frustrated; I wasn't sending the clearest signals. "You just want to be friends? I promise, it's fine. Pretend I didn't ... do anything."

"No, it's not that. Okay, it *is* that, but not in the way you're thinking." My head was spinning with all the disjointed thoughts and disconnected feelings. Nothing made sense.

He lifted an eyebrow and waited. It was impossible to tell whether he was mad, sad, or a combination of the two. One thing he wasn't, was happy.

I crossed my arms over my chest to hide the fact that my shirt was plastered to me in a very unflattering way and my hands were still shaking. "I ... I want to explain myself to you."

"Go for it." He wiped the sweat from his neck and glanced down at me as he did it.

I chewed my lip as I tried to figure out where to start, what to reveal, and what to keep hidden. I wasn't the best at sharing my feelings, especially with a guy like Jason. The only male person in the world who'd heard what went on in my head was Bobby and he was different. Way different. He didn't judge and I'd never wanted to kiss him on the mouth.

"You and I are like that Hootie song."

Jason frowned, obviously confused. "What?"

"That Hootie song. Two different worlds."

"How so? We live on the same street and go to the same school. We've practically grown up together."

Thank goodness he knew what I meant with that feeble explanation, because my brain obviously wasn't working on all cylinders today. That kiss seriously messed me up.

"No. We've grown up *around* each other. Bobby and I have grown up together. It's not the same thing."

"I don't see why that makes any difference." Jason dropped down onto a bench and looked up at me, waiting for me to start making sense.

"You know we move in different circles at school."

"So? Doesn't everyone, pretty much? So we have different friends, what difference does that make?"

I shook my head, frustrated with his ignorance. "I hate to be the one to break the news to you, Jason, but our friends, our circles, *do not mix*, okay? Someone from your circle does not mix with someone from my circle. It just doesn't happen. *Pretty In Pink* proves it."

He frowned, getting pissed maybe. "Circles? Pretty In Pink? What are you talking about? We're just people going to school."

"No, we're *not!* We're kids trying to figure out where we belong in a world that judges us by our looks, our bodies, our clothes, the cars we drive, the type of cell phones we have and purses we carry ... circles, Jason. *Circles*." I glared at him.

He lifted a brow, definitely mocking me. "Are you saying I'm one of the cool kids and you're not?"

I grabbed the nearest thing that wasn't a weight and threw it at him. "Jerk." The sweat-warped leather glove with the fingers cut off hit him right in the face.

I tried to storm by him and leave the room, but he grabbed me by the hand and held me back.

"Wait."

"Let go."

"No, don't go. Stay with me. Just for a minute. I want to apologize."

"Don't bother. It doesn't matter anyway." I refused to look at him. Not because he did anything wrong, but because I felt stupid. I'd gotten caught up in a teen movie drama that was playing in my head and forgotten that we were real people living a completely different life than Sam and Ducky had in that iconic but hopelessly unrealistic movie.

"I was just messing around, okay? I know what you're saying. Maybe last week I wouldn't have known, but I know now."

I had to look up at that. "What do you mean?"

He sighed out heavily and tugged on my hand. "Come sit by me."

Reluctantly, I took the spot on the bench that was far enough away that we weren't touching but not so far that it would look like I was avoiding him.

"Like you said ... there's a lot of pressure on us to be a certain person. At school, I mean."

"Yes." I nodded.

"And sometimes you feel that pressure, I guess, but for me, I mostly just moved through it without thinking too much about it."

"No wonder."

He looked at me sideways. "What's that supposed to mean?"

"Never mind." My mouth had gotten away from me again.

He twisted on the bench to face me. "No, really, I want to know."

"I really need to get going."

"Aren't you staying for lunch?"

I shrugged, feeling stupid. "I don't know." I wanted to stay but knew I should go. I'd never been so confused in my own head before. It was unnerving, like I wasn't in control of myself anymore.

"Stay for lunch ... but first tell me what you meant when you said 'no wonder'."

I looked up at him. "Promise you won't get offended?"

"No."

"Then I'm not telling you."

"Okay, fine, I won't get offended."

Looking into his eyes and staring at his face actually made it easier to tell him the truth. Seeing his impossibly handsome face reminded me of being invisible to him in the hallways.

"You're too good-looking and athletically talented to even notice the pressure. You could come to school with an orange clown wig on your head and everyone would think you were being cute. If I did that, everyone would talk about what a freaking idiot I am. People like you and Britt and Tiff and all your friends get a free pass. People like me get beat down. That's the way it works, but you wouldn't know that because you get to wear the orange wig whenever you want."

He shook his head at me slowly and it made me feel about two inches high.

"You really are pretty clueless, aren't you?" he said.

That made me back my head up a little. "Excuse me?"

He kind of laughed, but it was more the bitter variety. "No one has it that easy. It's just an illusion."

"I doubt it." I actually did kind of doubt it hearing him say that, but because I was interested in hearing his take on it, I challenged him. "Your life is nothing like mine."

"Haven't you ever heard that expression that things are tough all over?"

"No."

"Well, it's true. Being me ... it's not easy."

I couldn't help but laugh at that. "Yeah. Soooo tough. Being hot and smart and covered in muscles and the star of the football team every girl wants to sleep with. Must be reeealll tough."

His eyes went dark. "Have you ever thought about what it might be like to not know if anyone actually liked you? Like, ever in your life?"

That stopped my laughter short. "What?"

"You heard me. Let me ask you this ... does Bobby really like being your friend? Does he like you as a person, I mean?"

"Of course he does." I kind of laughed, kind of semi-snorted, thinking what a ridiculous question that was. "Why else would he text me a thousand times a day and be at my house every day for the last ten years?"

"Exactly."

Jason didn't say anything else so we just sat there looking at each other.

He lifted an eyebrow.

"What? Am I supposed to say something right now?" I asked.

"You don't get it, do you?"

"Get what?!" I threw my arms up.

"You know! You know that Bobby *really* likes you."

I narrowed my eyes at him. "I'm prrreeettty sure we already established that."

"See, I don't have that." He leaned in and pointed at my chest. "I don't have that. Never have."

I looked down at where he was pointing. "Sweaty cleavage?"

He gently tapped my chin on the side, pushing my face away. "Shut up, you know what I'm talking about."

I laughed. "No, I seriously don't. 'Splain yourself."

He paused and just stared at me. Slowly a smile spread over his face.

"Now what?" I asked. "You're making me nervous. You're not going to kiss me again, are you?"

He burst out laughing, leaning way back on the bench almost to the point I thought he was going to fall.

"You're going insane staying in this house all day," I said, playing off my latest gaff. "We have to get you out of here."

He straightened up at that and lost his smile. But he didn't look mad. "You're fucking awesome," he said.

I couldn't help but grin at that. "I am? How come?"

"Because. You like me."

I rolled my eyes. "Full of yourself maybe? Just a tad?"

"No, I mean you *really* like me." He swung his arm up and rested it across my shoulders. It was heavy, but I liked the feel of it anyway. Bobby's arm always felt like a skinny tree branch as opposed to this giant log.

"Yeah, I like you," I said, trying to ease myself past the awkward warmth flowing through my chest area. "I even brought you a sandwich. Want it?" I tried to stand, but his heavy arm held me on the bench.

"In a minute. I want to tell you what I was trying to tell you a second ago."

"Better hurry. My stomach's about to start eating itself."

He pulled his arm off me and started fiddling with his fingers in his lap. "When you're what people consider good-looking, all kinds of people want to be your friend."

"A very sad story," I said with my subdued, very understanding voice.

He talked a little louder, I think to drown my smart-ass out. "And when that happens all the time, you wonder if any of those people actually *like* you, like you, or just like being around you for what it will get them."

I nodded, trying to understand what that would be like. Since I'd never experienced anything like that before, it was tough to imagine it with respect to myself, but I could definitely see it with Jason.

"I know," I agreed. "That's what I was kind of trying to tell you earlier." I looked up at him. "I think your perspective on life is seriously skewed. How could it not be? I mean, probably very few people in your life have ever really been genuine with you."

"You might be right." He sighed. "I wish I had done things differently."

I stared at his strong jaw and lips, the ones that had kissed me just a little while ago that I sadly wished would come after me again. His problem was his face being so arrestingly handsome. There was way too much hotness going on there for any person to resist, really. People couldn't be blamed for that weakness.

"You should have uglied yourself up," I said. "That would have helped, probably."

He laughed, like he wasn't sure he'd heard me right. "Uglied myself up?"

"Yeah. Grown one of those nasty pube-like beards, like Jon Bertrand has."

"He's ugly even without the beard, trust me." Jason laughed.

"Yeah, but that's beside the point. Grow one of those face-muffs and no girl's going to want to kiss you." I literally shuddered at the thought.

"I had a beard for a little while. Didn't stop Tiffany from making her move."

I gasped and grabbed his arm. "No! Say it isn't so."

He smiled but he didn't look very happy. "It's so."

"She totally went after her BFF's man?" I shook my head, my hand slipping off his arm as I contemplated the third world war that would have broken out had Brittney ever found out. Talk about serious entertainment. "You people have no moral code at all."

"Hey!" he nudged me. "Don't include me in that mess."

"You were the centerpiece of that big mess," I said without thinking.

He instantly stopped laughing. Silence pressed down on us, and I hated myself for not controlling my mouth once again.

"I'm sorry. That sucked."

"No, you're right." He stood up and held out his hand. "Come on. Let's go eat a sandwich and forget about all this stuff." He sounded resigned to his fate of being an asshole, something I couldn't seem to quit reminding him that he was. What was wrong with me?

"You see the irony here, right?" he asked me as he moved down the hallway.

"No, not really. Enlighten me."

"If this shit hadn't happened, you and I would have never had this conversation and none of this stuff would have ever entered my mind."

"So, what's the irony?" I asked.

"The irony is, I had to murder a guy to become a better person."

I tripped on nothing at all and had to hold onto the wall or risk falling flat on my face. My feet didn't want to work right anymore.

"That is just ... so ... awful," I said, feeling the blood leaving my face. Reality had a way of taking my circulation away from me at the oddest times.

"You have no idea," he responded, his broad back slowly going lower as he descended the stairs at the end of the hall.

We went the rest of the way down to the kitchen silently, lost in our own worlds.

I PULLED THE SLIGHTLY SOGGY peanut butter and raspberry jam sandwiches from my bag and gave one to Jason. He ate it happily, like it was the best meal he'd had in weeks. I couldn't even touch mine. The butterfly battalions fighting for ground in my stomach made it impossible.

"You going to eat that?" he asked, gesturing at my plate.

"No. It's gross." For the first time in my life, I had no appetite.

"Want me to make you something?" he asked, leaning over and taking my sandwich. He bit into it as he waited for my answer.

"No, that's all right." I looked around the kitchen, still feeling terrible about his ironic admission and my lifetime of judging him and everyone I'd thought was like him. We're all human beings, just trying to make our way through the mess that's high school and society's unrealistic expectations. Why had I never noticed that before? Why had I put guys like him up on a pedestal and just assumed their lives were better for it?

"I could boil you an egg. You need some protein."

My eyes went back to him. "I do?"

He nodded, chewing away at the last piece of sandwich he'd crammed into his mouth in one bite. "Yeah. Helps build muscles."

I lifted up my arm and flexed. "I'm pretty sure I don't have any, actually. Today proved it."

He shook his head. "No, today proved you're strong. You have a great frame. Just work out with me five times a week and you'll see results fast. I promise."

"You promise? But what about all the sweat? I'm not really into that part of the equation."

He grinned, revealing mushy bread and raspberry seeds stuck in his teeth. "Sweating feels great. Gets rid of toxins. You'll see."

"You seriously need a toothpick," I said, laughing slightly.

"What are you talking about?" He smiled harder.

I looked away. "Gross. Forget what I said earlier. You're really not all that good-looking after all."

He stood up and took our plates, responding on his way to the sink. "Don't think for a single second that I'm going to forget all those things you said about me. My hot face and my muscles and all that."

I groaned. "I was just saying it for illustrative purposes. Don't let your head get too big over it."

He turned around and leaned on the counter. "So you're saying I'm not good-looking at all, then?"

I nodded. "Yep. Right now I'm actually picturing you with that snatch-beard on your face, and I'm thinking it would be an improvement."

His grin got way too evil for comfort. "I'll keep that in mind."

Worried he might actually grow one just to spite me, I changed the subject. "So, what's going on with your case, anyway? Any news?"

Jason pulled two apples out of a bowl on the counter and tossed one to me. I tried to catch it with one hand while he bit into his, but it bounced off my thumb and landed with a thunk on the table. Luckily I pounced on it before it rolled to the floor. *Yum. Bruised apple for lunch.*

"My case? Jesus. Talk about a mood breaker." He chewed a huge bite of apple, wiping his mouth off with the back of his hand when the juice splooged out.

I took a bite of my apple just to have something to do with my hands and waited for him to talk. I'd had enough with discussing his looks and our lame high school existence. Anything had to be better than that garbage, even his legal situation. Besides, it wasn't like we had a lot to talk about other than those two subjects.

"My lawyer says I have to plead not-guilty and give them a chance to build a defense while we wait for the trial."

"What are they going to build it out of? The defense, I mean."

Jason took another big bite of his apple and chewed it like he was trying to murder it, which was kind of disturbing, to be honest. He shrugged, not really answering.

"I mean, what *could* they build a defense of, really?" I was playing dumb, like I was just mulling the idea over in my head, when I was really just trying to pressure him into saying something. I hated that he was just so accepting of everything, especially when it made no sense.

He shrugged again, so I continued.

"I mean, you killed the guy, you have the bruises to prove it. No one else was there..."

Jason's gaze flickered over to the door and then came back to me, but it was such a telling gesture, he might as well have lit up a neon sign over his head.

My ears started to burn with the implications running through my head. I schooled my tone to remain normal, casual, somehow knowing if I acted too excited about his reaction that he'd shut down and refuse to talk to me anymore. Unfortunately, while my tone was casual and smooth, my choice of words was not.

"Who else was there, Jason?"

He blinked a few times and then tried to play it off. "No one. Just me and the coach."

"You're lying." I stood up and slowly made my way over to him, taking a bite of my apple on the way. When I got closer I pointed the fruit at him. "Why are you lying?"

He looked at me like I was nuts, frowning. This same look would have sent me cowering away from him in the halls of our school before, but not anymore. Now I knew he was full of shit.

"Lying to you? I'm not lying." He huffed out some air. "Get over yourself."

I laughed right in his face. "You are *totally* lying." I couldn't stop grinning. It quickly turned into a kind of angry grin, though. "Someone else knows what happened that night and you're covering up for him." I narrowed my eyes. "... or her. Was it a girl? Was Brittney there?"

He rolled his eyes and moved away from me. "Jesus Christ, give it a rest, would you? Brittney was with the cheer team. There wasn't anyone there. No one was there but us two, and that's it, end of story."

I followed him around to the other side of his kitchen island and trapped him next to the refrigerator. Staring up into his face, I refused to back down.

"You need to tell me right now who was there besides you and the coach." I was actually shaking a little, thinking about how finally this whole situation might start making sense.

He stared down at me, his nostrils flaring out a little. He looked ... dangerous. "Or else, what?" he asked. He was either angry or doing a very good impression of an angry person.

My heart was hammering away in my chest, like it was trying to escape or something. Jason had gone from being my laughing workout buddy to being an adult murderer in the space of half a second. I probably should have left right then, but my mouth wasn't finished destroying things.

"Or else I won't be your friend anymore." My voice didn't have a whole lot of strength to it.

He lowered his voice too. "That's fine, because I don't want to be your friend anyway." And then he was kissing me again.

His arms wrapped around me and pulled me in close. I could smell our sweat stink mingling in the small space between us, and for the first time in my life, I didn't think it was the worst odor in the world.

This time, I didn't immediately pull away. Because *this* time, it felt different. Gone was the tenderness. Gone was the spark. Gone was the hope. Now all I felt was a lie.

Jason pressed his lips harder against my mouth and he angled his head to the side to make it deeper. I did nothing but accept what he was doing. I didn't actually participate, but I didn't fight him off either.

He pulled his head away just a fraction of an inch. "You're not stopping me."

"And you're not really kissing me, are you?" I was starting to get mad at this point. He was ruining everything, being the old Jason, trying to make me do things that neither of us wanted just because he could.

He pulled back more, confused. "I'm pretty sure I was, actually."

"Nope." I shook my head, looking way more confident than I was feeling. "You were trying to intimidate me and distract me, but I'm not that easy to manipulate, sorry to have to inform you."

He let go of me and hissed out a whole lungful of air, running his fingers through his hair and making it stand on end. "Do you have any idea how annoying you can be?"

I smiled, feeling both embarrassed and a tiny bit proud. Hey, I might be a complete idiot but at least I have a skill. "Yes. Bobby tells me all the time, as a matter of fact."

Jason didn't say another word. Instead, he pulled the fridge open and blocked me from view with the door.

"I'm not going anywhere," I said from behind the stainless steel barrier. A picture of Jason and his father held to the fridge with a magnet was about an inch from my nose.

"Maybe you should."

I shrugged, even though he couldn't see me. "If that's what you really want." I didn't expect him to call me on it. Unfortunately, I underestimated him greatly.

The door shut and he was standing there glaring at me. "I like you, Katy. I really do. But I can't do this with you anymore."

My heart plummeted into my toes, leaving my chest an empty cavern filled with pain. I swallowed hard to get the lump in my throat to go down enough to let me speak around it.

So much for having a skill and feeling confident. Unfortunately, since rejection was something I was much more familiar and comfortable with, this situation felt normal. More normal than anything that had happened recently, anyway. Now Jason was acting like the Jason I knew before. It was devastatingly sad to me, but I kept my game-face on.

"Fine. I'll leave, then." I backed up and went around the kitchen island to grab my backpack, glad my hair was covering my burning ears so he wouldn't see how humiliated I was.

"And you probably shouldn't come back," he said, as I made my way to the front door. "No more picnics. No more work-outs."

Stab, stab, stab. More pain stabbing me in the heart with every word that came from his mouth. Who knew he had such efficient weapons at his disposal?

My face flamed hot red, thinking about how desperate I must have looked coming over here with my lame sandwiches and goofy smile. "That's fine too!" I shouted, opening the door and stepping out onto the porch. I couldn't get away from him fast enough. The cooler air outside did nothing for my beet-red face.

He didn't respond, and I let the door shut behind me. I didn't slam it like I wanted to, I just let it swing closed on its own. The latch clicking into place had a finality to it that made my entire insides ache.

I took a deep breath, trying to get control over my raging hurt emotions. *Just let things be,* I thought to myself. That was the adult part of me speaking sense. The girl in me wanted to scream and rant and break all the windows of his house in with a brick. A big, frigging, bastard of a brick.

My hair swung into my eyes, thank goodness, keeping the reporters from getting any clear shots of my face. With those stupid, high-powered lenses they'd for sure have been able to catch the tears swimming in my eyes.

I made it all the way to my bedroom before any of them fell. When they did finally escape, they came in rivers I thought would never run dry. I cried for myself and my sad little attempts at befriending a person who didn't want a friend, I cried for the coach and all the people who'd lost him, and I cried for Jason, a boy who was really and truly all alone in a world that had once revered him but now had turned on him with a vengeance. Life was so unfair.

I DIDN'T TALK TO JASON for the rest of the weekend. When Bobby texted asking me if I wanted to hang out, I lied and told him I had too much homework and my parents had forbidden me to go out. My room became my hideout, where I could lie in my bed and lick my wounds, trying to forget what a loser I was.

My mother was so worried about me, she let me have dinner in my room, which was normally a big no-no. I ended up eating two bites of my hamburger — all protein, Jason would have been so proud — and throwing the rest in the garbage. I fell asleep listening to the mix I made for him and picturing him having dance-seizures all over his kitchen. My eyes were pretty much swollen shut with all the boo-hooing I did.

Monday dawned dark and dismal, a perfect background for my mood. Rain ruined my hair and brought out the scent of the fabric softener my mother uses on my clothes before I was ten steps out the door. I was sweating and hating every drop of it, more so than usual. Sweat reminded me of Jason and Jason reminded me of the pain of rejection.

ELLE CASEY

People in the hallways stared and whispered as I walked by, but I ignored them and their tiny minds. I had nothing to say to anyone, or so I thought.

Mrs. Davis the civics teacher caught up with me on the way to fifth period. I'd made the mistake of taking the short way to class that led me right past her door during her off-period. She snagged me with a shout that pretty much alerted half the school that we were about to have a conversation.

"Katy! Hey, Katy! Could you come here for a minute?"

I tried to pretend like I hadn't heard her, but everyone else stopped and stared, so it would have been too obvious a snub to continue on. *Curse my parents for refusing to allow me to be rude growing up.* So much for personal freedom. I was starting to think that I had none at all, seeing as how most of my responses and actions were dependent on the approval or disapproval of someone else. I was starting to doubt if I'd ever had an independent or original thought in my entire life.

I sighed and turned around, making my way back to her door with my head down. "Hi," I said, still not really looking at her. I focused on the black cummerbund around her waist, lost in her eighties time warp that wouldn't quit.

"Would you come in for a minute? I promise I won't keep you very long."

"I have class..." I looked longingly out into the hallway.

"I'll write you a note if necessary." She backed into the room and hitched a buttcheek up over the corner of her desk. "So, how are things going with Jason?"

I shrugged. "How would I know?"

"The news channels show you going over to his house every day, so I figured you were at least talking to him, seeing how he's doing?" She leaned her head down, forcing me to look up at her.

Busted. Fuck the news.

I sighed, very put-out that she was using her teacher-power to force me into having a conversation I totally wasn't interested in having. Could this be false-imprisonment? It felt like it.

"He's as good as you would expect," I said with undisguised attitude. "Besides, I won't be going over there anymore, so ... whatever." I twisted to the side, looking out into the hallway. I couldn't have hinted any louder how badly I wanted to be gone from her classroom, but she continued to ignore my screaming body language.

"Why's that? Did your parents tell you they don't want you to go over there?"

"No," *not that it's any of your cummerbund-wearing business,* "they're fine with it." I finally looked at her, mad at her insinuation. "Jason's not dangerous."

"I wasn't saying that he is." She stared at me, like she was trying to see into my soul or something. It was annoying as hell.

"Can I go now?"

"In a minute. Did you give any more thought to what I said before? About how I might be able to help you?"

"I'm not the one who needs help."

I couldn't figure this woman out. Was she a sicko who got off on hearing terrible news? Was she looking for a story to sell? It never crossed my mind that she might actually care about anybody but herself. My time with Jason had turned me against the world.

"Help with understanding the whole process is what I meant when I said I could help. It can get very complicated and bewildering sometimes. Don't you have any questions? Any concerns about where this process will take your friend next?"

Friend. Now there was a concept.

"Yeah, I have a question." The statement burst out of me before I could stop it.

She grinned and folded her hands. "Okay, shoot." Her eyebrows were up, like she was anticipating my question more than Christmas vacation.

At that point, I was mad enough at her, at Jason, and at all the idiots who'd been whispering about me today in the hallways and classrooms to just speak without even trying to put a filter on my mouth first.

"What would it mean if Jason wasn't the only person there when the coach was killed?'

Ohhhhh shit. Did I really say that?

Yes, I really said that. Talk about feeding the monster. Now I was never going to get out of that room.

She blinked a few times and then leaned back a little. Her hands slipped away from each other. She kind of stuttered. "Do you mean ... if there was a witness to the murder?"

"Yes," I nodded, almost afraid to hear her answer, now that she'd put a familiar name to that alleged third person. *Witness.*

"What would that do to his case or his trial or whatever?" I was suddenly nervous.

She nodded, as if considering it, back in control of her facial expressions.

"Well, I suppose it would depend on what this witness had to say." She looked up at me. "It could help his case or hurt it. It could send him to prison or set him fee." She tilted her head to the right. "Did he tell you there was a witness?"

I shook my head emphatically. "No. Not at all. It was a hypothetical thing, completely. Totally." I was getting a headache from all the rattling around of my brain matter.

I knew Jason didn't want me even thinking about that, let alone talking about it. It was like I'd betrayed him by making this woman think that there was something to his story that wasn't being talked about in the news. I'd never forgive myself if I was the cause of a new rumor going around about him.

She continued. "Hypothetically speaking, if there were a witness, it could be really good or really bad. But frankly, I don't think it's possible that there is one in this case."

"Why?" I hitched my bag up higher on my shoulder, no longer as interested in the hallway and my escape as I was in hearing her explanation.

"Because there's been no mention of it in the news. That's a pretty big piece of evidence, so I can't believe it's been kept out of the public eye. Reporters follow detectives around, they're at the police station, they have sources ... they know when witnesses are interviewed. If there was one, we would already have a name."

My face fell. Even though Jason had completely rejected me and my lame friendship, I'd still been holding out hope that maybe there could be something or some*one* out there to save him.

"Unless of course this witness has not yet presented himself to the police..." She leaned in closer to me. "That does happen you know. People fear the publicity, the backlash ... they fear that they'll become embroiled in the charges, which is a very real possibility, by the way."

"What do you mean?" I stepped closer even though her breath kind of stank, wishing she'd stop talking so loud. People were starting to slow down in her doorway, trying to listen in on our conversation.

She glanced at the door and lowered her voice. "If a person witnesses a crime and does nothing to stop it, that person can be held liable as an accomplice."

I swallowed with difficulty, my throat suddenly dry. "So, if there *was* another person, it would help Jason's case, right?"

She shrugged. "It depends."

Her answer pissed me off. "Does everything depend on something else or what?"

She laughed. "Yes. 'It depends' is always the answer in a legal situation." She put her hand on my shoulder and left it there for a few seconds. I felt like I was being knighted by a very fashion-challenged queen. The Queen of Cummerbunds from the Land of Flowered Polyesters.

"Depending on who that person was, what that person was doing, what that person's involvement was, what his relationship was to the other people in the room ... it all depends. It could help or it could make things worse..." She leaned down and stared into my eyes. "...*It depends.*" Her eyes crinkled up in the corners and her expression clearly said she pitied me. She was trying to be nice, so I didn't feel the need to hold it against her.

I stared at the floor, once again battling tears. "I don't see how anything could possibly make Jason's situation worse."

"You'd be surprised." She let my shoulder go and stood. "You'd better get to class before you're late."

I nodded and turned to go.

"Do you want some advice?" she asked.

I stopped in my tracks, knowing that the answer *hell no, I've heard enough from you today* would be rude but also not wanting to waste my time saying the polite answer I didn't feel.

She continued without waiting for my response. "Keep your mind, your eyes, and your ears open. Things happen in cases like this that can completely turn a situation around. Nothing is over until it's over."

"Easy for you to say," I quipped as I walked to the door, feeling more bitter than I ever had in my entire life. "You're not the one on trial for murder."

I left before she could reply and spent the entire next period crying in the girls' bathroom.

THREE DAYS LATER I WAS on my computer clicking through photos when I came across the folder of shots taken by that photographer vulture guy. Football players and their fans flashed across my screen in various poses, caught in moments of candor interacting without knowing they were being watched.

The ones of Jason made my heart swell. My chest was filled with the sea and my heart was floating on top of it, a terrible inner storm tossing it around. It was sickening how just a photo of him patting a kid's shoulder could make me cry these days.

A text came to my phone making it buzz, and I glanced over at it.

I'm not taking no for an answer. Confess.

I hadn't yet told Bobby what was going on, and he'd been very un-Bobby-like in his patience at waiting for my explanation. It made me kind of sad actually, how willing he'd been to give me the time I needed. Normally he force-fed me his love, but this time he was letting me decide when it was the right moment to share. Suffice to say, absolutely *nothing* was right in my world.

I figured there was no use candy-coating it or avoiding it any-more, so I texted him back right away.

Jason told me to F off so I Fd off.

My phone rang almost immediately.

"He did not," Bobby said.

"Yes, he did." I was angry that Bobby was playing silly games, acting as if this were a joke. "And I don't want to talk about it or whatever. Believe me, I've cried enough tears. I'm totally dehydrated."

Bobby's tone immediately changed; pity filled his voice. "Was he rude about it?"

I'd gone over the situation in my head a thousand times, but it always came out the same in my analysis.

I sighed before replying, "No. He was just being cool. He doesn't feel like he deserves friends and I was kind of pushing him, so he cut me off. No big deal."

"Do you really think that?" Bobby's tone went all soft. "That it's no big deal?"

That was my undoing, Bobby being tender when normally he was as much a smartass as I was.

"Goddammit, Bobby, I told you I don't want to cry about this anymore!"

"Baby, baby, baby, don't crrrryyyy! I'll come right over!"

"No! Do *not* come over. I don't want my parents freaking out. My mom thinks it's my period and my father's completely oblivious. Just let it die."

"Die. That's an interesting choice of words."

I choked on my tears. "Give it a rest, Bobby, please. I'm not kidding. Don't analyze me, okay? I'll live."

"Live and die. Both interesting choices of words. I'll talk to you soon."

The line went dead, all the background noise of his television ceasing in an instant.

"What?"

Nothing.

"Bobby? Hello? What did you say?"

Nothing.

"Bobby, are you there? I think I lost you." I looked at my phone and saw the welcome screen. I tried to call him back, but it went straight to voicemail.

Figuring he was probably trying to call me at the same time, I put the phone down, a little confused about what had just happened but too upset over the resurfacing memories to fix anything. Instead of worrying about it, I went back to paging through the pictures on my computer.

I was buzzing through them pretty quickly until I came to one of Jason smiling. He looked amazing and obviously hadn't known that the camera was on him at the time. He was talking to a young boy with a poofy afro, maybe about twelve years old or so.

I went back through the photographs before it and after it to verify the scenery I was seeing, determining pretty quickly that this photo had been taken at that club or charity or whatever it was that the coach was involved in. This kid was probably one of the boys who got sponsored by a player for the year or for the season or whatever.

I frowned as my mind wandered. Jason never talked about that place, but it looked from the photos that he was friends with this kid in particular. I paged through all of them again and found four pictures of Jason with this one particular boy. Jason had his arm loosely over the kid's shoulders in two of them. In every single one, they were both smiling. A lot. If they'd had any physical similarities, I would have said they were brothers the way they seemed so at ease with one another.

My finger tapped the key that would scroll through the pictures. Back and forth, forth and back. Where was this kid now? Had he visited Jason? Had he been at the funeral for the coach? Was he as devastated as I was over what had happened to Jason?

I hopped online and searched all the news I could find on the coach's death. I didn't see the boy in any of the pictures. It wasn't really that surprising, though. He was only a kid. How would he even go to those things if he couldn't drive? And if he was part of that program Jason and the other players were in, it could have meant he really didn't have much in the way of parents who could drive him places.

I wasn't sure why this whole thing, why this *kid*, was sticking in my head, but he was, and the thoughts wouldn't leave. Jason said that no one really liked him, but surely this little kid did. And what twelve year old has ulterior motives? They don't care who a person is really, just so long as that person will throw a football with them every once in a while. From the pictures, it sure looked like that was the basis of their friendship. So if this kid was Jason's one true friend, where was he now?

My phone rang again and made me jump, cutting off my train of thought. I picked it up without looking at the screen.

"Bobby, I told you, I'm done crying, I don't want to talk about him anymore."

"Talk about who?" said the voice on the other end.

I pulled the phone away from my ear and saw a name there that made me cringe.

Chuck Bradley.

"Mister Bradley?" I asked, hoping against all hope it actually was him and not the person I suspected.

"No, this is Jason."

Heart ... sinking. Embarrassment. Pain. *Ugh*, I so wanted to hang up, but I didn't.

He sighed. "Listen ... Bobby called me and told me everything. I'm really sorry. Can you come over?"

I immediately hung up the phone and threw it onto my bed. Freaking out is probably the best way to describe what I was doing right then. It was like the phone was a snake all of a sudden, and I sure as hell didn't want to get bitten.

Reflecting back on what I'd said on the phone with him just now, I cringed all over. Had I just admitted to Jason that I'd been crying over him for, like, days on end? *Ergggh!! I hate myself!*

The phone rang again.

I threw three pillows on top of it and ran into the bathroom. No way in freaking hell was I going to have that conversation. I could just imagine it now:

"I heard you were all broken-hearted about losing me."

"No, I wasn't. I didn't cry at all."

"Then why is it all over the news that your eyes are puffy and you haven't eaten in four days?"

No. Way. No. Thank. You.

I plugged my flatiron in, deciding that putting a few hundred twists into my hair would be the perfect way to burn an hour of time and forget how much I missed being with Jason.

I was halfway done with the medusa-like mess when a knock came at my door.

"What?" I yelled, figuring it was my mother with another plate of food, trying to tempt me to eat.

"Honey, it's me," she said through the door.

Go away.

"I'm doing my hair. Come back later, okay?"

"There's someone here to see you."

I sighed with annoyance. Sometimes my BFF's love could be suffocating. "Tell Bobby he's supposed to call first before he comes over. I'm not in the mood."

I could only imagine how put-out he'd be over that statement, but oh well. I was done with tears and done with crying over Jason. Game over. *Be a winner, not a loser, Katy.*

The door opened and then shut, which pissed me off. I waited for Bobby's singsong voice to come around the corner as he pretended to not care that he'd totally just begged me for a fight.

"Bobby, if you so much as show your face in here, I swear to God I will straight-iron and back-comb your hair until you look like the nineteen eighties Tina Turner."

"That sounds serious."

I fumbled the flat iron in my surprise, and it burned my neck on the way down to the floor.

"Mother fudger!" I yelled as sweat popped out under my armpits.

The room went silent.

"Jason?" I prayed for an answer I knew I wasn't going to get.

"Yeah, it's me. Don't be mad. And please don't turn me into Tina Turner."

MY EYES WERE BUGGING OUT of my head. I had no make-up on, half my head was in curls and the other half was up in a clip, I hadn't brushed my teeth since what felt like a million hours ago before school this morning, and I was wearing my pajamas; they weren't even my nice ones.

I gritted my teeth together as I contemplated my image in the mirror. Conflicting emotions raged through me. He'll think I'm ugly. He'll laugh. He'll judge me. And then reality came back and saved my sorry butt. Who the fuck cares what I look like? Jason doesn't. He doesn't even want to be my frigging friend.

I stuck my head around the corner of the door. "What are you doing here?" I was pretending I was as cool as a chilly cucumber hanging out in the fridge. No ... the *freezer*. I was a frozen cucumber of a bitch. He couldn't hurt me anymore.

"I came over to apologize."

I pulled my head back into the bathroom so he couldn't see how freaked out that made me. He braved all those reporters to come over here and apologize to me? The frozen cucumber that was me started to thaw just the tiniest bit. Not a lot, but a little. I was a chilly cucumber now.

"Fine," I said, "apologize and go." I wasn't ready to make my heart so available anymore. It was way too easy for him to crack it wide open.

"And beg."

"Beg?" I looked out again, eyebrow raised in doubt. "You? Beg?"

"Yes." He looked very sorry. "For your forgiveness."

I snorted and pulled my head back into the bathroom. Chilly cucumber, my ass. I was a pitiful mess. But honestly, how could any girl stay cold to that? I was puddle of cucumber goo hating myself for being so easy, so weak, but it wasn't to be helped. I am only human.

I didn't know what to say to him, and I knew if I listened to my heart I'd probably be making out with him in my bed in about three seconds. No way was my brain going to let that happen, no matter how cute those stupid patented puppy dog eyes looked. I still had my pride, at least.

"I'm really, really sorry," he continued. "I shouldn't have said those things to you. I wish you'd ... come back. Come back and work out with me and have picnics with me."

"Why? Because you're bored?" I was a tad bitter, and when I'm bitter, I'm really not very attractive. It's a fact I've come to accept about myself.

It crossed my mind for a couple seconds after I responded with my bitchy attitude that heart attacks must be seriously painful, because I wasn't having one of those and yet my chest was positively aching. Since when was friendship so painful? Bobby and I had never come to tears over anything between us.

"Yes and no," he said.

That was enough of an honest answer to have me peeking my head out again. "What's that supposed to mean?"

He sat down in my desk chair backwards, facing the back of it and me at the bathroom door. "I am bored, but that doesn't mean that's the only reason I want to hang out with you."

I picked my iron up off the floor and started another curl. "I'm listening." I was, too, with every ounce of my eardrums' power, I was listening, a beggar starving for friendship from this boy. That was the pitiful truth of my life.

I pulled my hair extra hard, possibly trying to punish myself for being so stupid.

"I've had a hundred friends in my life before. People come and go, you know?"

I didn't respond.

"And you were only really in it for like, a couple weeks or whatever ... but when you're gone it feels like you should be there. Like there's something essential missing."

"That's because I was your only visitor."

"No, that's not why. And I've had other visitors."

I couldn't *not* look then. "Who?"

He shrugged, resting his chin on the top of my chair. "Lawyers. Tutors. Reporters. Crazy people."

"Crazy people? Am I in that group?" Thinking he was going to say yes made me queasy.

"No. You're like the only sane person in my life right now."

That warmed my heart a little. Just a little, though.

"What crazy people?"

He looked embarrassed. "You're going to laugh."

"No, I'm not. I promise." I put the iron down on the counter and came out of the bathroom a little, leaning on the door frame. "Who? Tiffany?"

I'd picked the least likely most pitiful person I could think of. Imagine my surprise when he answered, "She's one."

"No!" I gasped. "I would have seen that on the news!" *Oh, the scandal!* I lowered my voice. "Does Brittney know?" Bobby would totally pee his pants if he heard this. Keeping it a secret was going to be tough.

"No, she came dressed up like a tutor, business suit and big glasses and a hat. I didn't even recognize her when she came to the door."

I couldn't keep my jaw shut; it just hung there open while I was stunned into silence. It's crazy, but I was jealous. *Jealous!* How ridiculous is that? I instantly wondered if he'd been happy to see her, hugged her, kissed her, even. I wanted to punch her right in the boob. It was tempting to imagine printing fliers detailing her indiscretions and posting them all over the school. What a fake, back-stabbing, b-word she was. Good thing I wasn't a vindictive, flier-printing psycho or she'd be in big trouble with her friends at school, Brittney especially.

"A couple other women read about me and came over. Thrill seekers or something."

"What did they want?" I asked, coming into the room and slowly lowering myself to my bed.

He looked over at me with a sardonic lift to his brow. "Guess."

I couldn't help but look disgusted. "*Ew!* What's wrong with those women?"

He laughed. First it was just a little and then it was a lot.

"What?" I asked. "What'd I say?"

He got up from the chair and sat down next to me on the bed. Throwing his arms around me, he trapped me in a hug before I even know what was coming.

"Man, I missed you," he said, burying his face in my neck.

REACHED AROUND WITH ONE hand and patted him on the shoulder. It was all I could do in this awkward position, not that I would have hugged him back anyway. He had a lot more begging to do.

"Okaaaaay.... I'm still not sure what was so funny."

He let go and sat back a little so we could look at each other. "You basically said they're totally deviant because they want to be with me."

I thought about it for a second and then realized I kind of had. "I didn't exactly mean it like that."

"Nah, you're right. You're just being honest. I need honesty in my life right now."

"No, no, no," I grabbed his arm and squeezed it, "I meant that people who would just come to you now when you're a murderer, who are attracted to you *because* you murdered someone ... *that's* deviant. It's not you ... it's them."

He stopped laughing and lost his smile. "I went online while you were gone. That's what some people are saying about you. I saw it."

I lost my smile too. "Yeah, well ... fuck them."

He reached up and brushed some of the hair that had fallen from my clip towards my ear. "I'm sorry about that. I never wanted anyone to say anything bad about you. You're a good person. You don't deserve it."

I straightened up and shook my head a little to clear the sadness. "I can handle it."

He reached up and squeezed my bicep. "You're looking stronger already."

I flinched.

"Did that hurt?" he asked.

I sniffed. "If you must know ... I am still experiencing a little muscle pain from our workout."

"That was days ago. Did you stretch after? Eat a banana?"

I looked sideways at him. "No, was I supposed to?"

He leaned back and looked me up and down. "You've lost weight. Are you eating?"

I pushed him away and stood. "Go away. I have hair to curl."

"That's a good look for you," he said as I walked back to the bathroom.

My heart was soaring into the clouds. Jason was here and he wanted to be my friend again! The question was, did I still want to be his? And he likes my hair, too.

"Kind of reminds me of Medusa, though."

I rolled my eyes at my reflection in the mirror. As if wanting to be his friend was even a valid debate. I hadn't stopped crying except to sleep since I'd been away from him. Of course I wanted to be friends.

"What makes you think I still want to be friends with you?" I asked. Just because I was ready to forgive, it didn't mean I was above a little torture to appease my cracked heart.

"Bobby says you've been crying every day."

I growled. "I'm going to kill that pansy when I finish with my hair."

I was pulling another curl down when Jason appeared behind me in my bathroom.

"I've never watched a girl do her hair before," he said after a few seconds.

I played his confession off, pretending like it didn't sound tender and regretful. "That's weird."

"Why is that weird?" His eyes tracked my movements over and over. I took my time to make this particular curl perfect. It sprang up into a coil when the iron fell away at the bottom.

"Because. You've had about a thousand girlfriends and they're all high-maintenance types. Surely you would have seen them in action."

"Are you crazy? They never let me see them with their hair not perfect. And I don't have any sisters, and my mom was gone when I was really young, so ..." He shrugged.

I didn't reply to that. I was too focused on the fact that he'd pretty much just told me that most girls didn't let guys see them in the bathroom like this. Would there be no end to my social awkwardness?

"I'll bet I could do that," he said, watching my iron again.

"Do what?" I put the flatiron down and stroked the next bunch of hair with my brush to get the tangles out.

"Curl your hair. Let me try." He reached for the iron.

I regarded him suspiciously. Was he serous? "I don't want to get burned."

"Please. They call me velvet hands on the field, you know."

"On the field." I snorted like a pig. "Yeeeeeahh, right."

"Come on, let me try." He held his hand out for the brush.

I watched with trepidation as he took the flatiron and the hunk of hair I'd been holding and proceeded to set up the next curl.

"Start at the roots. Not too close! You'll burn my scalp. And twist the iron around the hair. And go slow!" I cringed, waiting for the pain.

He started following my directions. He was surprisingly gentle.

"Not *too* slow, or you'll burn my hair!"

"Okay, okay, just relax," he said, watching with full attention as the iron ran through my hair. He looked like a little kid, sticking his tongue out of the corner of his mouth in concentration.

It was pretty ridiculous, me standing there in my *Hot Buns* boxer shorts and his giant fingers holding what looked like a black chopstick in comparison next to my head.

"You have no idea how gay you look right now," I said, giggling.

"Bobby would be all over my ass, I know." He caught my eye in the mirror and smiled.

It made me happy, nervous, and sad all at the same time to share that moment with him. As soon as he was done with his big curling maneuver, I took the iron away from him. "Okay, thank you, good job, now go away."

He pointed at my head. "Hey look! I did one!"

"Yeah. Good for you. Now go." I started setting up my next curl.

He disappeared and then shortly thereafter returned, this time carrying my desk chair.

"What are you doing?" I asked, my hand poised above my head.

"Sit on this. I'll finish this for you." He put the chair down behind me.

"Are you insane?" I put the iron down and stared at his reflection.

He shrugged. "Maybe."

We looked at each other in the mirror.

"Please?" he asked.

He looked so vulnerable, I didn't have the heart to give him any more crap. "Fine. But if you burn my hair, I'm going to be seriously pissed."

"I won't, I promise. Just sit there and let me be nice to you for a little while."

I slowly took a seat, wondering what this was all about. I stared at him in the mirror and narrowed my eyes at his reflection. "Who are you, and what have you done with Jason Bradley?"

He just snorted, smiled, and took some hair, brushing it out. His movements were awkward at first, but became more assured. He finished six more curls before he spoke again.

"You have soft hair," he said. "It smells nice, too."

"Shampoo and conditioner. Available in all your local drug and grocery stores."

"Smartass." He grinned, pulling the iron through my hair. It tickled, sending shivers up my spine.

To distract myself, as more curls were developed and more shivers ensued, I played with a rubber band. "You have a special knack for this," I said.

"Yeah," he said, "maybe I can be the prison beautician."

I lowered my hands and flicked him on the leg with the rubber band.

"Ow!" he said, jumping to the side and taking my hair with him.

"OW!" I yelled, leaning my head over to lessen the pain.

"Oh, shit, sorry." He came back to stand behind me. "Keep your hands to yourself, lady. I have work to do here."

"Stop joking about your situation like that. It makes me sad."

He stopped and lowered the iron to the counter. "I don't want you to be sad."

My eyes filled with tears. It was all too overwhelming, to be sitting here with Jason Bradley curling my hair, telling me he didn't want *me* to be sad when he was about to be sent to prison or be put to death.

Our circles had *mixed*. A cataclysmic event in his life had caused the unthinkable to happen — circles mixing so much they fell apart and ceased to exist. Everything we thought was true about the world was revealed as a lie. Nothing that had felt important really was, and things we took for granted like friendship, real friendship, had become everything. And I'd blown Bobby off for no good reason, like, five times in the last two weeks.

"Oh, shit, you're crying."

"Of course I'm crying, you idiot!" I buried my face in my hands. "You're going to prison! You're going to miss out on everything! Your life is over!"

He leaned down and put his arms around me, hugging me into the chair. "Shhh, please don't cry. I won't joke about it anymore. I was just letting off some steam, but I won't anymore, I promise."

I knew I was being a selfish asshole, so I tried to make myself stop crying. But the harder I tried, the worse it got, to the point that I was choking and almost vomiting.

Jason pulled me to my feet and held me in his arms. I heard the door to my room open but then it closed again right after.

"Your mom is making sure I'm not strangling you or something, I think."

I punched Jason in the gut. "Shut up! Stop *saying* stuff like that!"

"Oooph," he said, exaggerating the effect of my abuse. "Man, do you work out? That's quite a punch you have there. I'm scared. She should be checking to make sure I'm okay."

I couldn't help but laugh, so then I was laughing and crying at the same time. I lifted my head to look to him.

"You are such an idiot." I stared up at his handsome face, loving that he'd come here in search of a friendship I thought I'd only imagined between us.

"And you are covered in snot. Stay right there." He leaned over to grab some toilet paper.

I wiped my face on his shirt. "Not anymore." Stepping back, I sniffed loudly and looked in the mirror. "Thanks for doing my hair." Only three quarters of it was done, but I didn't care. He'd done about ten of the curls and that was ten more curls than he'd ever done before.

He stood behind me and wrapped his arms around my waist. "Thanks for being my friend." His chin dropped to rest on the top of my head.

We stared at each other for a little while before he broke the silence. "You're not going to kiss me again, are you?" he asked, making a face.

I laughed, turning to go out the door and pushing him away. "You wish."

He grabbed my hand and pulled me back. Time froze and the laugher fell away as he looked at me and spoke. The laughter was gone, replaced with a gaze so intense I could literally feel it on my body.

"Any time you want to change your mind about that, just let me know, okay?"

I couldn't believe that he'd be serious about that, so I just laughed it off. "Yeah, okay, whatever." My pulse wasn't going to let me off that easy, though. It hammered away, sending my blood rushing through my veins along with a load of adrenaline. Did he mean what I thought he meant? That I could be more than friends if I wanted to be? And besides ... what did it matter? It would be the biggest mistake of my life to go there, so I just wouldn't.

I said that to myself like ten times to drill it into my head while I busied myself with dragging my desk chair back and then putting away all my hair stuff in the bathroom. This was no time to be thinking about kissing Jason, not with my bed and his prison sentence looming so closely.

Jason went back out to my room and was looking through my photographs on the computer when I finally joined him.

"Why do you have all these pictures?" he asked, looking at one featuring a former friend. "Were you there?"

"No," I said, flopping down on my back on the bed, "some dickcheese photographer was, though, and I got his memory card and deleted everything on it."

"Oh, okay. That makes no sense whatsoever."

"He followed me from your house and tried to get into my front door to talk to us, and my father grabbed his camera from him and shoved him outside. Before we gave it back, I did a little CSI Miami on the memory card and voilà ... I have the pictures and he doesn't."

"Hmmm ..." Jason turned around and smiled. It seemed forced. "So, you want to come work-out with me?"

I gave him the stink-eye. "Was this all some elaborate plan to find yourself another spotter?"

"Damn ... am I that transparent?" He stood up and held out a hand. "Come on. I do need a spotter. And *you* need to work on those spaghetti arms."

I held up an unenthusiastic hand. "I just got my hair did. I don't want to sweat. I'll lose all my curls."

"You look better without 'em anyway. Come on."

I shook my head as he helped me to my feet. "Not smooth at all, J-man. Not smooth. At. All."

"Hey, some chicks can rock the natural look and some have to dude their shit up for hours in the morning. Just pity those other chicks, don't hate the honesty."

I laughed, searching through drawers for something to wear that wouldn't look too awful when drenched in salty sweat. "You are really lucky ..."

"...that I'm so good-looking. I know, you already told me about ten times. Are you ready to go yet?"

I abandoned my search and opened my door, shoving him out into the hallway. "I have to get dressed. Give me five minutes."

He pounded down the stairs, and I quickly threw on my running shoes and my sweatpants from last year — the ones that magically fit me again since I'd lost some weight during my several-day mourning period.

As I was about to leave, my computer screen caught my eye. The picture showing was of Bobby wearing one of his righteous get-ups, not one of the photos from the reporter's camera. I went over to shut the program down, and a window popped up asking me if I was sure I wanted to delete the four photos in the trash basket.

I frowned, wondering what the hell the ghost in my machine was doing now. Occasionally my computer had a mind of its own and randomly did shit to make me crazy.

Going into the trash folder I expected to find nothing, but instead there were exactly four photos in there, which made zero sense since I hadn't deleted anything. I brought each of them up in turn and felt goosebumps coming out all over my body as I realized what they were.

All of them had Jason and that boy with the big afro in them. Every picture that the reporter had taken of that one boy had either magically ended up in my trash bin, or Jason had put them there himself intentionally; and I was pretty sure the ghost in my machine had nothing against afros.

I opened my mouth to yell down to him about it, but then closed it without saying a word. If he could be sneaky, so could I; and I had a feeling that I'd be able to get more answers if I didn't ask him directly.

A LITTLE OVER ONE WEEK later, Jason dropped a bomb on me. After hanging out with him for nine solid days, after school and on weekends, I was in his workout room doing the last rep of a horrible leg exercise, and he started up this conversation about his case — a subject we normally avoided judiciously.

"My lawyer says that I have a one-in-ten chance of getting anything less than twenty-five years to life."

The weights clanged down onto the rack as I lost all the strength in my legs.

"What?!" I was out of breath and freaked out, sending my volume way too high.

Jason turned around and lifted up some small barbells for my next exercise. "You heard me. One in ten. I'm pretty much doomed. But at least I won't be getting a lethal injection. I'm looking on the bright side of things. The trial is supposed to start in a few months since all the investigation and exchange of evidence is finished. Apparently they're fast-tracking everything. I could be in prison for my eighteenth birthday in February."

I slowly turned sideways on the seat and stared at him. "How is it that you're not curled up in a ball, crying on your bed right now? Cuz that's where I'd be." When your lawyer has that little hope for you, I was guessing there was none to be had. And all this time I'd been hoping for a miracle, for a lawyer like they have in the movies who uncovers some great piece of evidence and saves the accused from prison.

"I did that for about ten seconds, but then I quit." He shrugged, his face devoid of emotion. "I mean, what's the point, right? I did it. Do the crime, do the time. That's the way the world works."

I walked over and took one of the barbells from him. If I've learned anything dealing with Jason it's that he does way better with a conversation or the act of me extracting information from him that he doesn't want to share if I act like I'm otherwise occupied. I figured it was a side-effect of never having a real friend who paid him very close attention before. I worked with what I had.

I pumped a few reps before beginning my prying campaign. "That civics teacher at school, Mrs. Davis, she said that if you had a witness it could help your case a lot. Could set you free, even." I kept my eyes on the wall mirror, pretending like I gave a crap about my form when I was really just hoping he'd let his guard down and finally talk to me about that mystery person I absolutely knew had been in that room when he killed the coach.

Jason was always on me about *form*, about how I had to lift and lower the weights properly or I'd lose the full benefit of the workout. *Blah, blah, blah.* Today was no exception.

"Not so fast. Slow down. Use gravity..."

"...I know, I know, use gravity to aid the workout. Are you going to answer my question?"

"I didn't hear a question, did you ask one?" He was playing dumb and we both knew it.

"I know someone was there," I said with false bravado. Even though he'd proven to me about a hundred times that he really wanted to be a true friend to me, I still worried about saying the wrong thing and getting rejected again.

"There wasn't. I swear." This time he looked at me when he said it, so it sounded like the truth.

I let the weight hang by my side. "Are you sure?"

"Yes, I'm sure. It was just him and me in that office. No one else was around."

"No one who could *hear* anything, maybe?"

He shook his head. "No. I went there early to ..." He flared his nostrils and gritted his teeth for a couple seconds before finishing. "...I went there early. That's it. We were alone."

I put the weight on the ground and took him by the arm. "That's *not* it, Jason, I *know* that's not it." I was begging him with my eyes to tell me the truth — the whole truth, not a piece of it like I always felt I was getting.

"Are you hungry?" he asked. "My dad bought us some fried chicken for lunch."

Saturday had become a ritual picnic day for us. Every time we sat down in Jason's living room, that picture of the sun was there to keep us company. It always made a lump come up in my throat.

"Fuck the fried chicken. Are we friends or not?" I glared at him to drive home my threat. I was taking a risk, but one I felt was worth taking.

"Yeah, we're friends." I could tell he was on the verge of getting mad, but I pushed through anyway.

"Then be honest with me. Tell me exactly what happened, from start to finish, and leave nothing out."

"Why? It's not going to change anything."

"Yes, it will."

"I promise, it won't."

"You owe me, Jason."

His back went up. "How so?"

"Because." I put the other barbell down and gave him a double bicep flex. "I've been sweating and feeling sore for going on two weeks now and I have nothing to show for it. The least you can do is tell me the story."

He reached up and felt my arm. "You're getting stronger. You're already lifting twenty percent more than when you started and your form is excellent."

"If you say another word about my form again today I'm going to knock you out with your own weights."

He laughed. "You're a seriously violent woman, you know that?"

"That's why you like me."

Both our smiles kind of faltered as we thought about those words. Violence is what had brought us together, what ended up making us friends. The irony was not lost on either of us.

"Let's eat some chicken," he said, his voice softer and filled with regret.

"Yeah. We can talk about what happened at the picnic."

He left the room with me following. "Anyone ever tell you you're stubborn?" he asked.

"Everyone who's ever spent more than a day with me, yes."

"What did I do to deserve you in my life?" he asked as a joke.

I didn't give him the obvious reply. *You killed our high school football coach.* That would have been too terrible to even joke about. Even after I knew the *real* story behind his death.

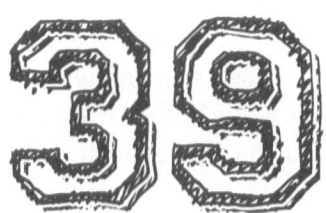

I WAITED UNTIL WE WERE digging into the potato salad Jason had made before I launched into my mission of *getting to the bottom of things*. That's what I started to call it, because it felt like we were always swimming on the surface of this very deep shit ocean and the truth was somewhere down where the water was cold and dark, and well, full of turds or sharks maybe.

"Tell me what happened." I shoved a giant forkful of salad into my mouth and didn't bother to wipe off the mayonnaise that I could feel hanging out on the corners of my lips.

Jason leaned forward and swiped at my face with a paper towel. "You are such a slob."

I waited for him to reply, ignoring his comment. We'd already come to the conclusion that I was a pig and he was there to clean up after me, and the arrangement suited us both fine.

He rolled his eyes and stared down at his plate, picking with his plastic fork among the bones and other scraps of food that remained there, as if finding just the right bite was critical to restoring happiness in his life.

"You're just going to get bored. There's nothing for me to say. You've read it all in the news."

"No one has your story, Jason, trust me. And when they don't have the story, they fill in the blanks with the most ridiculous stuff." I didn't tell him that people had conjectured that he'd had an affair with the coach's wife, that he'd been accused of being mad about the coach having a nicer car than he had, that his former friends were saying that he'd always had a bad attitude towards the coach from the beginning of high school.

All of that crap was lies, obviously, since years of contrary stories had been in the news before the coach's death. Jason had been the perfect football star — respectful, grateful, attentive, and dedicated. Only now that he was a murderer did he get to become a jealous, disrespectful, bitter adulterer. People are such assholes.

"Fine, you want to know, I'll tell you. And you can go out there and tell all those reporters and they can print it up and sell a million papers, I don't care."

I stopped him by putting my hand on his arm. "People could tear my fingernails out and I wouldn't tell them what you say to me."

He looked down at my hands. "Are you sure that hasn't already happened?"

I glanced at my hands, knowing what I'd see there. "So I chew my nails. Big deal. I'm upset over your situation and whenever I'm upset, my fingernails become very appetizing. Don't change the subject."

"You're the one talking about torture." He winked at me.

"No!" I pointed at his face. "The puppy dog winky eyes will not work on me today!"

"Today? Do they ever work on you?"

"No, especially not since you started growing that hellaciously awful hoo-hoo on your face." I pointed at the beard that was becoming way too bushy for my taste. It was only about a half-inch long, but still ... *ew.*

He laughed so hard he dropped his fork and flipped potato salad up at me. It landed in my hair.

I stared up at it and sighed. "First he lost his looks, then his coordination. It was all downhill from there."

He reached over and took the salad out of my hair and then held his hand out as he stood. "Come on."

"Where are we going?" I asked, standing with him after putting my plate on the ground.

"Out to the clubhouse."

"Clubhouse? Hmmm sounds interesting."

I followed him through the kitchen and out into his garage. He opened up the passenger door of his Camaro and waited for me to get in.

"Are we driving somewhere?" This was a bad idea, and we both knew it. Reporters still camped out just at the end of the driveway and they were all prepared to follow Jason should he ever try to leave. He was free to go anywhere he wanted, so long as it wasn't in public; they made sure of that.

"Do you trust me?" he asked, shutting the door behind me.

"I'm in the damn car, aren't I?"

My voice was muffled behind the closed window, but he nodded and then left me there, circling around the back of the car to get into the driver's seat. The door slammed with a heavy thunk, and Jason put his hands on the wheel.

I looked first at him and then out the front window, staring at the inside of the garage door.

"Where are we going?" I asked.

"Nowhere. I just miss driving my car."

I looked at him again. "Sucks being trapped in the house all the time, huh?"

"Yeah." He laughed but it wasn't happiness that came out with the sound. "I never thought I'd miss school so much."

"I never realized how much school would suck without you in it," I confessed.

He looked at me and gave me a sad smile. "Too bad we didn't know how awesome this could be before, eh?"

"How awesome what could be?"

"Me and you. You and me." He smiled like he was embarrassed.

I snorted. "Yeah, right. Like Brittney would have allowed that."

He looked back out the windshield, his jaw jumping a little. He might have been angry, it was hard to tell because he didn't say anything.

"So, are you going to tell me the story or not?" I was trying not to get excited about hearing the whole thing, but it was difficult. It wasn't that I was interested from a voyeuristic sense; it was more that I had this ridiculous idea that I would be able to uncover some otherwise overlooked evidence that could help him. My superhero complex would not give up the ghost.

"Yeah, I'll tell you. Just let me go back there and put it all straight in my head. I've been trying to forget it ever since it happened."

We both let out a long sigh and faced the front of the car. The only sound we could hear was the ticking of his non-digital clock on the dashboard. I counted out a full two minutes in seconds before he started talking.

I'D GONE TO THE STADIUM early. None of the players were there yet. The coach was in his office, going through his playbook and watching videos of the other team, something he did before every game."

"Was that normal for you? Did you always go in early too?"

"No. I usually rode over with Joe and Derek, sometimes Jamahl, and got there an hour before game time."

"Why didn't you go with them this time?"

Jason's jaw got tense again, but then he answered, something I hadn't expected him to do, since he'd been so evasive before. "Because ... I wanted to talk to the coach about something ... personal."

Jason looked down into his lap, emotions of all kinds fleeting across his face.

"What was it?"

Jason's eyebrow went up and he looked angry. "Something personal. That's all I'm going to say."

"Was it about football or something else?"

ELLE CASEY

"Personal. It was personal."

Sensing he wasn't going to go any further with this part of the story, I changed tack. "Okay, what then?"

"I went in there, to his office, and brought up this thing I wanted to talk to him about, and he just ... acted like an asshole."

"Asshole? Like what ... he was rude?"

"He was ...," Jason started punching the steering wheel over and over, first lightly and then harder, "...nonchalant ... like it didn't matter."

"Like what didn't matter?" My heart was going nuts. I knew I was about to hear something that no one else but Jason and the coach knew.

"The personal thing I needed to talk to him about!" Jason gave one more punch to the wheel and a loud beep came from the horn, echoing all over the garage.

I was a little scared at the violence, and I think he was too. We both stared at the wheel and then at his hand. There was a small dot of blood there where he'd opened up a cut on his knuckle.

I had a hard time swallowing when I saw that. All I could picture was that fist killing a man.

"Sorry," he said. "I guess I have a temper sometimes."

A shiver ran through me and I wondered for a moment if I should be scared to be in the car with him like this, with his dad upstairs in his office and no one around to see what was happening.

Then a second later I wanted to slap myself. Jason was my friend. Jason would never hurt me. It didn't matter to me that he had actually murdered someone. It was an accident, a mistake. He hadn't gone into that office that day to kill anyone.

He wiped the blood on his shorts and stared out the front window again. "Anyway, words got heated, the conversation went downhill fast, and then he moved and I moved and there was some shoving and punching and down he went."

"Down?"

"Yeah. He fell and his head hit the desk and he didn't get up."

"What'd you do?" I was having a hard time not being dizzy at this point. I felt like I was there watching it. And let me tell you

ALL THE GLORY

... if you've never had an actual murderer tell you about how he killed someone, I don't think you could understand what I was going through. Let's just say it wasn't anywhere near pleasant.

"I just stood there. I waited for people to come. I don't know how long it was before they were there, but they found me standing there doing nothing."

"Did anyone say anything to you?"

"Everyone just kept asking what happened, and then someone yelled out that I killed him and everyone started shouting and the cops showed up. They took me away, but not before half the guys I used to call my best friends were threatening to end me. They looked at me with such hate ..." He shook his head silently, staring off into space.

"Wow." I had to wipe the sweat off my upper lip. "That must have been intense. Just hearing the story..." I couldn't finish because it was completely insensitive and more than a little stupid to be comparing my hearing what he'd done to him actually living through it.

"Yeah. Intense. You could say that." He was lost in thought, nodding his head at nothing.

"I'm just wondering ...," I paused to make sure he was listening, "... I mean, if that personal thing you were talking about was something important, and he came at you ... did he come at you? I mean, maybe it was just self-defense or whatever. Just ... maybe he had a responsibility to do something that he didn't do, or maybe you felt ... threatened." I was grasping at straws, but at the same time I was waiting with baited breath, hoping that I'd struck on something that might help him. Teachers and coaches were supposed to help students when they went to them with personal problems, right? They have a responsibility, right?

"Responsibility..." He practically spit the word out. "Responsibility. Yeah. That's fucking awesome. Just great."

"Great as iiinnnn ... you think he had one or that he should have had one?" This was getting confusing, but he was talking and I knew of course that he was hiding something. *Getting to the bottom of things* had become my reason for being.

"Never mind. I'm done. Story's over." He threw his door open and got out. He didn't even wait for me before going back into the house.

When I finally got inside, his father was standing in the hall looking bewildered.

"What was that all about?" he asked, looking over his shoulder towards the front hall.

"I don't know." I didn't want to tell him what Jason and I had been talking about. He probably wished the whole thing would just disappear like pretty much everyone else on the planet had from their lives. I tried to think of a single person who would be happy that Jason did what he did and no one came to mind. Nobody was served by the coach's life being ended so soon. No wonder everyone was talking about sending Jason to the electric chair.

"I should probably get going," I said.

"Have a good workout?" he asked, walking me to the door.

"I guess. I'm always sore."

He looked down at me with his hand on the front doorknob. "Well, if it makes any difference, I can see your gains."

I looked down at my stomach. "My gains?"

"Muscle tone. And you've lost a lot of body fat. It's obvious."

"It is?"

"Your clothes are hanging off you. You have baggy-butt now."

I laughed. "Baggy butt? What parent says that?"

He looked so awkward as soon as I said that I felt bad.

"I'm sorry," I said, "that was rude."

"No, I just ... I realized that I'm not even sure what a parent is supposed to do anymore." His eyes got a little watery.

I put my hand on his arm. "No parent would. Don't be too hard on yourself."

"I try not to be. Thanks for coming over, Katy. It means the world to him, and that's saying a lot these days. You're the only one..."

"Don't get me started on those hypocritical assholes," I said before I could filter my mouth.

He laughed and pulled me into a hug. "You're a great kid, Katy. Never change."

I patted him on the back. "You're the only adult who's ever said that to me in my entire life."

He pushed me out of the hug but held onto my upper arms, looking me dead in the eye. "I am one of the very few adults who's had the horrible luck of having the veil that covers reality lifted. I see what others can't or won't. Trust me when I tell you that your honesty, your smart mouth, and your determination are going to take you a lot farther in life than anything those other kids at your school might boast about."

I gave him my most annoying suck-up expression. "You mean being prom queen *won't* guarantee me friends, financial success, and eternal happiness?"

He laughed and aimed me for the door. "You got it. Now get out of here. Your parents are probably wondering if they still have a daughter."

"Do I come here too often?" I asked, feeling just a little self-conscious about it.

"No. Come here as often as you like. More often if you want. Jason waits for you all day."

"He does?" My face went warm at that confession. Sometimes I still wondered why he even hung out with me at all.

"You bet. See you tomorrow?"

"Maybe. I have a monster final and physics hates me."

"Bring your books over here. Jason was a wiz at that stuff."

"You mean he *is* a wiz at it."

His dad leaned on the doorframe. "You're right. He is." His smile was sad.

I left without another word, for the first time not even noticing whether there were any reporters around. It was like they'd become a part of the landscape. Here on Chestnut Lane there were mailboxes, lawns, cars, lampposts, piles of dog doo here and there, and vultures. Vultures who carried cameras and microphones. This was my world.

IT WAS ALMOST THE END of football season and Bobby had been harassing me for a couple months to go to a game with him. It felt disloyal to watch any of those turd football players on the field when Jason was still locked inside his house, but Bobby was finally able to convince me that eating a paper bowl full of nachos and orange non-cheese would do my heart good. When he'd said heart, we both knew he hadn't meant the one pumping away in my chest that would surely be suffering from the onslaught of transfats; he meant the one that ached for a certain boy with a doomed future.

"I'm so glad you finally came," Bobby said, sliding the nachos off the counter of the snack stand and handing them to me. "You're turning into a total hermit these days."

"No, I'm focusing on my grades instead of football. Trust me, I'm better off for it."

"Grades? Is that why you're at Jason's every single day of every single week of every single month?"

I elbowed him in the ribs. "Shut up or I'm going home." I used a chip to move some beans, chili peppers, and orange non-cheese around. I have an issue with ratios being off in a bowl of nachos. Each chip must have a little of everything or my world feels completely off.

"Hey, I'm not arguing, okay? You look totally fab."

"I do?" I smiled, knowing for a fact that he wasn't blowing smoke up my butt. I'd weighed myself that morning and found that I'd officially lost fifteen pounds of fat and replaced it all with toned muscles. Jason had told me just yesterday that I was now in better shape than any girl at school, including everyone on the cheer team and the girls' basketball team. Adding a half-hour of the elliptical machine to my routine four days a week had made a real difference.

"Yes, you do. Totally fab-u-lous. I can actually see your muscles in your arms and legs. You're like … fit. Fitter than fit. Shakira-fit."

I grinned like crazy. "Thanks for noticing. I had to buy new jeans again last week."

"I saw." He leaned back to look at my butt. "They're good for your buns. Very flattering."

Happily crunching away on my nachos, I didn't even notice Brittney coming up on us until she was practically stepping on my toes.

"Excuse *me*," she said in a bitchy tone. She was all decked out in her cheer uniform, a small gym bag over her shoulder holding her pom-poms; I could see pieces of their plastic strips in our black and orange school colors peeking out from the partially open zipper.

"Sometimes there just is no excuse," Bobby said, raising an eyebrow at her in challenge.

My chip-crunching slowed as I came to grips with the fact that I was facing Jason's ex after spending nearly three months with him non-stop — a fact that the newspapers were still reporting fairly regularly. Was she mad about that? Jealous? I guessed we were going to find out.

"What's that supposed to mean?" she asked, looking first at Bobby and then at me.

I shrugged. "How'm I supposed to know? I'm just eating nachos." Having those reporters outside Jason's door for months had made me a lot more circumspect about engaging people in public. Before, I would have met a situation like this toe-to-toe, bitch-to-bitch; but today, not so much. I just wanted to claim our seats in the nosebleed section and pretend to enjoy football for an hour or so before I begged to be released from the boredom.

She turned her attention fully on me. "You know, everyone knows what you're doing," she said, her face all twisted up. "So *pitiful*..."

"She's not doing anything, Brittney," Bobby said, getting all riled up.

I waved my hand in the air between them. "Hey, listen, I don't mean to alarm anyone, but these nachos are already working their magic, so I suggest you be on your way, Britt."

She wrinkled her face at me. "What does that even mean?"

Bobby looked at me, his expression kind of blank. "Did you just threaten to pass gas?"

I shrugged. "I can't be held responsible for all these beans." I lifted up my paper box to show them how generous the lady behind the counter had been this evening. "Beans, beans, good for the heart..."

"Oh my god, you are so *weird*," Brittney said, before leaving in a hurry.

Bobby started giggling and eventually had to bend over to keep from busting apart.

"I can't believe you," he gasped out.

"What?" I crunched on another chip, waiting for him to recover. I was already bored with football and they hadn't even hiked the ball yet.

"You just ... you just ..."

My eyes scanned the entrance to the stadium and landed on a group of reporters surrounding some players. There were a few kids mingling with them, all of them wearing smaller versions of the team's jerseys.

I stopped crunching my chips.

"You just scared Brittney away with threats of farting on her!" Bobby was still laughing.

"No, I didn't. I issued threats of farting in her *general direction*. Not the same thing."

I left him there and started walking first slowly and then pretty quickly over to the group of players standing around. Some of them were posing for pictures with the kids, while others were tossing balls around. It looked like a publicity event.

When Bobby finally realized I'd left him behind, he jogged in my wake, arriving at my side panting for breath. "Where'd you go? You totally ditched me back there."

"What's going on here?" I asked, gesturing with my nachos at the scene before us.

Bobby pointed to a banner that had been strung up on the chain link fence next to them. "Charity thingy. You remember ... Jason used to be involved in it too. It's a team thing."

My eyes bugged out as I recognized one of the kids from the photos I had on my computer. It wasn't the one I'd seen with Jason, but that didn't stop me from being insanely curious about him.

"What's the big deal?" Bobby asked. "Can we go now? Have you finished ogling yet? The game's going to start soon."

I nudged him again. "The game can't start without all these guys out there. And besides, I'm not ogling the players, fool, I'm ogling the kids."

"Oh, that's not disturbing at all."

I sighed loudly. I used to have so much patience for Bobby's silliness but now I was just anxious to move on from it. "I've seen that kid before." I nodded towards the group.

Bobby moved in closer and dropped his voice. "Which one?"

"The one with the jersey. The black kid."

"Which black kid with a jersey? There are five of them over there."

"The little one. With the red shoes."

We both watched him smiling at one of the players and nodding.

"How do you know him?" Bobby asked.

"I don't *know* him, I've just seen pictures of him."

"In the news? In a magazine? In your dreams? Where?"

"Just ... hold these." I handed him my nachos and left him standing there, my eyes focused on the kid.

The boy didn't see me coming until the player he was talking to lifted his gaze and glared in my direction.

The boy turned around, his eyes going wide, probably trying to figure out why I was about to get pounded.

"Hey," I said to the boy.

"What're you doing here?" the player asked me.

"You're Jamahl, right?" I asked, turning my attention to him.

"Yeah? So?"

"So? Seen Jason lately? Your friend, Jason, remember him?"

The kid switched his bodyweight to the other foot and started looking around like he was trying to find an escape route.

"Fuck that," Jamahl said, putting his hand on the kid's shoulder. "Come on, kid, let's get outta here." He turned them both around and looked over his shoulder at me, lifting his lip in disgust. "Don't want you getting involved in some bad shit."

I reached out and grabbed the kid's hand before he could get too far away. "Wait! I want to talk to you."

Jamahl dropped the kid's shoulder and turned around to face me, his chest puffing out. He seemed to grow about three inches taller. I tried not to let it intimidate me, but it was difficult.

"You need to get gone, girl, before you get hurt."

"You're gonna hit a girl?" the kid asked, sounding shocked and maybe a little impressed.

Jamahl faltered. He looked embarrassed. "Nah, man, I don't hit girls. Never hit girls. That ain't cool."

I smiled as genuinely as I could at the kid. "I saw a picture of you once. At the boy's club place where you hang out sometimes. You were with these guys. You looked really cool in your new red shoes." I looked down at his feet.

The boy smiled a little. "Thanks. Coach got these for me."

"Really?" I nodded, acting impressed but inside feeling really sad that the coach wouldn't be able to do that for these kids anymore. "That's cool. He was a cool guy, huh?"

Jamahl let out a long hiss of air that sounded like steam escaping.

He turned slightly away to signal to a couple of his friends. I knew I had to hurry if I wanted to accomplish anything with this kid.

"So there was this *other* kid in all the pictures I saw too, but I don't know his name. Do you know who he is? He has a big afro, maybe about a couple inches taller than you?"

The boy smiled a little. "That's Leo. He's got some big ol' hair. He likes to pick it out all the time. Says the chicks like it that way." He rubbed his head from the back to the front. "My momma says no way can I walk around gettin' all kinds of lint in my hair like that. She says I play too hard to pay the right amount of attention to my head."

I laughed. "She's probably right. I think it's more fun to play sports than brush your hair all the time."

"Yeah. I guess." He looked at Jamahl and the three other football players who were approaching us. They were like a wall of angry muscle.

"I'd like to talk to Leo," I said in a rush. "Do you know how I can contact him?"

The kid shrugged. "He doesn't come 'round no more. But he lives near me. I never see him, though."

"Where do you live?" I felt like a total creeper, asking this little dude where he lived, but I wasn't going to let that stop me. I was on the verge of *getting to the bottom of things* and that kept me going even when Jamahl and his three friends stood there like Little Man's personal body guards.

"You need to get gone," one of them said to me.

"You need to ease up on the steroids," Bobby said from behind me.

I turned around to warn him away but I was interrupted.

"What'd you say, gay boy?"

"Gay boy? Seriously? What decade are you living in, anyway? That is *so* not p.c.. It's not even creative." Bobby rolled his eyes. "But I'm going to let it slide since you've obviously been injecting the 'roids right into your nut sack, and it's affected your ability to think properly." He turned to me. "Are we finished here?"

I looked at the kid who was now partially hidden behind Jamahl.

"She wanted to know where I live," the boy said in a tiny voice.

They all frowned at me, making me instantly feel like a total perv. Why did I want to know where he lived? What was I going to do ... stalk his friend? My brain wasn't putting all the pieces together yet, so I just ran on instinct until it was able to catch up.

"I just wanted to send them some gift certificates for more shoes, Jesus, ease up." I probably should have been a little disturbed at how easily that lie appeared and then rolled off my tongue, but I wasn't. It was time to be a super-spy, CIA-style, and I wasn't going to get there by playing a nun.

"If you want to donate shoes or whatever, you do it at the center," one of the less-intimidating looking guys said. "You don't get to pick which kid gets the money; it goes into a group fund."

I pointed to the boy now standing next to Jamahl. "He got shoes in his size. Looks like they were bought specifically for him by the coach himself."

The boy's head dropped, his chin resting on his chest now, but not before I saw the look of abject horror on his face.

I was completely confused.

"I gotta go," he said, right before he took off running.

"Where's he going?" Jamahl asked, sounding just as confused as I was.

"How the hell should I know?" answered the non-p.c. 'roid lover.

"Go get him and find out what his problem is." Jamahl turned his attention to me. "And you can take off too. Ain't nobody around here got any love for that murderer you're hanging out with."

He turned to go, so I raised my voice to make sure he could hear me.

"That guy used to be your *friend*. Don't try to lie and say he wasn't!"

"Everybody makes mistakes!" he yelled back.

"EXACTLY!" I screamed. I might have sounded like a deranged mental patient, but it didn't matter. He just kept walking and the rest of the crowd turned their backs on us. None of them were willing to forgive the kind of mistake that Jason had made, and I really couldn't blame them. I still wasn't exactly sure what made it so easy for me.

WHAT IN THE HELL WAS that all about?" Bobby asked, handing me back my nachos when we were climbing the stairs to the stands.

"I need to find that kid." I was running through my options in my mind, not paying any attention to where we were going.

"What kid? The one with the shoes?" Bobby pushed me to the right, selecting a row for us to sit in. Several kids saw us sitting down and got up to move, leaving the entire section empty except for Bobby and me. *Bastards*.

"No. The other one who wasn't there."

Bobby sat down and pulled me down with him. "Explain yourself or I'm taking all your nachos away."

I handed him the paper box. "Here. Take them. I don't want them anymore anyway."

Bobby took the paper and stared down into it with the saddest look on his face.

"What? What's the problem? You don't want them?" I started to take them back, but he pulled them out of my reach.

"You have changed, like *completely*." He looked up and stared at me. "You used to say I'd have to pry the nachos from your cold dead hands before I could have any. Now you're just giving them away."

Hearing I'd changed completely should have been a compliment, but the way he said it, it didn't feel that way. There was definite condemnation in his tone.

Trying not to get annoyed, I leaned back a little and asked, "What's going on with you?" This was my little deflection technique I brought out during those times I didn't feel like talking about me. The subject of *me* was too complicated right now for self-examination and Bobby picking at me was sure to bring out the angry version of my new self.

"It's not *me* that has things going on, soul-sister, it's *you*." He looked me up and down. "You're all buff and you're not eating nachos and you're picking fights with football players twice your size, and now you sound like you're considering stalking a child. I'm seriously worried about you."

The anxiety that had built up inside me over the confrontation with Jamahl and his meat-head buddies spilled over. "I haven't changed that much, okay? My eyes have been opened, but that's a good thing! And I'm not stalking anyone!"

Several heads from three rows down turned around to see what all the fuss was about.

I lowered my voice. "I'm fine. I'm better than fine. I would have thought you'd be proud of me for all the weight I've lost. I can bench almost a hundred pounds now."

Bobby put the nachos down on the seat next to him and pulled me into a hug. "I *am* proud of you. You look amazing, like I've already told you about ten times. And I know Jason is behind it, so I'm really happy towards him too."

"And yet you say he's a bad influence." I felt like all the wind had been taken from my sails. Jason had changed my life for the better and everyone in the world hated him except for me and his dad. In a sick and twisted way I saw that as the world preferring I'd stayed fat and alone.

"He's not really a bad influence, he's just ..."

I waited for the rest, but it didn't come.

"He's just what? Finish your sentence."

Bobby sighed. "I'm afraid it will make you angry."

"Since when has that ever stopped you?"

"Since you grew up!" he yelled.

We both stared at each other, searching each other's eyes. He had blue eyeliner on that day. I can remember it as if it were in front of me right now.

"I'm still three months away from my birthday," I said, trying to argue a point he was making that I didn't really understand. "I won't be an adult until then."

"You became an adult the minute you went over to see Jason in prison."

His words brought a profound sadness with them. After hearing Bobby say that, it all became very clear that the last bits of my childhood had been stolen away from me. The me that started high school this year was completely unlike the me who sat on the stadium bench waiting for a football game to start. I was a different person, outside and in. I used to pray that would happen, that adulthood would hurry up and get to me; now I wished it would go away and let me be a kid for a little while longer.

"Are you going to tell me what the big deal is with this kid or what?" he asked.

I was grateful for the change of subject, so I started talking immediately. "That kid with the red shoes knows the kid who I think was Jason's charity kid brother or whatever they call them."

"I believe the term is *little brother*."

"Whatever. I need to find that kid."

"Why?"

"I don't know." I started biting my fingernail, trying to find a spot that wasn't already gone. It was hopeless; at this point I was left with just cuticles to destroy.

"Is it something to do with Jason?"

"Yes, of course it is. Isn't everything?" I admitted then to myself and Bobby that Jason had become my life. I never went anywhere anymore unless it was to see him or get something for him. It probably should have made me bitter, but it didn't. It felt good. It felt *right*.

Bobby sighed. "Yes, *unfortunately*."

I ignored that comment.

"So what is it?" he pressed.

"I can't say."

"Why? Is it a big secret?"

The football players for both teams came out onto the field in a steady stream, and the school band began playing some horn-heavy song that got people stomping their feet.

"I don't know," I looked at Bobby and shrugged, "I just want to meet him and talk to him."

Bobby narrowed his eyes at me. "You're not telling me everything."

"I'm telling you that I want to meet him and talk to him. He was Jason's friend or little brother or whatever, and yet he's never contacted Jason that I know of and he's quit going to that club. That has to *mean* something." Everything means something. Nothing is random. Being with Jason and living through his trag-edy on the sidelines had taught me that.

"Maybe he got let down along with everyone else. Maybe he's broken-hearted. That seems like a natural reaction to me. Of course he'd want to be away from the source of all that pain."

"Sure, of course it is." My balloon burst. Bobby was making complete sense and I wasn't. A lot of the spark left my voice. "I guess I just want to know for sure, and I want him to know that if he wants to visit Jason, I could help with that."

Bobby crossed his eyes for a second. Then he frowned at me. "You want to bring a little kid over to visit a *murderer*?" He shook his head as he looked out onto the field. "Jesus, you really are losing it."

I stood up so fast I knocked Bobby sideways.

"What?" he said, surprised.

"You know what, Bobby?!" I was so upset I could hardly see straight. "Next time I want your opinion on anything, I'll *ask* for it." I sidestepped down the row until I reached the aisle. "In the meantime, you can *stick* it!"

"Wait ... what? Where are you going? Are you leaving?! But I don't want to stick it! Don't leave, Katy!" he yelled behind me.

I ran down the steps as fast as I could, ignoring the annoyed looks I was getting and the rowdy crowd farther down in the stands having a great old time while I fell part inside.

Bobby had always been my biggest fan and most loyal supporter, but now it felt like he belonged with all of these people and I belonged in Jason's house, living like a social hermit with zero chance at future happiness.

I had lost everything from my old life, and it was hard even for me to believe that I had gained anything by being Jason's one and only supporter. It felt like I had, but all the evidence in front of me said otherwise. I'd never been so alone in my life.

JASON TEXTED ME USING HIS dad's phone to ask if I want-ed to come over and work out, but I lied and said I had to go to Bobby's to work on a biology project.

It galled me to have to do it, but I texted Bobby and told him to cover for me if Jason called him. I hadn't spoken to Bobby since Friday when I stormed off at the football game, ignoring all his texts, calls, and emails. I hadn't cooled down enough to forgive him, and I didn't want to say anything else I'd regret. We'd both already said plenty.

I was walking out the door to get into my car when Bobby pulled into my driveway. I couldn't ignore him because he was blocking me in. He rolled down his window and stuck his arm and head out.

"What are you doing here?" I said in an emotionless voice. "I told you I needed you to cover for me."

"What's better cover than me coming to pick you up?" He grinned hugely.

I refused to be charmed. "If you're thinking that I'm blowing Jason off because I don't want to be with him, then you're wrong."

"I wasn't thinking that. I was thinking that if it's so important that you'd risk lying to your new best friend, then it must be something really big that I should be there for."

A lump grew to the size of a whole walnut in my throat. My eyes stung with tears. My voice was raw when it finally started working. "That was a low blow, even for you."

He rubbed his windowsill with his finger and shrugged. "Hey, what can I say? I'm not a very nice person when someone breaks my heart."

I hugged myself around the middle, turning a little so he wouldn't see my face.

"Are you going to get in the car or what?" he said a minute later.

"Why should I?" I asked, my voice still shaky.

"Because there's a telephoto lens pointed in this direction and your blotchy complexion is going to be plastered all over the front page of the paper if you don't hide it soon."

I choked out a laugh and then turned to go to my car. "I have to go. Move out of my way."

"Sorry. My car won't work unless you're in it."

"Bobby!" I screamed, spinning to face him.

"Katy!" he screamed back.

I could see tears in his eyes. That's when I knew I could push this too far, and hurting Bobby was the last thing I'd ever want to do in my life.

I swung my purse off my shoulder and slammed it down on my trunk, glaring at him. "You are so *pushy*, you know that?"

"Get in my car, bitch. I don't have all day."

I had to bite my tongue to stop from laughing. When Bobby called me bitch, it meant I was forgiven and life was going to go back to normal, and I really needed some normal in my life.

I grabbed my bag and wound my way around the cars to get to the passenger side of his. Opening the door I bent over and stuck my head inside. "You aren't going to be happy about where we're going."

He shrugged and looked out the front windshield. "Wherever you go, I follow. BFF Code. I don't play when it comes to The Code."

I got in and buckled up.

"Where to, Mistress Bitchness?"

"South side. Downtown."

Bobby tipped his head down and looked at me, pretending he was looking over glasses. "Are you completely off the range now?"

"Just go. And hurry up. It's almost lunchtime. Church is going to be over soon."

"Church? Oh boy. This should be interesting."

Bobby put the car in reverse and drove me downtown. I figured I'd start my hunt for the boy with the afro there and see what I could turn up.

YOU KNOW, YOUR FACE HAS been all over the news for months. People are going to recognize you." Bobby and I were sitting in his car, parked outside a Lutheran church just two blocks down from the Boys' Center.

"No they're not," I said, opening up my big bag. "I brought a disguise." I winked at him as I put on one of my dad's baseball hats and a pair of big sunglasses I'd taken from my mother's glove compartment.

"Do you have an elastic to put your hair up with?"

I nodded, finding a lost scrunchy in the bottom of my purse. I quickly threw my hair up into a bun and secured it under the bottom edge of the hat.

"How do I look?"

"Totally incognito. Who are you again?"

I grinned. "Guckenberger. Katy Guckenberger. Super spy extraordinaire."

He snorted. "Super dork, maybe."

Bobby and I got out of the car and went into the church, slipping into the last pew as quietly as possible. My eyes scanned the interior of the place, going from pew to pew, stopping whenever they got to a small kid about the size I imagined the boy with the afro to be.

"What are we doing exactly?" Bobby whispered.

"Looking for the boy with the afro."

Bobby pointed. "There's one over there."

I grabbed his finger and yanked his hand down to the spot between us. "Try to be a tiny bit less obvious next time," I said through gritted teeth.

"Ahhh, we're going super-spy on this one."

"Yes. Super-spy, super-chill, super-not-obvious."

An older lady with gray hair and a blue hat with plastic fruit on it turned around and glared at us.

"Sorry," I whispered, shrinking down into my shoulders.

All of the kids in this place were too little to be the one I was looking for, and we had three more churches in the vicinity to check out before I was ready to give up.

"Come on," I whispered to Bobby. "Let's bail."

He slid out behind me and followed me out of the church.

"And why exactly are we hunting down a boy with an afro?"

"I told you already ... he was Jason's friend and I need to talk to him."

"Can you tell me why?"

"No, I can't."

"I'm not gonna lie ... that hurts my feelings to know that you're keeping secrets from me. You've never done that before."

He said it in kind of a joking tone, but I knew better. I stopped and put my hand on his arm. "Jason told me some things in confidence that led me to believe I might learn some more things about what happened that night during the incident from this kid."

Why I thought Jason would have shared his personal problems with a kid, personal problems he talked to the coach about, was unclear even to me. But I had to know for sure that this boy had nothing to offer the people investigating Jason's crime. If he told me he wasn't Jason's friend, that Jason never shared any personal problems with him, then I'd let it go. But until I heard it straight out of his mouth, I wasn't going to be able to just walk away from it.

"Why do you think this kid has anything to do with anything?"

"Because, Bobby, friends don't just disappear like that without a reason."

"Uhhh ... I'd think the fact that a friend murdered a guy you respect would be reason enough."

"No, that's not why those guys on the team stopped being Jason's friend."

"It's not?"

I shook my head, frustrated with myself. I wasn't making sense, I knew that, but I kept trying to explain. "No. They were worried about what it would say about them, not what it meant about Jason and their friendship."

"I don't get it."

"Real friends, true friends, don't walk away without a word."

"Unless they see their friend murder someone."

"No, because first of all, they didn't see anything. All they saw was Jason standing there in the office and the coach on the floor. He hit his head on the desk and died. But they didn't know the facts. They still don't."

"But they thought they did."

"Maybe, maybe not ... but a real friend would have had at least one conversation with Jason to find out, to see him eye-to-eye and know for sure that their friendship needed to be over."

"So you're saying that none of those guys were his real friends."

"Yes, I'm saying that and I'm saying that this little kid wouldn't have the same issues as the players."

"What do you mean?"

"I mean that he's little. He's young. He's ... pure."

"*Ew.* I don't even know what you mean by that, but it sounds wrong."

"Argh, Bobby! Stop it! I'm just trying to say that if he was Jason's friend, and I think he was ... or is ... he wasn't one of those players all up in the coach's butt or worried about what people at school would think or what scouts would think or college entrance committees or whatever. That little kid would have made an effort to see Jason or talk to him or say something to him through a mutual friend, right?"

"He's just a kid. I think you're giving him too much credit. Kids are idiots."

"No, he's not a baby. He's, like, twelve or something. He probably even has his own phone. He could have texted Jason."

"Maybe he did. They took Jason's phone, right?"

I had nothing to say to that because Bobby was one hundred percent right, and I was completely crazy. Just hearing Bobby ask me the questions made that perfectly clear.

"Whatever. I just need to hear it from him that he's not Jason's friend and he doesn't want to see him anymore."

Bobby threw his arm around my back and started walking us to the car. "Okay, crazy lady, I'm in. Where to next?"

"The Baptist church just over there."

He altered our direction so we could walk to the church using the sidewalk on the opposite side of the street.

We reached the bottom of the stairs to the Baptist church. Singing could be heard even outside the doors. They were seriously rocking the party in there.

"You sure we need to do this?" he asked.

"Yep, I'm sure." My heart was beating way too fast. "Come on, let's go before I lose my nerve."

Bobby linked his arm in mine and marched up the stairs, fearless in pink and purple.

When we got to the top, I stopped him before he could open the door. "I love you, you know."

He leaned in and kissed me on the cheek. "I know you do. Come on, Gucky-Duck. Let's go find that kid."

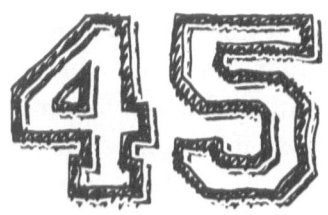

I DIDN'T RECOGNIZE HIM AT first. He'd shaved all his hair off, leaving just a light fuzz behind.

"There he is," I said, gesturing with my chin at the kid sitting in a pew just a few rows up from us on the other side of the aisle.

"I don't see any 'fros over there," Bobby said, scanning the crowd.

The preacher was saying something about loving your neighbor, his voice booming out over the small congregation. I ignored him, totally focusing all my attention on the kid.

"He cut his hair," I whispered.

Everyone stood up all of a sudden and started hugging each other. Bobby and I slowly got to our feet and just looked confused. Then someone tapped me on the shoulder and I turned around.

"God loves you, child," said a lady in bright purple behind me. And then she leaned in and enveloped me in a heavily-perfumed embrace, her bosom nearly suffocating me.

"Thanks," I said, "... uh, God loves you too."

She let me go and beamed at me. "That he does, that he does." She held her arms open for Bobby. "God loves you too, sweet pea."

Bobby grinned. "He does?" He tried to just shake her hand, but she grabbed it and pulled him in for a bosom-suffocation instead. "Indeed he does. He loves every last one of us sinners."

"Oh, I'm not a sinner," Bobby said, "I'm just gay."

She let him go and put her hands on either side of his face, pushing his cheeks in so hard it made his mouth pucker up. "We're all sinners and it doesn't have anything to do with who we're sleeping with, child. Every day you wake up, you probably sin again and again, but God loves you anyway. Have a blessed day." And then she was off to hug her neighbors behind her and give them a little boobie suffocation action too while she was at it.

Bobby looked at me, barely containing his laughter. "God loves you, Katy."

I wanted to laugh along with him, but for some reason the sentiment was messing me up. I wanted Jason to be here, to feel this, to experience this. I decided then and there that I would make that happen, even if he fought me on it. Before he went away to prison for life, he would come to this church and get a hug from the big-boobied purple dress lady.

The preacher said something about services next week and then everyone started filing out of the pews.

Panic set in. "We have to get over to him!" I said in a whisper-shout. "He's leaving!"

Bobby stood up super straight and side-stepped over to the end of our row. I held onto his shirt as he made his way past everyone.

"Excuse me, pardon me, coming through," he said. "Thank you, oh, I'm sorry, was that your toe? Oh my god, I love your hat! So cute! Excuse me, need some fresh air, pardon me..." And so it went until we were outside the doors in a crowd of people chatting in small groups.

"Where'd he go?" I asked, standing on my tiptoes, scanning the front lawn of the church.

"There!" Bobby said, pointing off to our right.

The boy was walking with an older lady, leaving the church, headed down the sidewalk.

We followed without any further discussion.

"Operation stalking a child has now officially commenced," Bobby said under his breath as we walked down the cracked and uneven sidewalk.

"Shut up, I'm not stalking anyone. I just want to talk to him."

"So go up to him and talk. He's right there." Bobby made a sweeping gesture with his hand like he was bowling.

"Shhhhh, not so loud. I don't want him to hear us."

Bobby put his hand on my arm to stop me. "I don't get it. Why aren't you going up there to talk to him now? Why are we just following him?"

I brushed him off and started walking again. "I need to wait until he's alone."

Bobby caught up to me, talking in a sing-song voice. "Aaaand the creepy just keeps getting creeeeepier."

I ignored him and everything else around us, totally focused on getting this kid's address. We were rewarded a couple minutes later when he turned up a small driveway and went through a chain link fence that ringed the house before disappearing inside with the woman.

I stopped and held my arm out so Bobby would stop too. "Memorize this address," I said, staring at the number on the outside of the house. "Fifty-three Shady Oak Drive."

"Got it. Now what?" Bobby was looking up and down the street. "This isn't the nicest neighborhood in the world, you know."

I chewed my lip as I considered our next move. "I don't know what to do next. Wait?"

"Wait? For what?"

"I don't know ... for something to happen."

"Seriously?" Bobby moved to cut off my line of vision. "That's your plan? Stand out here on the sidewalk and wait?"

The door to the house opened, and I had to shift to the side to see who was coming out over Bobby's shoulder.

"That's him!" I said in a loud whisper. "He's outside!"

Bobby twisted his head to look for himself. "Wow. Your non-plan actually worked. Color me impressed."

I slapped him on the arm with the back of my hand. "Come on. Let's follow him."

The kid turned left, heading away from us. Thank goodness, because I didn't think my next idea — to act casual by staring up at the sky and whistling — would have worked. He looked pretty street-smart.

"Are we going to catch up to him?" Bobby asked. We had to hustle; the kid was moving fast.

"No, not yet." I really had no idea what I was going to do, figuring the universe or God would somehow point me in the right direction at exactly the right time. So far, so good.

There was a basketball court up ahead, and the boy started to slow.

"Maybe he's going to play basketball," Bobby said. He slowed down too, breathing kind of heavily. "Good thing, because I was almost out of gas."

"Man, you're out of shape." It felt good to be able to say that. I wasn't even winded or sweating yet. Score!

"Not everyone has a personal trainer making him work out every single day, excuse you very much."

I grinned, thinking of Jason as my personal trainer. He was that and more.

When the boy got to the basketball court, his head dropped and he sped up.

"What's he doing?" Bobby whined. "Why is he going faster?"

"Shhh, just keep following."

When it got to the point that I had to jog to keep up, the kid turned around and saw me. A look of panic crossed his face and he ran faster.

"I can't ... I can't ..." Bobby dropped back, panting like a dog.

"Go back to the car!" I said without looking behind me. "I'll meet you back there!" As the kid picked up speed, so did I.

Adrenaline fueled my legs and kept me going, even when normally I probably would have been gasping for air. Even with all my workouts, I wasn't exactly prepared to beat a twelve-year-old in an all-out sprint through a neighborhood I didn't know.

When he got so far ahead I was afraid I'd lose him, I shouted, "Wait! I just want to talk to you!"

The kid looked over his shoulder at me but kept on running. If anything, he went faster.

"I'm not going to hurt you! I just want to talk!"

He kept going.

"Jesus Christ, you're too fast! I want to talk to you about Jason!"

The kid tripped on a bump in the sidewalk and fell forward, catching himself with his hands and then falling to the side as he cried out and rolled over. He was in the process of trying to get up and escape, but his hands and feet didn't look like they wanted to cooperate. He kept falling until I got there and stopped just behind him.

"I swear," I said between gasps for air, "I'm not going to touch you. I just ..." *Gasp, gasp, gasp,* "...want to talk."

"I ain't got nothin' to say to you!"

He said it with anger, but I heard a tremor to his voice and his eyes filled with tears too.

I ignored those tears. It's not that I was happy he'd fallen, but it energized me, sending a surge of excitement through my chest; at least now I felt like I would have some answers.

"Why don't you want to talk to me? I thought Jason was your friend."

The kid slowly got to his feet, his nostrils flaring and his lips pressed together. His chin trembled. He looked like he wanted to say something, but he didn't. He just stared at me mutinously.

I took off my hat and my sunglasses and rolled them up together. The boy's facial expression relaxed just the tiniest bit, but when I removed the elastic from my hair and put it in my pocket, he started to talk.

"It's you."

I blinked a few times, waiting for him to finish. But that's all he was going to say apparently, because he just stood there staring at me.

"My name is Katy."

"Yeah, you're that girl with the crazy last name. Like Gookey-burgers or something."

"Guckenberger, actually. Yeah, that's me. I'm Jason's friend."

The boy looked down at the ground, his face contorting several times. It finally stopped on the expression of someone supremely sad.

"You're Jason's friend too," I said. "He told me." I figured a little white lie wouldn't hurt, but boy, was I wrong.

The kid lifted his head immediately and glared at me, angry tears falling out of the outside corners of his mouth. "He told you?!"

I backed up a step or two, surprised by the fury I saw there. The boy's arms were rigid at his sides and his hands clenched in fists.

I held up my hands in surrender. "Hey, ease up, little man, he didn't tell me anything. I just saw some pictures of you two together, before ... well, before all that stuff happened with the coach, and I figured..."

"What stuff?" The kid was still angry.

"Uhhh ...," I looked at him like he wasn't all there, because of course that's what he was acting like, "... the stuff where Jason accidentally killed him?"

"Oh." The boy looked down at the ground again. "Oh."

"Oh." I was mimicking him, hoping it would prompt him to say more, but once again, my shit wasn't working.

"So, are you friends with him or was I wrong about that?"

The boy started to walk away, but I walked with him, working hard to stay shoulder-to-shoulder. He stared at the ground the entire time, his chin almost to his chest.

"Hello? Is anybody in there?" I leaned down to try and catch his eye, but he wasn't going for it.

"I thought you were friends because he spent a lot of time with you at the Boys' Center and there were all those pictures of you together and he seemed to really think you were someone special."

The boy said nothing, but his speed relaxed just the tiniest bit.

"I know you've heard a lot of bad things about Jason in the news, but I just wanted you to know that he's not a bad person. He's just a guy who made a big mistake."

"I know he's not a bad person," the kid said. He spoke so softly, I barely heard it, but the words were clear.

"When I was little, Jason once saved my friend from some bullies."

The kid looked at me for a split second and then went back to staring at the ground. I took that as a sign to continue.

"See, my friend is gay, so these other kids were being mean to him, and Jason made them back off."

"I'm not gay!" the kid yelled at me. His fury was back.

I frowned at him. "Dude, chillax, no one said you were gay."

The boy shook his head and sped up once more. "I have to go," he said. "See ya later."

"What's your name?" I asked, no way that easily dissuaded. I'd trained for this moment for months, running a thousand miles on that damn elliptical machine. No way was I going to let this kid just disappear now.

"Don't matter."

"It matters to me."

He sighed. "It's Leonard."

I laughed.

The boy slowed down and looked at me, confused. "You laughing at my name?" He stopped and I followed suit.

I shrugged. "You have a lot of nerve mocking Guckenburger when your name is Leonard."

He was about to get all mad at me for a second, I could see the fury crossing his features, but then it all fell away and he smiled just a tiny bit. "Yeah, I guess you're right, Gookeyburger. I got named after my grandad and he's real old."

I knocked him in the shoulder. "That's Guckenberger, *Leonard*."

"My friends call me Leo."

"Leo the lion. Fearless." I nodded. "Cool."

He dropped his gaze to the ground. "I ain't fearless."

"Meh, who is?" I shrugged. "Everyone's scared shitless every once in a while."

He looked up and frowned. "Didn't anyone ever tell you you shouldn't swear around kids?"

"Nope. I consider swear words like salt and pepper. They spice things up a bit, make 'em tastier." I glanced around the neighborhood, wondering if I was being watched. "Just don't tell anyone I said that. I'll lose my babysitting license." Not that I babysat kids, but it did strike me that the way I was running after this boy and interrogating him with my spicy words didn't speak well for my maturity level. Maybe he was right. Maybe I shouldn't be saying *shitless*.

"Jason's never scared," the boy said. "He's fearless, just like a lion."

I nodded. "I know what you mean. He's like ... completely tough."

"Yeah, but he ain't violent."

The defense of Jason I heard coming through in his tone made me want to dance and sing, but I kept it cool. My eyebrows came together in a thoughtful pose and I nodded slowly. "Yeah, he's actually pretty gentle. He's been helping me work out." I gestured to my body. "I used to weigh like thirty pounds more and be all fat and he's slowly helped me get stronger and faster."

He nodded. "You're pretty fast for a girl, that's for sure."

I grinned. "Thanks. You're pretty fast yourself, though."

He glanced up the street. "I gotta go."

I stood there watching him walk off, kind of stunned that he just ended the conversation without any of the normal segues, but then I followed. I'd come all this way, there was just no way I could let it end without *getting to the bottom of things*.

"I know Jason's got a really bad rep now, but if you ever want to visit him, I could pick you up and bring you over."

He said nothing for a while, taking a right turn and then a left one. I had no idea where we were going.

"No thanks."

"How come?" I had to speed up to keep up with him. "I thought you guys were friends."

"We are. Or we were. Whatever. I can't go."

"Is it your parents? Because I could talk to them."

"My parents are dead. I live with my grandma, but it's not her, it's me."

"What do you mean, it's you?"

He started to jog. "I gotta go, okay? Could you stop following me, please?"

I jogged at his side. "No, I can't just leave you alone. I think Jason misses seeing you and right now he has only me as a friend. He's lonely. He needs support. I thought you'd want to do that if you were his friend... you know, support him and stuff."

His feet were slapping the ground, and as I looked down, I noticed what bad shape they were in. They had duct tape around both toes.

"How come you don't have a pair of those cool red shoes?" I asked.

He stopped running immediately, coming to a complete standstill. I hadn't been expecting it, so I kept going for a few steps until I realized I was alone.

Stopping to turn around, I caught the expression on his face before he could think to erase it.

Fear.

"What?" I asked. "What'd I say?"

"Why're you asking me about those goddamn shoes?" He was back to being furious and on the verge of tears.

Obviously I'd hit a nerve, but I had no idea why. Maybe he lost out on a shoe lottery or something. "If you want a pair I'm sure we could get you some."

"I wouldn't wear those nasty shoes if they were the last shoes on *earth!*" he shouted. Spit flew out of his mouth and landed on my arm.

I looked down at it, mystified, confused, and a little bit scared. Something was going on here, and I knew it was big but I had no idea what it was.

"Why are you so angry about some stupid red shoes?" I asked, feeling like an idiot.

His face looked like it was made of brown putty, the way it morphed and changed its shape over and over. His eyebrows pressed in and then drew apart, his mouth pinched and then smoothed, his chin trembled and then folded up, his teeth showed and then disappeared. He was obviously running through just about every emotion a human being can have, all in the space of about five seconds.

"I don't want to talk to you anymore." His voice started to crack. "Could you please just leave me alone?" He was openly crying then, and I felt terrible.

"I'm sorry! I'm sorry!" I glanced around me worried one of these neighbors was going to call the cops on me. And wouldn't that be awesome, me being on the news for being a child stalker. *Ack!* "I'm really, *really* sorry, I didn't mean to make you cry."

I must have looked desperate, because he calmed down a little. "I ain't crying." He hiccuped, trying to control his emotions. Swiping his hand over his face, he looked anywhere but at me.

"I know what Jason did was awful, and you hate him for it, but please don't give up on him."

The boy shook his head as he gritted his teeth together. He was looking off into the distance for so long, I thought he'd never come back. But then he did and he blew me away with what he said.

"What Jason did ... it wasn't awful." He turned and looked me right in the eye. "And I don't hate him. I hate the coach, and I'm glad he's dead."

He took off running so fast, and I was so shocked, I didn't have the energy to chase after him. I watched his back until he disappeared off in the distance.

I COULDN'T WAIT FOR SCHOOL to be over on Monday. As soon as I was done, I hauled buns over to Jason's house, not even stopping at my house for permission first. This was the first time I'd ever defied my parents' rule, but it was worth it. They were at work anyway, so they'd never know where I was when I got in touch.

I was standing in Jason's front hall when I called my mom. "Can I go to Jason's?"

"Not today. I need you to do some chores at home."

"What chores? I've done all of them ... ahead of schedule, I might add."

Jason stood there giving me a questioning look. There may have been some disapproval there too, but I ignored it.

"There's a list on the counter. Take a look."

"Okay fine. If I finish the list can I go over after?"

"You won't finish the list today. I'll see you in a couple hours. I left you a snack in the fridge."

I hung up the phone without responding, rolling my eyes in frustration as I put it away in my bag.

"What'd she say?" Jason asked, scratching at his nasty beard.

"She said I can't come over today."

He grinned. "Ooops."

I grabbed him by the arm and dragged him down the hallway.

"Where are we going?" he asked, humoring me.

"To the clubhouse."

"Uh-oh ... sounds serious."

"It is."

He stopped and refused to go any farther. "What's this all about?"

"I'm not saying anything until you're in the clubhouse, Jason. I'm not kidding, so don't try the puppy dog eyes on me. It won't work."

He leaned his head down and blinked a few times, making his face as cute as he possibly could. The beard was crushing it completely.

I stared at him, expressionless. "Not working."

He tilted his head another way and tried again.

"Still not working." I pointed to the garage door. "In the club-house or I'm outta here."

"Threats? We're down to threats now?"

"Okay, fine. If you go into the garage, I'll let you kiss me."

He barked out a laugh. "You'll what?"

"You heard me. I know you've been dreaming about it for months, so you can just get it over with." I had no idea where this nonsense was coming from, but I ran with it anyway. As usual, my ridiculous sense of humor was enough of a distraction that he forgot to fight me.

He turned around and started walking down the hallway. "I thought we decided we weren't going to go there."

"And we aren't. Just get in the car, would you?"

He stopped just outside the passenger door. "I'll get in if you promise to kiss me after."

I grimaced. "If I must."

He laughed again, opening the door for me. "You have no idea how awesome it is to see that look of disgust on your face."

"You're seriously messed up, you know that?" I got in the car and shut the door, waiting for him to go around to his side.

When he got in and shut the door, I turned in my seat to face him. "I met Leo yesterday."

Jason's smile disappeared and his jaw dropped open. He looked confused and then cautious. "You what?"

"I met Leo. Your old buddy from the Boys' Center."

Jason's jaw muscle twitched, but it was the only sign I got from him that what I was saying meant anything. Otherwise, he was a cool cat.

"Oh, yeah? How's he doing?"

"He's not doing good, actually."

Jason looked at me closer. "He's not? Why?"

I shrugged. "You tell me."

He frowned. "How would I tell you? How would I know? I'm stuck in here."

Maybe it was my imagination, but I could have sworn I heard evasion going on in his tone.

"He shaved his hair off, he doesn't go to the club anymore, and he refuses to wear the red shoes."

Jason shrugged and stared out the front window. "Did he tell you why he's done all that? Maybe it's just random shit that kids do."

"He didn't exactly tell me, but he kind of told me some things."

"Some things like what?" Jason started squeezing the steering wheel over and over. Then he leaned over and started fiddling with the buttons on his radio. The engine wasn't on, though, so it made no sense to do that. It wasn't like music was going to start playing.

"He told me you're still his friend, that you're fearless ...," I paused, wondering if I should say this part, " ... and that he's glad the coach is dead."

Jason's hand stilled on the volume button. Slowly, his hand retreated and he rested it on the steering wheel. He said nothing for the longest time.

"Did you hear what I said? He's glad you killed the coach. He's your friend."

"Katy?" he said, very softly.

"Yes."

"I need you to stop."

I blinked a few times, absorbing what he'd said. I wasn't sure I understood.

"You want me to stop what? Stop talking?"

"Yes, and I want you to stop talking to Leo and I want you to stop talking about what I did and I want you to stop *talking period*." He banged his hand on the steering wheel with the last two words, making me jump.

The old me might have run out of the car and the garage at that loss of temper, but the new me stuck. I knew Jason well enough to know that he wouldn't hurt me. He was freaking out and trying to intimidate me, but I was too strong for that now.

"Sorry, no can do." I crossed my arms, maybe a little afraid I was pushing too hard.

He turned his head to face me. His skin above his beard was a mottled red and his mouth was drawn in tight. When he finally spoke, his words blasted out at me.

"Why can't you just leave things alone?!" He shouted way too loud for inside the car. My ears were ringing from it.

"Because you're my friend," I said in a normal tone. "And friends don't let friends go to prison for something they didn't do."

He leaned in close and shouted for all he was worth. "I did it, Katy! I murdered him! I fucking killed him with these hands!" He threw his open hands up into my face, an inch away. "You can't change that and you can't make everyone forget how much they loved him! They think I killed a saint!"

"Leo doesn't!" I screamed back, finally snapping over all the violence. "Leo thinks you're fearless!!"

Jason grabbed me on either side of my head and pulled me in, slamming his lips into mine. It was the most violent, hairy kiss I'll ever experience in my life, but I remained still. I let it happen. I let Jason take all his anger and frustration out on me, because I knew he wasn't hurting me, he was hurting himself. He was the sacrifice.

He pushed me away and looked out the front window. "There. I got my kiss, you said what you wanted to say, now get out."

"No." I looked out the front windshield too. "I'm not going anywhere."

"Fine."

He got out of the car and walked around the back.

I licked a drop of blood off my swollen lip where it had hit my teeth.

"I'm not coming back out here with you," he said at the door.

"That's fine."

"Ever!" he added, stepping through the door.

"That's fine!" I shouted.

I waited in the car for about ten minutes, but he never did come back. Eventually I left his house and returned home to a chore list obviously designed to keep me away from him for the next few days.

I TRIED TO GO OVER to Jason's house about five times after that, but he refused to see me. Each time his father answered the door and told me Jason was sleeping, or in the shower, or busy with homework. His expression told me the truth though, that Jason was avoiding me. It cut like a knife, it hurt so much.

He wouldn't see me in person, but I had hope deep in my heart that he'd still read my emails. Each day I typed out at least one to him, filling him in on what I was doing, how my workouts were progressing at the local gym, how many miles I was logging onto that damn elliptical machine.

He never answered, but that didn't deter me. When the news of his upcoming trial came into the papers, I told him that I'd be there every day, that I'd skip school and repeat senior year if I had to. Even if he wasn't going to talk to me, it didn't make our friendship null and void in my eyes.

The night before his trial was to start, he finally answered me back. I cried for hours after I read what it said.

Dear Katy, You've got to stop emailing me. I know you mean well, but our friendship is over. I think it's best for everyone involved if you don't come to the trial. I'm glad you're still working out. You look great and I know it makes you happy to sweat, even if you like to say it doesn't. Bobby's your friend and the person you need to be focusing on. Just leave me be. I'll be fine. — Jason

I SKIPPED SCHOOL TO GO to the opening day of Jason's trial. I didn't care that he'd cut me out of his life and told me to go to hell. I'd made a promise to myself that I'd be the kind of friend I'd want to have in this situation and that's who I was going to be.

Apparently, the first several hours of the day were taken up by selecting a jury, something I wasn't permitted to see, so I hung around the courthouse until almost eleven before the trial actually started.

The first twenty minutes featured people shuffling papers around and employees of the court coming in and out of a door behind the judge's bench. Talk about boring. People around me were whispering about how fast the jury selection part had been completed, but it seemed like it took forever to me; hours felt like days in this place. I just wanted everything to hurry up and be over.

I watched Jason steadily for the entire time I sat there, chanting over and over in my head *turn around, turn around*. But he never did. He whispered to his attorney once in a while, giving me a glimpse of his profile, but he never looked back. It made me so sad to be this close and yet so far away. He might as well have been on an Alaskan cruise.

At least he'd shaved off that nasty beard. I'd been worried that thing would make him look even guiltier, like some kind of crazed mountain man or something. He was back to being too beautiful for his own good. I started to think maybe he should have left his face-snatch on.

The courtroom was loaded with people from the press and a few onlookers, people curious about this boy who'd killed his coach, probably all of them hoping he'd fry. The outcry over the trial no one felt Jason even deserved was beyond just negative. They called it a waste of taxpayer money, that they should short-cut the whole process and let him die just like the coach.

The coach's wife was there along with two of his three grown sons. When they turned around their red-rimmed eyes practically glowed with pain. When they noticed me, they shot me looks of pure hatred that made me want to shrink down inside myself and disappear.

I guess everyone knew who I was by then. Jason and I were pretty similar in that way; both of us had exactly two friends left in the world. Bobby hadn't come with me today, but he'd already sent me eight text messages of support. My parents had no idea I was here but there was nothing they could say to keep me away.

When other people noticed the coach's family hating on me, it seemed to give out some sort of blanket permission for everyone to stare me down. To avoid all their mean looks I kept my eyes focused straight ahead on the back of Jason's head and his attorney's sagging shoulders. Jason's dad was in my line of sight too, sitting in the front row just behind Jason. I could tell he was tense by the way he wouldn't lean back in his bench seat. His head was bowed and he never moved.

Finally the door behind the bench opened and the judge came out in a black robe. The bailiff dressed in a cop's uniform said in a booming voice, "All rise, the honorable Judge Melanie Radcliff is now presiding."

I didn't even have time to get up before she started talking.

"Have a seat," she said, without even looking at us. She picked up some papers on her desk, put on some reading glasses, and proceeded to ignore the entire room. The power wave she was sending out was palpable. It made me sick to my stomach. I hoped she hadn't read the papers and already decided Jason was guilty and should be put away for life.

No one spoke. There were sounds of people moving around in their seats, a lady coughing, and camera shutters going off, but that was it.

"No cameras in here," she said without looking up. She sounded pissed. "You want to illustrate, be my guest, but no photography or filming. If I catch you, you'll be in contempt and you won't be welcome in my courtroom for a year."

I didn't hear any more cameras after that. This woman apparently scared everyone, not just me.

She finally looked up maybe ten minutes later and addressed the bailiff. "Ralph, please bring the jury in."

He walked over to a door that was next to the jury seats and knocked on it before opening it. Fourteen people of various ages, sizes, colors, and gender filed out and took their seats in the jury box.

I knew from reading on the court's website that two of them were alternates, whose opinions about Jason would only matter if one or two of the real twelve jurors were dismissed for any reason. I wondered who they were, but there was no way for me to know.

I searched the jury members' faces, clothing choices, and body language with eagle eyes, imagining I could determine their character and the way their minds would work during the trial by how they looked to me. Were they fair people? Open-minded? Already set against Jason from things they'd invariably seen on the news?

Jason's attorney had tried to get the court to move the trial out of town for fear of a tainted jury pool, but his request was denied. I wondered if these people who would decide his fate were football fans or anti-sweating types like I used to be. I wondered if any of them would look at Jason's perfect face and decide before they even heard a word that he had to be guilty, that a boy that good-looking with that much going for him could never have a valid reason to kill a person.

Once the jury settled in, the judge addressed the whole room. "We are here for the case of the State of Florida versus Jason Bradley, the accused being charged with murder in the first degree."

My heart cracked hearing that from her. She looked like God herself up there on that high pedestal where she sat, her stern face and black robes looking so *final*. A glance at Jason told me nothing. He faced her with his hands folded on the table in front of him, his suit jacket pulled tight against his back. I wanted to tell him it was all going to be okay, even if I knew in my heart it was a lie. Nothing was going to be okay ever again. My throat burned and my stomach churned. If I didn't barf today it would be a miracle.

She turned her attention to the jury. "Ladies and gentlemen of the jury, you have been sworn in already. You are here to listen and observe. Do not speak unless you are in the jury room. Do not ask questions. Do not make any signals or gestures to anyone in this courtroom. You may take notes about what you hear today and you will be allowed to take those notes into the deliberation room along with all of the evidence. You are charged with determining whether the prosecutor has proven beyond a shadow of a doubt that Mr. Bradley committed the crime of which he's been accused, which is murder in the first degree. Before we send you in for deliberations, I will give you specific instructions guiding you in following the law."

She didn't wait for any response before turning to face the two tables in front of her. "Attorneys for the prosecution and for the defense, be warned, I'm not in a good mood today. The last trial I had in here was a three-ring circus and I'm not going to stand for it with this one. No histrionics, no games, no dancing the line, are we clear?"

"Yes, Your Honor," they both said in unison.

"Good. Opening arguments, then, Mr. Prosecutor?"

I watched with a vague sense of unease as the two attorneys laid out their cases summary-style, telling the jury what they were going to prove. The prosecutor said that Jason had gone to the stadium early with the express purpose to confront the coach about a disagreement they were having about the way he was coaching the team and that he killed the coach in a fit of rage. It wasn't an accident, it was something he planned to do when the coach didn't respond the way he had wanted.

Jason's attorney responded by saying that the prosecution had to prove without any doubt that Jason had gone there and meant to kill someone. That he had intended to do it. He kept talking about *intent*, like it mattered. It seemed to be what his entire case hinged on. He mentioned self-defense, but he didn't focus on it like I thought he should have.

To me, it didn't sound all that convincing. Whether Jason had meant to do it or not, he had done it, so it seemed as if this stupid defense attorney was setting Jason up for a big fall. I hated him immediately. He was weak and stupid, I could tell by his sloping shoulders and the ugly green tie he'd worn. I'm no fashionista, but even I knew to wear an honorable-colored tie when facing a jury looking for a murderer. Puke green? Bad, bad choice, asshole. He might as well have tattooed *ignore everything I say* on his forehead.

As the lawyer droned on and on, I scanned the crowd. Not one of Jason's old friends was here. I knew no one other than Jason's dad. I was just about to twist back around in my seat to face the front again, when I noticed the doors opening in the back of the room. A small figure slipped in and sat in the back row.

Leo? I squinted my eyes to see better, but there was a big fat man in my way blocking my view. I was sure it was him, though.

Impatience started eating away at me. I had to talk to Leo and ask him why he'd finally come. Had he re-established his friendship with Jason while I was away? Is that part of the reason why Jason blew me off, because he had his friend back and he only had room for one? I knew it was silly, but I was willing to give

Jason any possible excuse for breaking my heart that I could. If he wanted Leo to be his friend instead of me, I could live with that; as long as he had a friend, I would be able to sleep at night again.

The judge called for a lunch break and everyone stood. Looking at my watch, I was shocked to see it was one o'clock already. I couldn't believe those lawyers had talked for so long. Quickly making my way out of the bench seat to the back of the room, I scanned the crowd for a little person, but Leo was already gone by the time I got to the doors.

"Katy!" said a voice from behind me. It was Jason's dad.

"I'll be right back!" I said, running out the door as fast as I could without looking like a lunatic. I felt bad that he might think I was running from him, but there was nothing I could do about it. Something told me Leo being here was an occurrence I wouldn't be seeing again. If I didn't love Jason so much I wouldn't have wanted to come back either; the lawyers were as dry as overcooked toast.

The hallway was filled with people who'd left the courtroom. Leo was nowhere in sight, but I took off towards the front hall of the courthouse to see if he was on his way out.

I caught sight of him as he was going through the turnstiles at the exit to the main building, but I waited until he was outside and just a few feet in front of me before I said his name.

"Leo!"

He turned to me, his face frozen in shock.

"Don't run away, I'm not going to do anything to you." I held my hands out, hoping it would make me look less threatening.

"What are you doing here?" he asked.

"Same thing you are. Watching Jason's trial. Hoping they don't send him to prison for the rest of his life."

Leo moved on and I caught up to walk next to him.

"I have to go. I'm s'posed to be in school," he mumbled.

"Me too. How'd you get here?"

He looked up, facing where he was walking. "Bus."

We were quickly approaching the stop and a bus was waiting there. I panicked, thinking I'd never see him again.

"Jason's life is ruined," I blurted out, tears filling my eyes. "Have you talked to him?"

Leo stopped. He wouldn't look at me. "No."

"Me neither. He won't talk to me anymore."

Leo looked up at me. "Why not?"

"I don't know." It was embarrassing to be crying in front of this kid, but I couldn't stop. My heart was broken for about ten different reasons. "After I talked to you, he got so mad at me, he told me I couldn't be his friend anymore."

"You serious?" Leo looked as if he didn't believe me. The bus pulled away.

"Yes." I looked down at him. "And I was the only friend he had left."

Leo's chin started to quiver.

"Why didn't he want me talking to you, Leo? Why did he cut me off for that? Was it about the shoes?"

I don't know why I was so fixated on those damn shoes. I just kept seeing their bright color and the flashy look they had on those little boy's feet. Shoes meant for an older guy. Shoes meant for a serious athlete who spent a lot of money on his equipment. Shoes that looked so out of place on a twelve year old who lived behind a chain-link fence.

Leo surprised me when he started bawling. Right there on the sidewalk, his face collapsed in tears and snot started running out of his nose. He wrapped his arms around himself and turned away, but the sounds coming from him were devastating to hear. He sounded like a tortured animal.

Something came over me and I forgot society's rule that I keep my distance. I put my arms around him and squeezed him tight. "Please don't cry," I said through my own tears. "It's going to be okay."

"It's never going to be okay!" he yelled. "Never! Do you hear me! Never!"

"I hear you, I hear you, but I don't understand." I released my grip enough to turn him around. Bending down so I could get on my knees in front of him, I looked him in the eye. We were a mess, both us covered in tears and boogers and pain.

"I don't understand, Leo. Please tell me what happened. Were you there? Did you see it happen?"

Leo shook his head. "I wasn't there."

"You weren't? Are you sure?" I so wanted him to be a witness, to save Jason from this horrible fate.

"I'm sure." He nodded. But tears kept coming, and his face was a mess of misery.

"Tell me what's on your mind. I know there's something wrong."

"I can't."

I squeezed his arms hard. "Yes, you can, Leo! Tell me!"

"Excuse me," said a voice behind me, "is there a problem here?"

It was a police officer with his hand on his hip, his feet spread apart a little. He looked ready for action.

I stood up and stepped to the side of Leo. "No, no problem here. I was just talking to my friend, Leo." I wiped my nose with the back of my wrist.

He looked at Leo. "Sounded more like you were yelling at him and being a little rough about it."

Leo's chin came up. "No, she wasn't. We were jus' talkin'. We're friends." His hand slid into mine and I squeezed it, my heart filling with hope.

"Yes, we're friends having a conversation about someone we care about, that's it. We got a little over-emotional, and I'm sorry if that freaked you out."

The cop smiled. "Happens at the courthouse. Have a good day." He walked away and left us standing there. Our tears had mostly dried but there was an acre of unspoken terrain between us.

I looked down at Leo and our clasped hands. "Leo, you really need to tell me what's going on."

He looked down at our hands. "I know," he whispered. "But I'm afraid."

I let him go so I could put my arm over his shoulders. We turned to face the courthouse. "You don't have to be afraid. Jason's your friend and he's fearless. And I'm your friend too."

"You seem pretty fearless," he said, sounding much younger than his twelve years.

"Nah. I'm scared shitless most of the time, but I go into things anyway. I guess that makes me brave."

"Or maybe stupid," he said.

I laughed. "Or that." I started walking with him next to me. "Come on. Let's go get a Coke and we can talk."

"I'm not going to talk in there," he said, tensing up as we got closer to the courthouse.

"We can talk outside. Look, there's a vending machine. Sit here on this bench and I'll get you a drink."

He sat down and I walked over to get a drink, but by the time I had two cans in hand and had turned around, he was gone. I collapsed to the ground in tears.

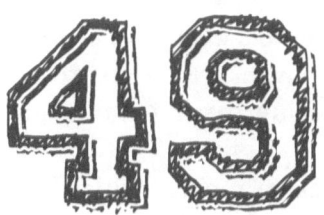

THE TRIAL ENDED THAT DAY with the prosecutor questioning a witness, the guy who maintained the stadium and who'd opened it up early for the coach. Other than Jason, he was the last one to see Coach Fielding alive. He testified that the coach acted totally normal that day, that nothing was amiss before Jason arrived. The defense attorney didn't cross-examine him.

I stood up after the judge went into her chambers for the day feeling let down. Not only had Leo disappeared, but Jason's lawyer had done nothing to help his case. This whole thing was a mess, like a long waiting period before Jason inevitably went away. Pointless.

"Thanks for coming, Katy," Jason's father said, coming up from behind me. He nodded and then made as if to move away, but I put my hand on his arm to stop him.

"Sorry I took off earlier. I wasn't running from you. I was ... running after someone who was leaving."

Mr. Bradley paused and gave me a sad smile. "You haven't come around in a while so I just figured..." He shrugged.

"Jason didn't want me around, but that doesn't mean I'm not his friend anymore."

"He wouldn't tell me what that was all about."

I couldn't meet his eyes anymore, feeling embarrassed. I looked over at Jason, but he was deep in conversation with his attorney, still sitting at his table. He probably didn't want to see me anyway, so I shifted my gaze away.

"I think he's just feeling very fatalistic about everything right now. He's trying to protect everyone around him."

When I said that, echoes of Leo's words came back to me, calling Jason fearless, saying that he was glad the coach was dead. What kid says that?

My heart was back to racing, which was a welcome change from the coma the lawyers had put it in. I needed to talk to Leo. He had answers to questions that were swimming around in my head and drowning everything else out.

"Mr. Bradley, I need to go. There's someone I have to talk to."

"Sure. See you tomorrow maybe? Or no, you probably have school."

"Screw school. I'll be here tomorrow."

He chuckled. "Am I going to be getting a call from your parents tonight?"

"Just blow it off if you do. This is my life and I'm calling the shots on this one."

He leaned in and kissed my forehead. "You're a gem. I miss having you at the house. Come and see me one of these days and we'll have some cake."

"Count on it," I said, actually looking forward to chatting with him at his kitchen table. Even if Jason ignored me and stayed upstairs the whole time, I still wanted to be a part of his life somehow. I hoped that didn't make me a stalker nut job.

I texted my parents telling them I'd be at Bobby's working on an art project and then texted Bobby and told him to cover for me. Two return texts and I knew I was in the clear at least until ten o'clock.

I left the courthouse using the bus and took it all the way over to the Boys' Club. It was dark by the time I got off in a neighborhood full of barking dogs. Sticking to the sidewalk and areas thick with hedges, I made it to fifty-three Shady Oak Drive without being accosted or bitten. There was a light on in the living room.

I started to sweat from the pressure. Thinking about going to Leo's house and confronting him was one thing, but to actually *be* here out on the lawn while the neighbor's pit bull drooled and dreamed of eating me for dinner was a whole other thing. I was on the verge of chickening out when the front door opened.

"Lawd have mercy, what in the name of all that is holy is goin' on out here? Mavis! Shut yo' damn dog up already, 'fore I come over there and put him outta my misery!"

I stood there like a deer caught in the headlights.

"Who you?" she asked as the porch light lit my face up. There was nowhere for me to hide.

I said nothing. Maybe I thought if I stood really still, she'd think I was a new lawn ornament or something.

"Cat got yo' tongue? I asked who you is." Her accent got thicker as she walked down her front porch stairs.

"Giiirl, you better not be playin'. I ain't in the mood for no playin' tonight. My bunions be acting up and my sciatical nerve been screamin' for goin' on a week now." She reached the gate to her fence with a pronounced limp. "You hear me, or you deaf or som'in?"

"I can hear you just fine. I was just trying to decide if I should run away or not."

She laughed, her round, light-brown face illuminated by the streetlamp across the road. "Well, at leas' you honest. Good thing you didn't run tho', cuz Mavis's dog likes to chase things that run." She lifted her chin and narrowed her eyes. "What's a nice white girl like you doin' in this hood? You lookin' for drugs? Cuz I'm sorry to tell you but we got ourselves a neighborhood watch up in here. Ain't no drugs, ain't no prostitutes, ain't no gangs. We practice clean livin', thanks to Jesus Christ our Lord and Savior, amen."

"Uhhh ... I'm not here for drugs or prostitutes. I'm here to talk to Leo."

She backed her head up a little. "Leo? *My* Leo? What you want with my Leo? He done somethin' wrong?"

"No, no, not at all. He's a sweet kid."

"Damn straight. Boy's a straight-A student, honor roll and everythin'." She put her arm up on the top of the fence. Lots of extra flab jiggled around when she did it, making me a little worried it was going to get caught in the chain link. "So what you wanna talk to him about, then? You not a social worker, I hope."

"No, I'm in high school. I just ... can I come inside maybe?" The dog next to me sounded like he was foaming at the mouth. I glanced over, hoping the fence keeping him away from me was sturdy enough. When I saw how wide his jaw was, I decided it probably wasn't sturdy enough at all. He looked like he could eat a hole in that metal and then me for dessert.

"Dammit, Fluffy, shut yo' mouf!" She swatted at the dog and he ran away for two seconds with a yipe before coming back and starting all over with the I'm-going-to-eat-you-and-gnaw-on-your-bones barking thing.

"Okay, come on, then. Come inside, 'fore Fluffy be dinin' on your carcass. You ain't got much meat on you anyways."

As we walked in the front door, I heard Leo.

"What's got Fluffy all crazy, Grandma? Is it that cat again?"

"No, it's a white girl, says she wanna talk to you." We stopped in the front living room.

A pot or something heavy clattered into the sink into the kitchen.

"Come on out here, and don't play like you didn't hear me, neither."

Shuffling footsteps came next and then Leo's face. He was obviously scared shitless, but I didn't know whether it was me causing his distress or his grandma. She was kind of scaring me.

"What's wrong wit' you, boy? You look like you's seen a ghost." She looked at me. "You sure you not a cop or somethin'?"

"No, I'm a friend of Jason Bradley's." I nodded at her grandson. "He was the guy from Banner High School's football team that was Leo's big brother at the Boy's Center."

She frowned, confused. "Big brother? Leo ain't got no big brother. It's jus' him and me. Always has been, always will be. His momma passed jus' after he was born."

"It's not that kind of brother, Grandmomma."

Her eyebrows went up and her head started bobbing. "Oh, shi...ply's baked beans, he jus' called me Grandmomma." She shook her head. "Mmmm, mmm, mmm, somethin's goin' on, now I know it." She was getting riled up and I didn't have a clue what she was talking about. *Baked beans?*

"Grandmomma, I'm sorry I didn't tell you before..."

Leo was clearly going into fight or flight mode, and the way his feet were dancing around, I was pretty sure which option he was going to choose. I was panicked that I was going to lose him again.

I held out my arms. "Okay, people, let's just take it easy, here."

"Take it easy? Take *what* easy?" Leo's grandmother put her hands on her ample hips. "Boy, you better come clean, right this second, 'fore I put my spatula on your backside and wear it out."

Leo started crying. "I can't tell you, Grandmomma, cuz you'll go to jail and I'll go to jail and the whole world will *know!*"

"Will know what?!" She looked at him and then me. "What's this child hawin' about?"

I took a deep breath and let it out before I answered. "I think what Leo is trying to say is that he knows something about the murder of Coach Fielding."

"MURDER?!!" she screeched, looking first at me and then him. Her eyeballs were bugging out of her head and somehow her hair had come out from its bun and was flying around her head. "YOU MURDER SOMEONE?!!" She charged after Leo and he screamed and ran back to the room behind him.

I screamed and ran after them both.

We all ended up in the middle of the kitchen, everyone in a giant hug, wrestling for purchase on Leo's body.

WHEN THINGS FINALLY SHOOK OUT, I ended up the meat in a good, old-fashioned, Katy Guckenberger sandwich. Grandma was one slice of bread and Leo the other. It got hot really quick, especially with her yelling her steamy breath on everyone.

"Boy, when I get my hands on you..."

"No one's getting hands on anyone until I get some answers," I said, frustrated that time was ticking by and I was here wrestling in a kitchen that smelled like fried fish. "I just want to talk to you Leo for ten minutes, fifteen tops, and then I'll go."

Grandma didn't appreciate my request. "I don't know who you think you is, telling us what you gonna do in my house, but you better back up."

I ducked down and moved to the side, leaving the two of them to hug it out. Grandma grabbed Leo by the back of the neck and squeezed.

Leo leaned over. "Ow, ow, owwww, okaaaay! Okaaaaay!"

"You're hurting him," I said, worried I was about to witness some serious child abuse.

"You ain't seen nothin' yet." She shoved him towards the hallway that I assumed led to the bedrooms. "Go get Grandpa's belt."

Tears were streaking down his face. "Yes, Grandmomma." He left us alone in the kitchen.

She turned her ire on me, but her tone went down to whispering levels. I felt like I was hearing the Devil Himself.

"You gots ten seconds to tell me what the holy hell is going on with my grandson before I lose my mind. And trus' me when I say, you do *not* want to see this woman lose her mind."

With her hair flying out in gray tufts all over her head and her crazy bug-eyes, I was absolutely sure she was correct in that.

"You're right," I nodded like crazy, "I don't want to see you lose your mind."

"Now what's this about murder?" She jutted her chin out, I think daring me to accuse her boy of killing someone.

"Jason Bradley, my friend, a guy I go to school with, killed the football coach about six months ago."

"You mean that white boy? Good looking boy? Big ol' football star?"

"Yes, that's him."

"What's that got to do with my boy?"

"Jason and Leo were friends."

"That ain't possible. You mus' be crazy." She folded her arms across her boobs, somehow defying the laws of physics in doing so. There's just no way those arms could have fit around that bosom, but she made it happen. It made her even scarier, like she had superpowers or something.

"Leo was part of, or a member of, the Boys' Center. Jason was a big brother there. Leo was his little brother."

She frowned. "Leo ain't at no Boys' Center. He go to school, he come home. That's it."

"Are you home all day?"

"No." She said it with attitude but then she backed down. "No. I work, ten hours a day, four days a week. I clean rooms at the mo-tel down the street."

"So he could have been at the Center and you wouldn't have known."

"You sayin' my boy lied to me?"

I gave her a sly look, telling her we were in this together. Teammates not enemies. "I'm saying he might not have mentioned it."

Leo came out dragging a long leather belt behind him. He held it up but kept his eyes on the ground. "Here you go, Grandmomma."

"You go sit. I can't even look at you right now." She pointed towards the living room, and Leo disappeared.

She lowered her voice again. "Why he wanna do that? Lie to me and spend time with those white boys."

"I don't know ... they're not all white boys." It seemed like a weak thing to say and those damn red shoes popped into my head again. "They give the boys stuff like new shoes for playing sports and they throw the ball around with them."

She hissed out some breath and shook her head. "Charity. I don't go for that charity. No foodstamps, no welfare, no free shoes. I pay my way and so do Leo."

"I know. He didn't take the shoes."

She looked over her shoulder. "So what's this all about, the murder an' all?"

"I'm not sure, but I think Leo knows some things about it that no one else knows."

"He was there, like a witness?"

"I don't know. Maybe. Maybe not. But he has something to tell. I know he does." I took her by the hand, desperate to get her cooperation. "I know he's just a kid, but Jason is on trial for murder, *right now,* and his lawyer sucks and I'm worried he's going to go to jail for the rest of his life."

"He guilty?" she asked, patting my hands that were gripping onto her.

"Maybe. But not exactly. Can we talk to Leo?"

She thought about it for a few seconds and then stood up, letting my hand go and pulling away from me. "We can try. But that boy can be mighty stubborn when he wants. Jus' like his momma, God rest her soul."

We walked out into the living room and Leo was sitting on the couch, staring at the floor.

"I want to die," he said, without preamble.

"Leo!" his grandmother shouted, sounding shocked. "Why you say such an awful thing?! You know better than that!"

He started crying again, loudly. "Cuz that's what I want! That's what I *want!*"

She trundled over and sat down on the couch next to him, taking him into her arms. She leaned back and pulled him against her chest. He got swallowed up into her boobs. I noticed he hung onto her like a drowning man.

I slowly walked over and took a seat in the armchair. When I had to peel my leg off it a second later due to instant sweating, I realized that every piece of furniture in the room had what looked like custom-made plastic covers on them. Were they planning on murdering someone or what? I'd never seen anything like it.

"Tell Grandmomma everything. I know you don't want to die. Ain't nobody gonna kill hisself in my house. Now you tell me what's happenin' and Grandmomma gonna fix it right up. Tell Grandmomma." She sounded like she was about to cry.

"I can't," he said in weak, agony-filled voice. "I can't. You won't love me anymore."

"Pssshhhh, child please. Grandmomma ain't never gonna stop loving you, never, ever, ever. You hear me? Now stop talkin' foolish and tell me what you did. Be honest. You know we tell the trufe in this house."

The trufe, the whole trufe, and nothing but the trufe ... come on, Leo. I gripped my hands together so hard it hurt, but I couldn't make myself stop.

Leo wiped his eyes on his grandmother's shirt a little before sitting up. He glanced at me and then kept his gaze fixed on the floor.

"I wasn't there."

"You wasn't where?" she asked, sitting up and taking one of his hands in hers.

"I wasn't there when Jason killed Coach Fielding."

"Well that's good news, right?" She looked first at him and then me.

I shrugged. To me, it sounded like bad news, at least for Jason. Maybe I'd been wrong about everything. Maybe Jason really was one hundred percent a cold-blooded killer like everyone said he was.

"But I'm glad he killed the coach. *Glad!*" He said it with such vehemence, with such fury, I knew then that something was very, very wrong with this situation.

Leo's grandmother's voice went very even and very low. She looked right at him and leaned in. "What that coach do that was so bad you be glad he's dead, Leo? You tell Grandmomma."

Leo started crying again. "He did a bad thing, Grandmomma. He did a really, really, really bad thing!"

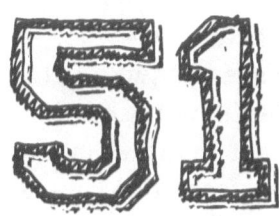

MY FINGERS WERE SHAKING SO bad, I couldn't press the numbers on my phone. It was my worst nightmare come to life.

"You want me to do that for you?" Grandma asked me. She had instructed me to call her that. *Grandma*. She was surprisingly strong, considering what she'd just heard from the love of her life.

"Please." I sniffed, wiping the four millionth tear from my eyes. "Just click that arrow until you see the name Chuck and press the green button."

"Here you go, baby," she said after following my instructions. "I'm going to go check on my boy. I'll be right back."

I put my hand on her arm. "I'm so sorry," I said, my face crumpling again.

She patted my cheek. "Not your fault, baby, not your fault. We'll make this right. You and me and my baby Leo and our Lord God and his son Jesus Christ. We will make this right." She nodded once before leaving me for the bedrooms.

I nodded too as the phone rang, leaving her to check on Leo while I called Jason's dad.

"Katy?" he said, coming onto the line sounding tired. "Are you all right?"

"Yes, why wouldn't I be?" I tried to sound perfectly fine and not totally wrecked. It was after eleven, but I wasn't completely out of my mind just because of the time.

"Your parents called here looking for you."

I rolled my eyes. "Great. Listen, forget them for a minute, I need to talk to you."

"Okaaay, what's up?"

"Can you call Jason's lawyer, like right now?"

"Uhhhh, I guess. But I'm not sure why I'd do that."

"I need for you to get that lawyer over to your house right now. Like right this very second." My breaths were coming out as dog pants. Fluffy and I were like brothers right now.

"Katy have you been drinking?"

"Listen, Chuck, *I'm not playing!*" My voice came out a little too shrieky, so I took a moment to breath in and out and then tried again. "I'm sorry. I'm a little freaked out, but you will be too when you hear what Leo has to say."

"Who's Leo again?"

"You've never met him. He was in the courtroom today. He's the one I was chasing after when I blew you off."

"Sweetie, I'm sorry, but you've lost me. Do you need a ride home?"

"Mr. Bradley!" I screamed. "I'm not drunk or high or crazy, okay?!"

Leo's grandmother came out of the kitchen and held out her hand. "Let me have a word with the man."

I handed her the phone, my hand shaking so bad I almost dropped it.

Grandma took the phone from me with one hand and with the other pulled me against her hip. She held me there tightly as she talked to Jason's dad.

Her voice was a smooth as silk. "Mr. Bradley? Yes, hello. My name is Dolores Williams, and I have a grandson named Leo who I have recently learned was a friend of your son Jason." She paused as she waited for Jason's dad to speak before continuing again. "Nice to meet you too, but I have to say I wish it was under better circumstances. From what I understand, time is running out, and I think Katy is right. We need to have a talk to*night*. And you need to bring that lawyer o' yours with you. You come to my house because my grandson needs to stay in bed as much as he can. He sick. My address is fifty-three Shady Oak Lane." She paused. "Yes, that's right. Shady Oak ... Lane. You got it. You can park on the street right in front of the house."

Sick. Sick was not the word I'd have used to describe Leo right then. *Destroyed* would have been closer. *Devastated* not as good. Really, no words could describe what Leo was now or what he would be for the rest of his life. *Changed*, maybe, but that didn't seem to do it justice either. It was too ... innocent.

Grandma nodded a few times and then said her last bit before hanging up. "Bring your boy too. This involves everyone. It's time for justice to be done."

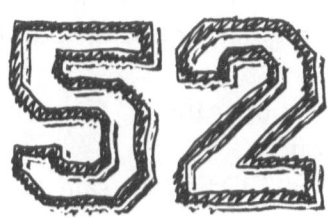

I COULD NOT SIT STILL. Jason and his dad were coming over. *Jason.* The boy who was my second best friend, the hero of elementary school, defender of innocents ... and he'd told me he never wanted to see me again. He told me to let things drop. He told me to leave it all alone.

But I had to *get to the bottom of things*. It's a personality flaw of mine, to not be able to let things that weren't right go. I prayed he wouldn't hate me for the rest of his life. But if he did, I would have to live with it, because down to my soul and with every fiber of my being, I knew I had done the right thing. I just hoped no one else would end up dying over this.

Two cars pulled up outside at the same time. They both turned their engines off and their headlights went out in synch.

"What's that other car?" I asked.

Then a third car pulled up behind those two.

"What in the hell?" I said absently.

Grandma went to the door and opened it up wide, stepping to the side to let all the visitors in.

The first one in the door was Mr. Bradley. He shook her hand and introduced himself. He nodded at me as he came in and moved over to stand by me.

"I'm glad to know you aren't drunk," he said, I think trying for a joke.

All I could do was shake my head. I was panicked about seeing Jason.

Jason's lawyer came in next. He looked different, not wearing a suit. "This is very irregular," he said, "but if it'll help my client, I'm willing to listen."

"You just have a seat over there," Grandma said, gesturing to the plastic-covered couch.

"You must be Jason," Grandma said as he passed over the threshold.

"Yes, that's me," he said, his voice making my heart squeeze painfully in my chest.

Grandma wasted no time, pulling Jason into a bear hug. Then she started crying, and it was loud. "You my angel, Jason Bradley. You my angel sent straight from heaven. God forgives you and Jesus Christ forgives you, you can believe that."

Jason stood there, stiff as a board. I could see the expression on his face. He was made of stone and he said nothing.

She pulled away and wiped at her face. "Come in, come in, sit, sit." She waved over at the couch.

Jason took a few steps and then stopped, staring at me.

I stared back, tears filling my eyes. He hated me. He wished I wasn't here. I could see it all over his face.

Then he walked over and sat near me on a chair that really wasn't big enough for two people. He reached up and took my hand, pulling me down to sit with him. My butt landed half on his leg and half in the seat.

"Move over, would ya?" he said quietly.

I wiggled into the tiny spot next to his tree-trunk legs. "Jason, I'm ..." I wanted to apologize, but I wasn't sorry. I didn't want to lie. There had been enough lies in Jason's world for one lifetime.

"Shhhh ... we'll talk later." He took my hand in his and held it tight. I wasn't sure who needed the reassurance that his strength gave us, him or me, but it didn't matter. I gave as good as I got. I held onto him like he was the only thing keeping me from floating away.

My parents came in last. "You have some explaining to do, Missy," my father said. He barely acknowledged the other people in the room, so focused as he was on making me scared shitless to go home. But nothing he said could burst my bubble. Jason was my friend again and this lawyer was going to fix things.

My mother thanked Grandma for allowing us into her home and took a seat next to my father in chairs brought in from the kitchen.

Grandma stood and clasped her hands together. "So, you all want to know why we asked you to come here in the middle of the night." She pointed both hands at me. "You can thank Katy here for that, and I'm gonna let her tell her story and then I'll get my Leo up to talk to this here lawyer." She nodded at the attorney and then sat down in a chair I was sure would collapse under her weight.

But it didn't and all the attention shifted over to me. My face flamed up as I started my story.

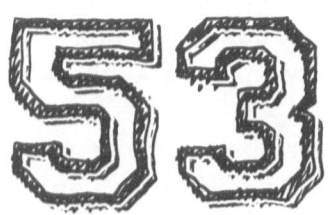

A LL THIS TIME THAT I'VE spent with Jason, I knew he wasn't telling me all of the story."

I glanced at him before I continued, to see if he was angry. He stared at the floor, but held onto my hand. I took that as a good sign.

"He told me over and over again that I had the story, the whole story, but I didn't believe him."

"She's very stubborn," he said in a subdued voice.

"That's my girl," said my mom with a sigh.

My father grumbled but then she cut him off with, "She takes after you, Mike, so watch it."

I rolled my eyes and continued. "Anyway, one day Jason told me part of the story that he hadn't told anyone else."

His lawyer got visibly agitated at that, but I continued without stopping.

"He told me that he'd gone to speak to the coach about something personal, and that the coach hadn't reacted right and then they got into an argument and ... well ... we all know what happened after."

"You killed that man," said Grandma, "praise Jesus."

When everyone looked at her, my mother with shock in her expression, Grandma looked at the ceiling and said, "Lord, I'll beg forgiveness for that evil thought at church on Sunday, I promise, but let me be a sinner for jus' a little while longer." She shook her head and shifted her gaze to me. "Tell your story, baby, tell it."

Jason took his hand away from mine and put it around me, pulling me against him. He set me on fire with that. I was warm from head to toe with his love and friendship. I felt like I could fly.

"Dad, remember that photographer who came to the house that one night?"

"How could I forget," he said wryly.

"I took the pictures off his camera and kept them." I looked around the room. "They were pictures of the football team at the Boys' Center, the charity place not far from here. Jason was a big brother there. It was the coach's pet charity."

"He made all the players participate," Jason said, his voice rough and low.

"There were several pictures of Jason with Leo, and I could tell they were friends from the way they smiled at each other."

Jason smiled, but he seemed very sad.

"Anyway, one day when Jason came over, he was looking at the pictures. And after he left, I noticed that he'd tried to delete all the photos with Leo in them."

My mom frowned. "Why would he do that?"

I looked at Jason as I answered her question. "He was trying to protect Leo."

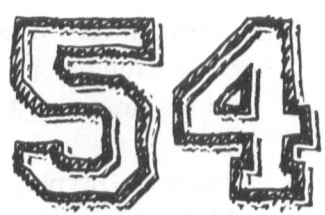

I DIDN'T SLEEP THAT NIGHT. After Leo was roused from bed and had a private conference with the attorney, we all went home and I spent the entire night and morning at Jason's kitchen table, talking with him and his dad.

"We need to get going so we're not late to court," Chuck said. "You sure your parents are okay with this?"

I nodded. "Do you honestly think they could stop me at this point?"

He laughed. "Uh, no. You're unstoppable." He pulled me into a hug. "Thank God." After he let me go, he walked down the hallway. "You kids have ten minutes before this bus is leaving."

Jason and I sat there looking at each other across the table, the first time we'd been alone in what felt like forever.

He just stared at me, his head kind of tilted.

"You're making me paranoid," I said, feeling my face pinking up. "Say something."

"You are ... the most beautiful, amazing person I have ever known in my entire life."

Why I was suddenly shy with him after all we'd been through, I have no idea, but there was no denying it. It felt like a first date.

"Shut up," I said, ever so eloquently.

"I'm serious." He got up and walked over, taking my hand and making me stand in front of him.

We stared into each other's eyes for a long time.

"I love you, Katy."

"I love you too, Jason." I knew he probably meant *as a friend* and even though that's not how I meant it now, it didn't matter. Being his friend was an honor for me.

"I really want to kiss you, but I don't want to screw things up," he said.

I tried to smile but my lips were too trembly to do it without looking like a lunatic. "How could you screw things up by kissing me?"

He huffed out a single laugh. "If I remember correctly, the other times I tried I managed pretty well to completely suck at it."

I lifted my chin. "Those weren't kisses. Those were you trying to fight me off with your weapon of choice."

"My weapon of choice." He said it like a statement.

"Yeah. Before you used to think I was hanging around because you're cute. You were kissing me with your ego. Now you know different."

He moved closer so we were almost touching body to body. "So you're saying now that I know you actually *love* me, I can kiss you without my ego?"

"And you love me too. That's the key." I winked, acting waaaay more confident than I was feeling.

"Close your eyes," he said.

I did as I was told without arguing, pretty much a first for me.

"Pucker up."

I laughed but then stuck my lips out.

I could feel his breath before anything else. It was warm and smelled of blueberry muffins.

"Okay, kids, time to go!" said his dad from the hallway.

My eyes flew open and I pulled away, just as Jason's lips were touching mine.

"Great timing, Dad," Jason said, stepping back and running his fingers through his hair.

"Sorry, but we need to get the lead out. You know what the traffic is like downtown." He came into the kitchen, oblivious to what he'd just interrupted.

I grabbed my bag and threw it over my shoulder. "You ready?" I asked Jason as we walked down the hall to the front door. There was a mass of reporters out there, waiting to hear the big news that Jason's attorney had hinted was coming, last night when he spoke with his contacts in the media.

"As long as you're there, I'll be able to handle anything," Jason said, leaning over and giving me a quick kiss on the lips, just as the front door opened.

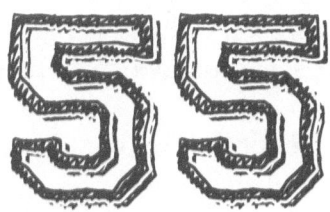

THE COURTROOM WAS PACKED. THE judge had come in extra early to deal with the procedural issues that she was notified of, last night around midnight by the prosecutor's office.

After the judge came to the bench but before the jury was allowed in, Jason's attorney addressed the court. "Judge, we have a motion we'd like to make before we get started."

She looked over her glasses at him. "So I gathered." She held out her hand for his documents and he walked up to hand them to her.

"Sorry about any spelling errors ... my assistant didn't have time to proofread for me."

"She's probably still in bed," the judge said dryly. "Give me a minute to read through this."

Jason was turned in his seat so he could watch me watching the judge. I could tell he was nervous; he kept rubbing the top of the seat like he was trying to take the wood stain off.

"Okay, let's hear your argument," she said to the defense attorney.

Jason turned around and faced the front, his hands folded in his lap. His leg bounced up and down rapidly in time with mine doing the same thing.

"Your Honor, last night I was alerted to the presence of a witness, a critical witness, one that could not possibly have been discovered previously, and this witness absolutely must be allowed to testify."

"Go on," she said, putting the papers down.

"Your Honor, this is a very sensitive matter."

"Murder is always a sensitive matter," she said, her tone scolding.

"Of course, Your Honor, but we're talking about a minor here and allegations of sexual abuse."

Everyone in the entire courtroom gasped, me included. I knew the story from start to finish and yet it still shocked me to hear the words spoken out loud in such a public place.

The judge looked at the prosecution. "Your counter?"

"Your Honor, really, the State asks that you deny this motion on the basis that this witness should have been presented to us long before this day when we're in the middle of making our case." The prosecutor shook his head and threw his hands up. "I mean, come on. We're completely prejudiced by this situation. If I had known about this person, I would have deposed him."

"Fine." The judge took her glasses off and gestured to the prosecutor. "I'll give you two hours. Depose him."

L EO WAS LED INTO AND out of the courthouse under armed escort, using side doors and underground basement parking to ensure his face never figured in the lens of a photographer. No one ever knew his name or saw him live except for the prosecutor and the defense attorney. But it didn't matter; his words were plenty powerful enough.

"I understand we have another issue," the judge said after everyone minus the jury was back in her courtroom.

"Yes, Your Honor," the prosecutor said. He looked pissed. "We need some time to determine whether we're going to ask for a mistrial, drop the charges, or continue and ask for conviction on a lesser charge."

"The lesser charge being ...?" The judge raised an annoyed eyebrow at him.

"Manslaughter."

"You have two minutes. The clock is ticking."

He looked like he wanted to argue, but she wasn't going to listen and he knew it. Instead, he sat down at the table with his team of two other lawyers and discussed it in whispered tones.

"What's happening?" Jason asked his lawyer.

I was sitting in the front row now so I could hear everything when they turned around to share the information with Jason's dad.

"The charge of murder includes the lesser charge of manslaughter, so they can continue the trial and ask the jury to find Jason guilty of that instead of murder."

"What's the prison sentence?" I asked.

"Could be less than ten years. Much less. But I'm going to argue justifiable homicide. He has a very strong defense. I think the prosecutor is going to drop the case."

I felt like I was going to have a heart attack, so I could only imagine what Jason was going through.

"That would be ... that would be wonderful," Jason's dad said, getting choked up over the idea.

"Don't count your chickens just yet. That prosecutor is a real asshole." Jason's attorney sat up and turned around when the judge started talking.

I loved him for saying that. The prosecutor *was* an asshole.

"Mr. Prosecutor, do you have anything for me?"

He got up from the table where he'd been arguing heatedly with his colleagues and approached the center of the space in front of the judge's desk.

"Your honor, the State of Florida would like to drop the charges against Jason Bradley."

"Are you certain? Because we've already spent quite a bit of the taxpayer's money here."

"I don't feel as though I have a choice," he said, hanging his head.

The courtroom blew up with noise. The most vocal were the family members of Coach Fielding. The biggest son made a leap for the table where Jason was sitting, but he didn't get very far. Three bailiffs jumped on him and dragged him to the ground, handcuffing him and taking him away.

The judge banged her gavel over and over.

"Order!" she yelled. "Order! The next person who acts out of turn goes to jail!" She glared out at the crowd. "Any takers?!"

Everyone calmed down immediately and she looked at Jason. "Mr. Bradley, the charges against you have been dropped and you are free to go. However, be advised that if the prosecutor's office discovers new evidence against you, you can have charges brought against you again and you can be tried again. Double jeopardy does not apply in this situation."

"Yes, ma'am," Jason said, nodding at her and standing. He turned around and pulled me into a bear hug. I began to cry because it was the only thing left to do. Jason was coming home.

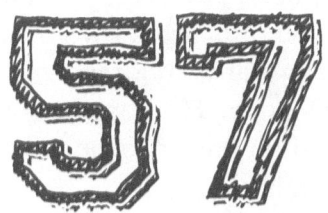

"I DON'T GET IT," I said in the car ride home. Jason and I were in the back seat holding hands. "How come they dropped everything entirely? It seems so impossible."

Jason's dad answered. He's spent an hour with the attorney after the trial was called off getting all the details while Jason and I stared at each other and smiled like goofballs in love in the cafeteria, because that's exactly what we were. In love. I grew two inches taller that day.

"The lawyer said that with Leo's testimony it was very likely, highly likely, that Jason would be found not-guilty based on some statutes that say it's legal to kill someone if it's in the defense of others. And if there's a situation where a person is confronted with the things Jason confronted the coach with, and that person becomes violent, a person is within his rights to defend himself with deadly force." He shrugged. "And let's face it, when a person did what the coach did, there's really not any jury in the world who doesn't want him dead. No one would convict."

"Except his family." Jason got sad all of a sudden.

ELLE CASEY

"Don't be too sure about that," said Jason's dad. "I heard rumors about the son that wasn't there. This stuff doesn't happen in a vacuum. You wait and see. Things will start coming out of the woodwork now that the truth is out. The lies are coming undone. Everyone is going to see you as the hero you are." Chuck looked at his son in the rearview mirror and winked.

"I'm no hero, Dad, I killed a man."

"Jason, you are a hero. And yes, you killed a man. But you saved lives, I know you did. *You* know you did. How many lives did he destroy? How many children will *not* have their lives ruined now that he's gone? He was a monster. You slayed that monster. I know you didn't mean to, but it happened, and I'm not going to say it was a mistake."

Jason shook his head. It was impossible to know right now how many lives had been ruined or saved and we probably never would. But at least I could finally say that Jason's life wasn't ruined. Not anymore. It was changed, yes, but he was free.

THIS IS THE PART OF the story that Jason should tell, but since he keeps insisting that I'm way better at it than he is, I'm going to go ahead and do it. But I really wish you could have seen the look on his face when he told me the first time, in full detail, what actually happened that evening in the coach's office at the stadium. The night that all of our lives changed forever.

Jason had gone to the Boys' Center the afternoon of the big game to ask Leo if he wanted to come and watch from the sidelines, but when he went to the Center, he couldn't find him. Kids from the neighborhood said that he was at home and that he'd quit the Center entirely.

Jason got his address and went over to see him. Leo at first refused to come out, saying his Grandma was working and didn't want any strangers coming in, but Jason convinced him to come out on the porch for a chat. That's when he noticed something was wrong.

Leo wouldn't look him in the eye. He refused to say why he didn't want to be at the Boys' Center anymore.

ELLE CASEY

Jason thought he'd get Leo to talk by changing the subject. He talked about how much fun Leo'd be missing by not coming to the game that night. He mentioned how all the scouts were supposed to come out and then maybe contact him about college scholarships. He figured the kid's hero worship would be enough to get him to come.

"You like football?" Leo asked.

Jason was confused about the question at first. "Sure, I love football. It's my life."

"But aren't there things you don't like about it?"

Jason thought about it for a few seconds and shrugged. "Sure, I guess. I mean, to be good you have to work hard. That's a lot of practices, a lot of drills, and lot of hits to take."

"Yeah." Leo seemed lost in his own world. "Is there anything else you don't like?"

Jason laughed. "Nah, man, it's all good. You get the girls, you get the fans, you get free stuff all the time. Like those red shoes. You want a pair? I can get you a pair if you want."

Leo looked up at him, his mouth quivering. "You want to give me a pair of red shoes?"

Jason shook his head at the boy's expression. "Why are you acting like I just offered to kill your pet hamster?"

"Coach offered to buy me a pair of them shoes."

"Yeah, he's a good guy like that."

"He buy you shoes? Red ones?"

"No, not red ones, but other ones. Blue ones, black and white ones ...what's the big deal?"

"And you do whatever the coach tells you to do? Cuz he buys you those shoes?"

"Sure I do whatever he tells me to do. He's the coach. Every team has a coach. And he's the best coach I've ever had. He's like a father to me."

Jason remembers Leo's face going very pale at that point. "I gotta go," he said. "See ya."

He stood up and went into the house without saying another word.

Jason could have left. He was tempted to. But that look on Leo's face was just killing him. He went into the house and called out his name.

"Leo," he said, "where are you, man? Come out and say good-bye, at least."

Jason followed the sounds of sorrow that came to his ears and found Leo sobbing in bed.

"Dude, what's wrong with you?"

Leo sat up and screamed, "I can't do the things he asks me to do anymore, okay?! I can't do it anymore!"

Jason said he stood there confused for the longest time. First he thought to himself that this kid was upset because the coach had told him to do some pushups or something, or had told him to run sprints. He liked to make the young kids run the bleachers over and over until they were ready to collapse. He said his job was to make men of them.

But then other thoughts entered his head and made him extremely uncomfortable. Leo was way too upset to be freaking out about pushups.

"Leo, what did the coach ask you to do?"

"He didn't ask me, he *made* me. He *made* me do it!"

"Okay, what did he *make* you do?" Jason distinctly remembers feeling physically ill at this point. He didn't yet know the truth, but deep down inside, he knew the truth was bad. Very bad.

LEO SPOKE IN A MONOTONE, staring at the wall as he lay on his side.

"The first time, he touched me ... on my private parts." Leo whimpered a little but kept talking, trying to maintain the disaffected tone he started with. "The next time, he made me touch him. He said all the guys do it. It's part of being on the football team."

"Oh fuck," Jason said. He had to sit down on the floor because he felt faint.

"And he told everyone afterwards that I was going to be a big player at the school and I was going to go all the way. That made me feel important."

"I'll bet," Jason said, barely able to get the words out.

"Then he ... then he ..."

Jason reached up and patted him on the back. "You're okay, Leo. It's never going to happen again, I swear it to you. I'm going to take care of this."

Leo continued as if he hadn't heard Jason at all. "He took me in the shower. He hurt me. He said if I told anyone, I would never get to play football, that everyone would say I'm gay. He did it so many times..."

Jason dropped his head in his hands and cried. "I'm sorry, Leo. I'm so sorry this happened to you."

Jason wanted to put all his hate on the coach, but he couldn't do that. He blamed himself too. He'd come to the blindingly painful conclusion that he was part of the problem.

He'd ignored signs. There had to have been signs, right? Why hadn't he paid better attention? And because of guys like him, boys like Leo were easy victims. Easy to draw in and convince to do things they'd never normally do. All they wanted was to be put up on that pedestal and be admired by everyone. They wanted to be like him.

What a tragedy, he thought, to base your life dreams on such an illusion of grandeur.

Leo lost his monotone and spoke softly, all of his emotions wrapped up in every syllable. "I'm afraid I'm gay, Jason, and I don't *want* to be gay. I like girls. And I used to like football too. But I don't anymore. I hate it. I hate it!"

Jason stood up all of a sudden, knowing he had to fix this. "Leo, I'm going to go take care of this, right now. And you need to get up out of that bed and talk to a grown-up about this. Tell your grandma or your priest or someone."

Leo sat up and shrieked, "No! Don't you tell anyone, Jason! If you do ... if you do ... I'll *kill* myself! Just like my momma did, I'll kill myself!"

"What? Oh my god, no." Jason sat down on the edge of the bed and hugged Leo. Then he shook him to make sure he was paying attention. It was freaking him out that the kid looked so *absent*. "You aren't going to do that, man!"

"I will." Leo looked him right in the eye. "If you tell a single person in the whole world, I will kill myself. I swear it."

Jason was caught between a rock and a hard place. Try to get Leo some help and find him dead from suicide? That wasn't even an option. The best decision he could make right then was to solve the most immediate problem first and then convince Leo to get help after. Jason needed to stop the predator in his tracks, let the coach know that he knew the truth and he wasn't going to quit until the rest of the world knew it too. Then it would be safe for Leo to find help. To heal.

"All right, listen, I won't tell anyone. Not a word. But I *am* going to tell the coach that I'm watching him and that he's not allowed to ever touch anyone ever again."

"I'm not the only one," Leo whispered. "I saw him with other boys. Sometimes he makes us watch... and other stuff..."

"Oh god, oh god." Jason stood, sick to his stomach and torn between comforting Leo and needing to do something to fix things, to stop the pain from escalating, from spreading, from infecting everything that he held dear. *Football.*

Boys who used to be like him, dreaming of their big days ahead, were hiding in plain site, mourning the loss of their innocence, questioning who they were, going along with horrible awful things for a dream that Jason himself helped create and kept alive. The camaraderie, the loyalty, the feeling of the win. All of it was a lie. He felt like a fraud, a fake, a monster himself.

"Leo, I'm going to go take care of this. You stay cool. Don't freak out and whatever you do, do *not* hurt yourself. This is not your fault. The coach is a predator and an evil person who I am going to make sure is put in jail for the rest of his life. He'll never touch you or anyone else again."

"You promise?" Leo asked, his voice just a shadow of its former self.

"I promise."

JASON PRETTY MUCH BROKE THE sound barrier driving to the stadium. He wondered on his way there if he should have gone to the police first, but his promise to Leo told him no; it was better to confront the coach and keep him from doing anything else and then get Leo some help. The professionals dealing with Leo would get the police involved in a way that didn't destroy Leo's life. Jason would be there to help, he vowed to himself and any god that might be listening.

He watched the janitor leaving as he pulled in to the stadium parking lot. He waved and acted as calm as possible under the circumstances. After parking his car, he found Coach Fielding in his office.

"Coach, I need to talk to you," he said, sweating with the raw emotions that were eating him up inside, and trying like hell to keep a tight rein on his anger. His disillusionment was literally painful, his heart aching for Leo and all the other boys and young men who had been led astray by this man. The entire city believed his lies. It was beyond sickening how everyone had just allowed this to happen.

But no more...

ELLE CASEY

"Just a minute, son, I'm in the middle of something."

Jason slapped the power button on the TV to shut it off and stood in front of it. "No. *Now.*"

The coach slowly sat back in his chair. "You okay, son? Something bothering you?"

"Yeah, I'd say so." His nostrils were flaring with the effort of keeping his temper under control. All he wanted to do was break every single trophy in that room and tear down all the photographs of the young boys that hung on the wall. Coach with his arms around their shoulders and that slick smile took on a whole new meaning that day.

"Have a seat. Talk to me." His voice was all smooth and slimy, according to Jason. He seemed to know why Jason was there and he didn't act like he cared one bit. If anything, he was cocky.

"No thanks, I'll stand."

The coach smiled and rested his hands on the arms of his chair. "I'm all ears."

"I talked to Leo today. He told me *everything.*" Jason was trembling with anger. He could picture Leo's tear-streaked face as the boy threatened to end his life at the age of twelve.

"Who's Leo?"

The casual answer threw Jason off. All he could see was a demon sitting there in that chair; a demon who abused children and then didn't even remember their names. There must have been too many to keep track of, he thought to himself.

"Leo is the twelve year old boy who you sodomized and abused several times and tried to bribe with a fucking pair of *shoes!*"

The coach kind of laughed and then frowned. "Well now ... those are some serious accusations, son."

"Don't call me son! My father's name is Chuck and he doesn't ruin kids' lives like you do. He has honor, and honesty, and ... and ..." Jason couldn't think straight he was so upset.

The coach slowly got to his feet. "You think you know everything, don't you?"

"I know right from wrong." Jason stood straighter, even when the coach's attitude went alarmingly cold.

"Maybe you do, maybe you don't. Or maybe you're just jealous. Is that it? You missing my attention? Want more of it for yourself? Not happy with just being first string, getting all the news coverage, being captain?"

"Don't be ridiculous," Jason said, disgusted with the way he was coming closer and closer while talking in such a sleazy tone. Jason backed up a step towards the door.

"Or maybe you talked to Leo and you felt left out ...like you should have been invited to our private coaching sessions, is that it?"

Jason's face crumbled in disgust. "Private coaching sessions? Are you *serious?* That's what you tell those kids? God, you're sick, you know that? You're fucking sick in the head."

The coach took two big steps forward, putting himself right in Jason's face, towering over him. "That's it. You're jealous. Well, don't worry, son, I can fix that."

The coach reached down and put his hand on Jason's crotch.

And that's when all hell broke loose.

ASON SHOVED COACH FIELDING WITH all his might and sent the guy back a couple paces, but the coach wasn't that easily brushed off. Even though he was in his late sixties, he still had a lot of muscle on him and at least three inches of height to work with. He came at Jason faster than Jason could have imagined possible.

Coach slammed Jason into the wall, knocking most of the air from his lungs, causing him to hit his eye on the corner of a shelf. Then he shoved his forearm up against Jason's throat and growled in his face.

"It's my word against his, asshole, and no way is anyone going to believe you or a bunch of welfare losers that I did anything wrong. This city loves me. This city *owes* me. I bring them to State championships every year. We *compete* when I'm in charge."

Jason could barely talk with the pressure on his windpipe. "People's lives are being ruined by you, and I'm going to the cops as soon as I leave here, as soon as Leo is safe from you, you monster."

"Over my dead body," the coach said, releasing Jason long enough to take a swing at him.

Jason moved to the side, and the coach missed, hitting a coat rack and sending it across the office in pieces.

Jason tried to run out of the office, but the coach came after him, pulling him by the shirt back towards him.

Jason twisted around and swung out, panicked the coach was going to kill him to shut him up. He caught the coach in the cheek, a hard crack that broke one of his knuckles. Fear and revulsion had given him a strength he'd never known, even on the football field.

Unfortunately, the blow only stunned the coach, so he was able to launch himself at Jason again. Jason said he felt like a tackle dummy when his thighs slammed into the desk and he bent over backwards.

Jason rolled off the desk and leaped up to punch the coach once more, this time with his other fist. It got the coach in the stomach, slowing him for just a second or two before he was upright again and coming at Jason with blood in his eyes.

Jason swung as hard as he could, knocking the coach sideways with a solid hook to the jaw. The coach tripped on his way down, catching his toe in a rug he had custom made to celebrate his latest State win. It had the Boys' Center logo in the corner of it. He fell to the ground, hitting his head hard on the corner of the desk on his way down, and he never got up on his own again.

That was how Jason's teammates found their beloved coach ten minutes later, with Jason standing over him, his knuckles cut and bloody.

Jason hid the bruises on his back and ribs from them and the police so that he could keep Leo's secret from everyone, just as he'd promised. He was carted off to jail and turned into everyone's most hated citizen overnight. One minute he was in all his glory, and the next he was less than nothing.

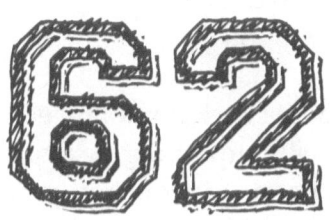

THE DAY AFTER THE CHARGES against him were dropped, Jason showed up at my front door, a giant bouquet of pink and red roses in hand.

"What in the heck are you doing?" I asked, a huge grin splitting my face. He couldn't have looked more handsome standing there in his shorts, muscle shirt, and running shoes.

"I've come over to ask you to go jogging with me."

I looked pointedly at the flowers. "It's going to be awkward running with those."

He thrust them towards me. "This is a thank you from me and my dad."

I took them from him and went to the kitchen. "Thank you for what?"

He waited until I put them in water before he pulled me into a hug. His arms wrapped all the way around me until he had his hands on my ribs. He spoke over my shoulder.

"Thank you for being my friend. For never giving up on me. For not listening to me when I was being stupid. For forgiving the unforgivable."

I hugged him back as hard as I could. "That's what you do for friends."

"I hate to say it, but your definition of friendship is a lot different than most people's."

"Well, most people suck, what can I say."

Jason released me and then got down on his knees.

"What on earth are you doing, fool?" I panicked. If he pulled out a ring I was going to deck him.

"I wanted to know if you'd do me the honor of going to prom with me."

My heart did a double back flip followed by a triple axle.

"Prom?" My normally supercalafragalistic sense of humor had escaped me. I'd never gone to prom before and never ever would I have imagined going with someone like Jason. It seemed like such a foreign concept now. Prom was for kids and I didn't feel like a kid anymore.

"Yeah, you know ...," he said, "...the dance? Dresses, tuxes, shitty music, awkward dancing, chaperones, dinner ..."

"I get it, I get it. Would you stand up, please? You're making me nervous." I pulled on his t-shirt to make him go faster.

He stood and took me into a light embrace so we could face each other and look into each other's eyes.

"I love you and I want to show the world how much," he said.

"You don't need to do that, you know." Imagining myself on his arm and both of us all dressed up made me a little light-headed, actually. Maybe I wasn't totally grown-up yet.

"I want to. Unless you don't want to..." He leaned back a little to look at me. "Are you worried about what people will say?"

I raised an eyebrow at him. "I *will* slap you, you know."

He grinned. "That's my girl. So, I was thinking we could go shopping for a dress today if you want."

I laughed. "Bobby would kill me if I went with you and not him."

"Okay, fine. He's probably got better taste than me anyway." He pulled away and started walking towards the front door. "Come on, let's run."

"I need to get dressed."

"I'll be stretching out on the front lawn."

I was down there in ten minutes, which was apparently exactly how much time it took for a whole gaggle of reporters to realize Jason was there and gather on my front lawn to talk to him. He was still front-page news.

I walked out the door right into the middle of the circus.

"How does it feel to be cleared of all the charges?" one of them asked.

"Do you think it's fair that you got released when you killed him?" asked another.

"What are you going to do now?" Someone from behind the crowd shouted.

Jason put his arm around me and nodded to the reporters. They all went quiet and listened.

"I'll answer those three questions and then I'm done. Forever. So don't bother showing up here or at my house, because this is the last time I cooperate with you people."

He stared at everyone, giving them his full attention. "First of all, it feels good to be free. Great. Until you've had your freedom taken away, I don't think it's possible to truly appreciate it. But at the same time, it's hard for me to appreciate it because there are so many kids who aren't free now, because of Coach Fielding and what he did to them. They're prisoners of those memories and I doubt they'll ever be free of that."

He swallowed with effort and continued on, his voice strong. "I feel terrible for all those kids whose lives were ruined by the monster who took advantage of them and of his position in our community. We put that man up on a pedestal and look what he did. There's a danger in that, and I hope all of you guys who put people's pictures in the paper and build them up to be some kind of god will think about that little bit harder from now on."

He paused to let his words sink in before continuing. "You asked if I think it's fair that I'm not in jail. Yes, I think it's fair, while I also think this whole thing was a terrible tragedy. Do I wish things had gone differently? Yes. I wish the coach were in jail right now answering for his crimes. But would I do what I did all over again if given another chance? Yes, I would. I didn't go see the coach with the intent to harm him. I went there to confront him about what he'd done. I did it because people can't be afraid to confront monsters, to call them on their bullshit, to stand up and say *no more* when things are happening that hurt kids."

He put his arm around me and pulled me in close. "And what am I going to do now? I'm going to go jogging with my best friend in the entire world ... the girl who never gave up on me and the person who is responsible not only for me being free but also for all those kids getting the help they need. She's the real hero here. And we were all victims."

"What are you going to say to all those people who say you're lying about what Coach Fielding did?"

I didn't think Jason was going to answer at first, but then he stopped trying to walk off. His arm dropped from my shoulders and he stood very straight. "Anyone who will look one of those kids in the eye, hear his story, and then say that Coach Fielding did nothing wrong, belongs in a cold grave right next to him. And that's all I'm going to say on the matter. Please go home to your families and stop harassing me and these good people here."

He grabbed my hand and pushed through the vultures on the steps, pulling me behind. We started jogging before we hit the sidewalk, the wet grass making our ankles damp and itchy.

"Come on, race you to the corner," he said.

"I've been working out," I said, taking off at a dead run. "Catch me if you can!"

We ran for miles that day in silence, just enjoying each other's company. I imagined that with every block that went by, we left behind a little bit of the sorrow we'd been gathering for the last six months. It was only a dream, but at least I knew it was okay to have hope. Jason was free to move on with his life and so was I.

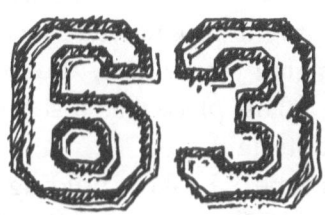

OUR FIRST DAY BACK TO school together wasn't really a school day. Jason took a couple weeks off and then decided his first introduction back into the system would be better if it didn't involve classrooms of students staring at him like he was some kind of freak.

The night of prom he picked me up in his Camaro.

"Have her home by midnight," my dad said. He'd begrudgingly accepted the fact that Jason was going to be a permanent part of my life. He wasn't ready for smiles and hugs yet, but I had hope that he'd get there eventually.

"You two have fun," my mom said, hugging Jason. "And be safe. Watch out for the press. They're still out there."

"We're yesterday's news," Jason said, "but I'll be careful."

He turned to me and grinned. "You ready, beautiful?"

I smiled back, unable to stop myself from looking like a happy fool. "Ready as I'll ever be."

My mom snapped a picture of us standing there in love, ready to face the world that had until recently considered us the worst humanity had to offer.

We arrived at the hotel where the prom was being held about an hour after it started. Hoping to avoid a mob was our plan, but we might as well have spit into the wind and hoped to stay dry. It seemed like every single student at the entire school was waiting for us to show up.

The first people we saw, thankfully, were Bobby and his date Stephen. Stephen was new to the school, so he had no preconceived notions about Jason or me. It was kind of refreshing not to be wondering how much he might have hated us a couple weeks ago.

"Oh, I'm soooooo glad you're here," Bobby said, getting all of us into a group hug. "This place was just buzzing with rumors. Time to set everyone straight."

"What was it this time?" I asked, holding Jason's hand. I was nervous. So far I'd heard that I was pregnant, one of the coach's victims, and several other equally ridiculous things I'd managed to block from my memory.

"You don't want to know. But just watch your back where Britt and Tiff are concerned."

"Watch her back? What's that all about?" Jason asked.

"Oh, you know. Mean-girl stuff." Bobby waved it off like it was no big deal. "Come on. Let's go get something to drink."

"We're glad you're back, Jason," Stephen said. "Everyone feels really bad about what happened."

"Not everyone," I said under my breath. Jamahl was standing off to the side in the lobby staring at us. He made no effort to approach.

"Save the drama for your momma," Bobby said as three guys from the football team came walking up from the other direction.

"Nah, man, it's all good," said one of them. "Yo, Jace, good to see you, man." He held his hand up for some sort of man fist pounding or whatever.

Jason just looked at him. "How've you been?" he asked politely.

The guy stood there with his hand out for another second or two before giving up on the social greeting he expected to receive. "I'm good. How 'bout you?"

An awkward silence ensued.

"Did you seriously just ask that question?" Bobby said.

"I'm good," Jason said, diffusing the awkward. "Listen, we're going to get some drinks, so ... see you around."

"Yeah, sure." The three guys watched us walk by, mystified.

"Holy awkward moment," Bobby said, snorting. "They just don't get it."

"It's hard for anyone to get," Jason said, squeezing my hand a little. "We don't live in the same world as they do anymore."

"You can say that again," I said under my breath as Brittney approached from across the room. She was covered in a white dress that looked suspiciously like a wedding gown and she had more makeup on than a tranny.

I watched her set her sights on Jason and felt a sharp stabbing pain in my chest area. What if he decides he wants to be with her again? I wasn't sure I could handle that. Not after all we'd been through.

"Jason, oh my god, you're back!" she squealed, coming for him with her arms open. She ran on tiptoes, her grin stretching from ear to ear.

She fully expected him to drop me and take her in a bear hug, obviously, so she was totally shocked when he backed up, took me with him, and then pulled me in really tight to his side.

"Hello, Brittney." His voice was dead, zero emotion lighting it up.

She came to a halt and glared at me, dropping her arms. "I see you brought your friend to prom," she said, her voice saccharine sweet. "What a pretty dress you have. I've seen three others just like it so far tonight."

"I guess I have good taste," I said, giving her my eat-shit smile.

"So, when are we going to see you back in school?" she asked Jason. "We've really missed you, you know."

"Monday."

"Oh, that's so exciting." She stepped in closer. "I'll save a spot for you at our table in the cafeteria."

"No thanks. I'll be eating with Katy and Bobby."

"And me too," Stephen said, raising his hand.

Jason smiled at him. "Stephen too."

"You're eating with them?" she asked, her distain on display for all of us to enjoy.

"Yes."

"But ... what about the team?" She looked genuinely confused.

"What team?" Jason asked.

We were the only ones who knew what he really meant when he asked that question.

"Jail really messed you up," she said, turning bitchy.

"He's not the one who's messed up, actually," I said, ready to go toe-to-toe with her.

"Easy," Jason said, pulling me back and turning us to go around Brittney. "She's not worth it," he said quietly.

It wasn't quiet enough to escape her ears, though.

"Not worth it?" she asked, as if she couldn't believe what she'd heard. "Not worth it? Oh my god ... that's hilarious." She started laughing, but it sounded more like a witch's cackle than anything else. "Wow, have you got your priorities turned around."

"God, I hope so," Jason said with a sigh.

I couldn't stop laughing after that. My abs were sore by the end of the night, from laughing at Brittney and from all the twisting and booty shaking we did on the dance floor. It felt amazing to be able to do this in public and not just in Jason's kitchen.

When Jason dropped me off at my front door that evening, five minutes before midnight, he pulled me into his arms and kissed me long and slow. The moon lit up the front lawn and made the wet blades of grass sparkle a little.

"You are the coolest girl in the entire school," he said, touching me forehead to forehead.

"You're pretty cool too."

"My constant gardener," he said. "I'm glad I finally got to know you. When are you going to plant some more of those pink and purple flowers, anyway?"

"Funny you ask ... I was planning a trip to the garden store for next weekend."

"Can I come?"

I grinned. "Do bears poop in the woods?"

"Uhhh ... I think so, yeah."

"Okay, then. Bring some gardening gloves."

"It's a date."

He kissed me again until I went warm everywhere. A small moan escaped my lips and then the front porch light went on sending a flood of light into our eyeballs.

"I think your dad wants you to go inside."

"My dad can suck it," I said, looking to kiss Jason again.

He laughed and pushed me from him gently. "One of these days I'm going to take you away from here and get you naked. But not tonight. Tonight your dad's the boss and I have to go home."

I pouted, but inside I was secretly happy that he was so respectful of my dad's antiquated attitudes. "Promise?" I asked.

"You bet your sweet buns," he said, walking down the stairs backwards. It was like he couldn't take his eyes off me, which of course made me feel like a million bucks.

"You were beautiful tonight," he said.

"You were pretty okay yourself."

"See you tomorrow?" he was halfway across the lawn.

"Aren't you tired of me yet?"

"Never. I'm waking you up at seven for a run."

I laughed, pulling open the door. "Good luck with that."

As I was stepping inside, inspiration struck. "Hey!" I shouted.

He was on the street, but he turned around. "What?"

"I want to go to church tomorrow after our run."

"Seriously?"

"Yes."

"Okay, if that's what you want to do."

I blew him kiss. "See you tomorrow."

He reached up into the air and pretended to catch my kiss. He put it on his chest. "See you tomorrow, beautiful."

I had the best sleep of my life that night. Not a single nightmare came to steal away my happiness for the first time in months.

WE WALKED INTO THE CHURCH just as it was starting. I took the same pew I had before, ending up right next to the same big lady with the same purple dress. I cast my eyes around the room until I found the people I'd been looking for. Leo and his grandmother were across the aisle again, both of them standing very close to one another.

The priest talked about community and brotherhood, about loving thy neighbor and cherishing our children, of love and loss and forgiveness. Jason and I held hands throughout the entire service and when it came time at the end to greet our neighbors, he held me close and inhaled deeply. "I love you, neighbor," he said.

"I love you too, neighbor."

Someone tapped me on the shoulder. "God loves you child," the woman said, pulling me into a hug. She smelled of roses and soap.

"God loves you too," I said.

"That he do, that he do," she responded. She looked up and saw Jason and her eyes teared up a little. "Come over here and give me a hug, son."

Jason and I switched places and I watched as they embraced. The woman didn't want to let him go. She cried too.

Slowly the people around us started to notice. People whispered. Others who had started to file out of the church stopped and realized what was going on and came back.

Pretty soon the entire congregation was there, everyone wanting to give Jason and me a hug.

I couldn't stop crying. I'd never actually physically felt forgiveness and love before like I did that day. Waves of warmth and joy and kindness enveloped me and surrounded everything around me.

"Thank you, Jason, thank you," they said.

"Thank you, sweet girl, you are a blessing," they said to me.

And then the crowd cleared and let Leo and his grandma through. She looked at Jason for a long time and then started crying. "You my angel," she said, opening her left arm up for a hug. The right one she kept around Leo's shoulders.

Leo tried to smile at Jason, but he couldn't do it. All he could manage was to cry.

Jason hugged them both, crying himself by now. I joined them behind Jason and tried to get in on it. I wanted to heal the world with the power that congregation's love had given me, even though I knew we were missing that one vital ingredient: time. Leo was going to need a lot of time to get past this.

"Thank you, baby girl," Grandma said to me. "You my hero."

"She's fearless," Leo said in a small voice. "Just like Jason."

"Just like you," I said, shifting so I could hug him alone. "Just like you, little man."

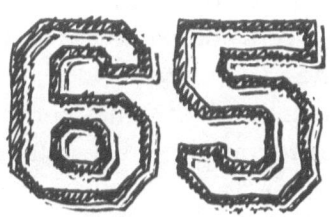

JASON AND I GRADUATED FROM high school with decent enough grades. Neither of us were ready for college, though, even though for most of our lives that's what our families had planned for us, and Jason still had several offers from really good football programs offering him a full ride.

Something about having our worlds turned upside down made it difficult for us to imagine continuing on with the old plans we'd made, and Jason had sworn off football for the rest of his life.

The press had called it a shame, what had happened to Jason and his future as a possible NFL player. But we knew differently. We knew that what happened had happened for a good reason and there was no point in living with regrets. We had too much going for us to get bogged down in that regret garbage.

"You ready?" he asked me, slamming the door down on the moving truck.

"As ready as I'll ever be."

He draped his arm over my shoulders. "You sure about this? I don't want you to do anything you don't want."

"Yes, it's what I want." I reached up on tiptoes to kiss him. "I hate having to walk across the street to find you."

He winked as he opened my door. "Up you go, roomie."

I climbed up into the truck and took out the map. "We're off to see the wizard!" I exclaimed, going over our itinerary in my head again as my parents came out the front door.

"Here," my mom said, handing me a tin foiled package through the window. "For your trip."

I peeled back the layers and smiled at what I saw there. "Rice crispie treats. Sweetness."

"We're going to miss you," she said, her eyes watery.

My dad put his arm around her waist. "We'll be fine. You'll be fine. You have each other."

Jason climbed up into the driver's seat. "I'll take great care of her, I promise."

"We know you will," my dad said. He turned his attention to me. "You call us when you get there. And call along the way too so we don't worry."

"You got it," I said, sending a text to Jason's dad telling him we were leaving. He had to work out of town that week, so he was missing the Big Goodbye.

Jason started up the small van and backed down the driveway. "See ya!" he yelled, turning out onto the street.

"I can't believe we're moving to Seattle," I said, grinning like a madwoman.

"I can't believe we both got hired to work in the same place," he said.

"I guess publicity has its benefits."

Jason reached over and squeezed my hand. "We're going to kick ass for those kids."

"Hell yeah, we are." I was one-half of the dynamic duo, the two teenagers hired right out of high school to run a program for inner city kids in Seattle, the Emerald City.

Jason and I had gotten this wild idea to submit a proposal to the city after reading about it online and had actually impressed them so much they flew us out to discuss it. And now we both had jobs that were guaranteed to last at least two years and money for moving expenses and an apartment.

"Last year this time I thought my life was over," he said.

"Last year this time I thought your life was over too."

"Good thing you didn't give up on me," he said. He looked over at me, like he always did when he said that. "I thank God every day for you."

"Stop, you're making me blush."

"Blush? Just wait until I get you alone in that apartment. *Then* we're going to see real some blushing."

I couldn't even look at him I was so happy and nervous at the same time. Today I was finally an adult. Our lives were once again changing in fundamental ways we could only partially comprehend right now.

The road spread out before us and the sun shone in the window, bringing out the highlights in Jason's hair. I used to think he was in all his glory out there on the football field, running blindingly fast, catching balls that should have been impossible to catch; but I was wrong. Now I was really seeing Jason at his best — free to live his life in the service of others, fearless and compassionate, beautiful from the inside out.

Now *that* is glorious, all right. This is Jason in all his glory.

Being an independent author, I depend entirely on *you*, the reader, to get the word out about my books. If you liked this book, won't you please leave a review online and recommend it to a friend? The more you spread the word, the more books I can write, and nothing would please me more than to put a new book in your hands every single month.

I read all my reviews!

Find more Elle Casey books at the following retailers:

Amazon
iBooks
Barnes & Noble
Google Play
Kobo
Walmart
Your Local Library via the OverDrive ebook platform

Want to get an email when my next book is released?
Sign up here: www.ElleCasey.com/news

ABOUT THE AUTHOR

Elle Casey, a former attorney and teacher, is a NEW YORK TIMES, USA TODAY, *and Amazon bestselling American author who lives in France with her husband, three kids, and a number of horses, dogs, and cats. She has written more than 40 novels in less than 5 years and likes to say she offers fiction in several flavors. These flavors include romance, science fiction, urban fantasy, action adventure, suspense, and paranormal.*

A personal note from Elle ...

If you enjoyed this book, please take a moment to leave a review on the site where you bought this book, Goodreads, or any book blogs you participate in, and tell your friends! I love interacting with my readers, so if you feel like shooting the breeze or talking about books or your family or pets, please visit me. You can find me at ...

www.ElleCasey.com
www.Facebook.com/ellecaseytheauthor
www.Twitter.com/ellecasey
www.Instagram.com/ellecaseyauthor

Other Books by Elle Casey

CONTEMPORARY URBAN FANTASY

War of the Fae (10-book series)
Ten Things You Should Know About Dragons
(short story, The Dragon Chronicles)
My Vampire Summer
Aces High

DYSTOPIAN

Apocalypsis (4-book series)

SCIENCE FICTION

Drifters' Alliance (ongoing series)
Winner Takes All (short story prequel to Drifters' Alliance,
Dark Beyond the Stars Anthology)
The Ivory Tower (short story standalone, Beyond the Stars: A
Planet Too Far Anthology)

ROMANCE

By Degrees
Rebel Wheels (3-book series)
Just One Night (romantic serial)
Just One Week
Love in New York (3-book series)
Shine Not Burn (2-book series)
Bourbon Street Boys (4-book series)
Desperate Measures
Mismatched

ROMANTIC SUSPENSE

*All the Glory: How Jason Bradley Went from
Hero to Zero in Ten Seconds Flat*
Don't Make Me Beautiful
Wrecked (2-book series)

PARANORMAL

Duality (2-book series)
Monkey Business (short story)
Dreampath (short story standalone, The
Telepath Chronicles)
Pocket Full of Sunshine (short story & screenplay)

www.ingramcontent.com/pod-product-compliance
Lightning Source LLC
Chambersburg PA
CBHW021526250626
47154CB00006BA/1985